THE END
OF THE
WORLD

Also by Don Hertzfeldt

The Mystery of Ghost Airport

Difficulties on Planet X

The Screaming Woman

Glare of the Dangling Cat

The Case of the Missing Screams

Hot Tongues of Screaming

Screams of the Screamer

P.S. You're Dead, and Screaming

The Uncomfortable Seat

Blooooood at Midnight

Cave of the Jumping Beetle

Blind Man's Teepee

The Screaming Man with Little Dog Feet

Scream and Scream Again, Screamy

The Screaming Ghost Skeleton is Holding a Grenade

Hell Sock

published in the united states by random house,
an imprint and division of penguin random house LLC, new york
random house and the house colophon are
registered trademarks of penguin random house LLC

printed in china on acid-free paper
printed in hell on horrible acid-soaked paper

originally printed in hardcover by antibookclub, new york, in 2013

a few pages that were edited out of that 2013 edition have been added back to this edition
because the author can't seem to stop fucking around with the book

a very small portion of this book appeared in embarrassing rough draft form
in *flight: volume two* in 2005, published by image comics and villard books,
an imprint of random house, a division of random house LLC

other portions of this book appeared thousands of years ago on the ocean floor,
where sea slugs sadly rap their heads against things in the darkness

one day, many years from now, this book will be discovered beneath a fading, forgotten pile of
dusty, long-lost ephemera belonging to someone who is no longer around and a person will
pick it up and think, what on earth is this? and then they will read this and they will think, ha

hardback ISBN 978-1-9848-5535-0
ebook ISBN 978-1-9848-5536-7

please note, due to a minor traffic accident involving a mysterious gypsy woman this hardcover edition has been "cursed for all time throughout the universe": the author assumes no legal responsibility for any malevolent supernatural activity that occurs during or after use of this book, including but not limited to book bites, leaking pages, book screaming loudly both day and night, the shedding of excess book fur in the summer months, reader's limbs falling off, book suddenly turning into a pile of floppy eels, book snapping at you during dinner, book growing distant and spending more and more time at work, ink spraying across the room, book changing netflix password, strange new friends showing up at weird hours, book unable to spend more than six months out of prison, book always apologizing but refusing to change, book constantly hitting you up for cash, mysterious bruises, clammy hardcover, nightmares about lost teeth, book being somewhere in florida these days, or lingering little paper cuts that never want to heal

please enjoy some more numbers
246897531

it's ok that you are sad right now we can be sad together

random house 2019 edition
randomhousebooks.com

this book will slowly fall apart

the SUMMER is FILLED with
the LITTLE "FFFT, FFFT"
SOUNDS OF CHILDRENS'
MOUTHS BREAKING the
SURFACE OF SWIMMING
POOLS

MANFISH MISLEADS the PRINCESS, SENDING HER in the WRONG DIRECTION.

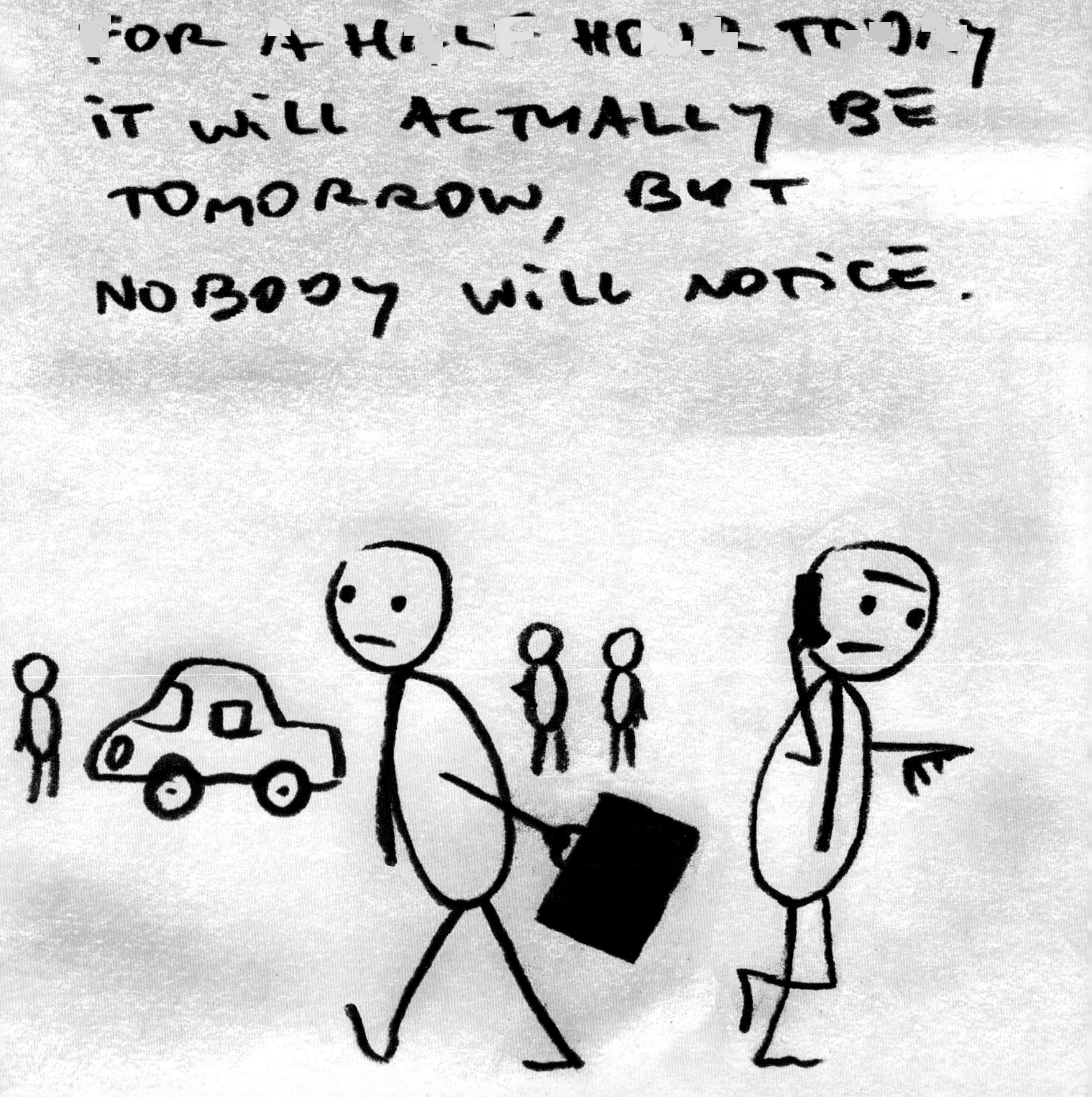
FOR A HALF HOUR TODAY
IT WILL ACTUALLY BE
TOMORROW, BUT
NOBODY WILL NOTICE.

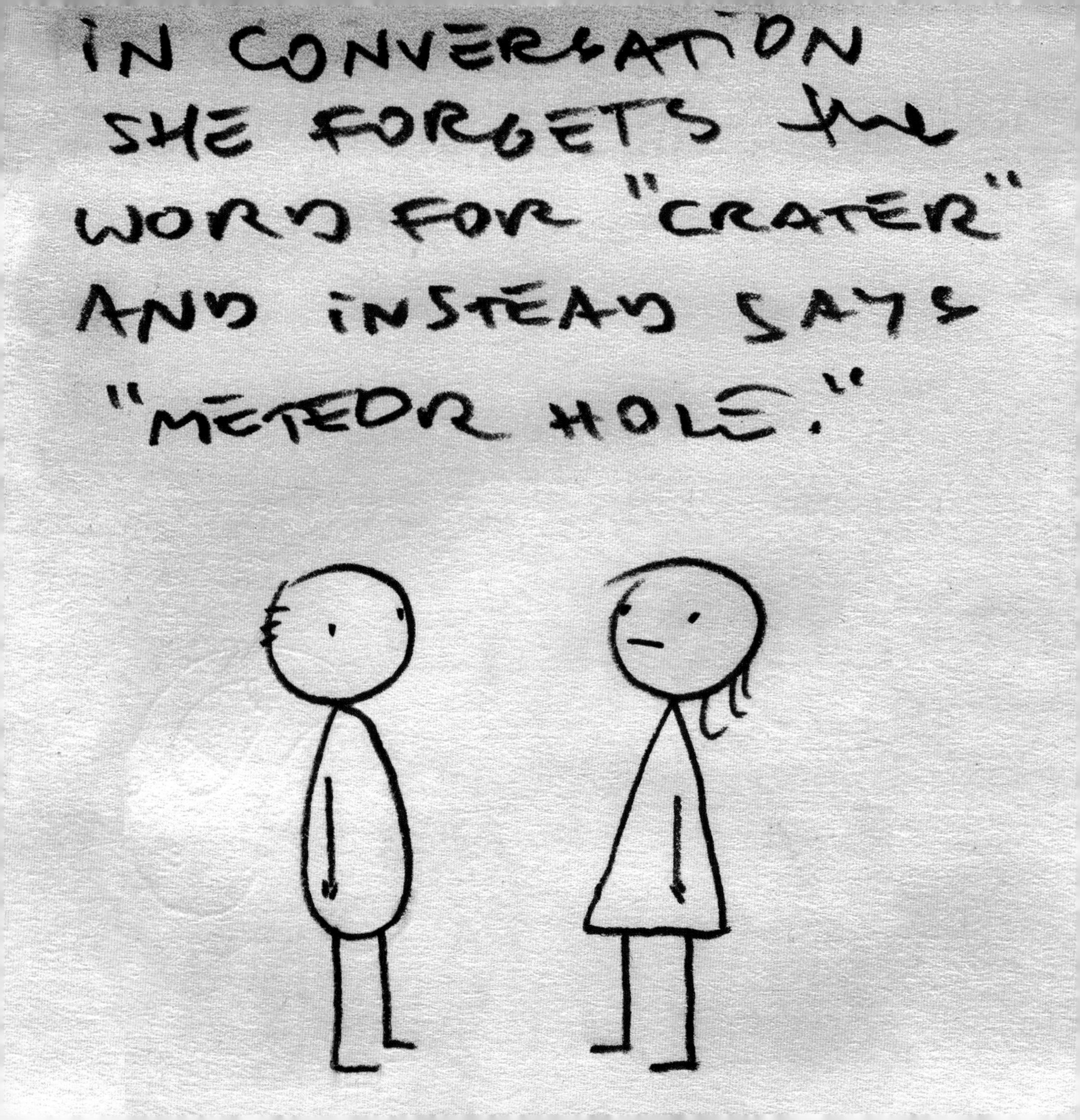
IN CONVERSATION
SHE FORGETS the
WORD FOR "CRATER"
AND INSTEAD SAYS
"METEOR HOLE."

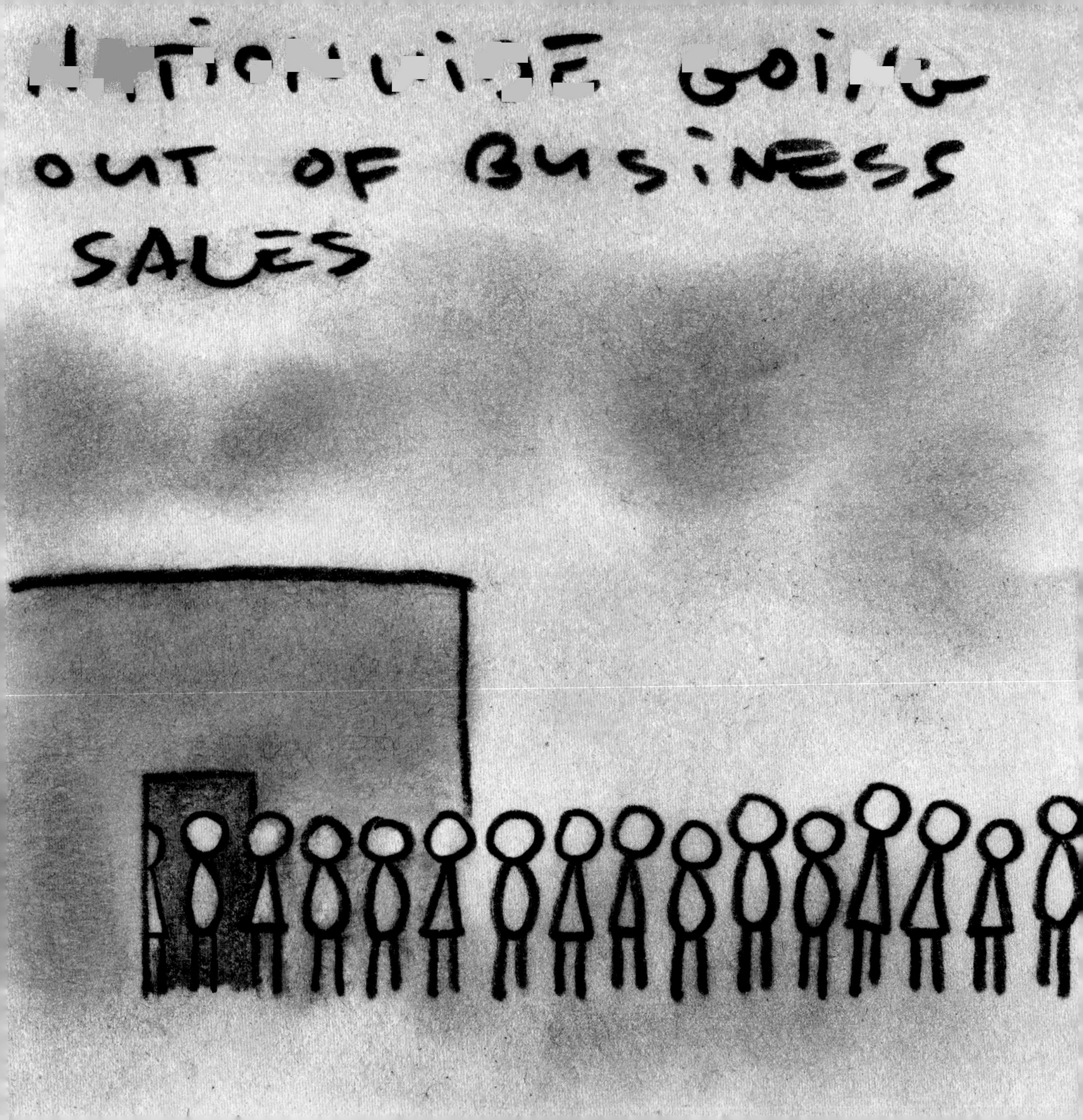
GOING
OUT OF BUSINESS
SALES

A FRINGE GROUP GENERATES GOOD WILL

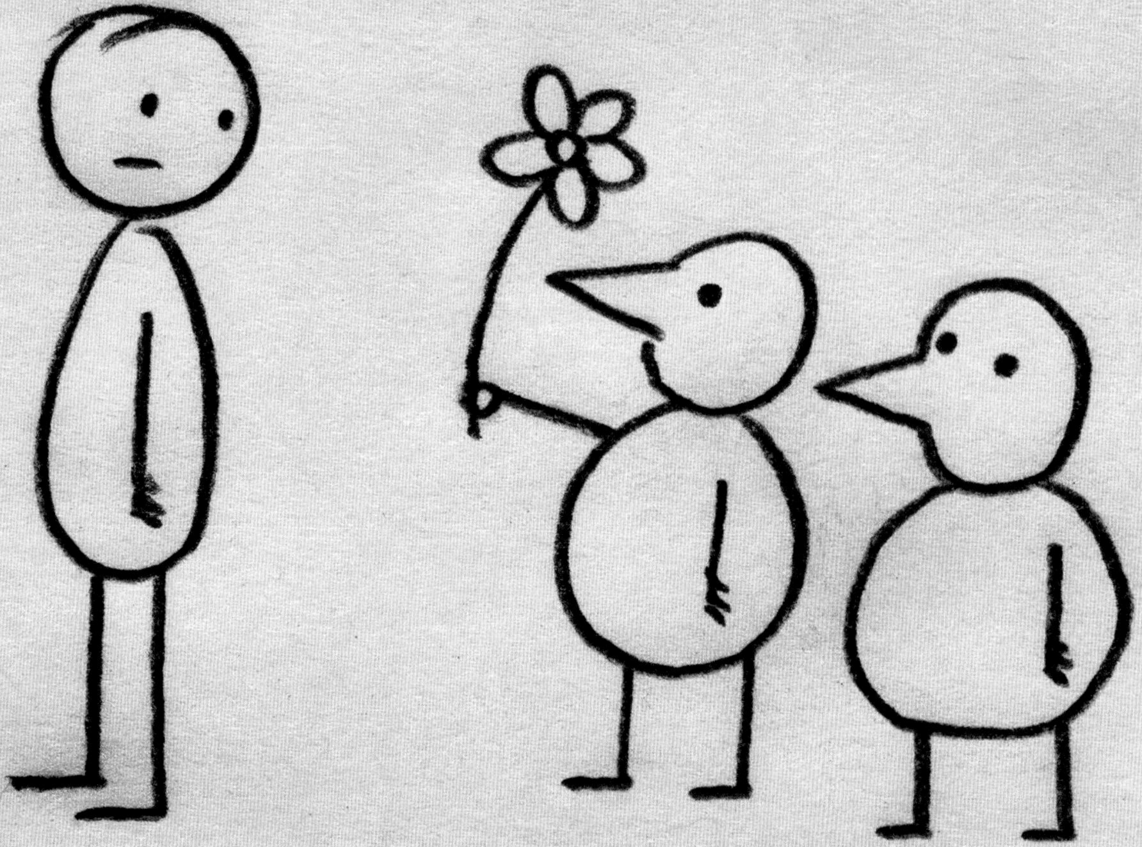

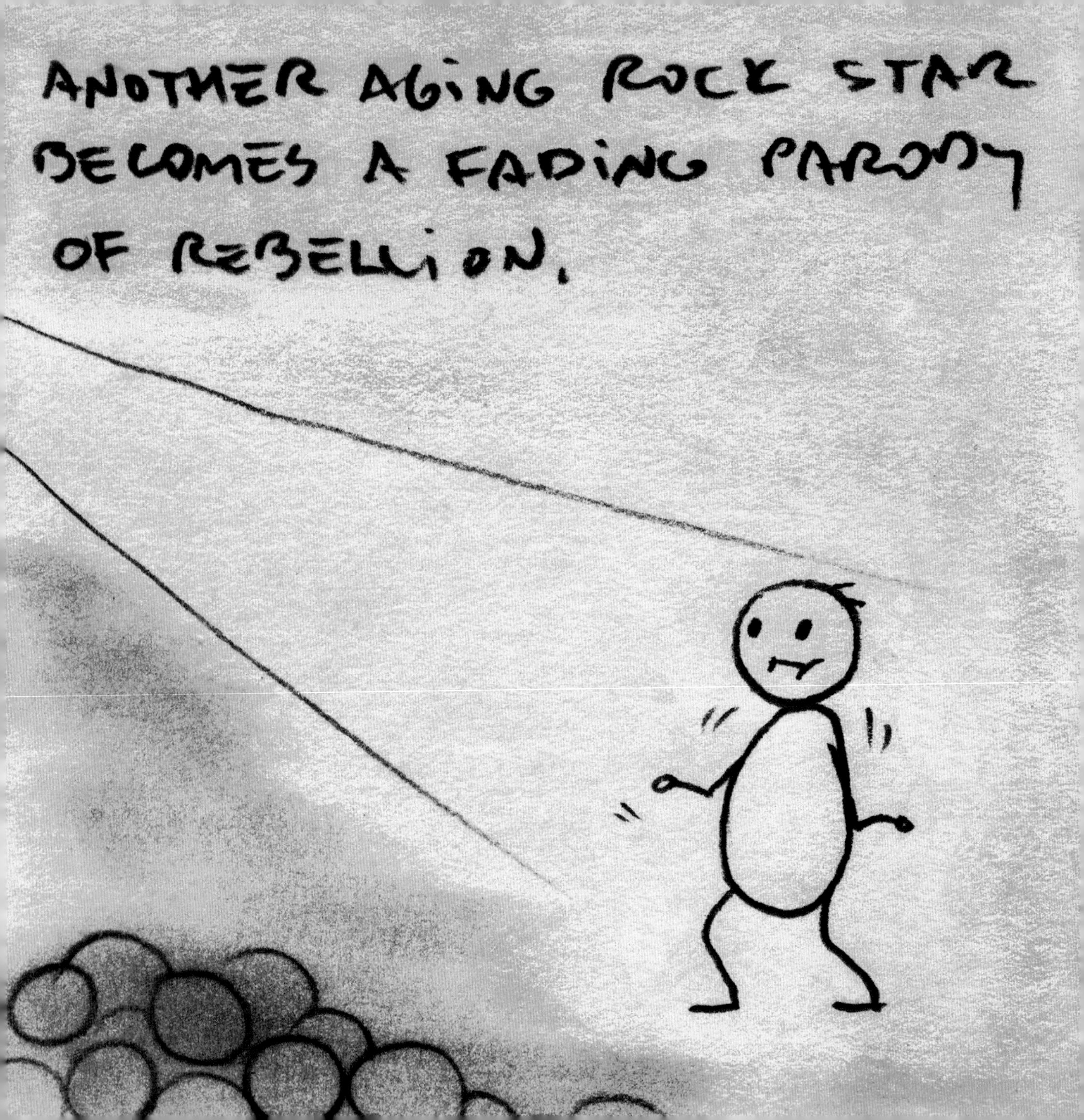
ANOTHER AGING ROCK STAR BECOMES A FADING PARODY OF REBELLION.

"IT'S ALL FUN AND GAMES UNTIL SOMEBODY GETS HURT," HE SAYS, SOME AQUATIC CREATURE STUCK TO HIS FACE.

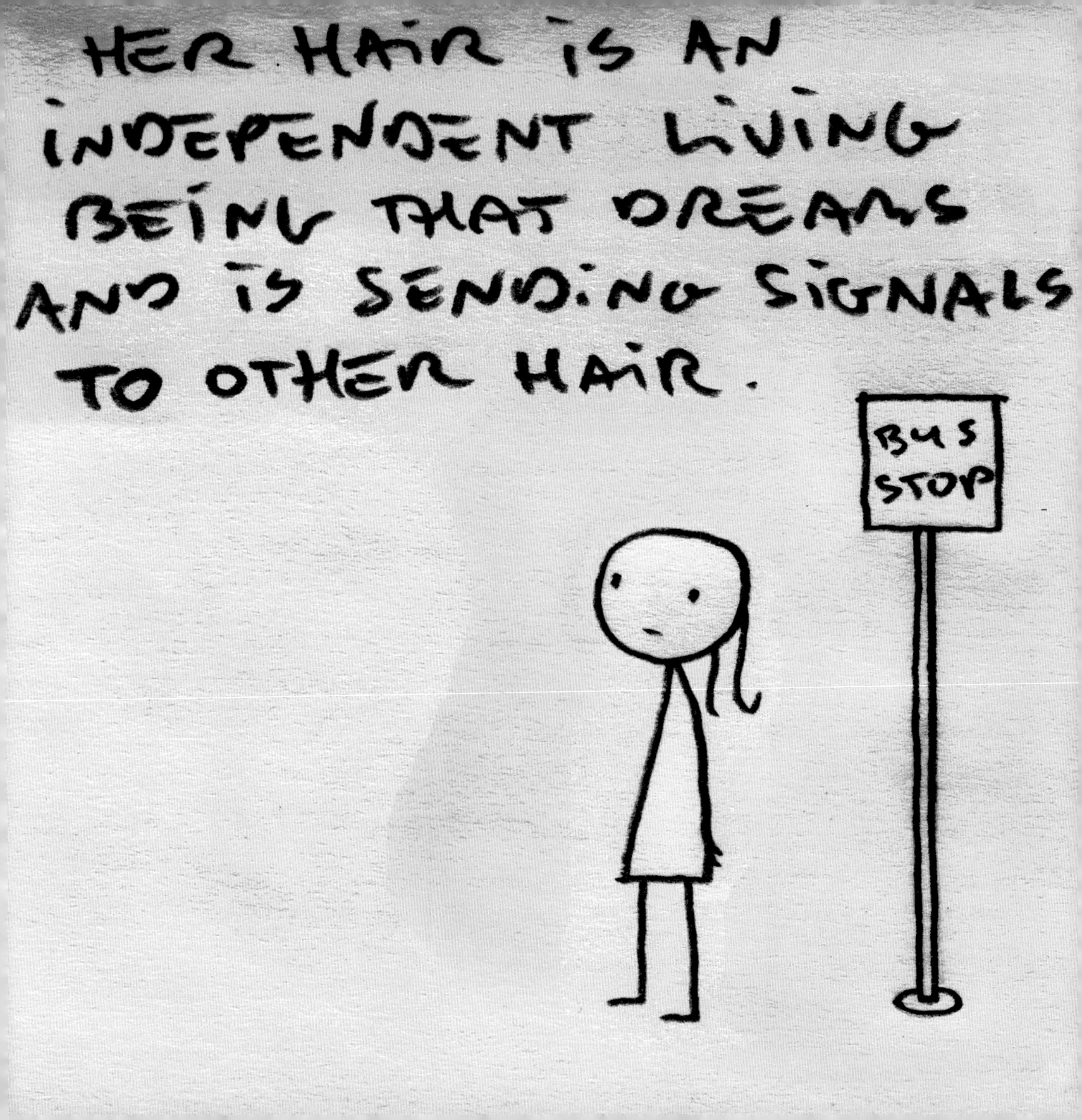
HER HAIR IS AN INDEPENDENT LIVING BEING THAT DREAMS AND IS SENDING SIGNALS TO OTHER HAIR.
BUS STOP

the SUPERMARKET is ALL OUT OF CANDLES OTHER THAN the SCENTED APPLE SHAPED ONES

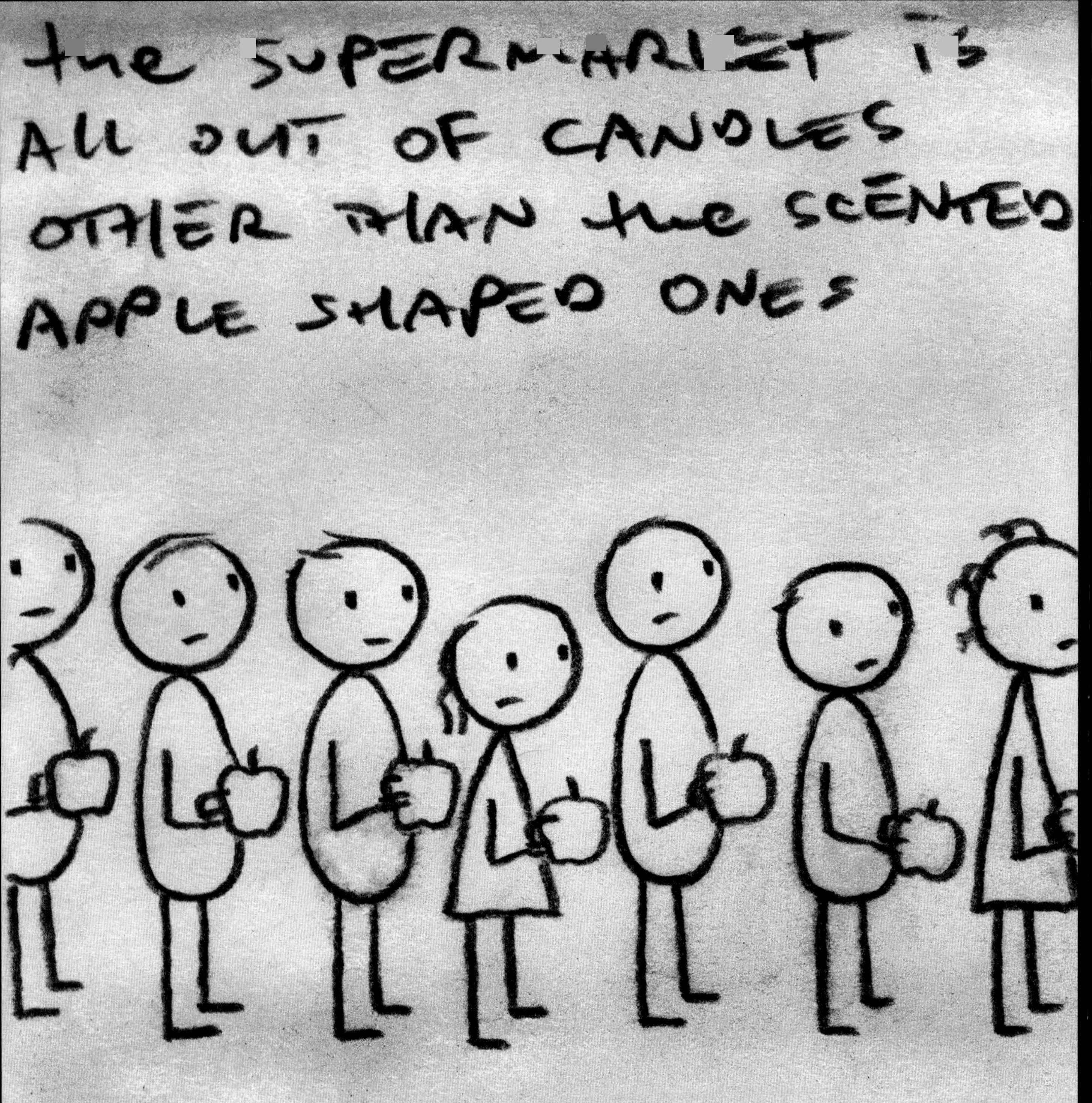

THE REFLECTIONS OF SUN-LIGHT OFF THE TRAFFIC BELOW CAST KALEIDOSCOPE BANDS ACROSS THE CEILING

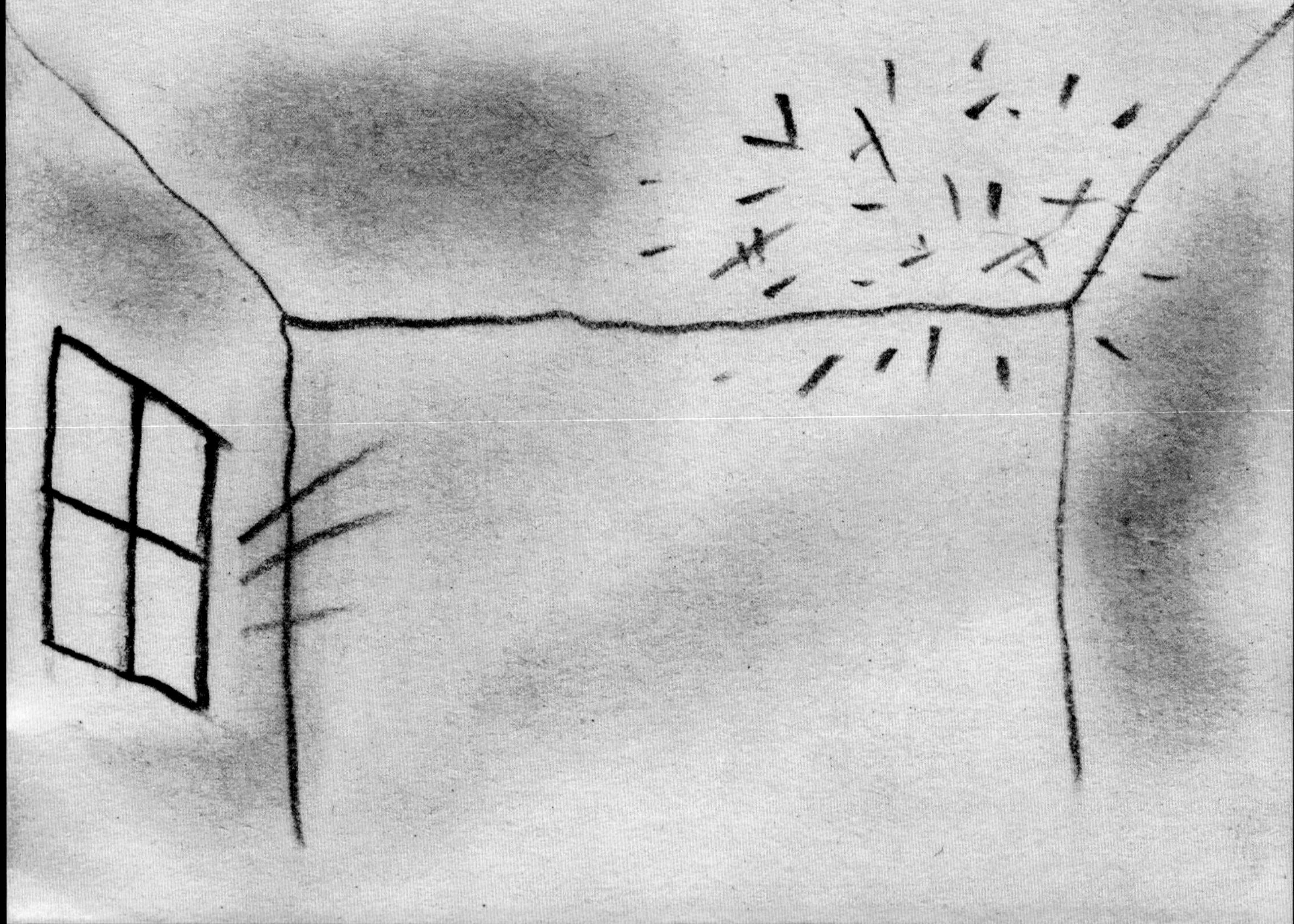

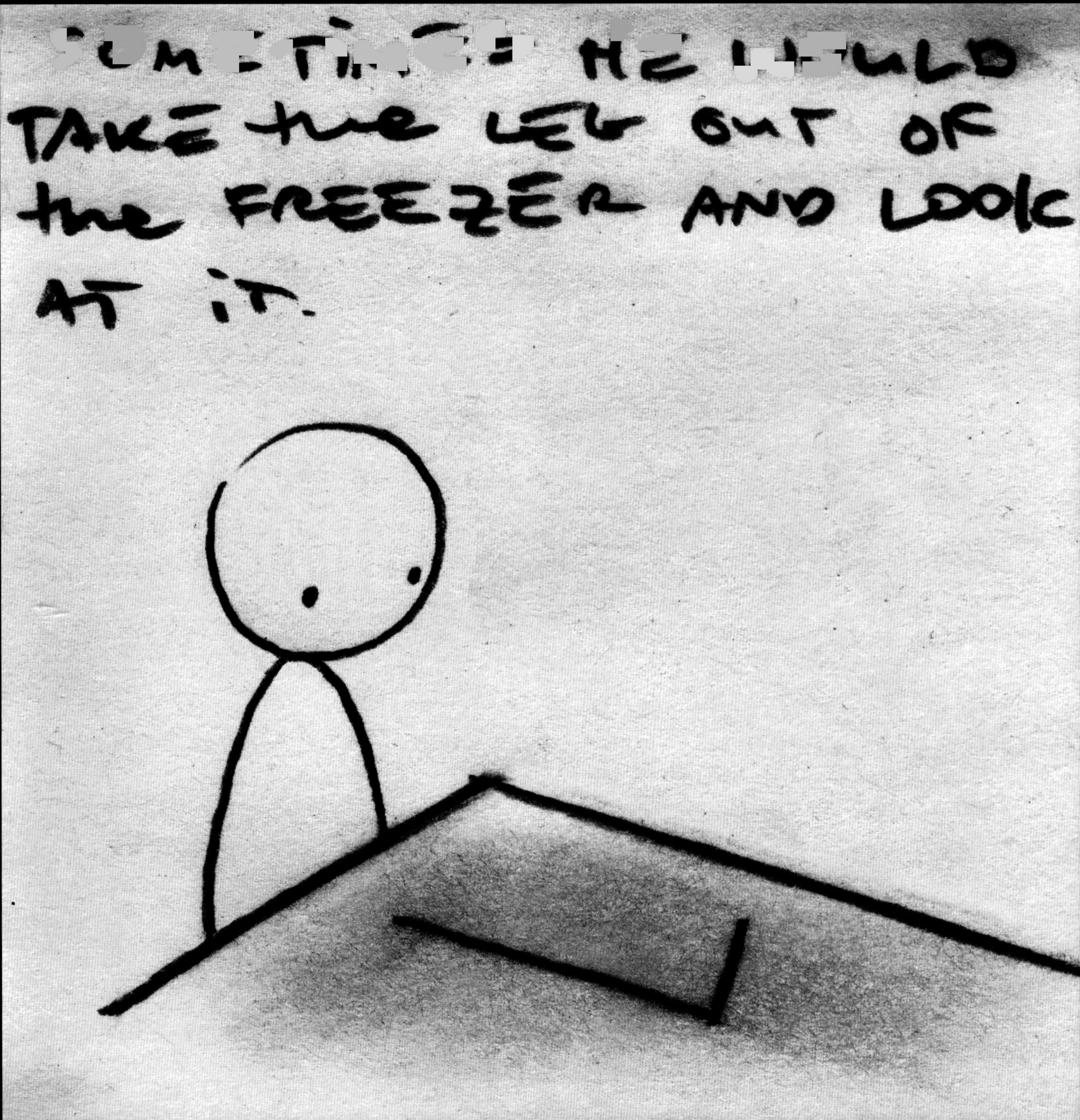
SOMETIMES HE WOULD TAKE the LEG OUT OF the FREEZER AND LOOK AT IT.

OUTSIDE SOMEONE GOT
STABBED AND PEOPLE
ARE DRIVING CARS VERY
STRANGELY

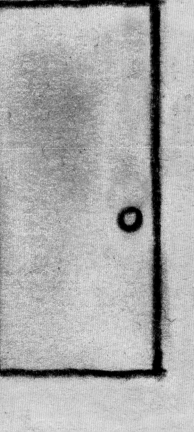

ETHNIC CHILDREN AND SMALL BIRDS STARVE THEMSELVES AND DART AROUND THE ROOM

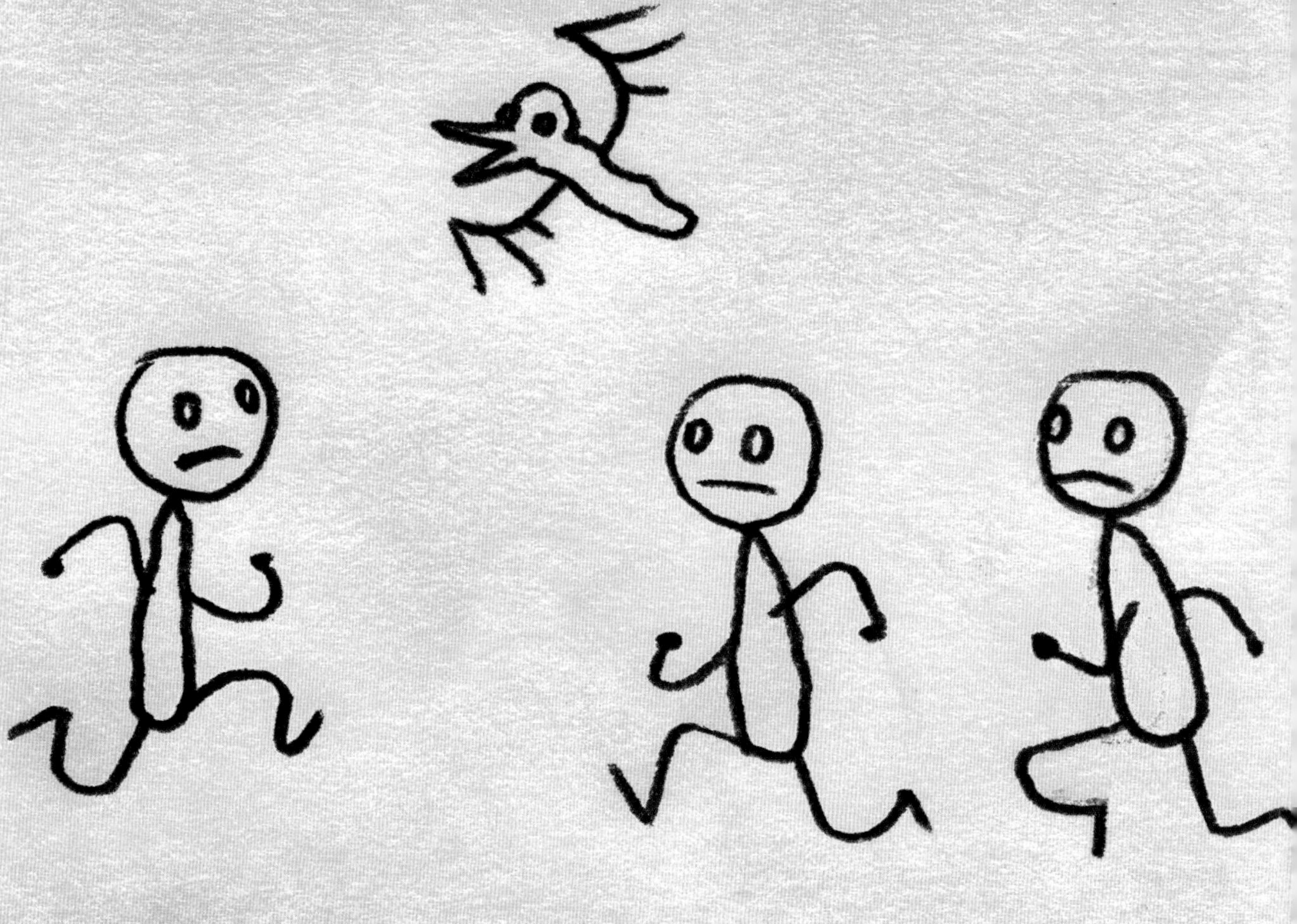

MARTIN SEARCHES FOR PORN AS ALL OF HIS DEAD RELATIVES LOOK ON

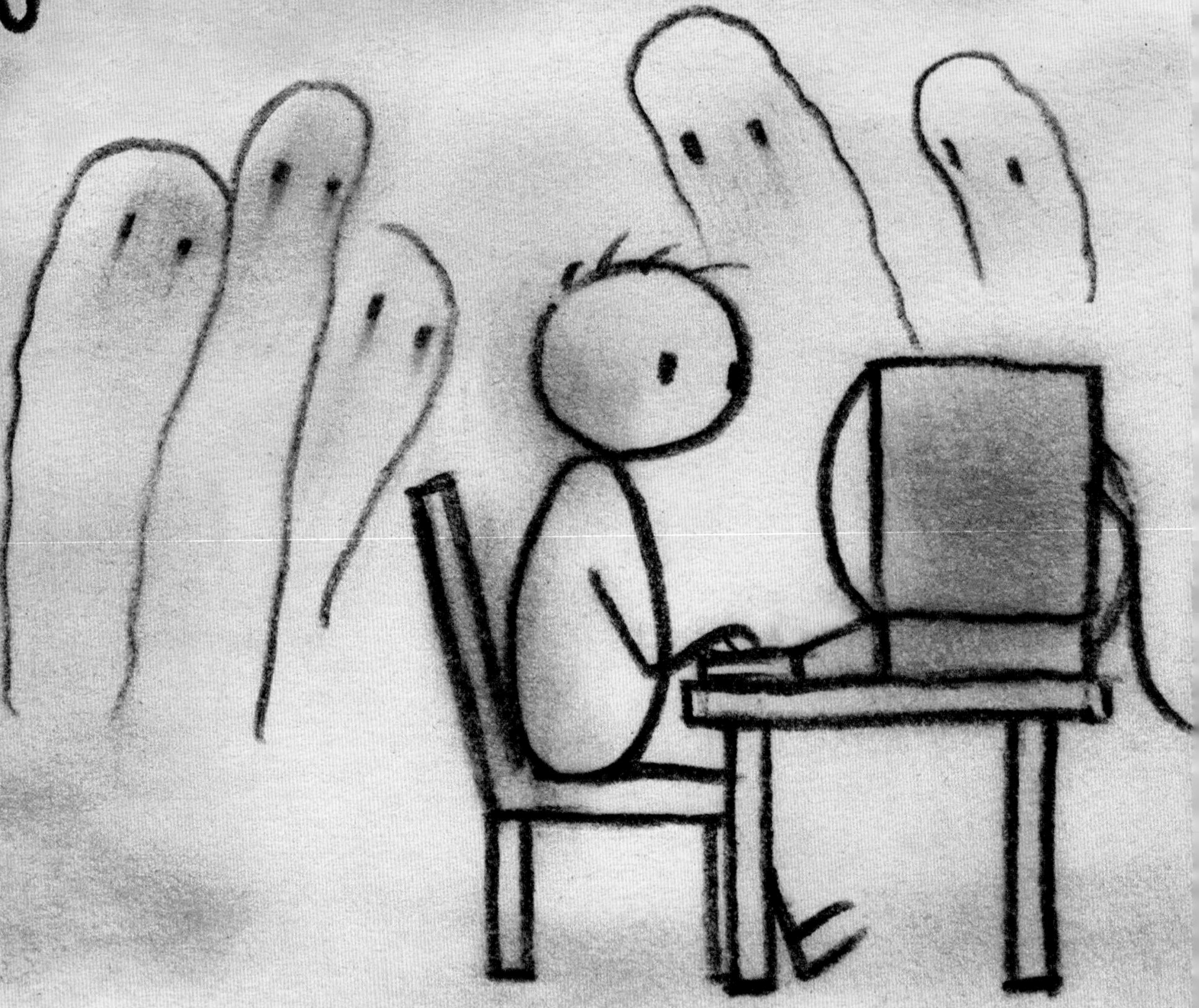

THE PRINCESS
DISAPPEARS INTO
A CREVASSE.

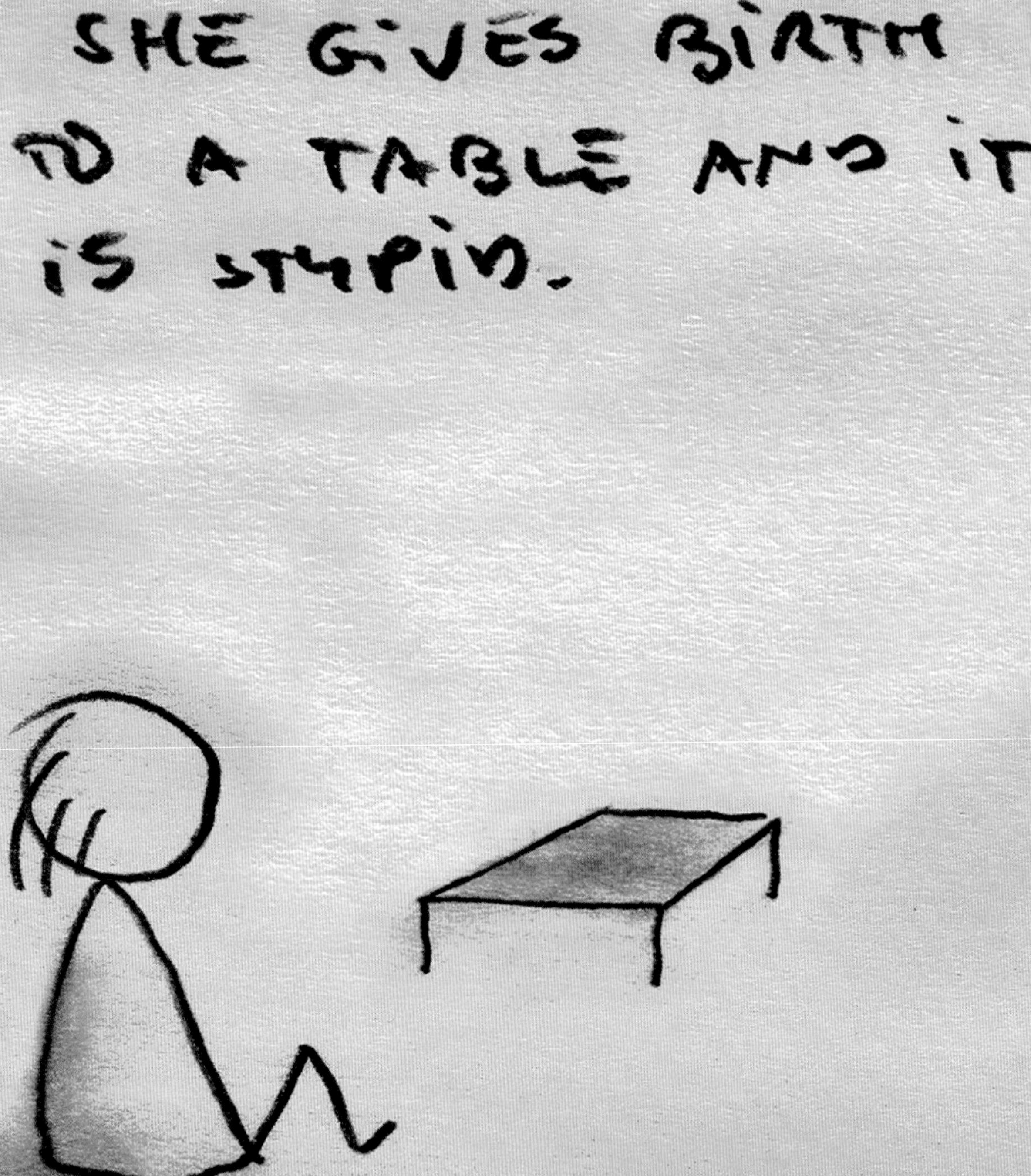
SHE GIVES BIRTH
TO A TABLE AND IT
IS STUPID.

A CURIOUS MEMENTO FROM A MEMORY GAP

THE SUN SETS FOR
TWO MONTHS.

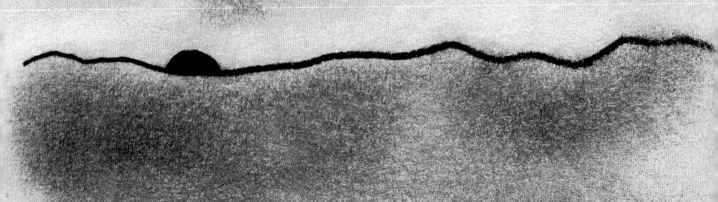

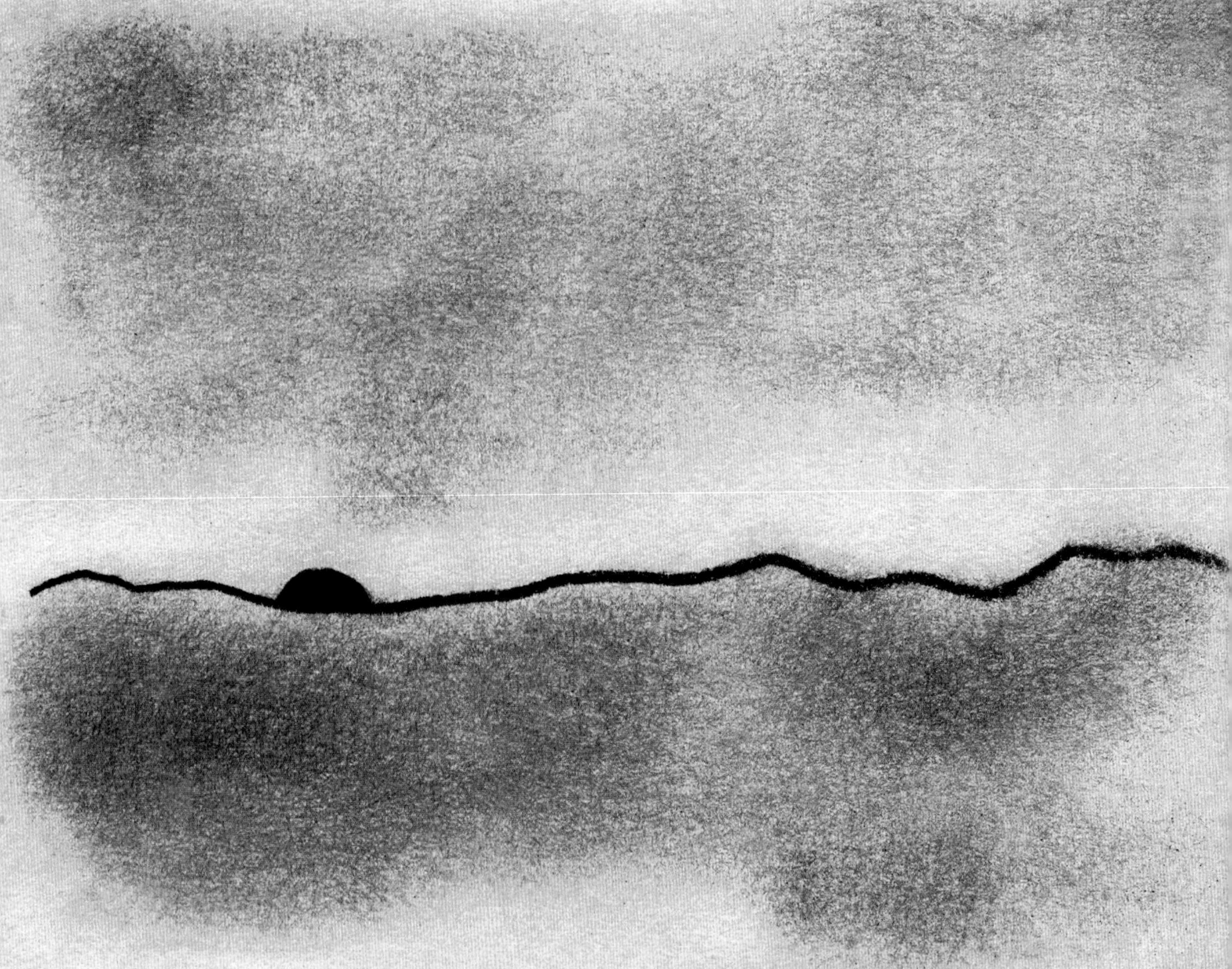

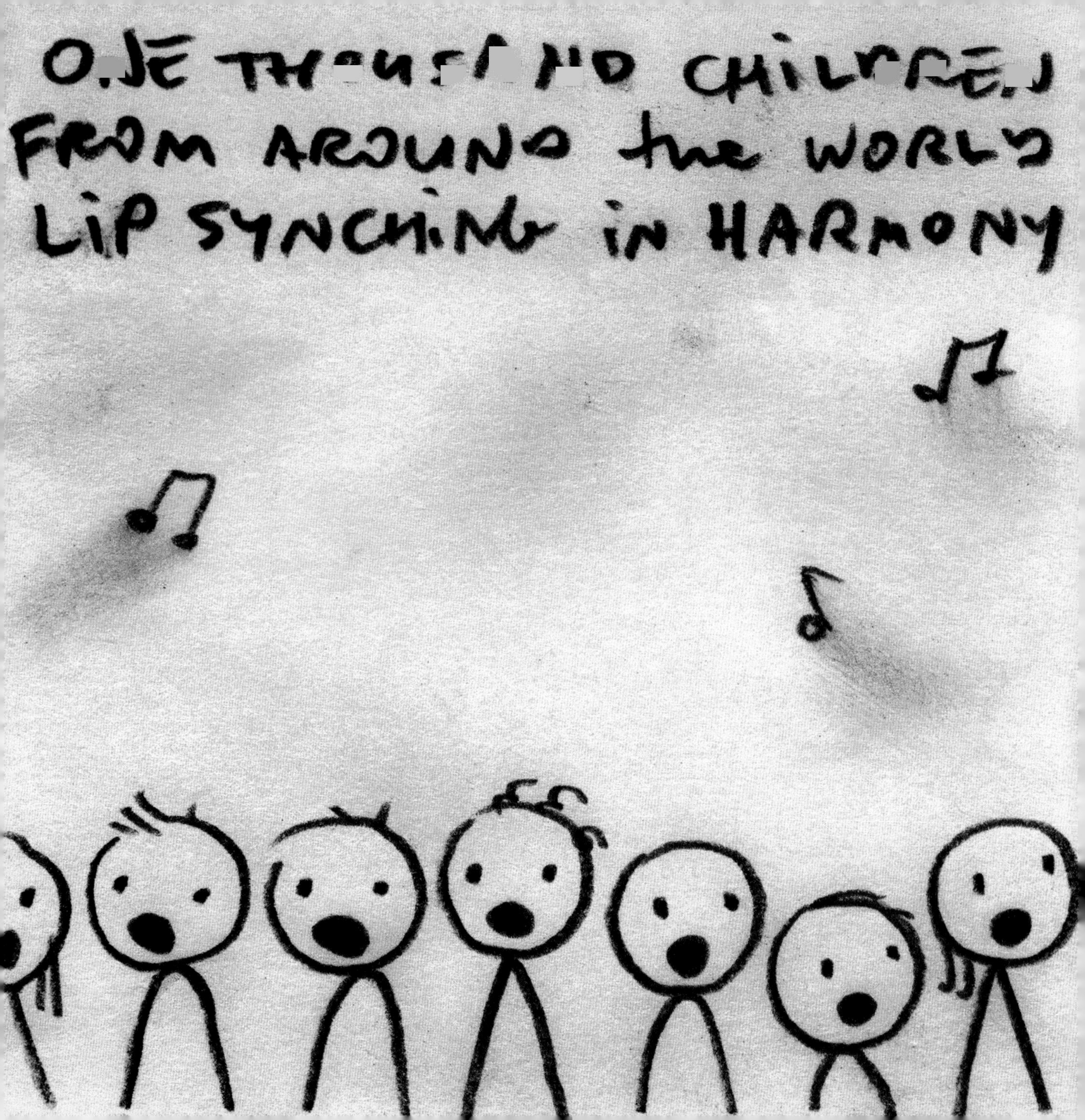
ONE THOUSAND CHILDREN FROM AROUND the WORLD LIP SYNCHING IN HARMONY

SCIENTISTS HAVE IMPREGNATED HER WITH A PERFECT CLONE OF HERSELF.

ONE DAY SHE WILL UPLOAD ALL OF HER MEMORIES INTO THIS HEALTHY NEW BODY. ONE DAY LONG AFTER THAT SHE WILL REPEAT the PROCESS ALL OVER AGAIN. SHE IS GOING TO LIVE FOREVER.

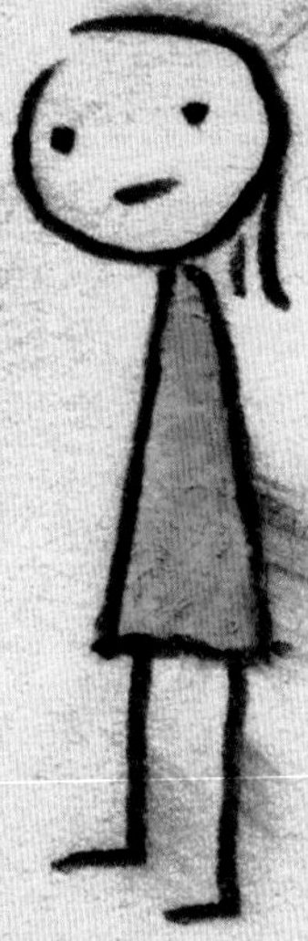

A MYSTERIOUS CORPSE APPEARS IN ORBIT

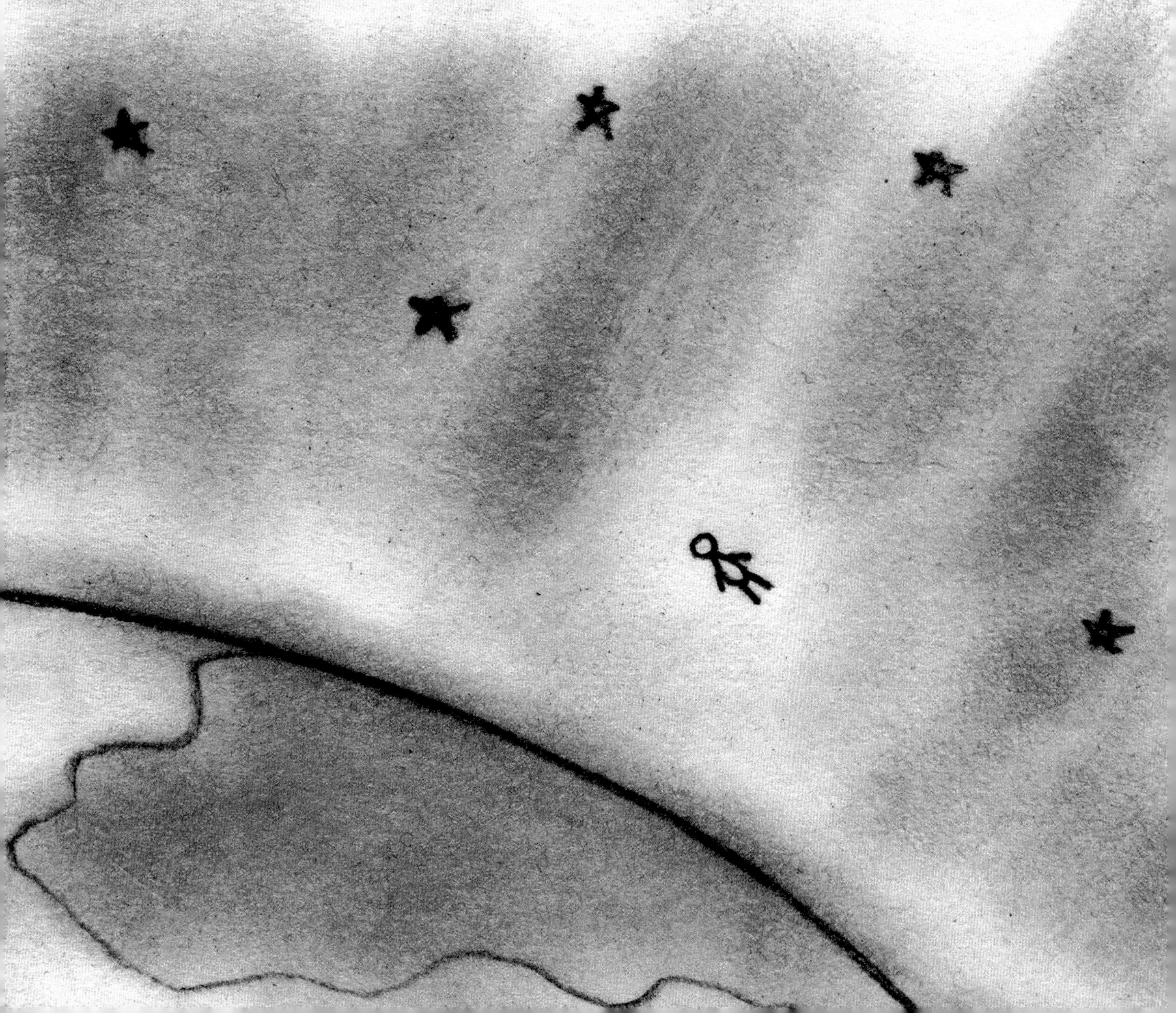

THE POPE DOES SOMETHING.

SUSAN "COLLECTS THEM ALL!"

HIDING IN HOMES AND
SAYING GOODBYE

CARTOON MARATHON ON TELEVISION.

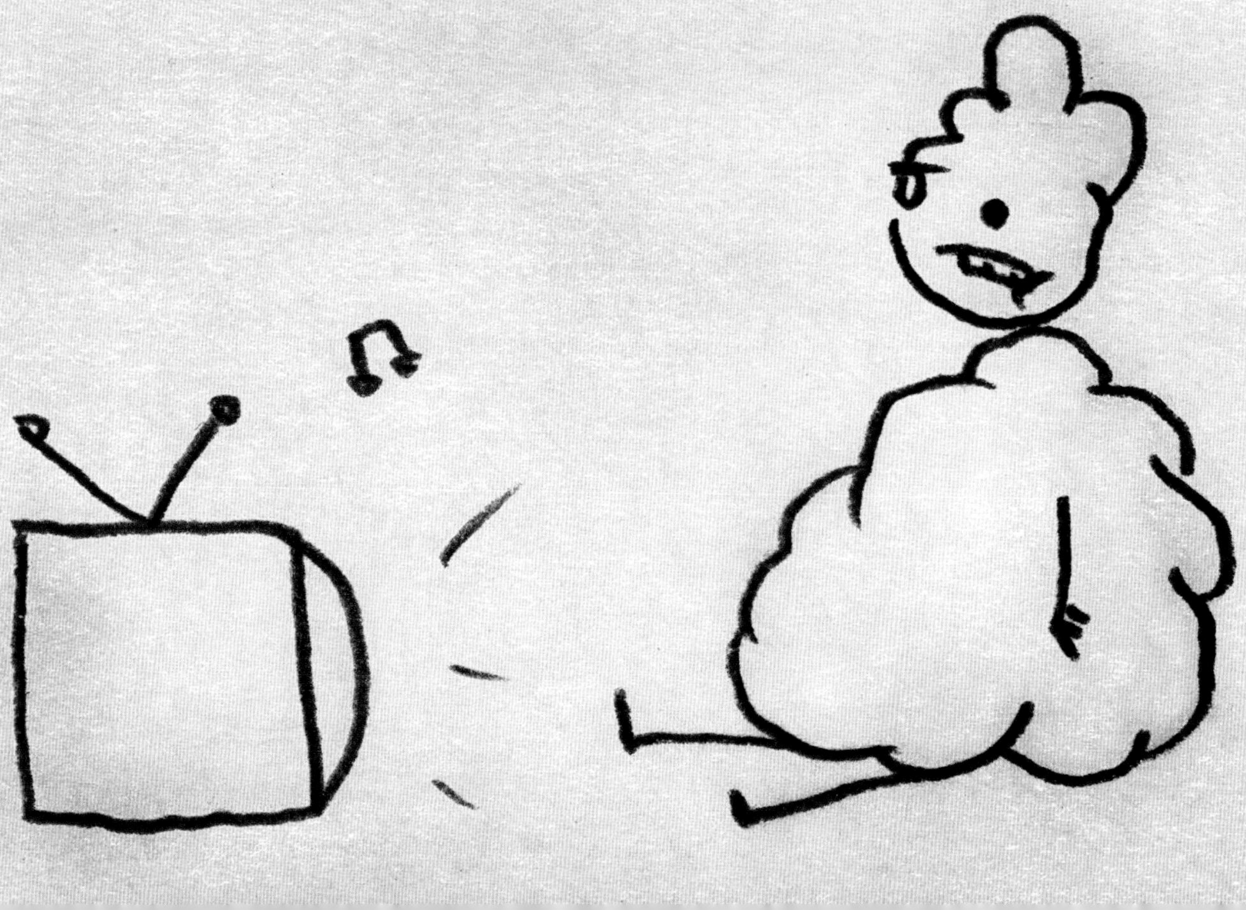

SHE HAD ARRANGED
FOR the FACE OF HER
DEAD HUSBAND TO
BE STRETCHED OVER
the HEAD OF A SIMPLE
ANIMATRONIC ROBOT,
SO SHE COULD STILL
SORT OF BE WITH HIM.

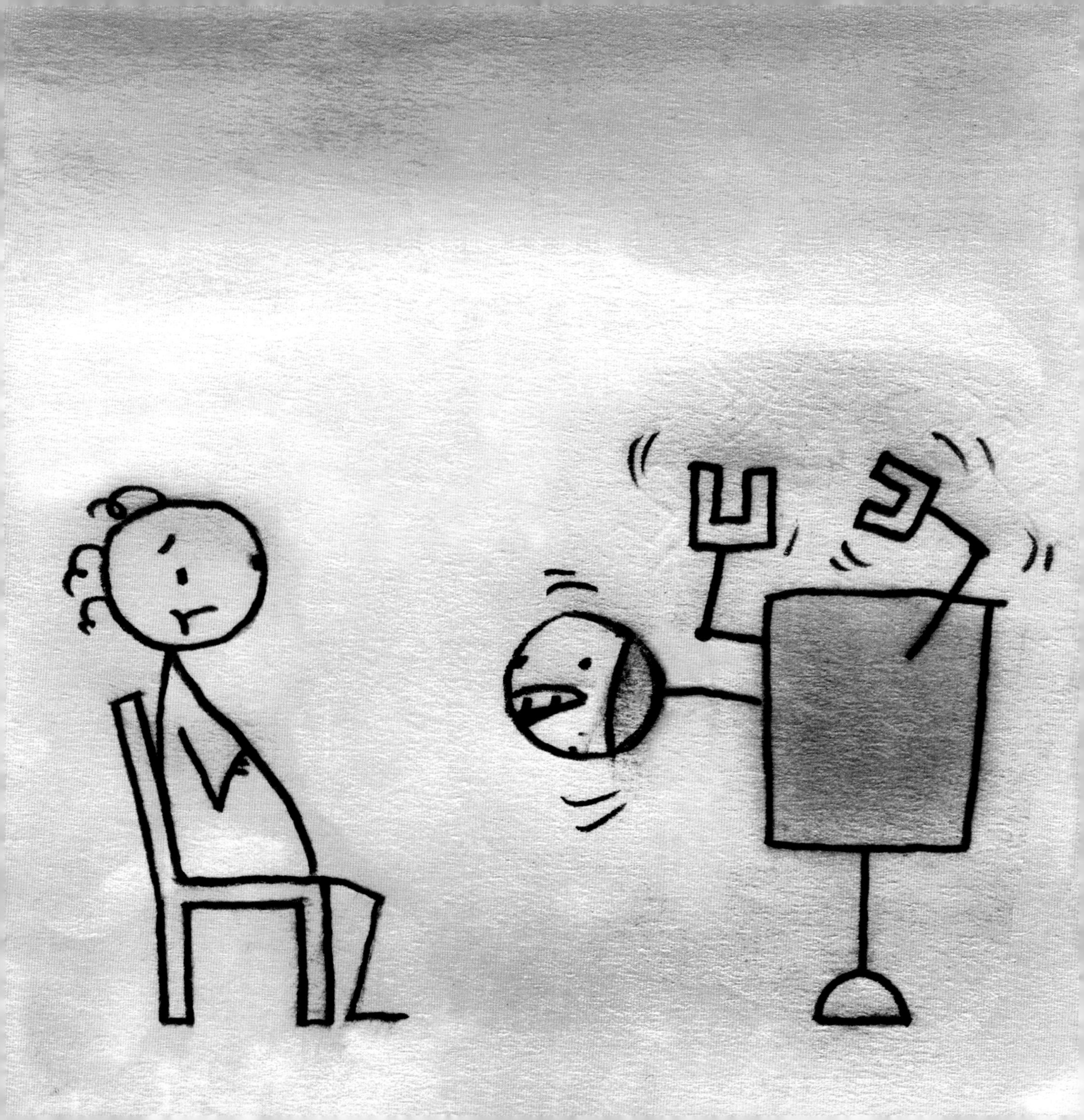

TO A DISTANT OBSERVER, the
BLAST MOMENTARILY SEEMS
LIKE A SCENE FROM A
MOTION PICTURE.

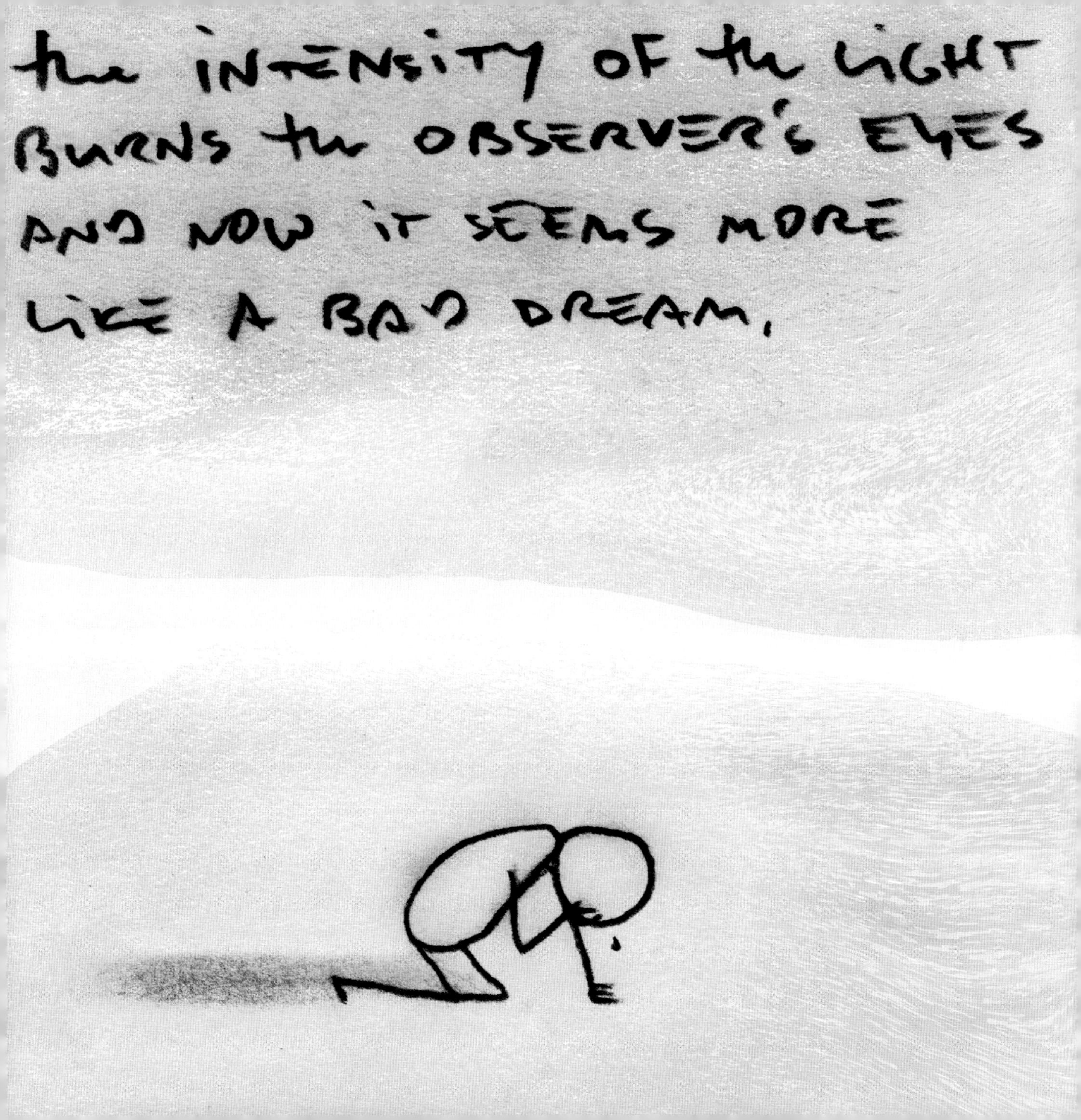

the INTENSITY OF the LIGHT
BURNS the OBSERVER'S EYES
AND NOW IT SEEMS MORE
LIKE A BAD DREAM,

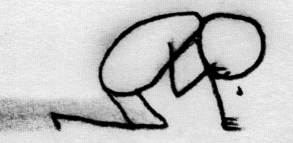

MASS CRUSTACEAN SUICIDES

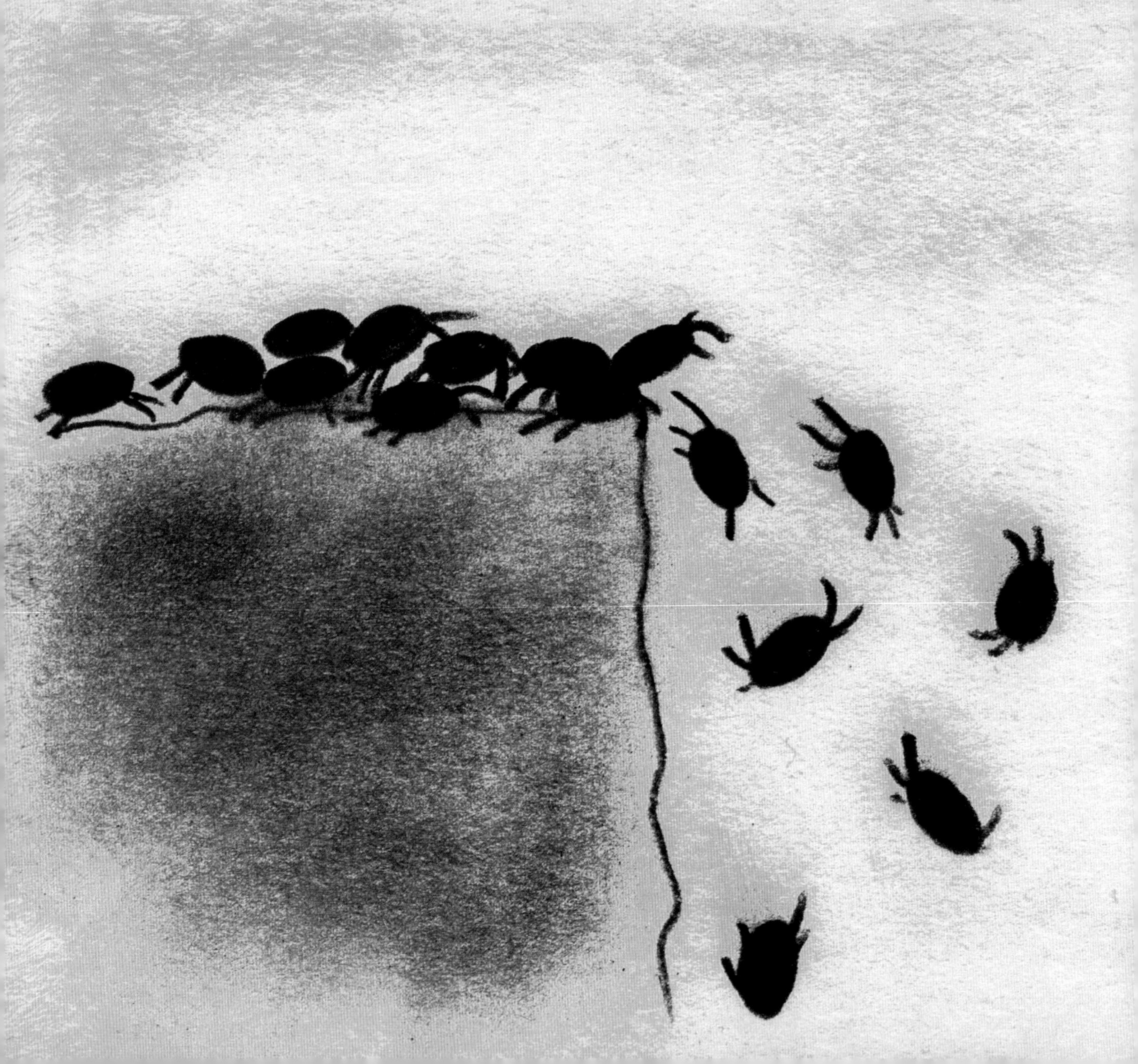

ADVERTISEMENT:

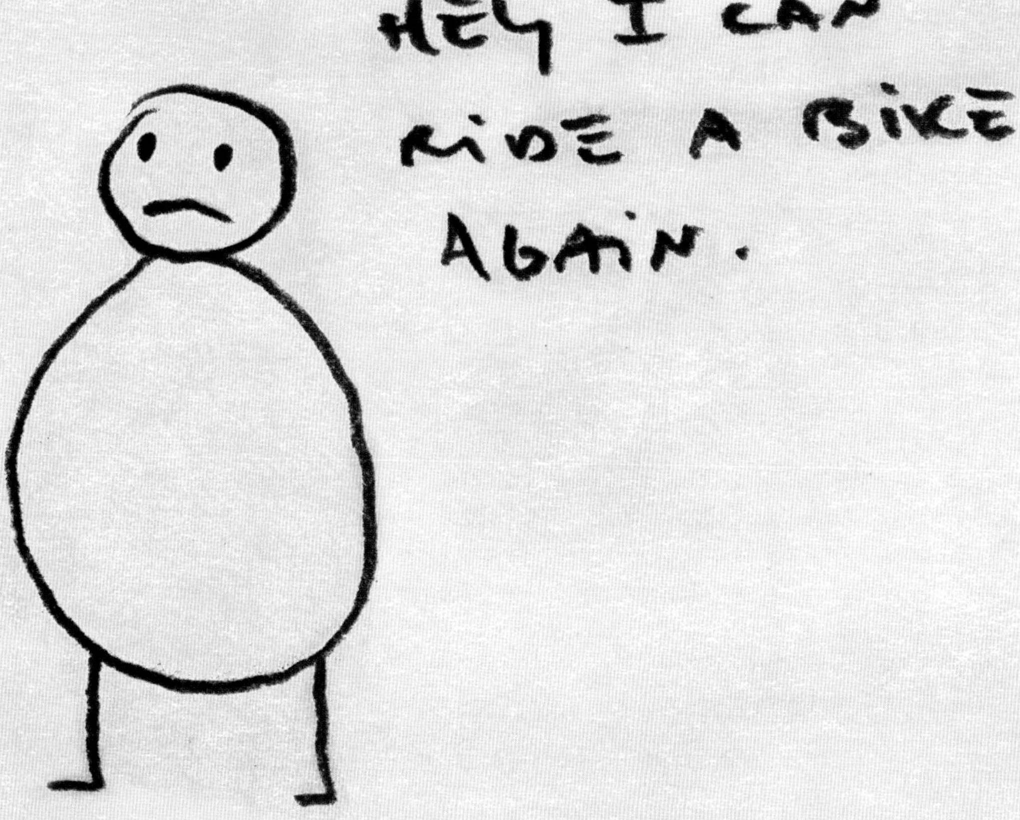
HEY I CAN RIDE A BIKE AGAIN.

"WE ARE FLOATING IN
the MIST OF UZBEKISTAN."

A FAT GUY JOGS AIMLESSLY DOWN THE STREET WITH AN EMPTY CUP.

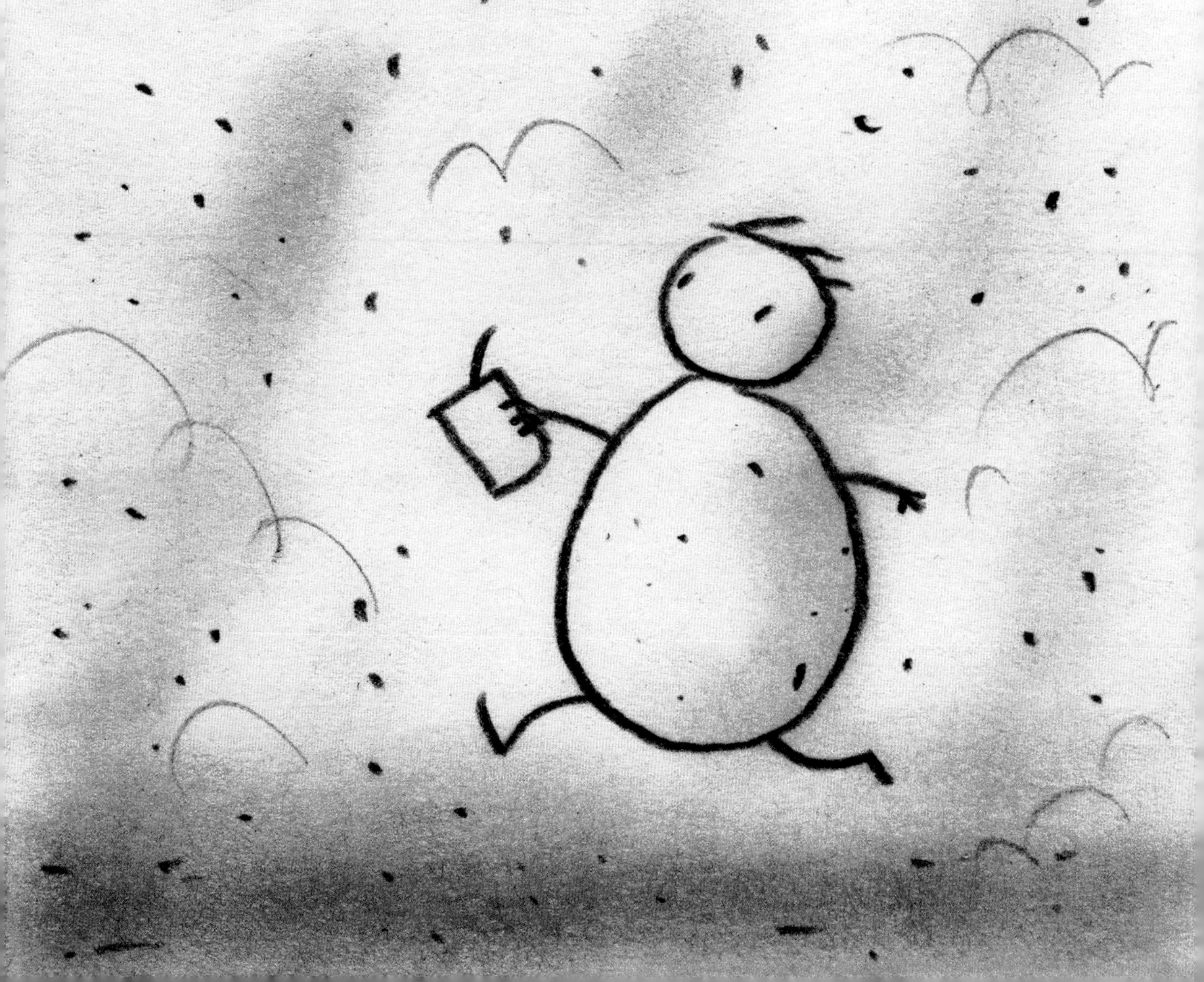

BEFORE the FIRST SHOCKWAVE HITS THEY ARE MOMENTARILY WEIGHTLESS.

YOUNG PEOPLE ON TV FROZEN IN A MID AIR LEAP OVER the TASTE OF COLA

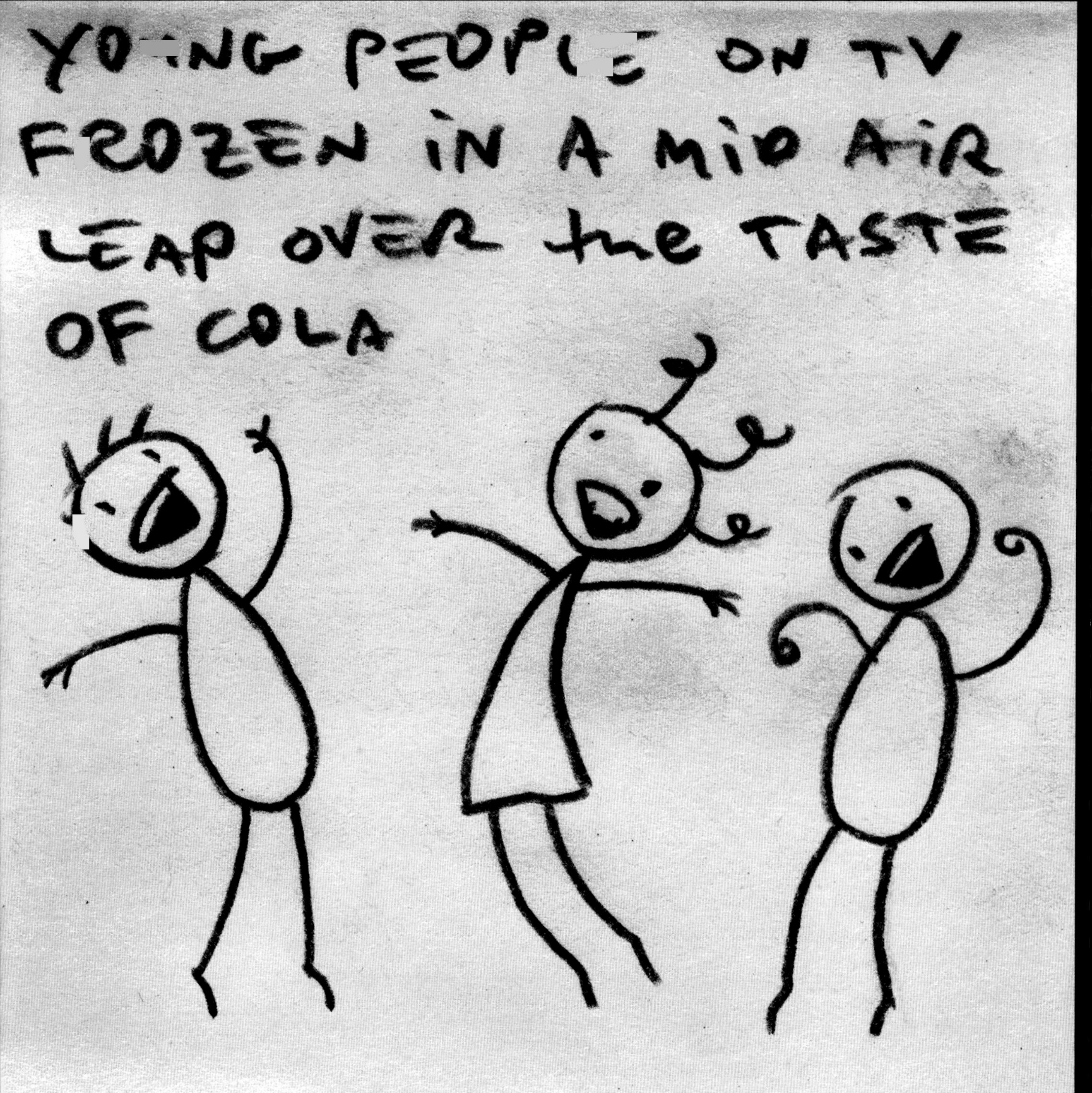

DEAD LIVESTOCK BLOWN into the POWER LINES

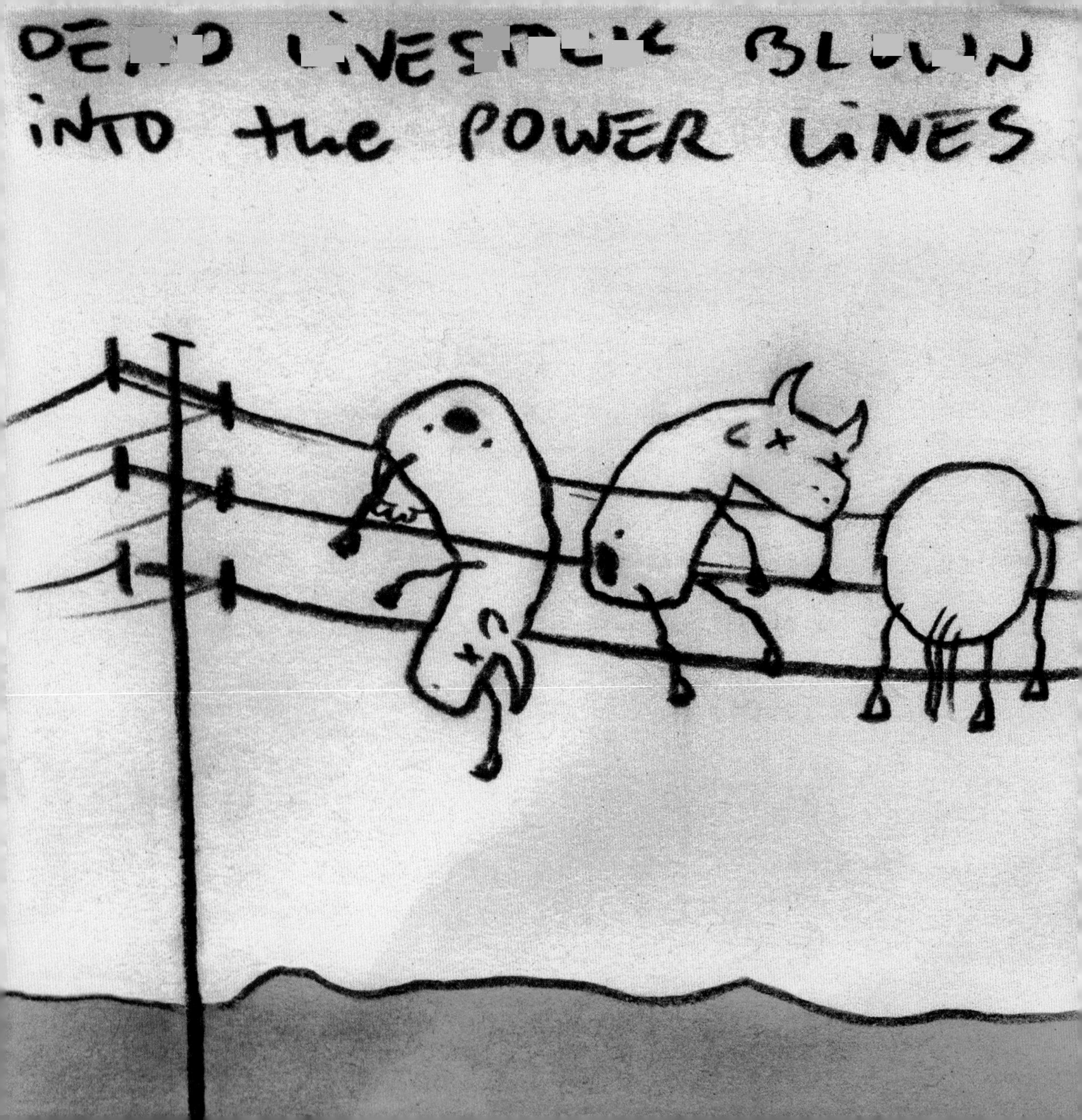

A SUDDEN CHILDHOOD MEMORY AS PIECES FALL

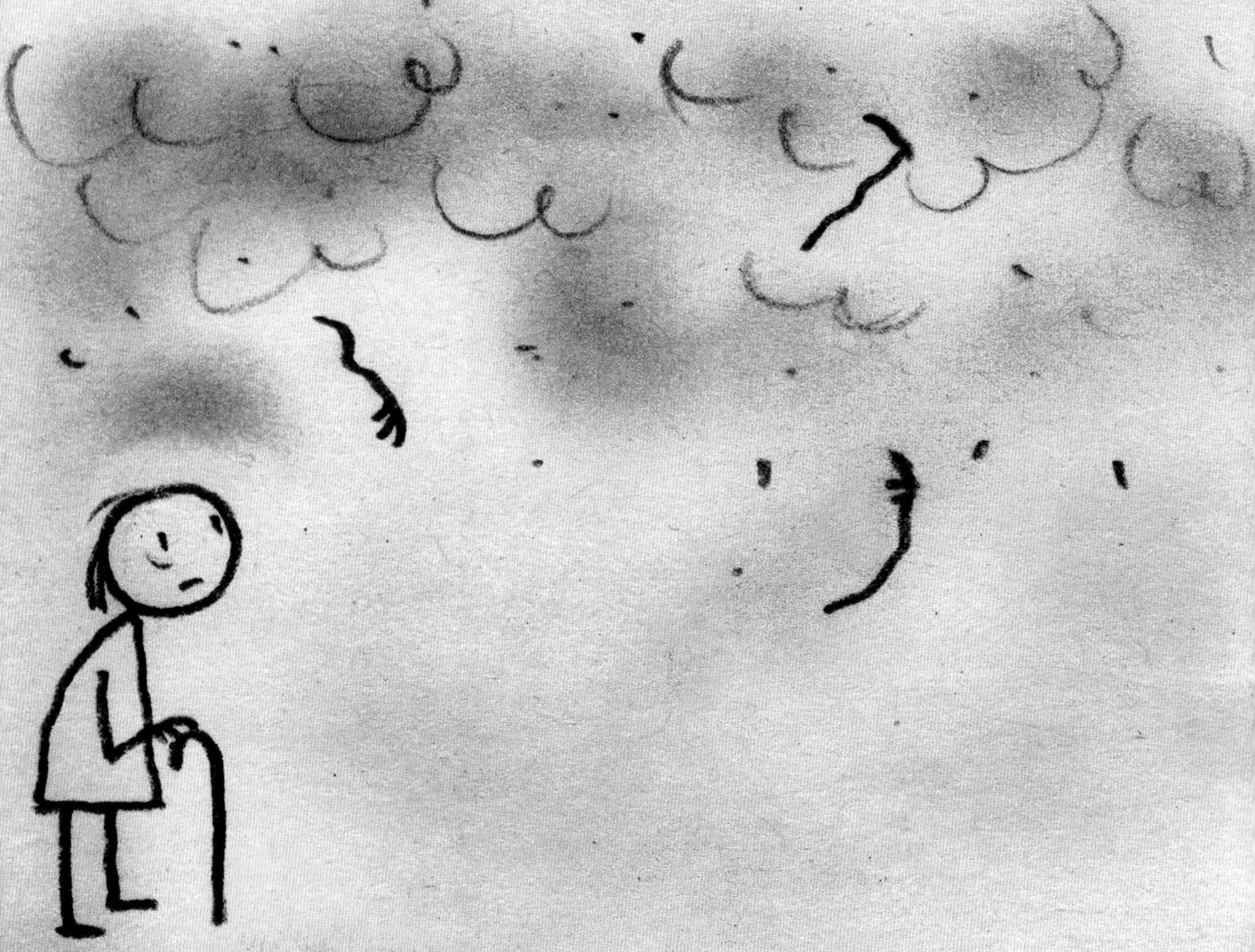

"CURSED BY GOD, WITH A BUCKET AND THE MILK CAN," HE SAYS, THROUGH THE FALLING ASH.

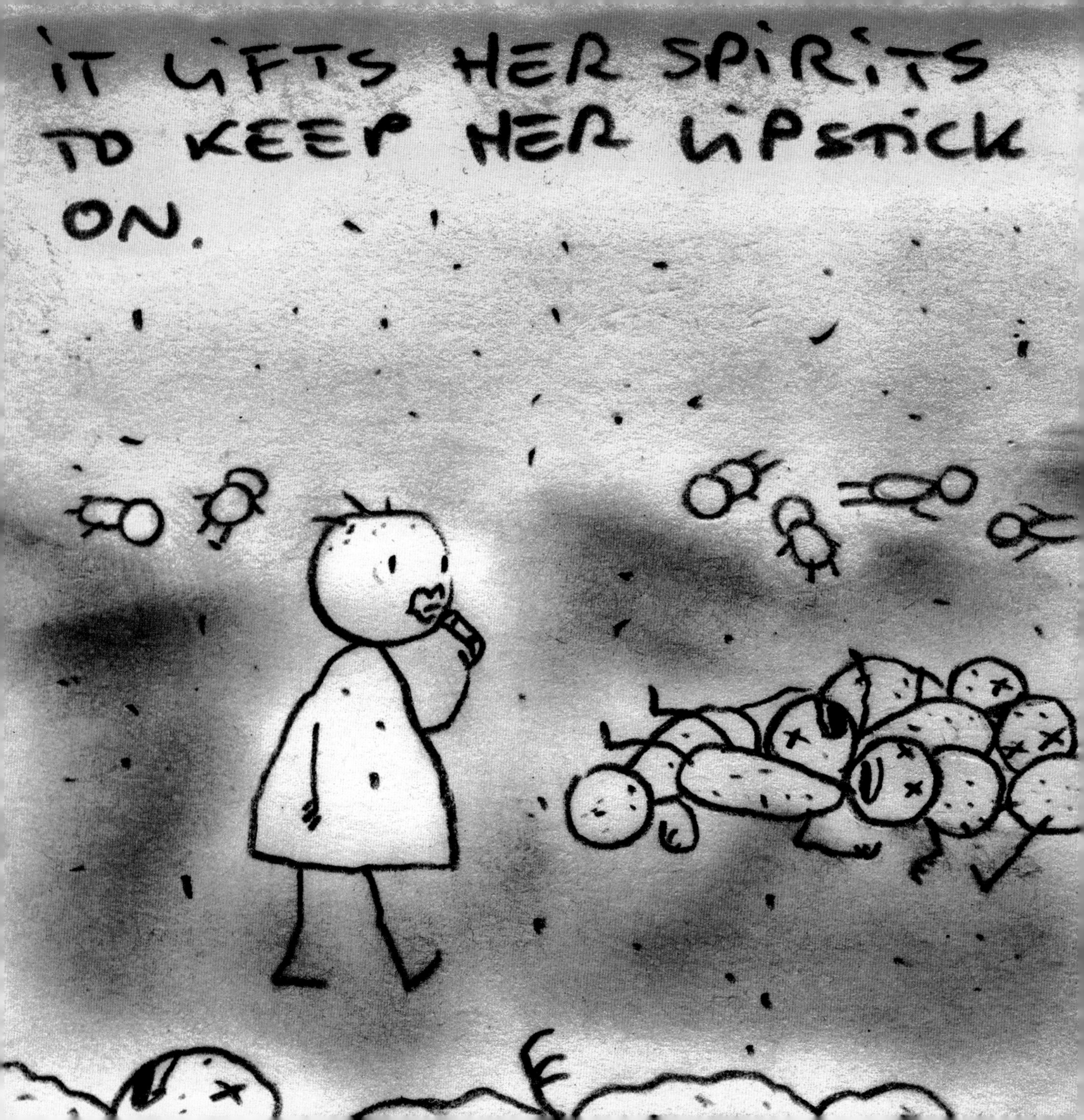
IT LIFTS HER SPIRITS TO KEEP HER LIPSTICK ON.

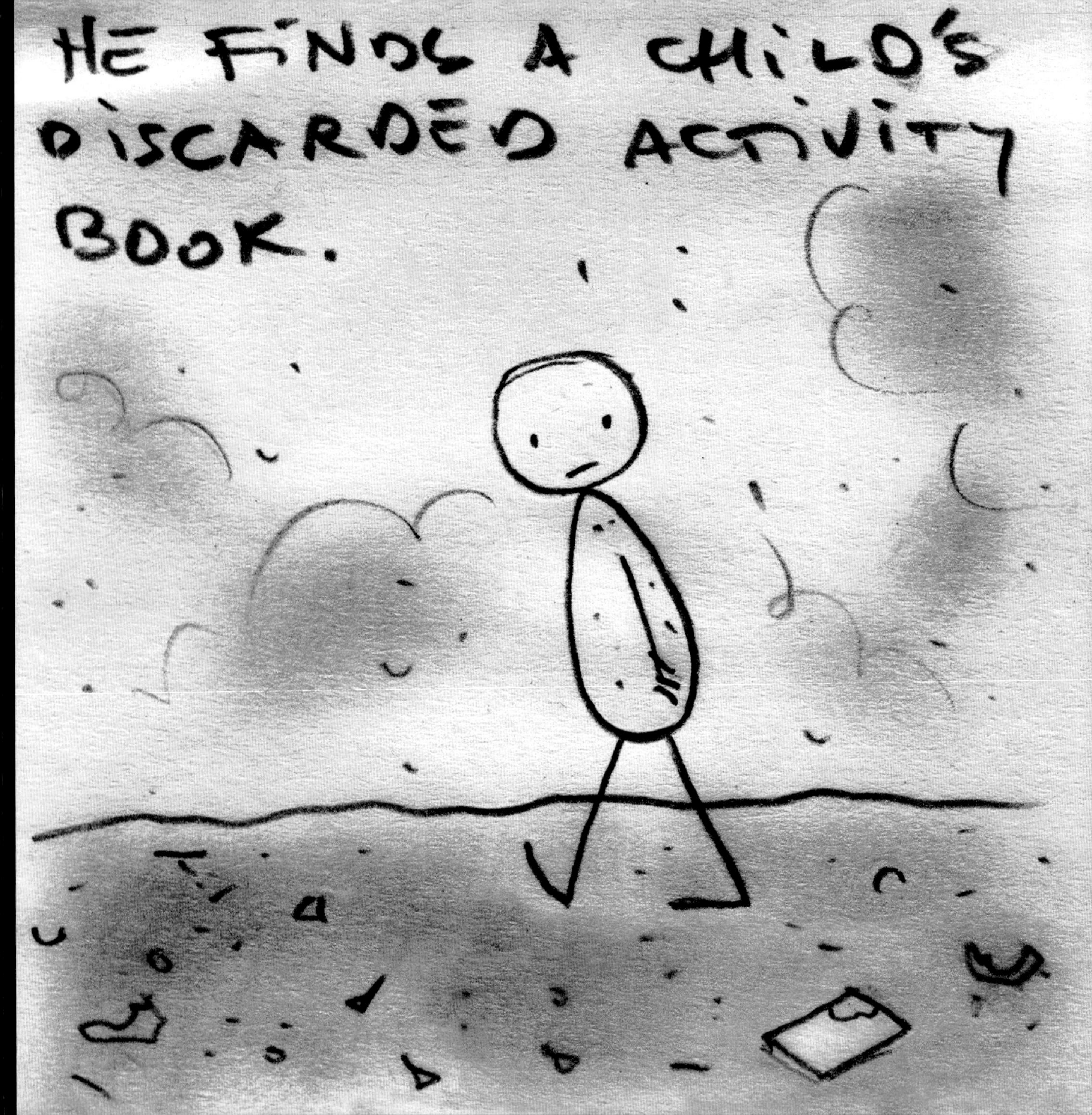
HE FINDS A CHILD'S DISCARDED ACTIVITY BOOK.

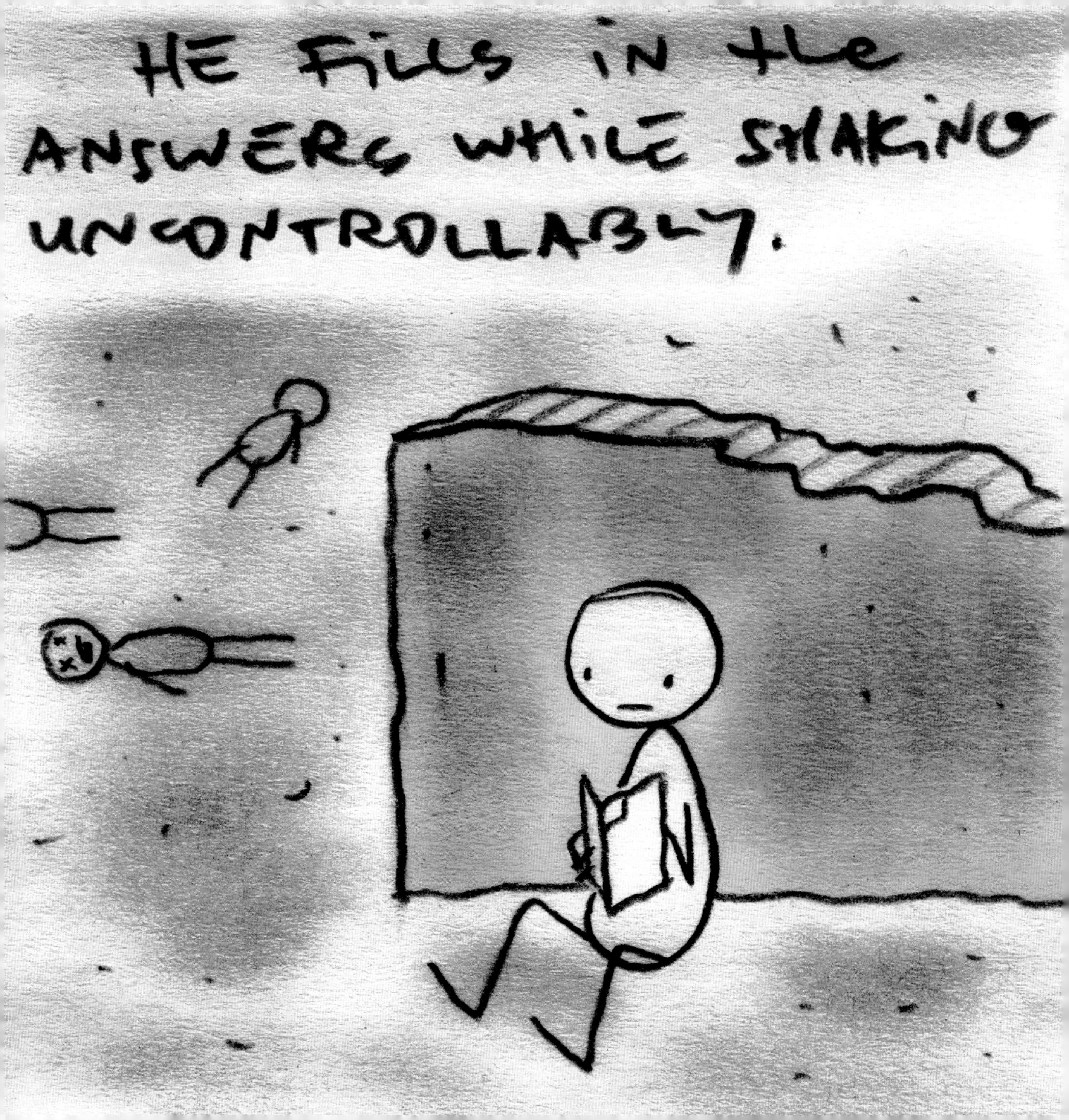
HE FILLS IN THE ANSWERS WHILE SHAKING UNCONTROLLABLY.

HAIR FALLS OUT IN IRREGULAR CLUMPS

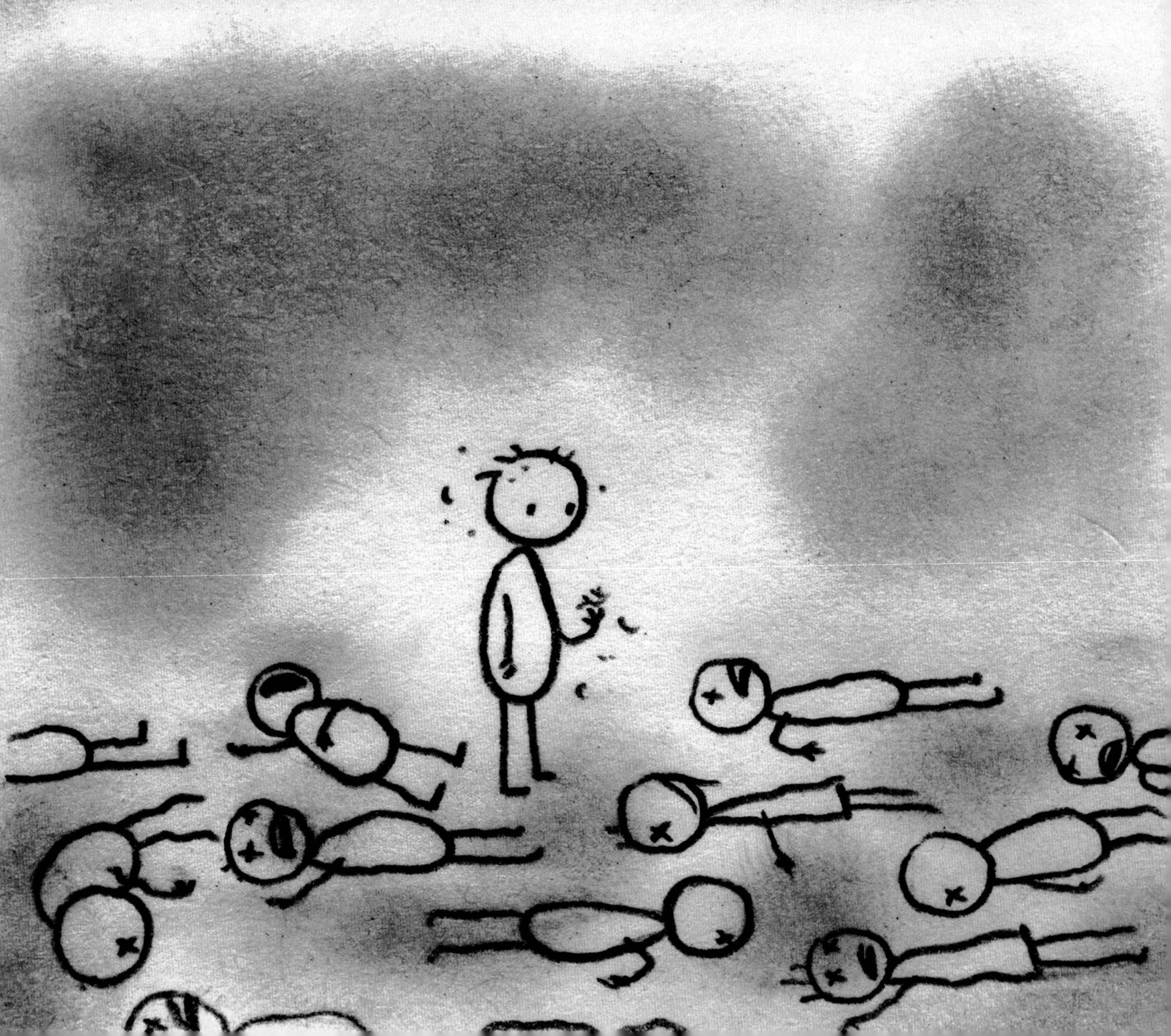

LITTLE PACKAGED HOTEL
SOAP BARS AS FAR AS
the EYE CAN SEE

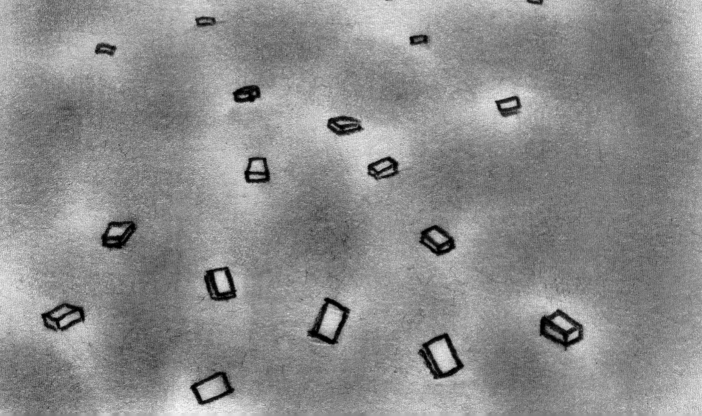

the LAST OF the STREET LIGHTS FLICKERS OUT

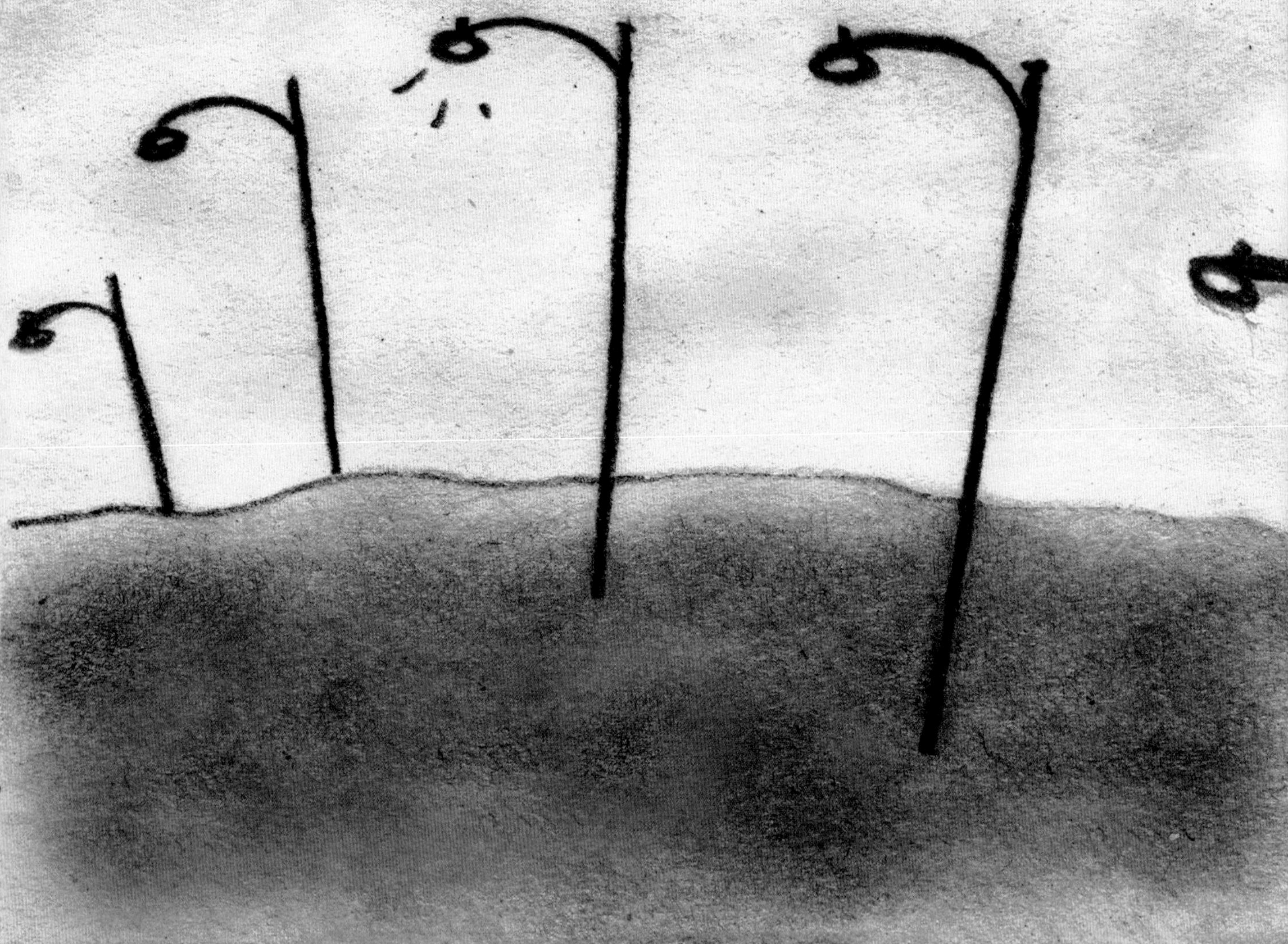

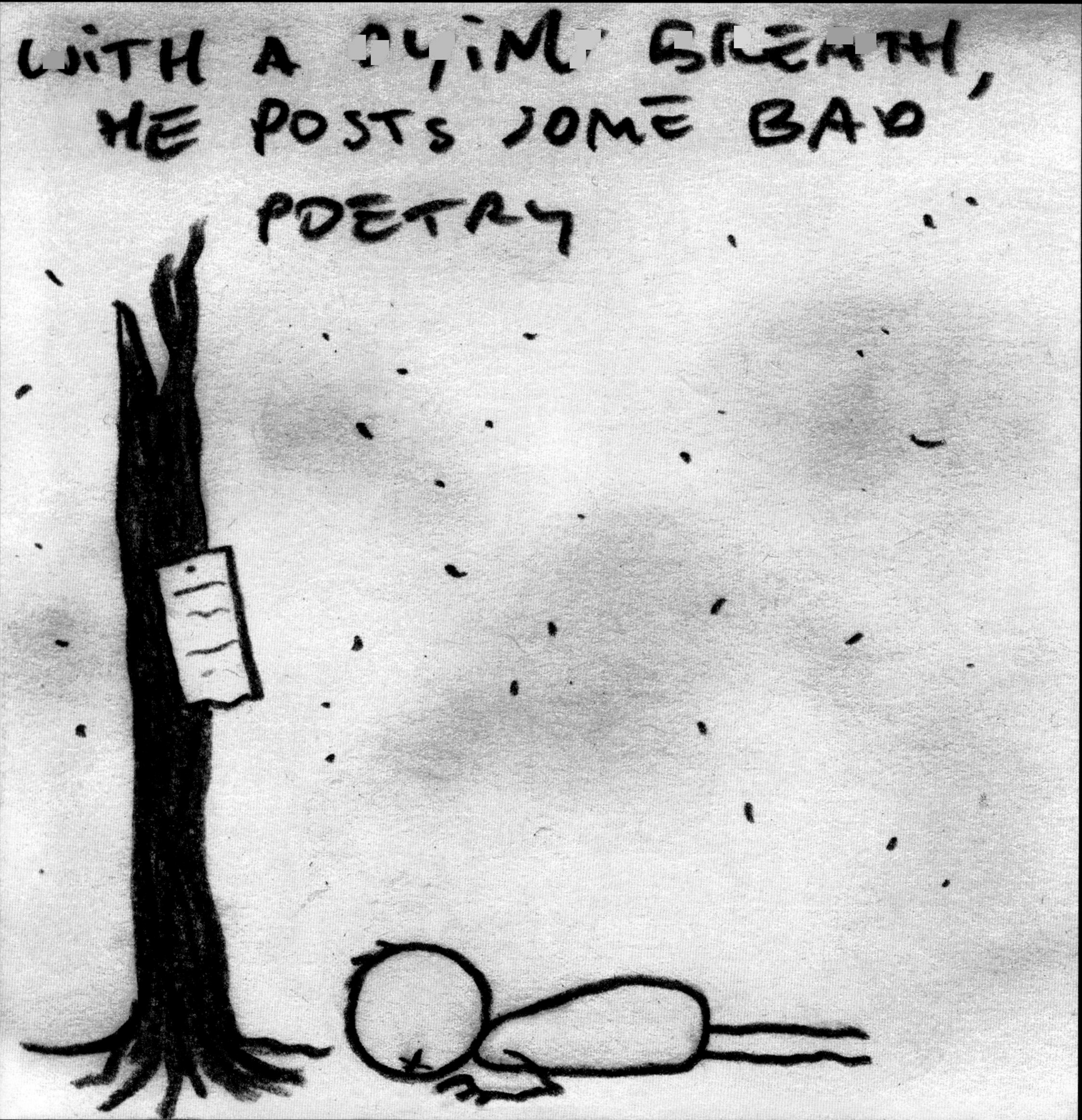
WITH A DYING BREATH,
HE POSTS SOME BAD
POETRY

THINGS ARE GROWING
OUT OF the EARTH

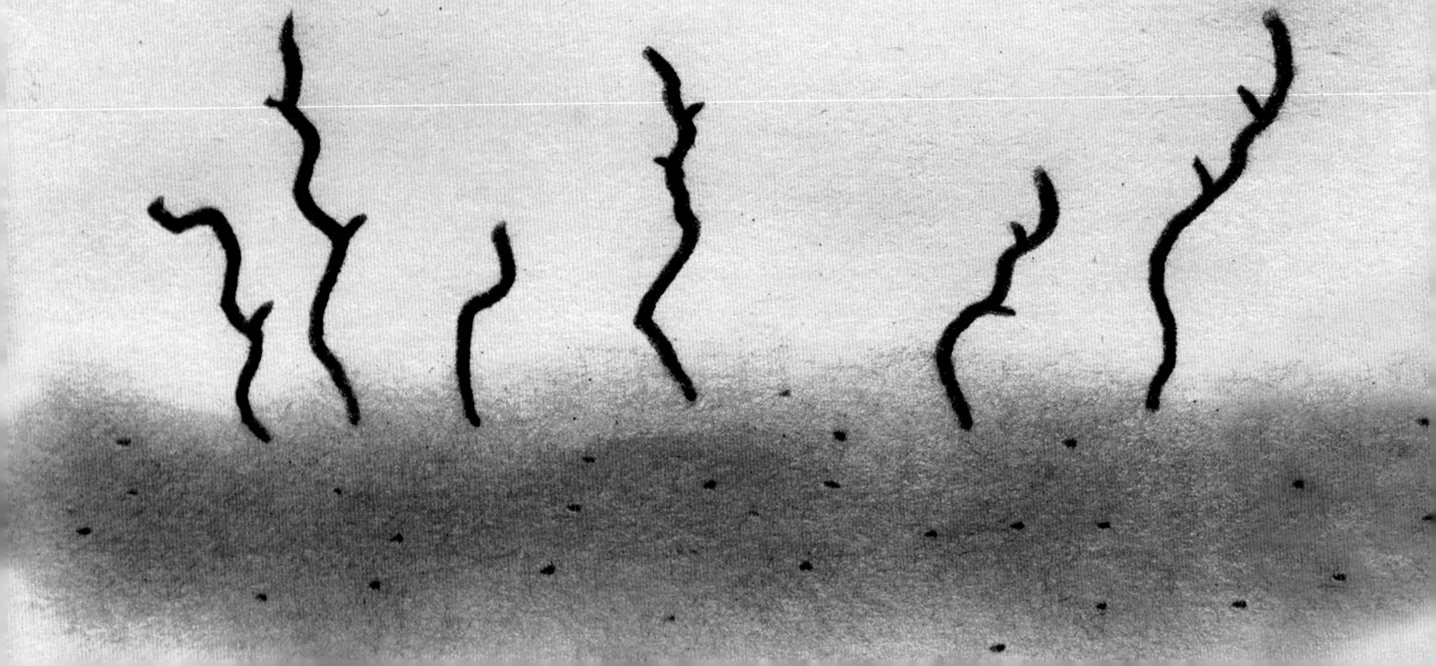

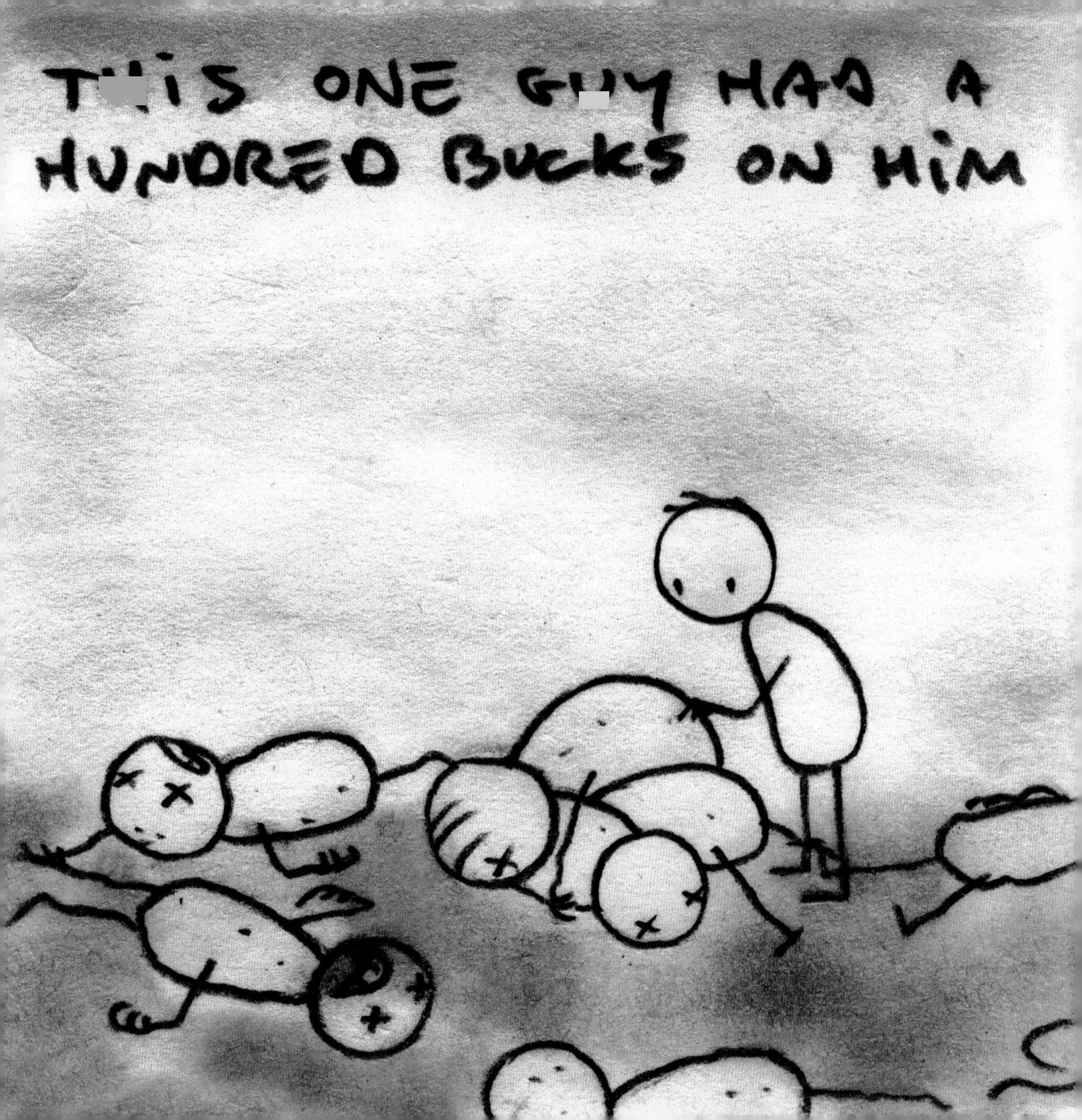
THIS ONE GUY HAD A
HUNDRED BUCKS ON HIM

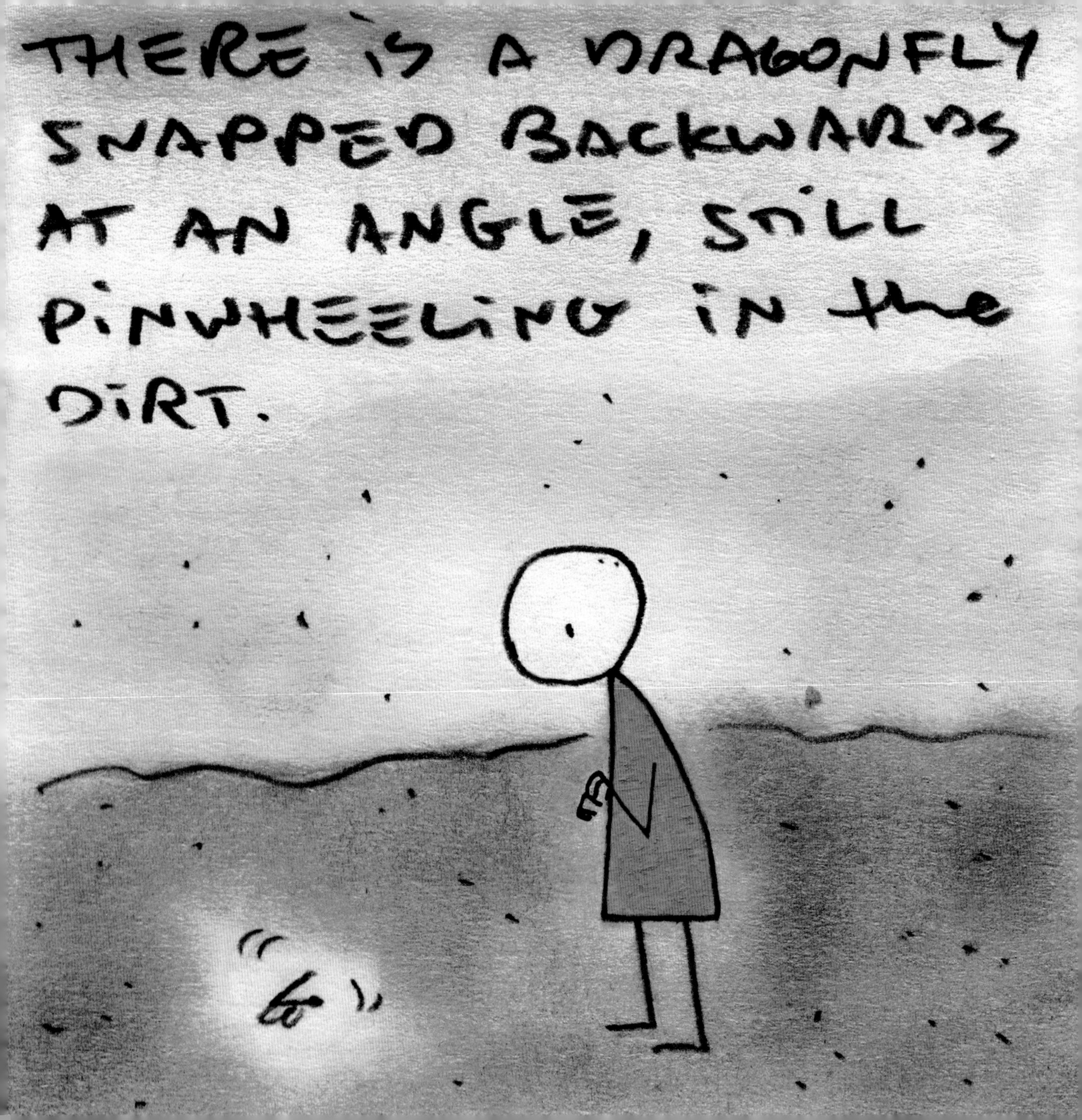
THERE IS A DRAGONFLY SNAPPED BACKWARDS AT AN ANGLE, STILL PINWHEELING IN the DIRT.

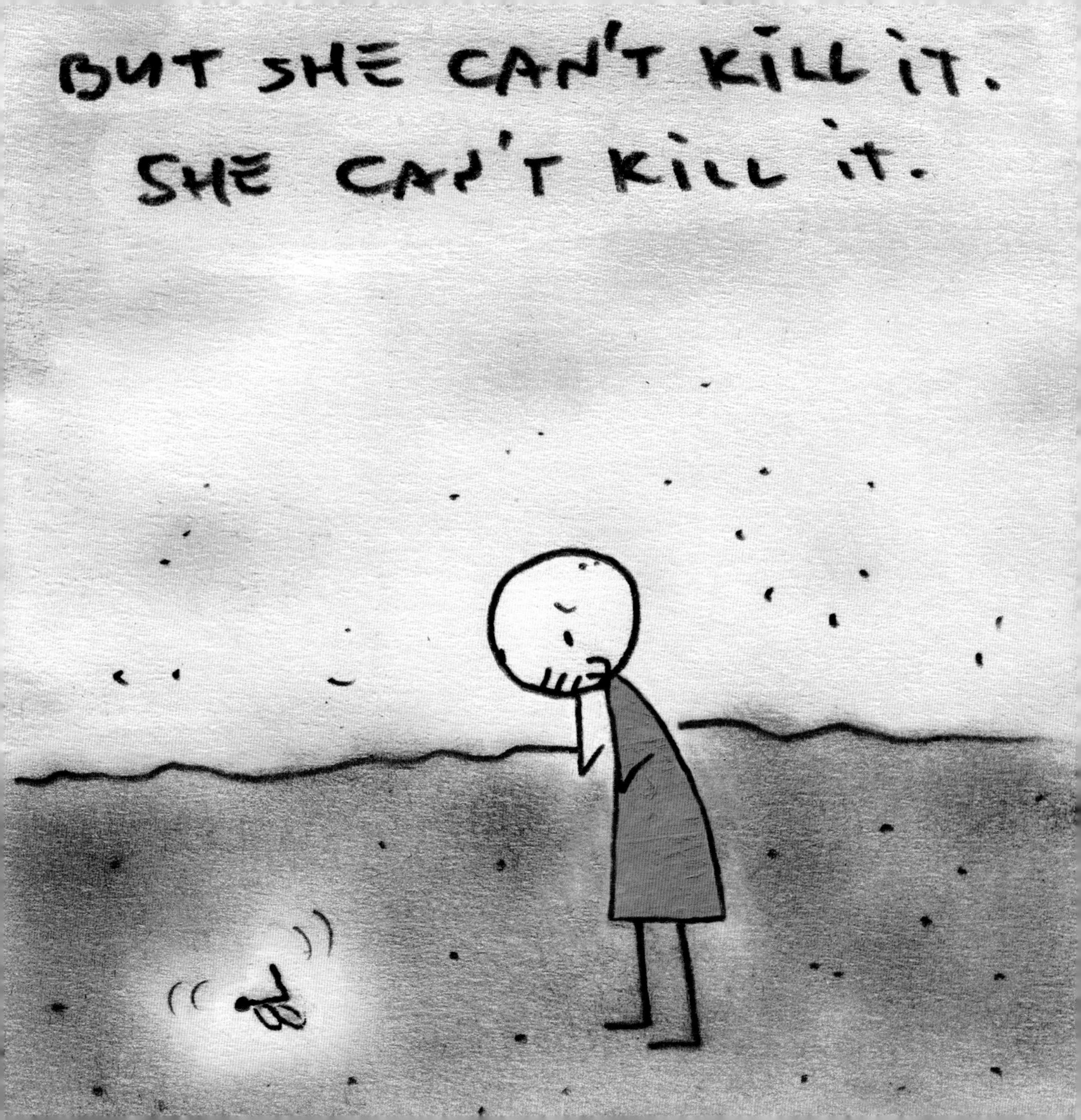
BUT SHE CAN'T KILL IT.
SHE CAN'T KILL IT.

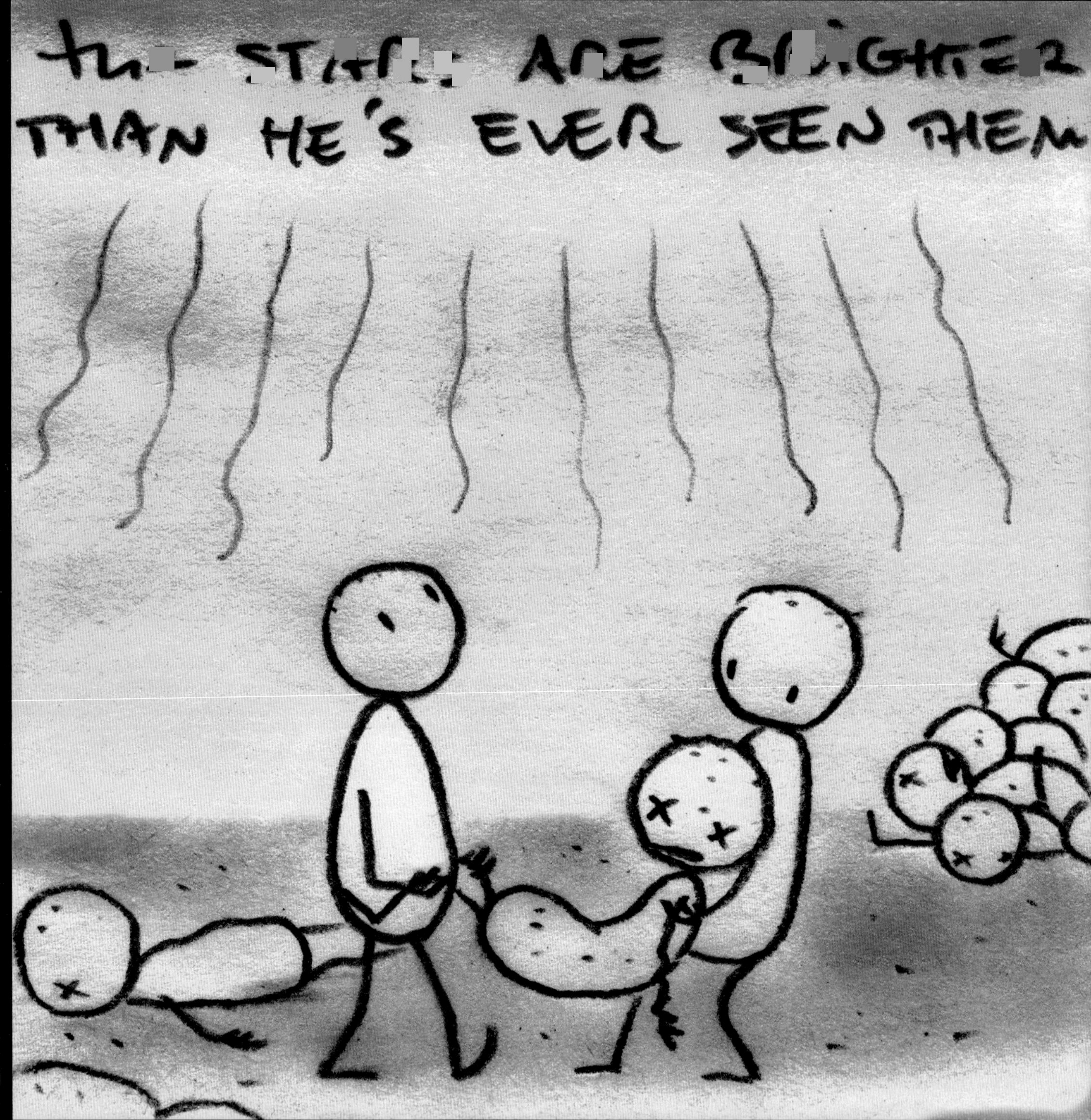
THE STARS ARE BRIGHTER
THAN HE'S EVER SEEN THEM

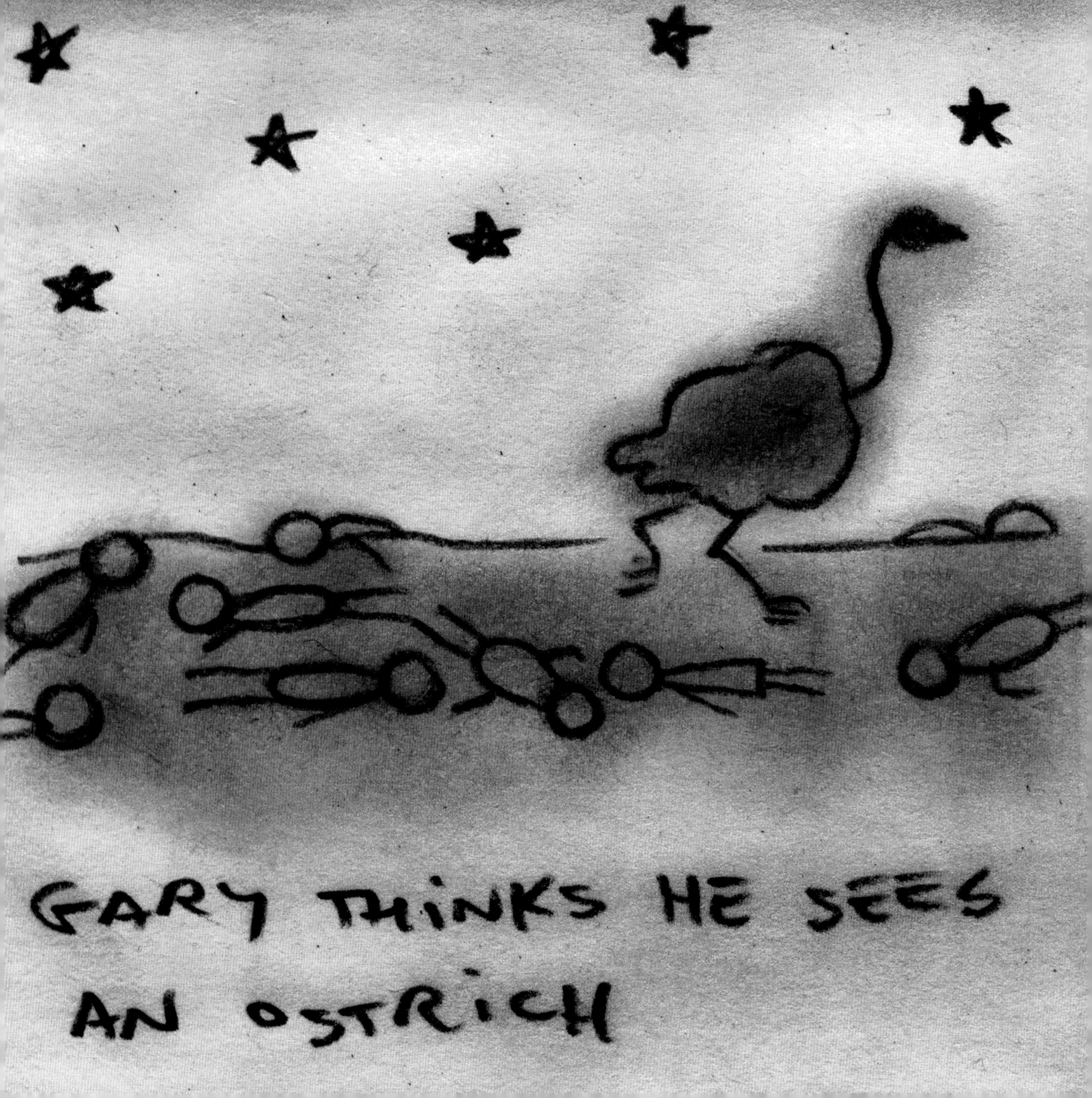

GARY THINKS HE SEES AN OSTRICH

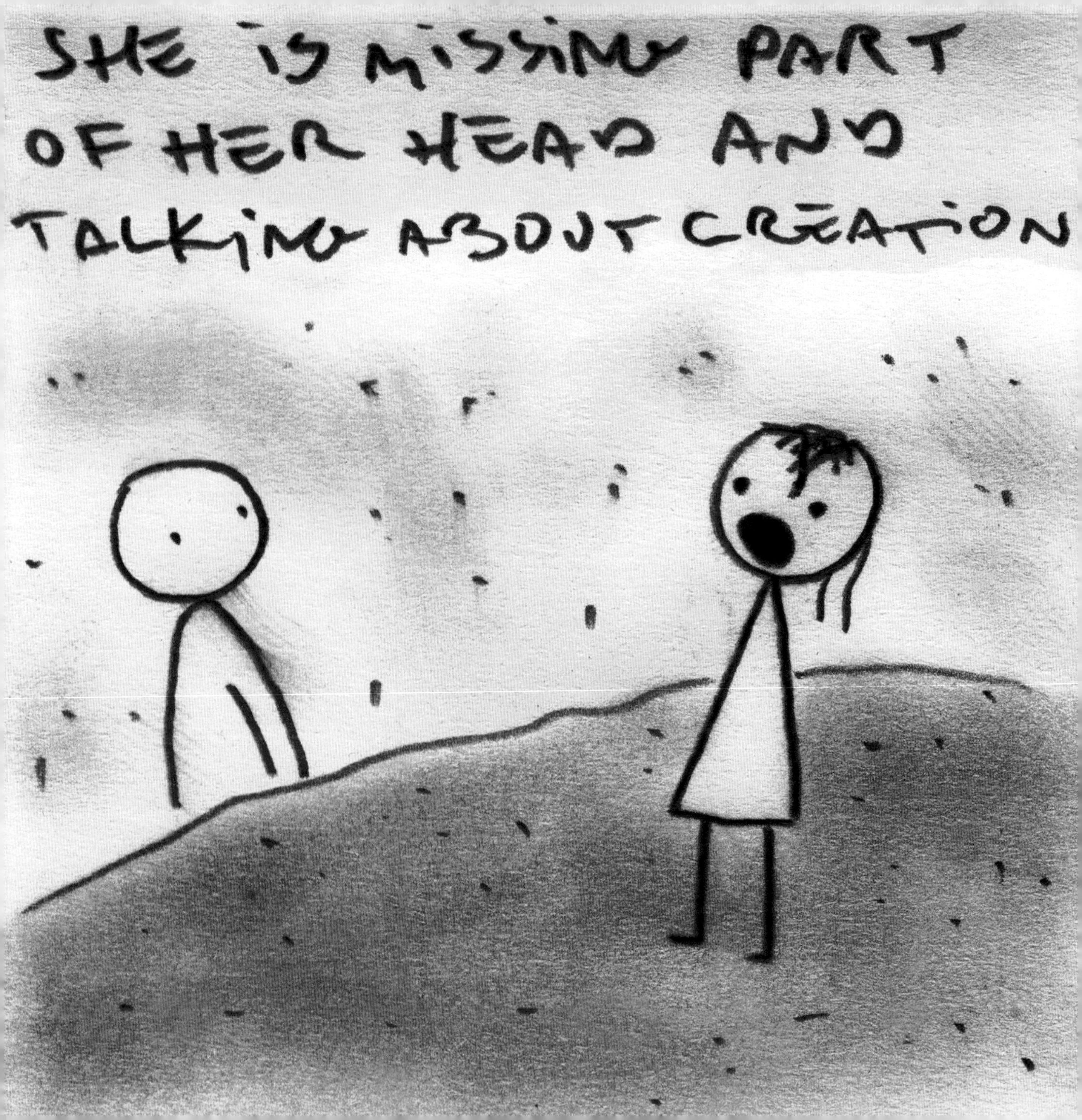
SHE IS MISSING PART OF HER HEAD AND TALKING ABOUT CREATION

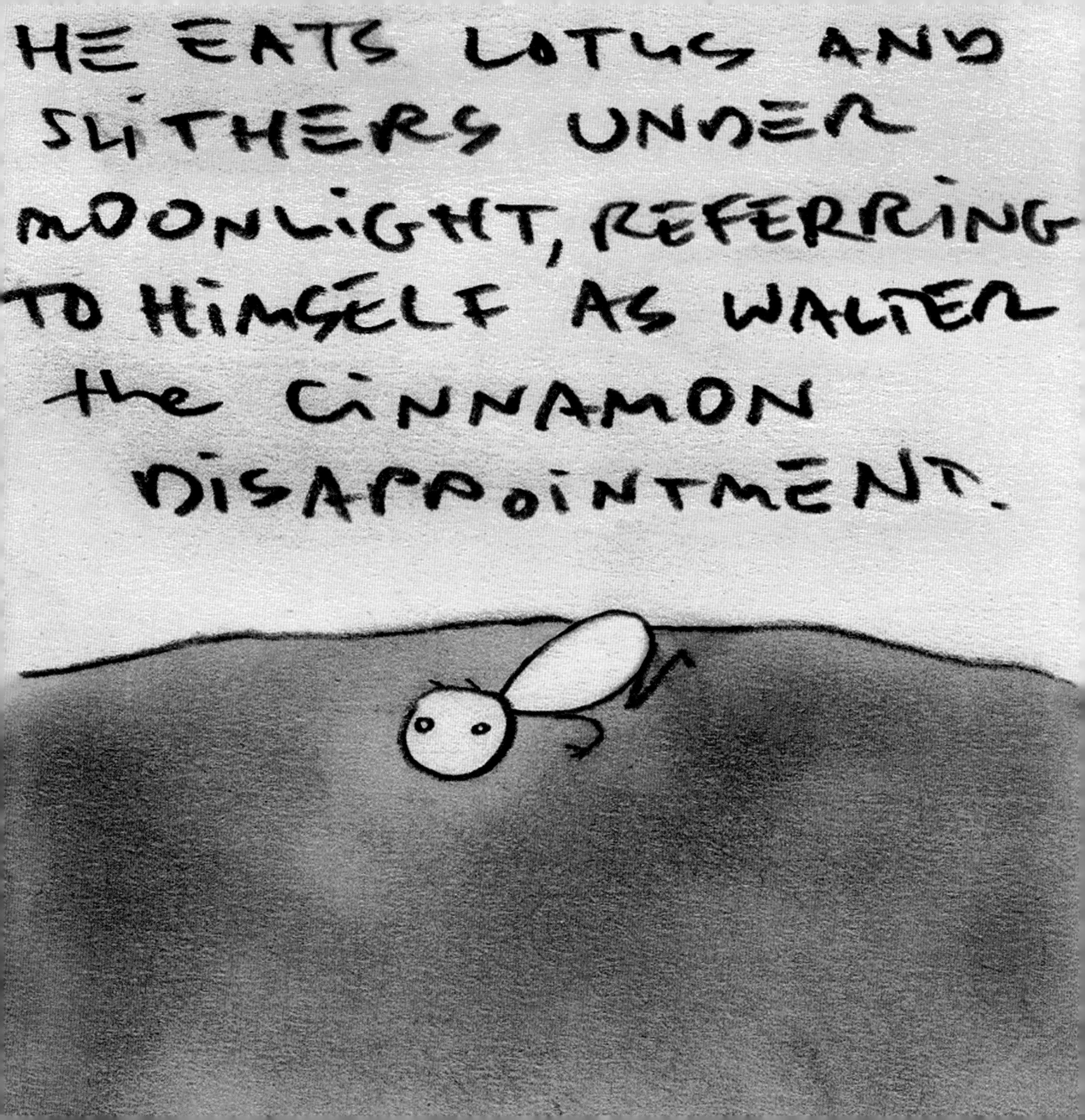
HE EATS LOTUS AND SLITHERS UNDER MOONLIGHT, REFERRING TO HIMSELF AS WALTER the CINNAMON DISAPPOINTMENT.

A BUCKET OF WEDDING RINGS IS PLACED BESIDE EACH PILE TO AID FUTURE IDENTIFICATION.

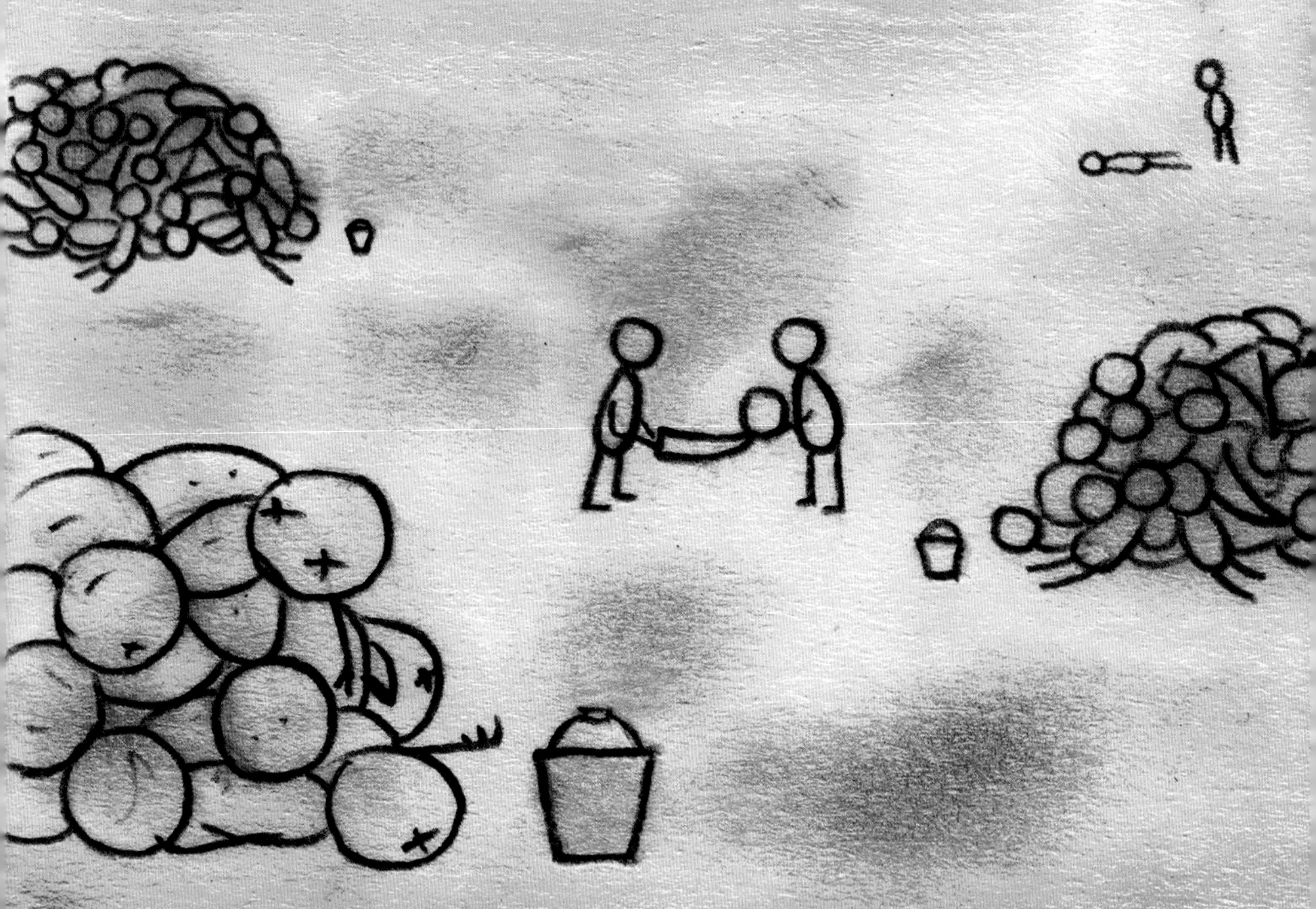

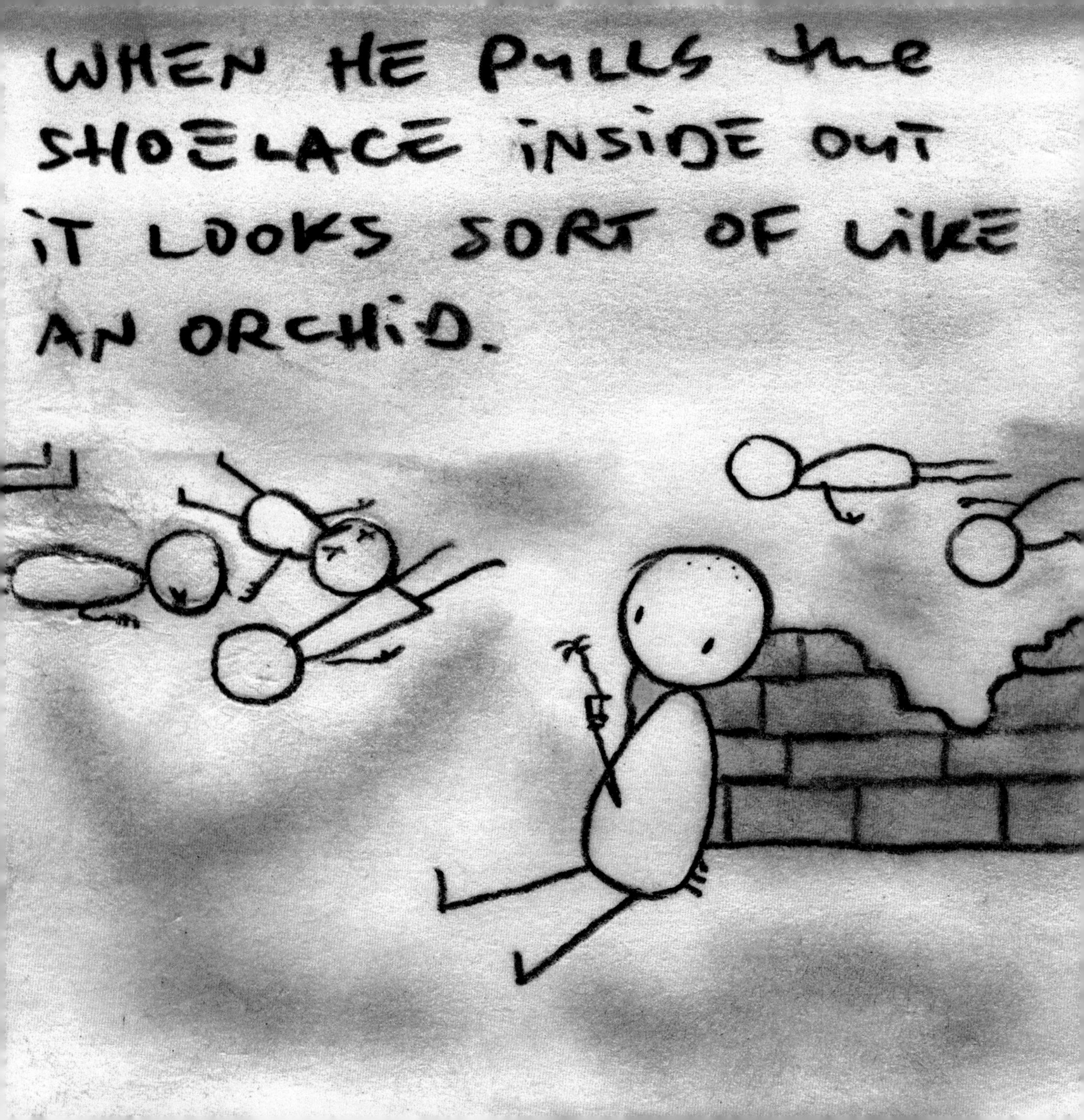
WHEN HE PULLS the SHOELACE INSIDE OUT IT LOOKS SORT OF LIKE AN ORCHID.

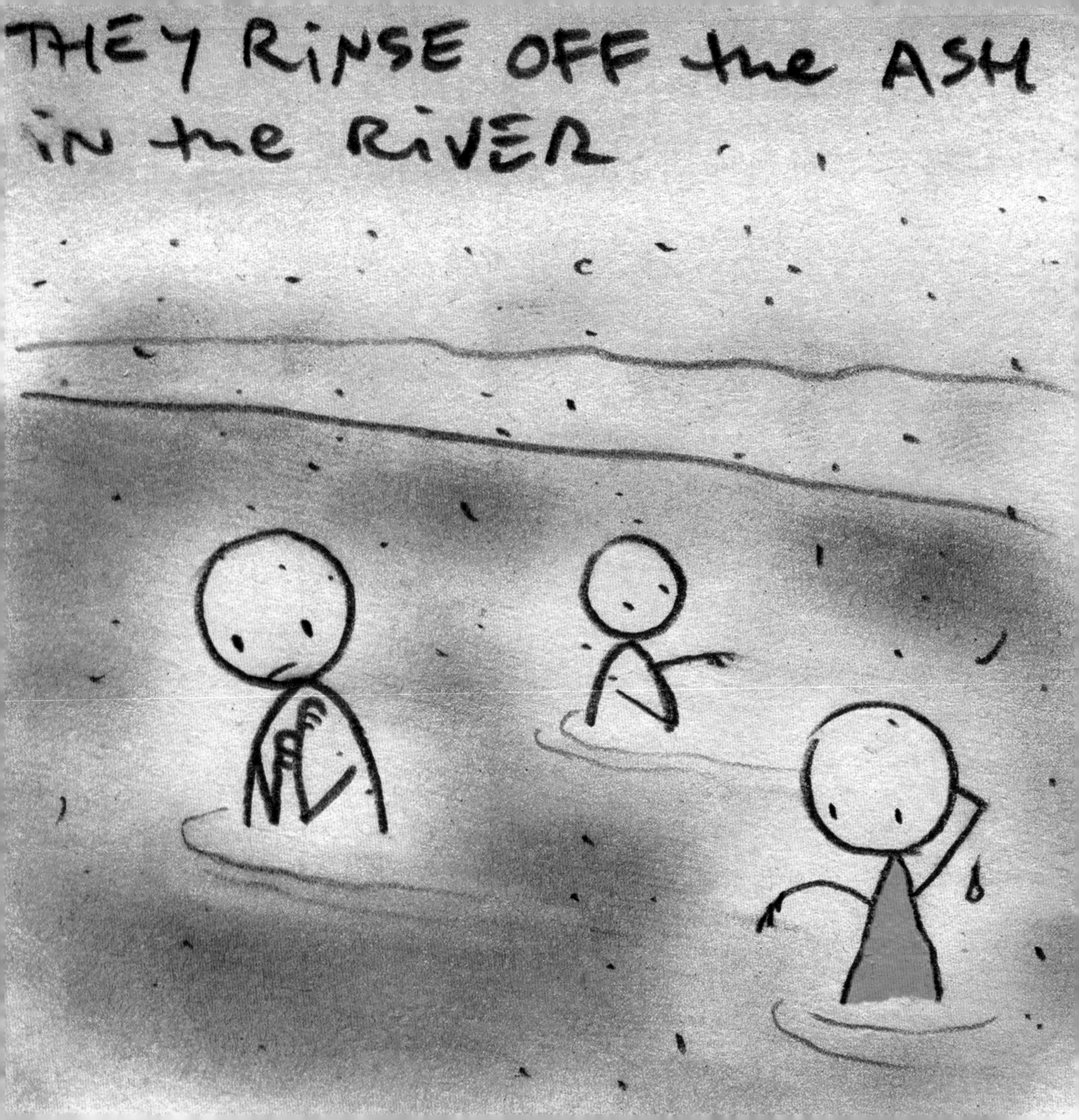
THEY RINSE OFF the ASH
in the RIVER

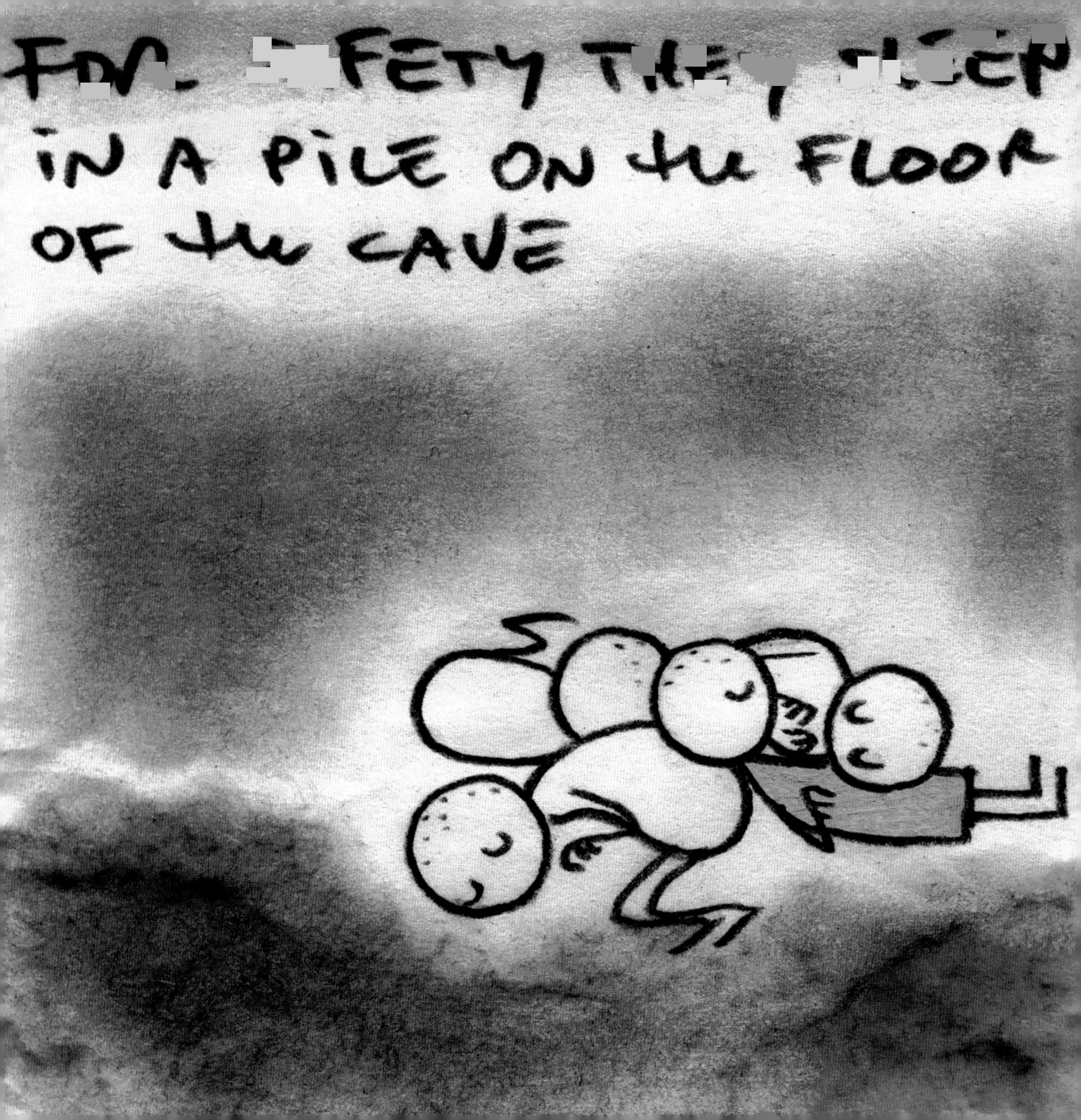
FOR SAFETY THEY SLEEP
IN A PILE ON THE FLOOR
OF THE CAVE

SHE DREAMS OF FOUR PEOPLE BURIED HEAD-FIRST

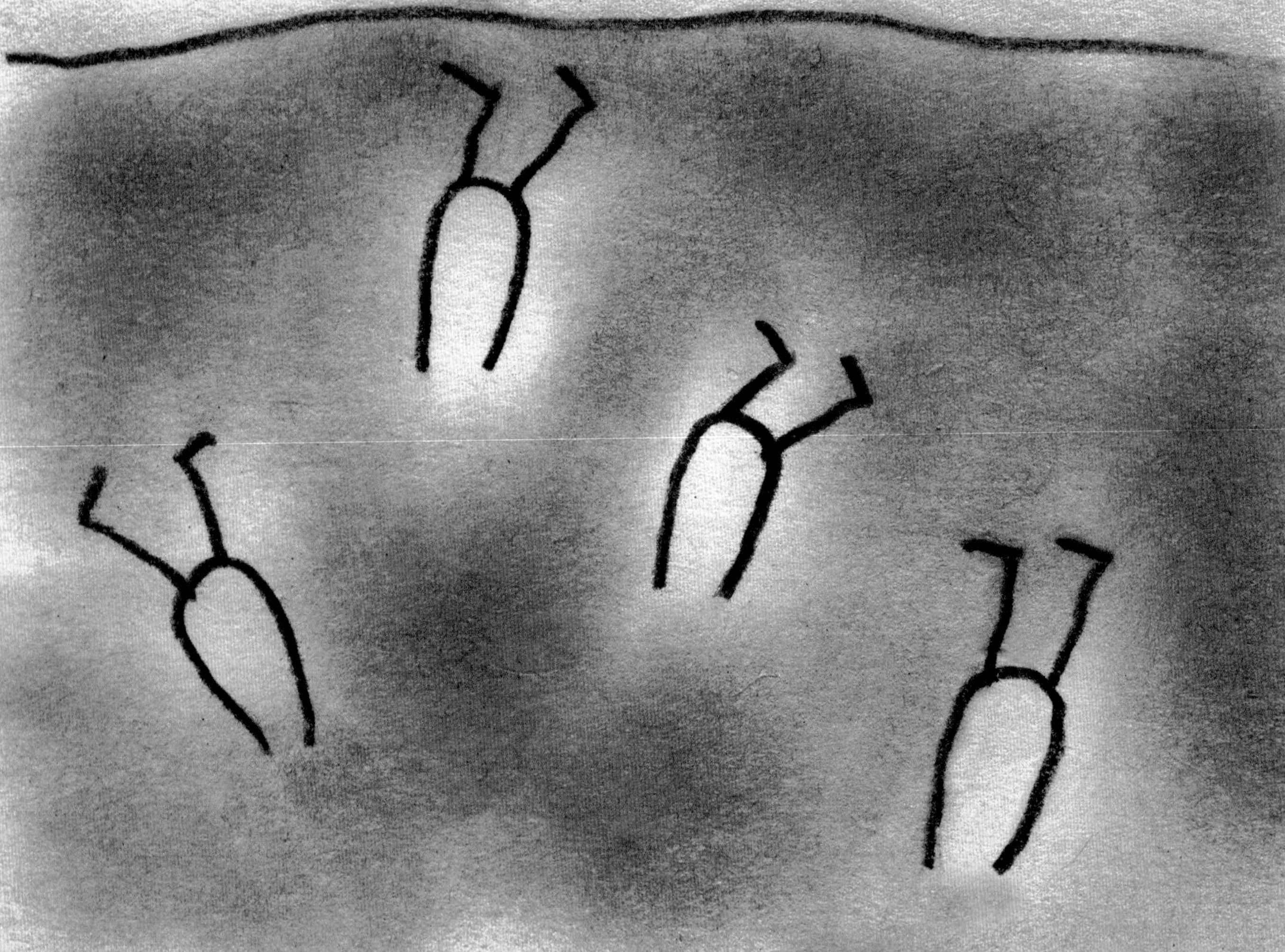

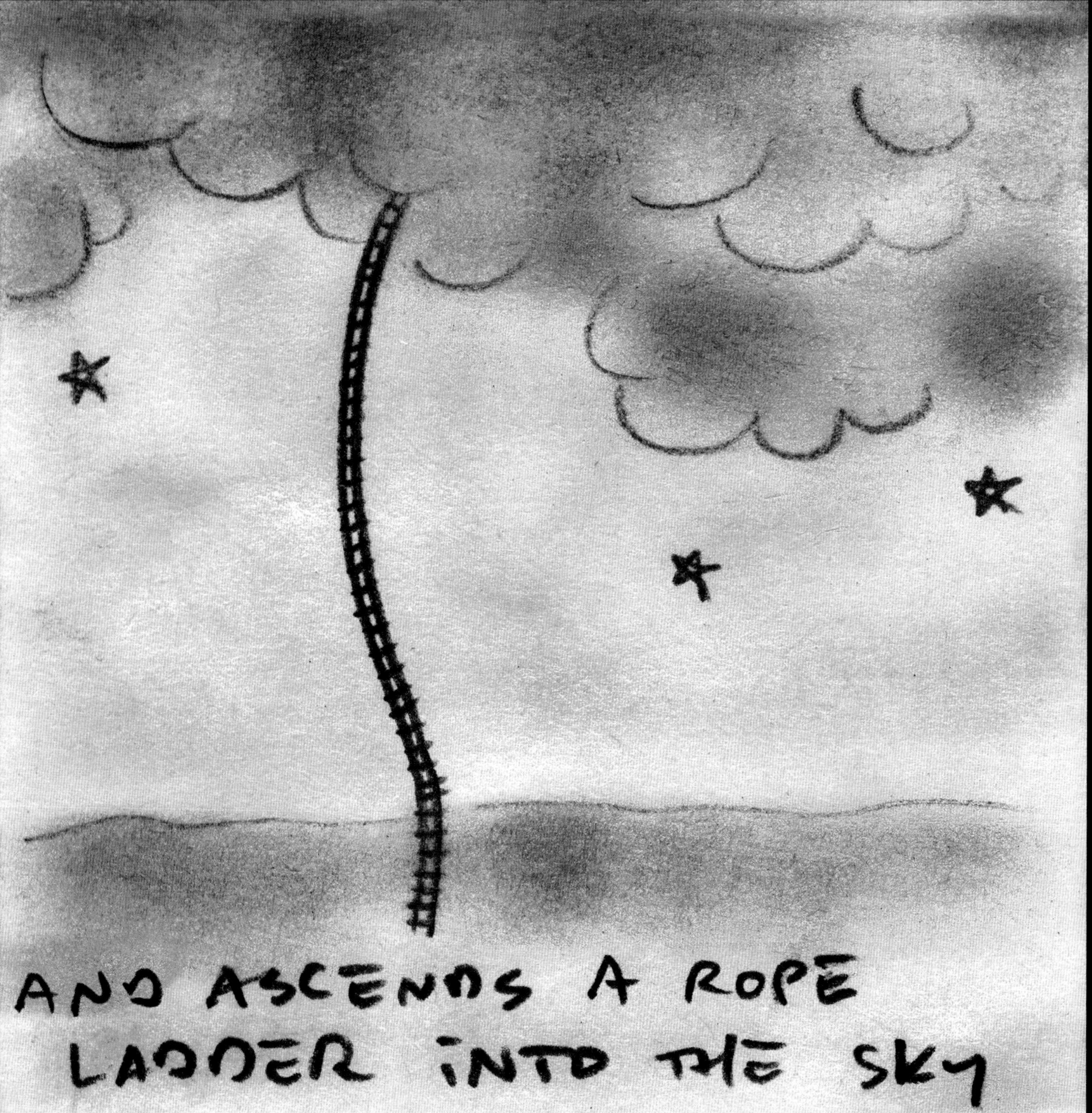

AND ASCENDS A ROPE
LADDER INTO THE SKY

THE STARS ARE COVERED
WITH RAIN CLOUDS AND
SOMETHING HOWLS IN THE
DISTANCE

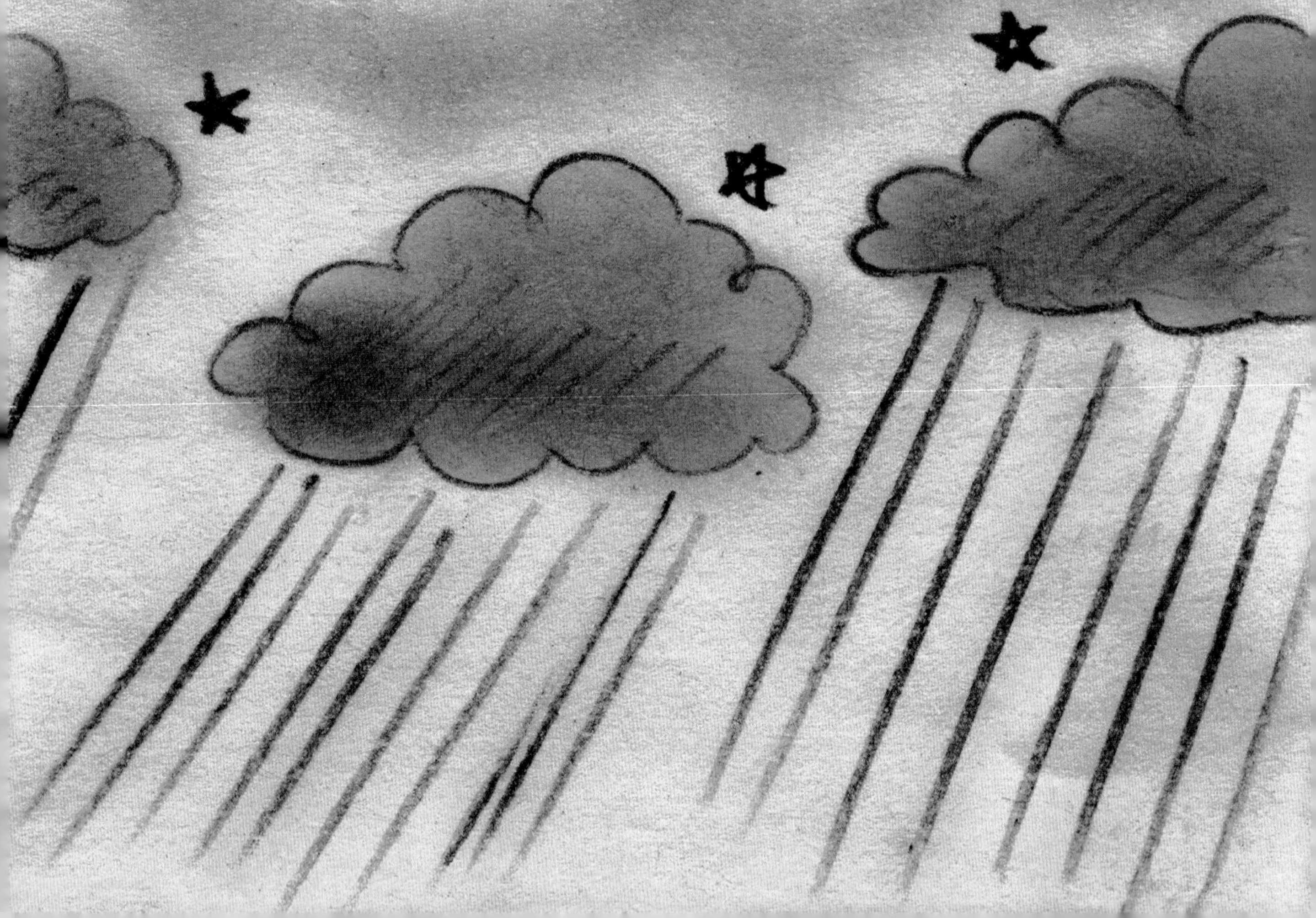

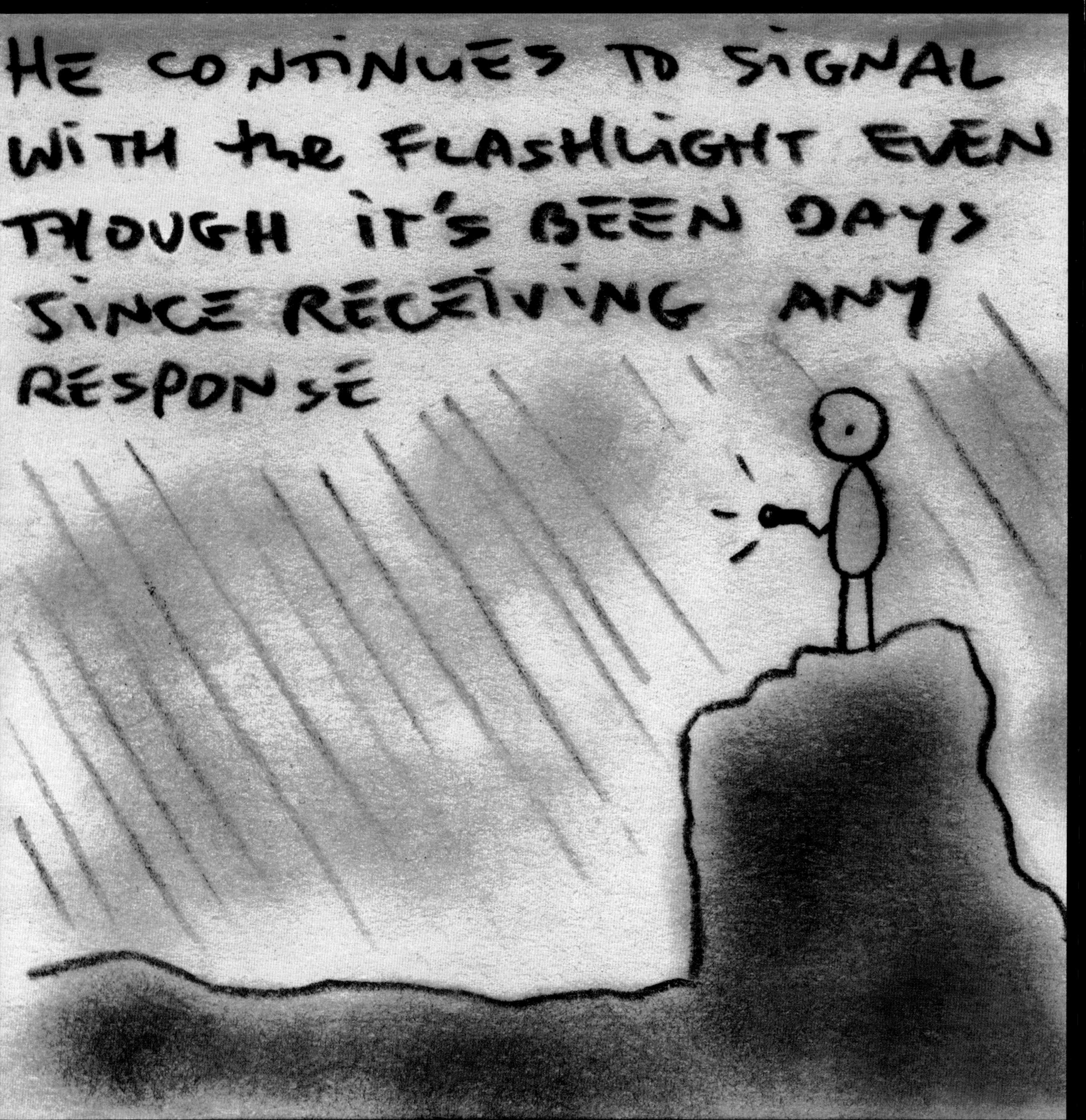
HE CONTINUES TO SIGNAL WITH the FLASHLIGHT EVEN THOUGH IT'S BEEN DAYS SINCE RECEIVING ANY RESPONSE

SOMETHING IS SINGING A LITTLE SONG BENEATH the EARTH

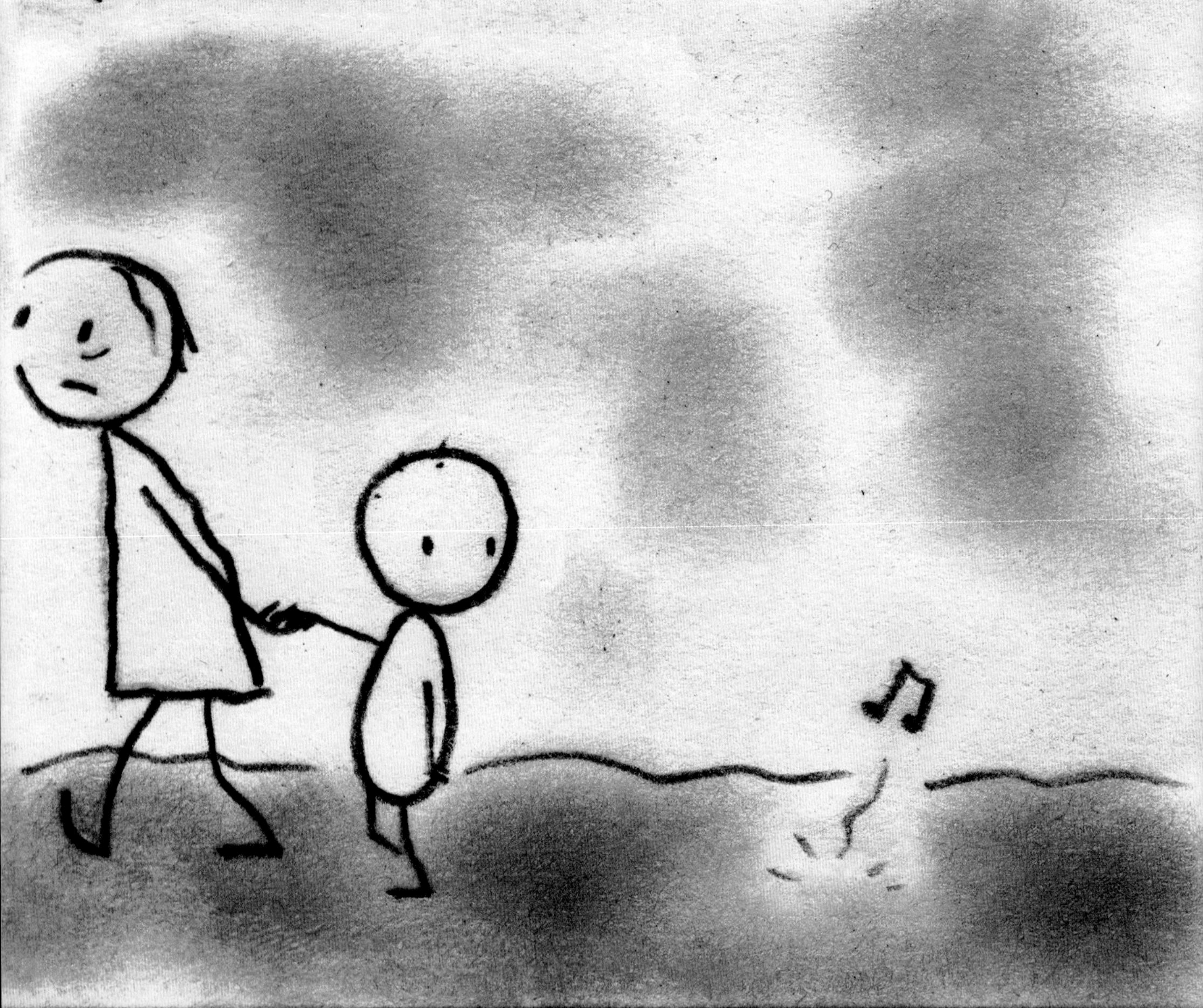

THERE ARE DRIED UP
EELS IN the GRASS.

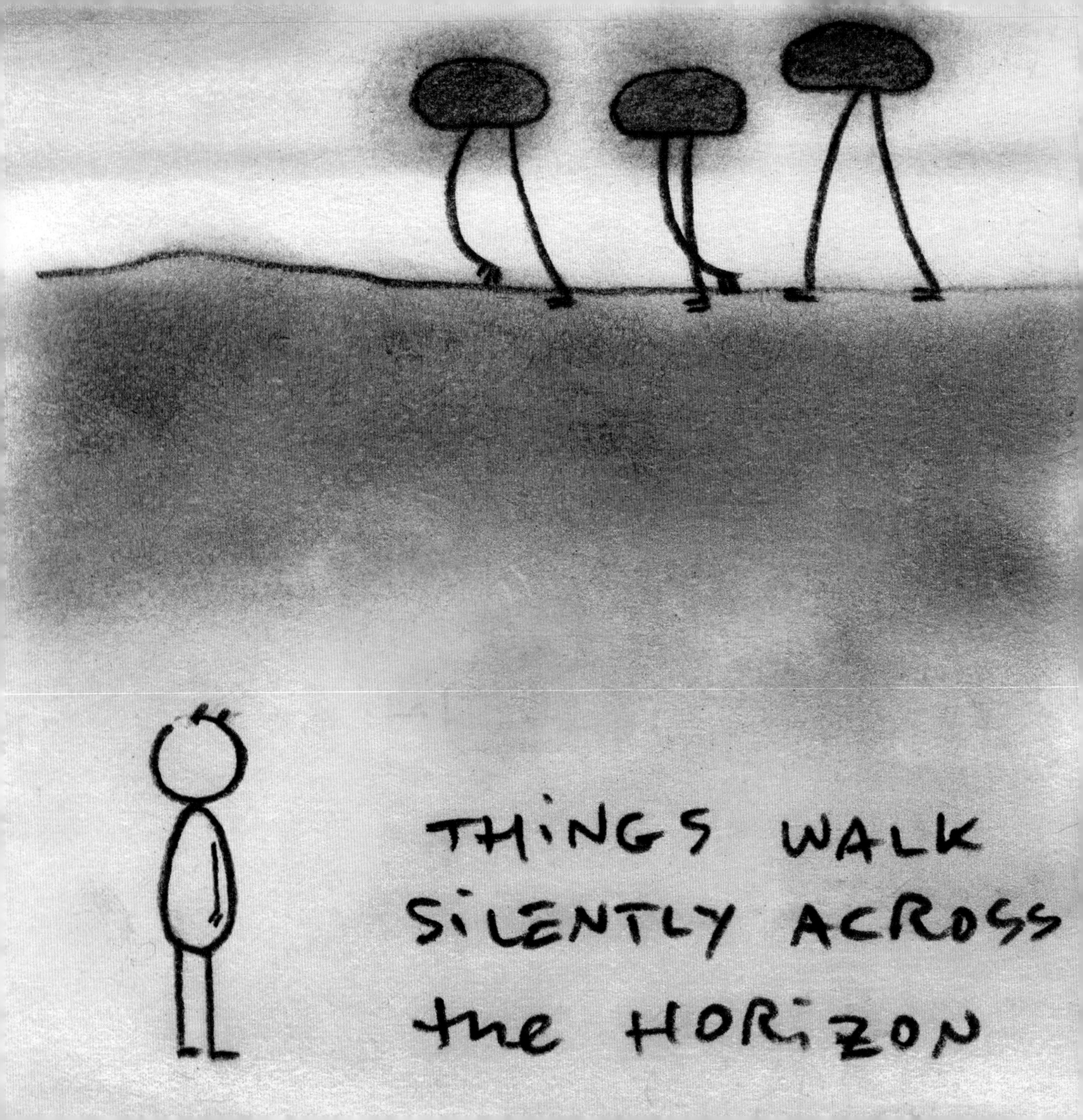
THINGS WALK
SILENTLY ACROSS
the HORIZON

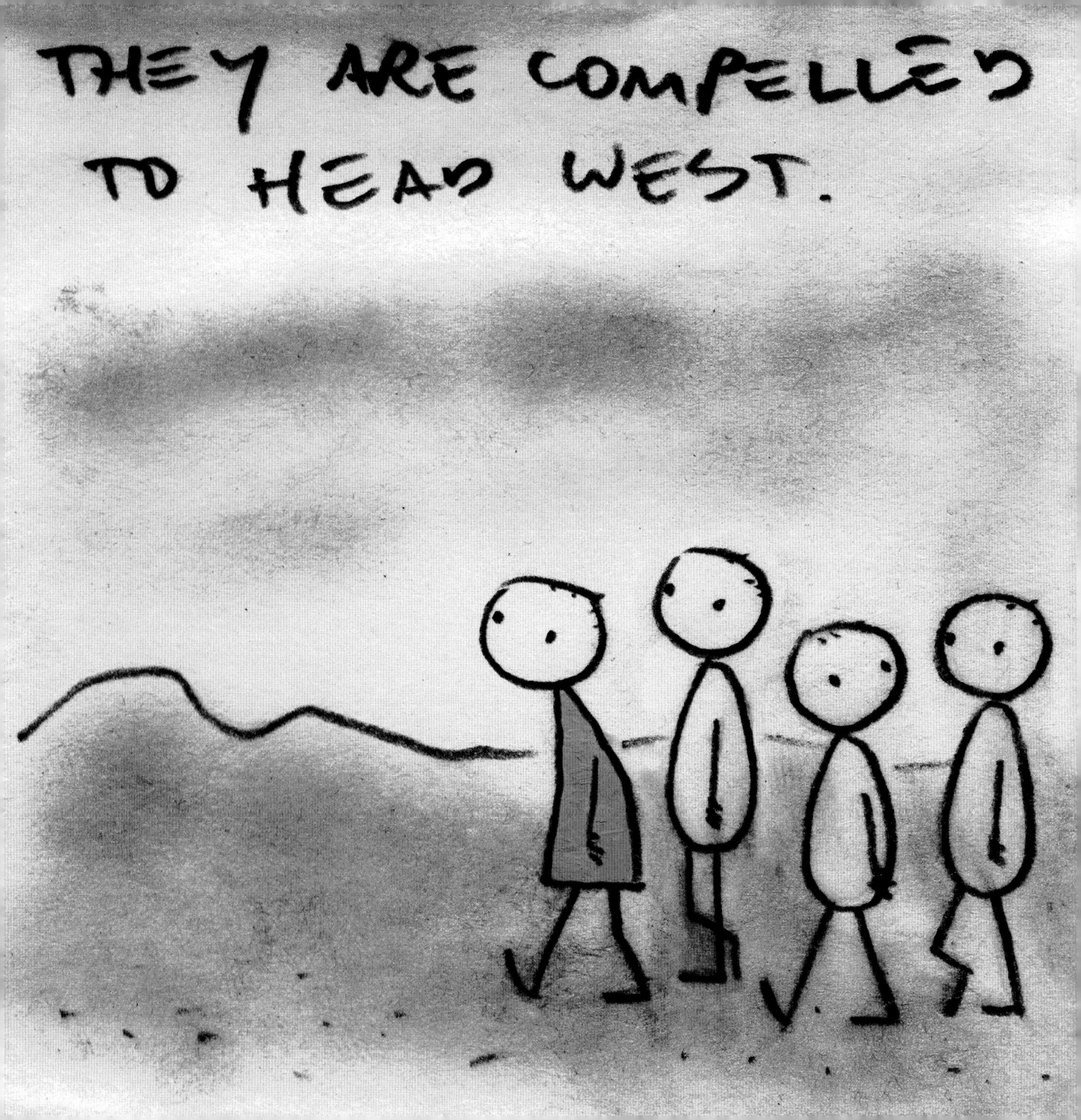
THEY ARE COMPELLED
TO HEAD WEST.

the IMPRESSIONS OF
LEAVES, FOSSILIZED LONG
AGO ATOP the BROKEN
CEMENT

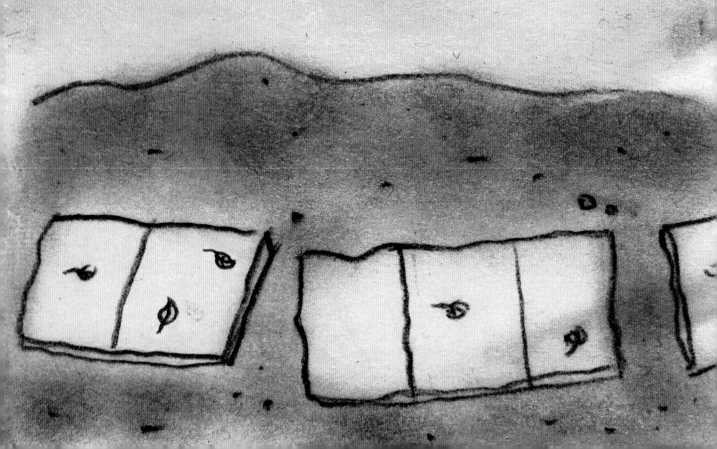

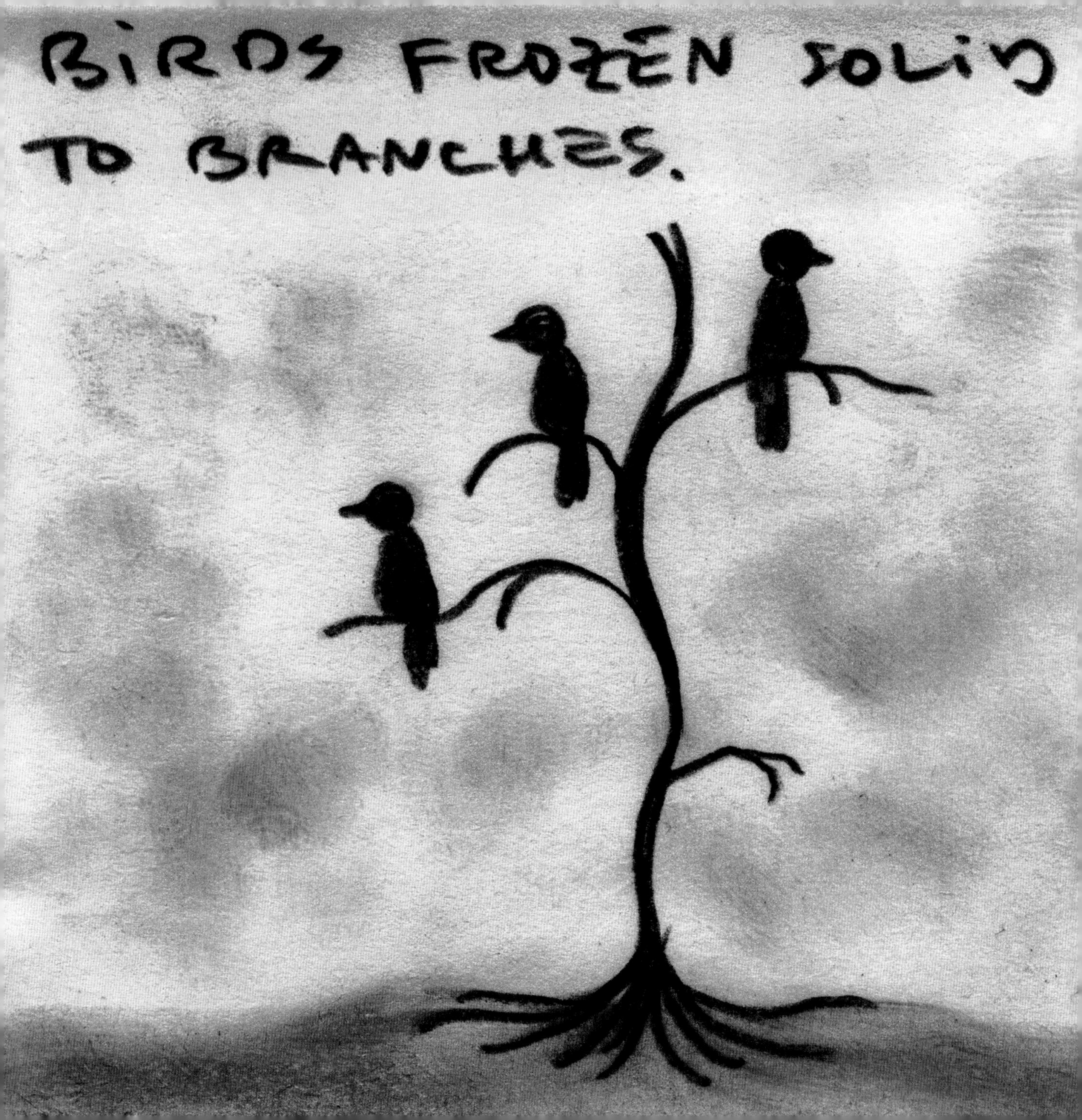
BIRDS FROZEN SOLID
TO BRANCHES.

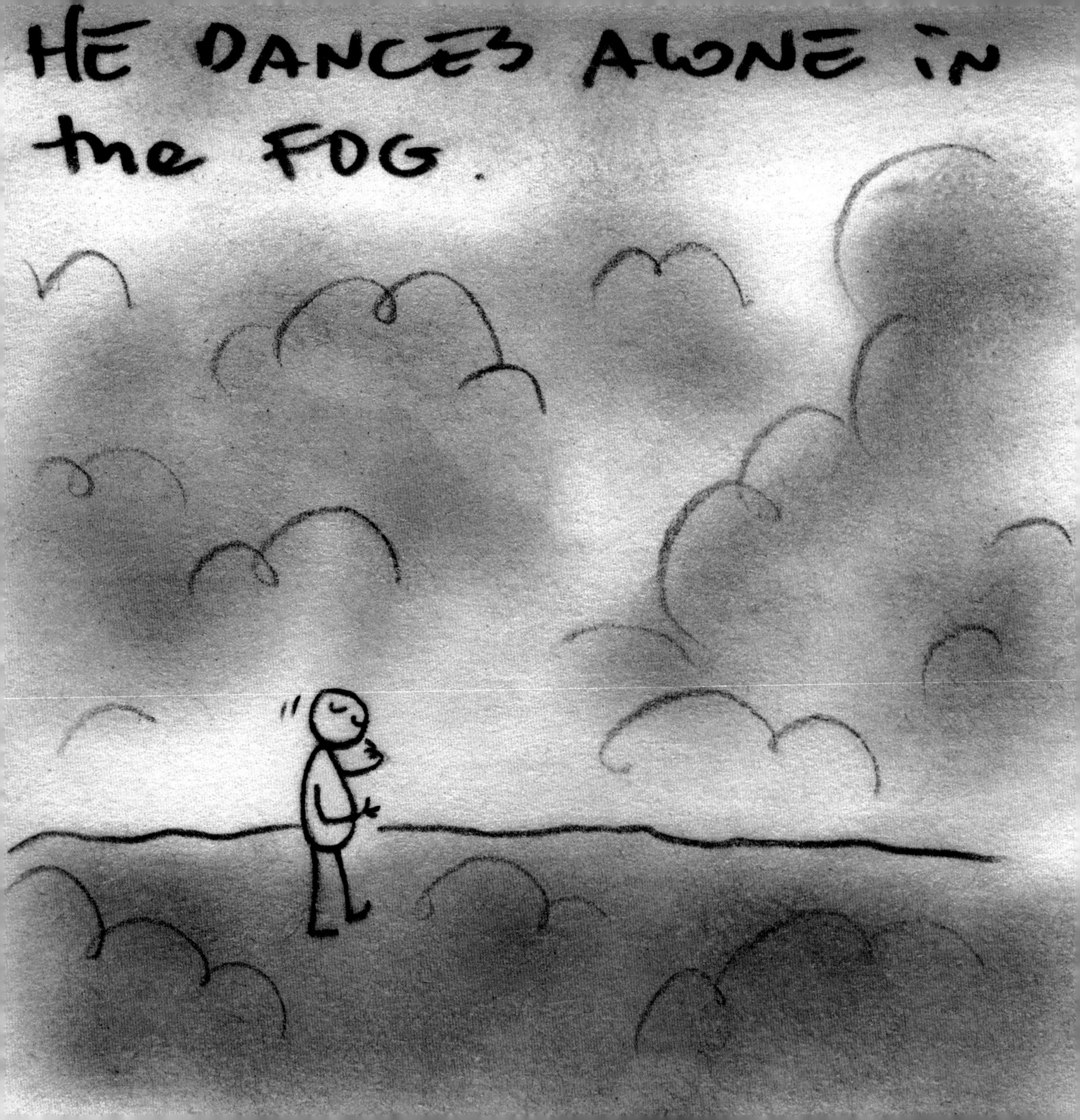
HE DANCES ALONE IN the FOG.

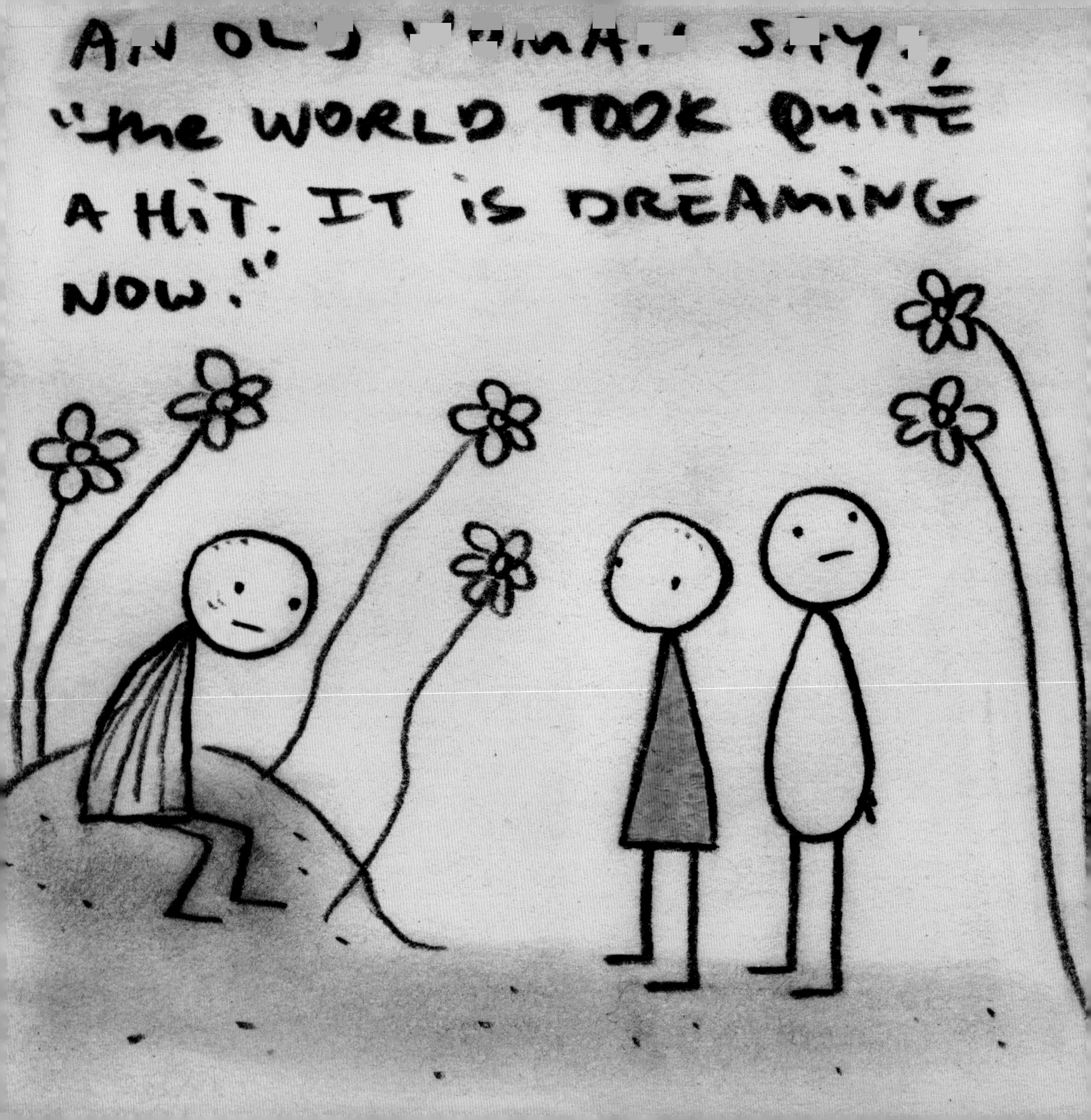
AN OLD WOMAN SAYS,
"the WORLD TOOK QUITE A HIT. IT IS DREAMING NOW."

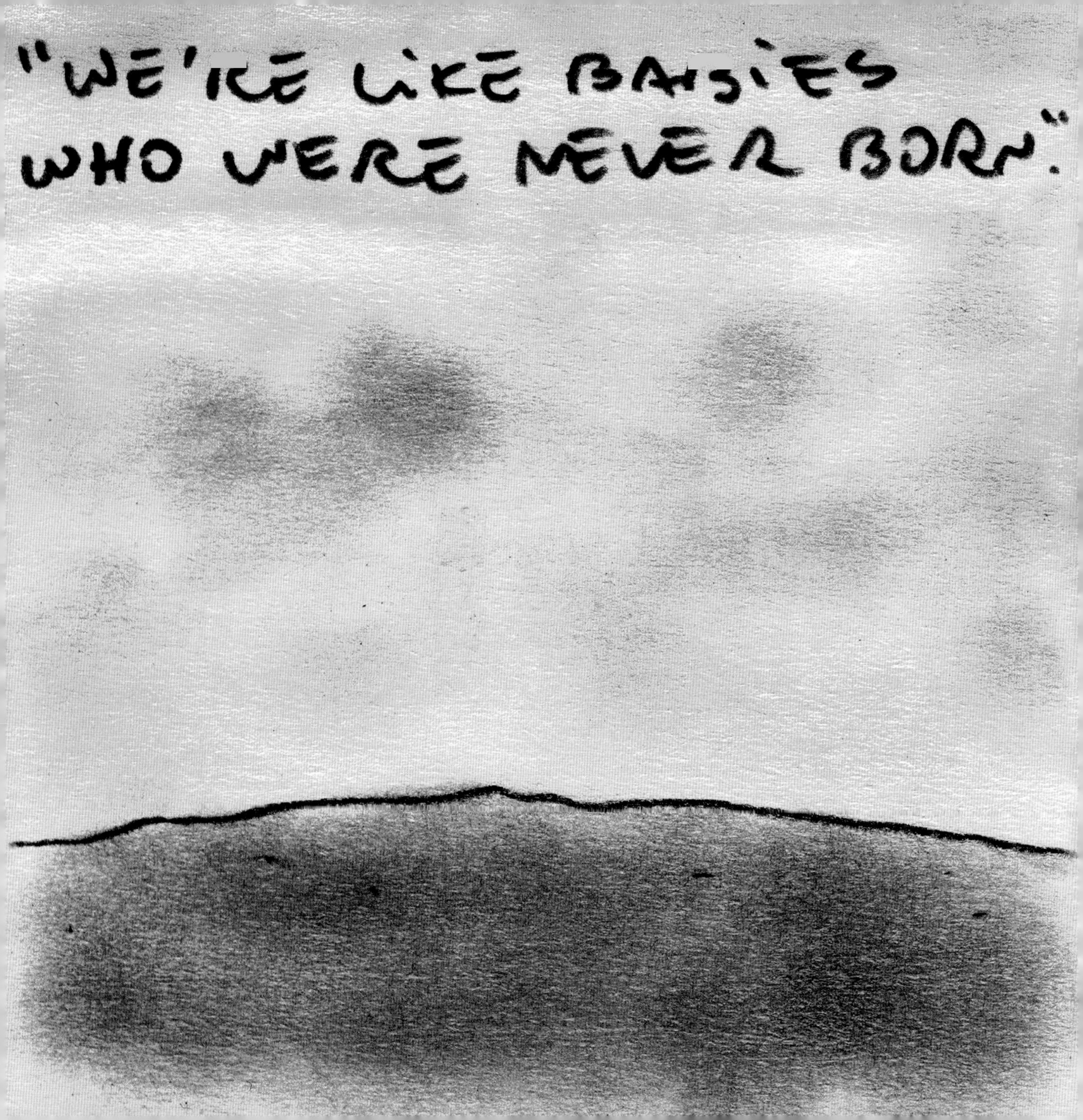
"WE'RE LIKE BABIES WHO WERE NEVER BORN."

"ALL THEY EVER KNOW ARE DREAMS AND DARKNESS AND THEN THEY'RE GONE."

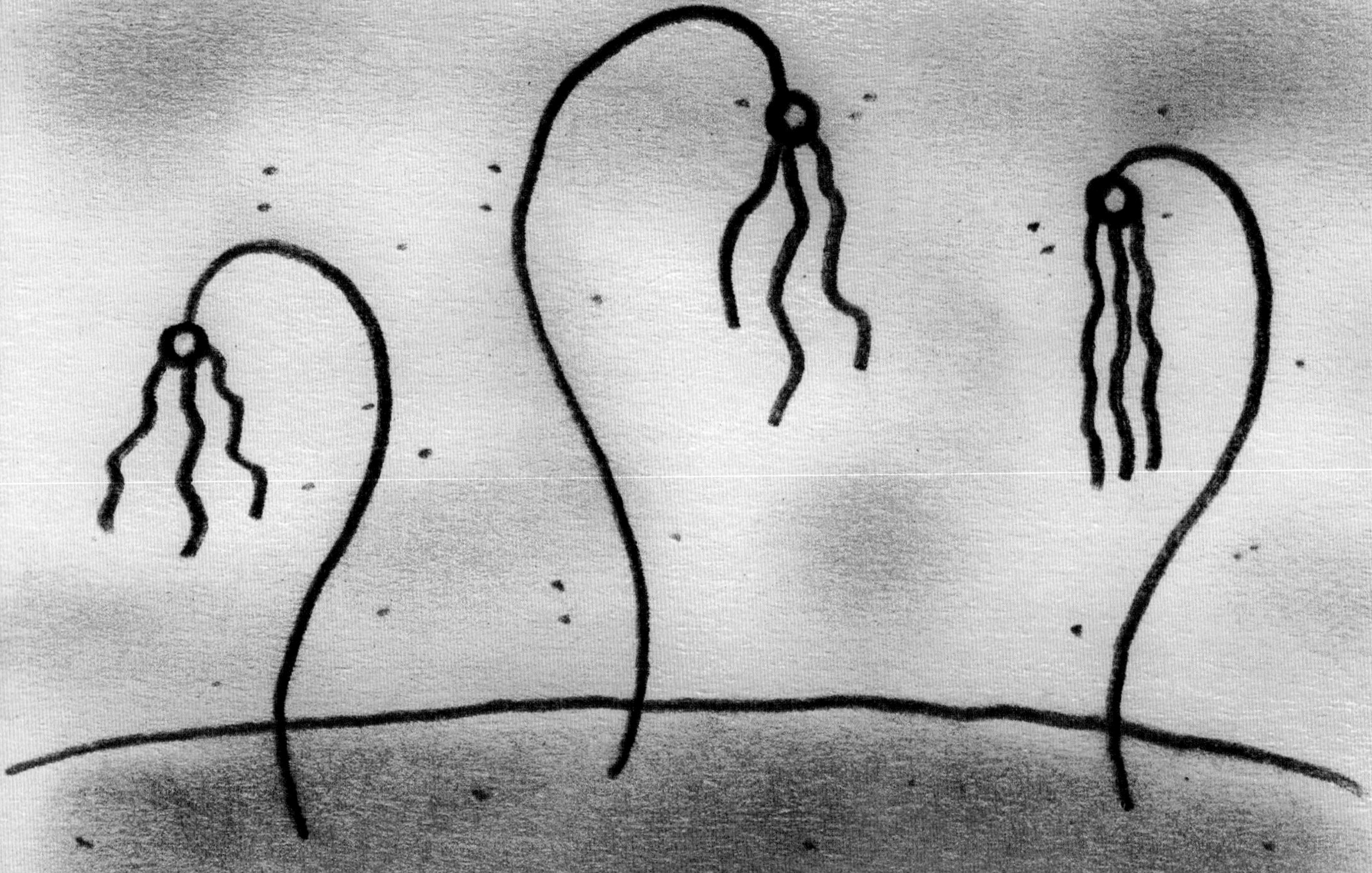

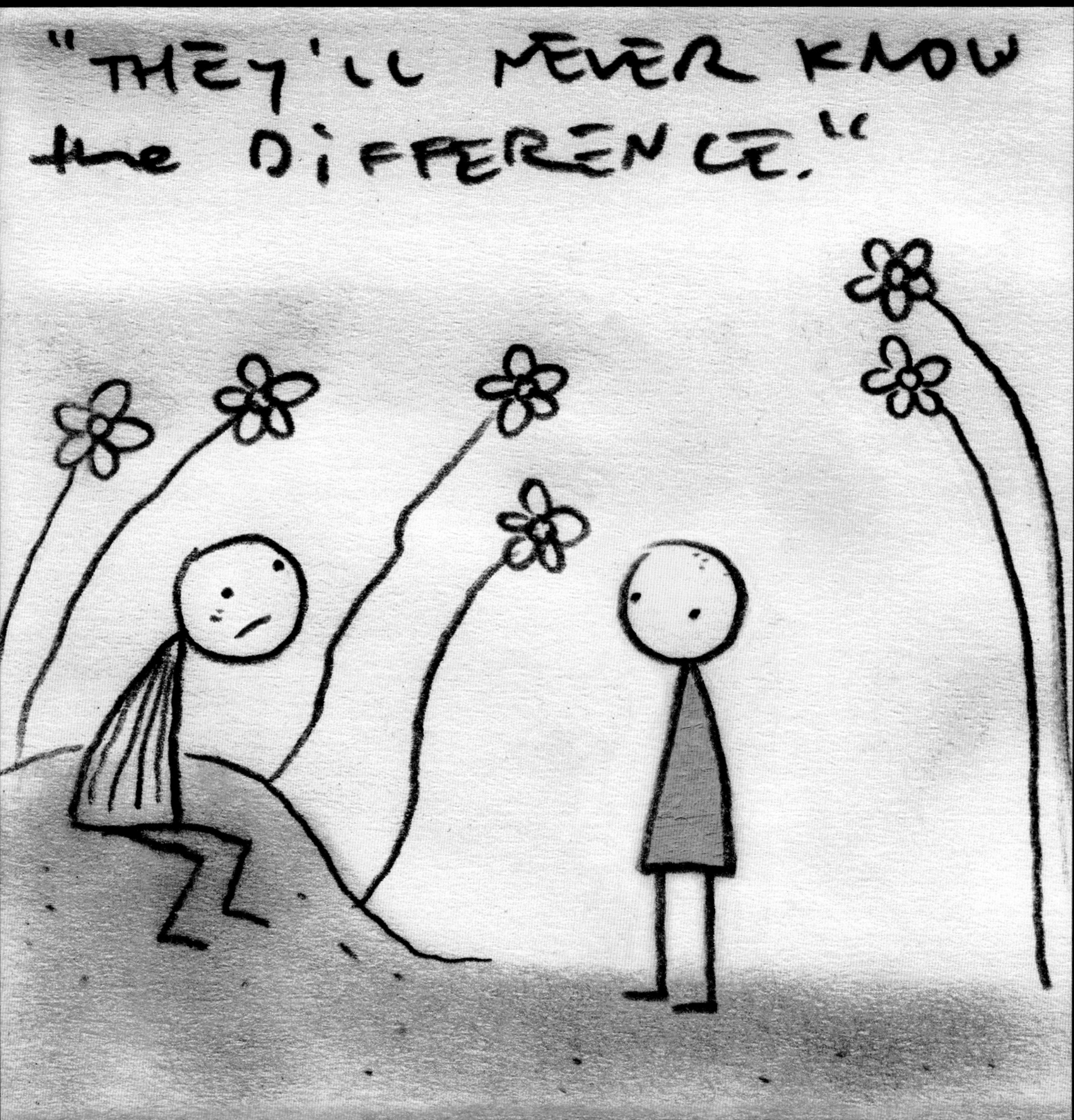
"THEY'LL NEVER KNOW the DIFFERENCE."

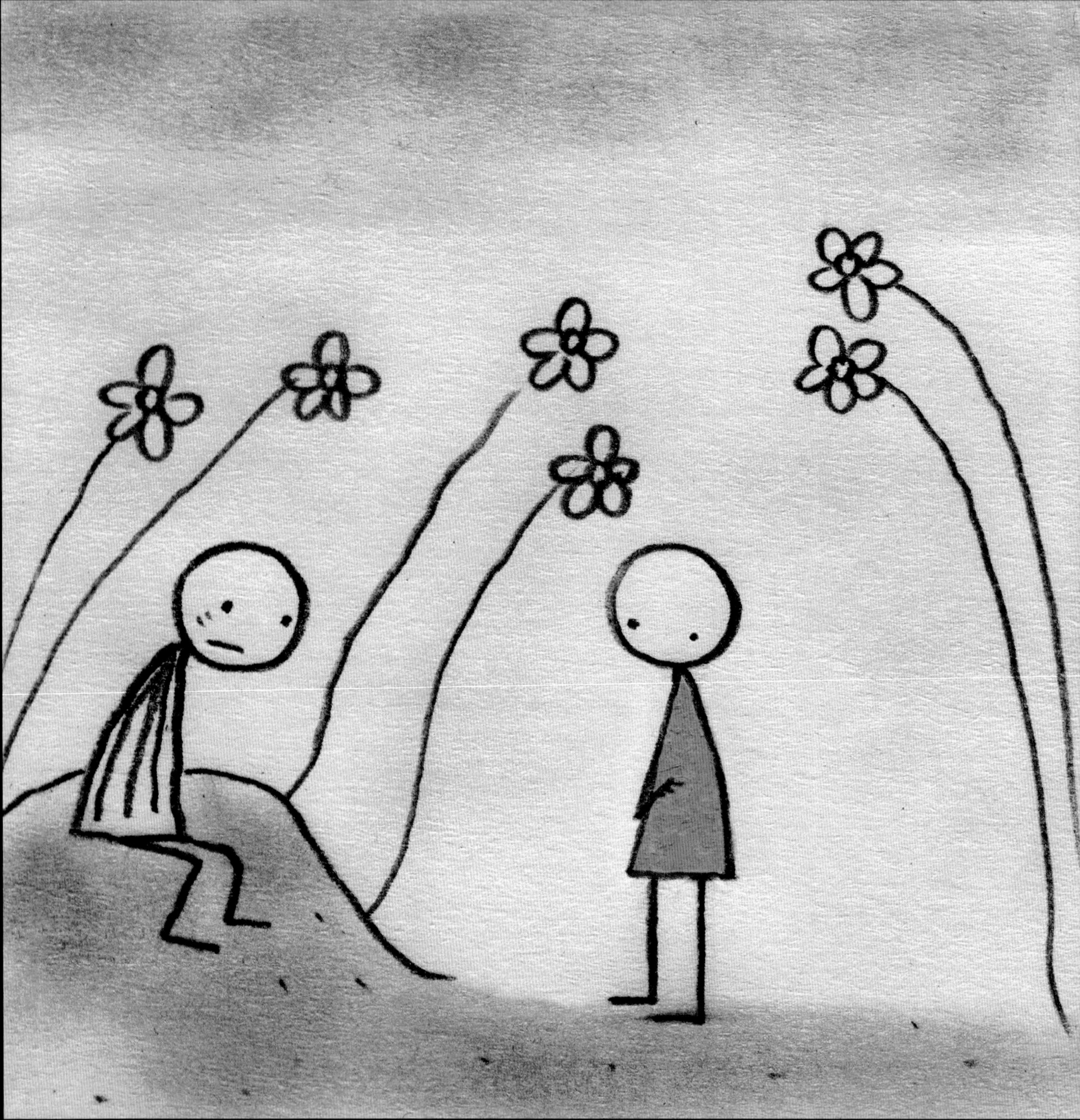

A BAG OF SALAD IS
TURNING BROWN IN
A FORGOTTEN SPACE,
SLOWLY, SLOWLY.

THERE WAS ONCE
A CONTROVERSIAL
NEW EXHIBIT IN
the MODERN ART
MUSEUM

AN ARTIST PLACED A CLONE ON DISPLAY IN A STASIS TUBE.

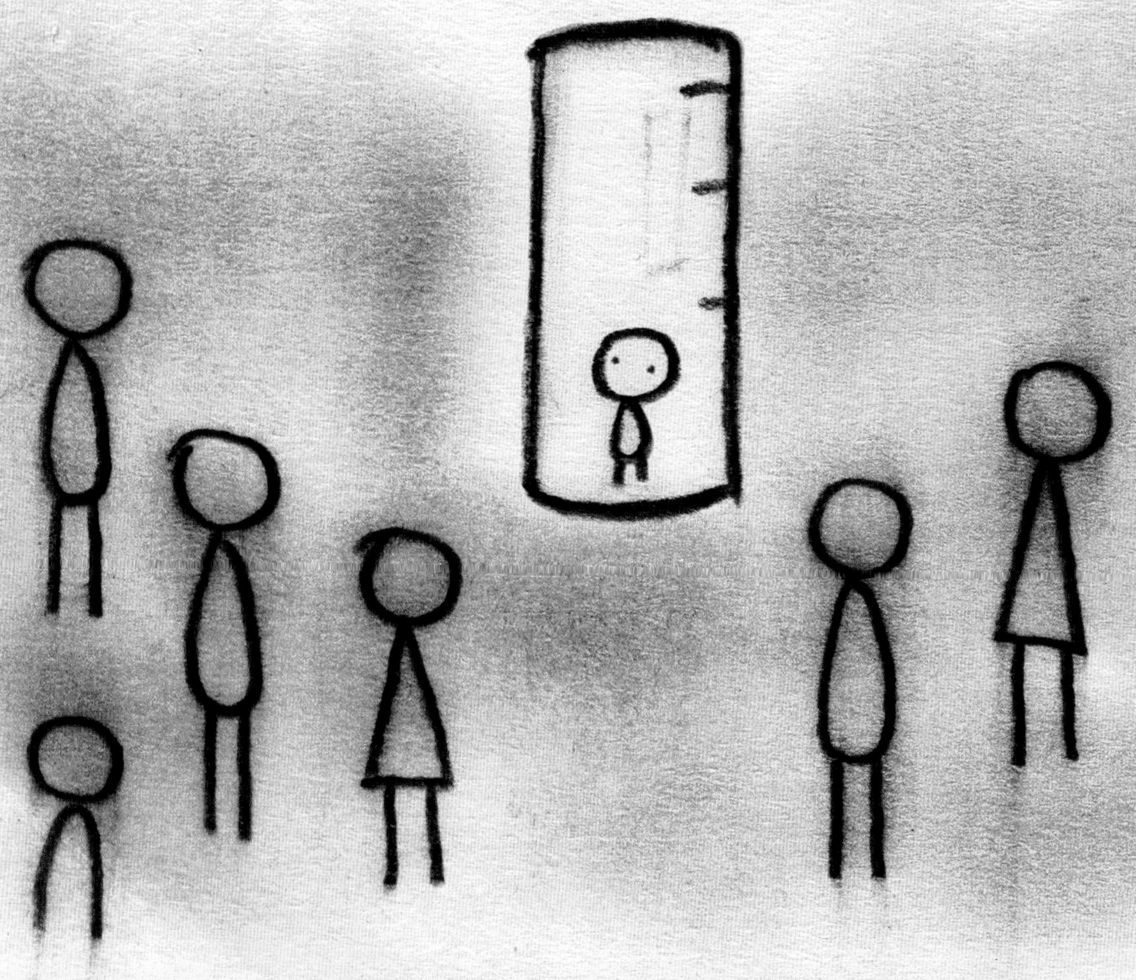

A CHILD WITHOUT A BRAIN THAT the PUBLIC COULD WATCH GROW OLD OVER the YEARS IN REAL TIME.

MUSEUM VISITORS NICKNAME the BODY DAVID AND IT BECOMES A POPULAR ATTRACTION...

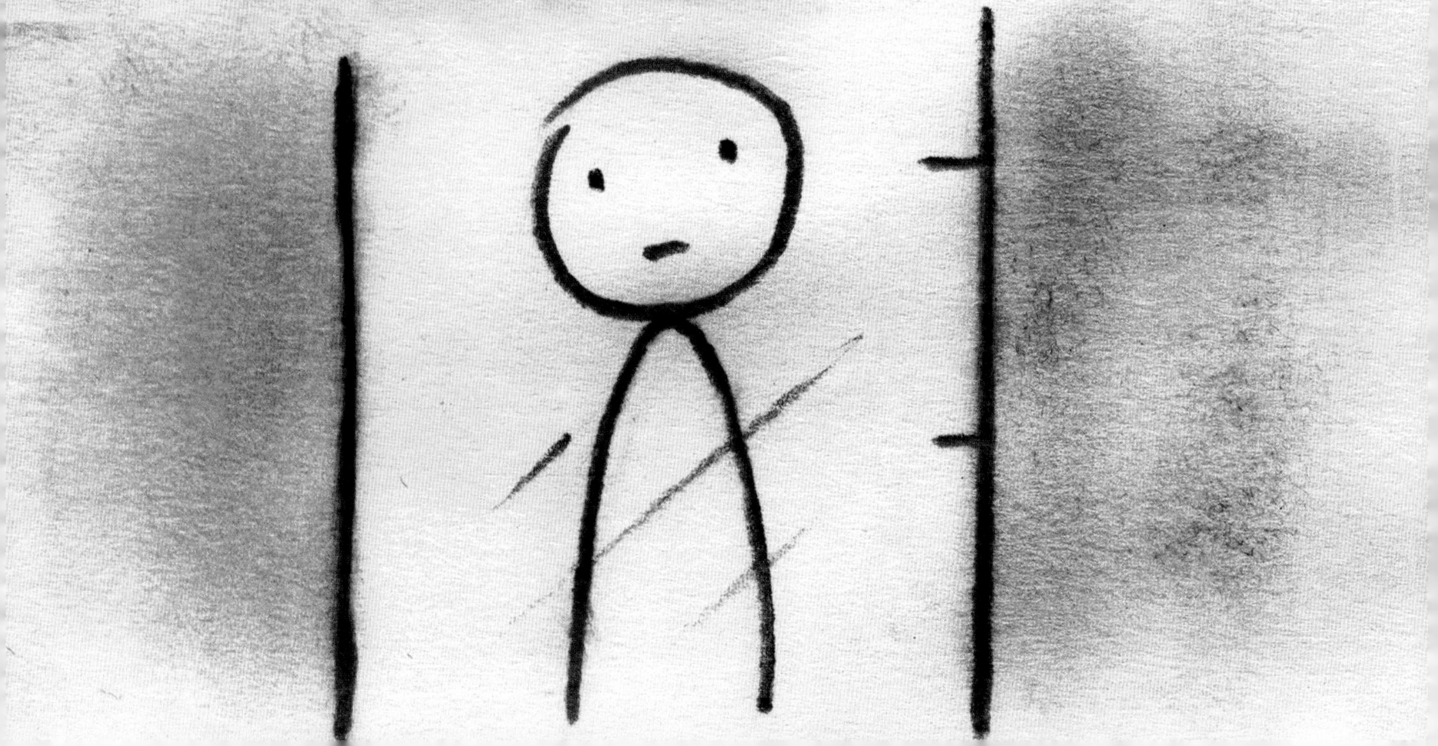

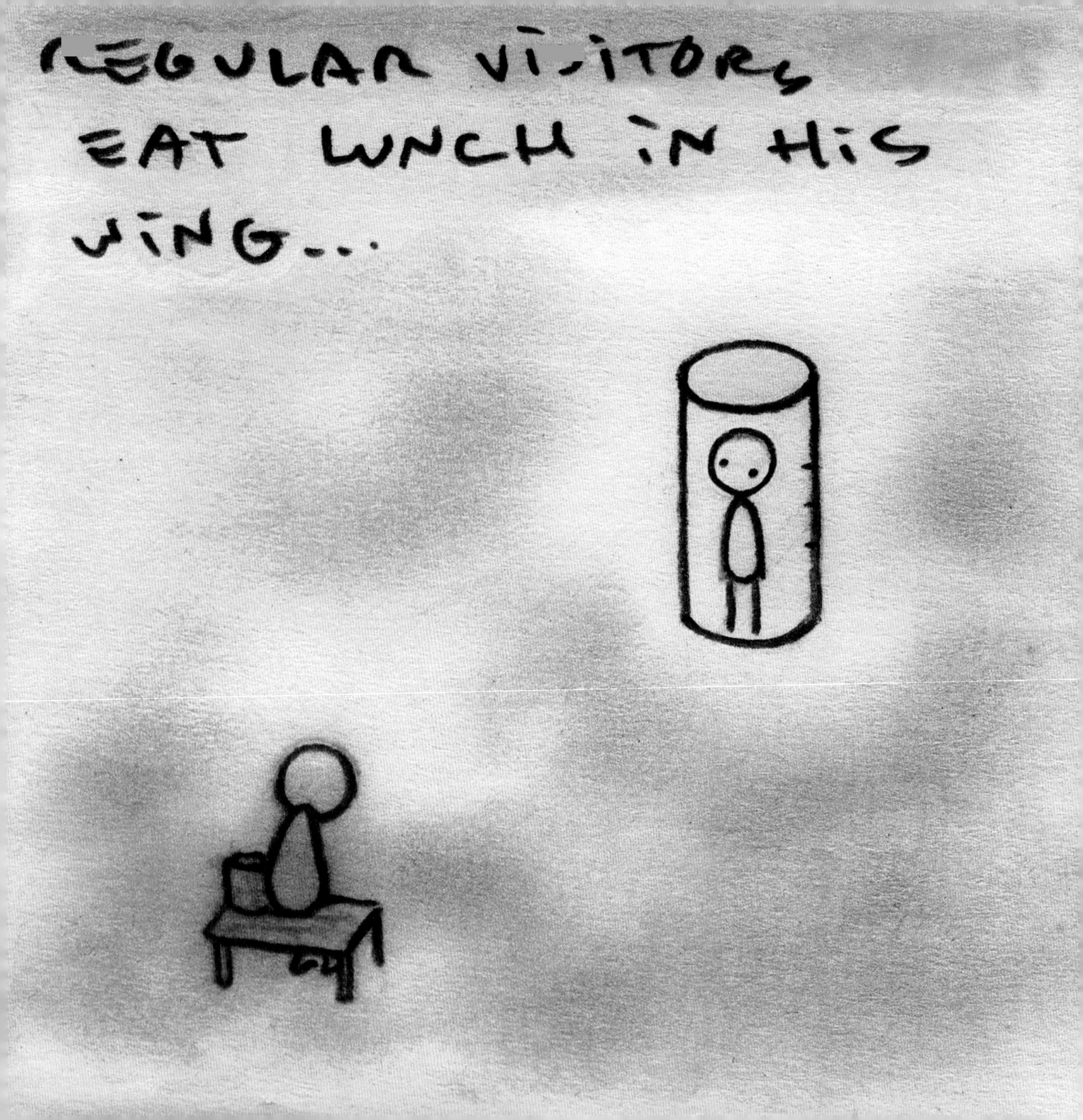
REGULAR VISITORS EAT LUNCH IN HIS WING...

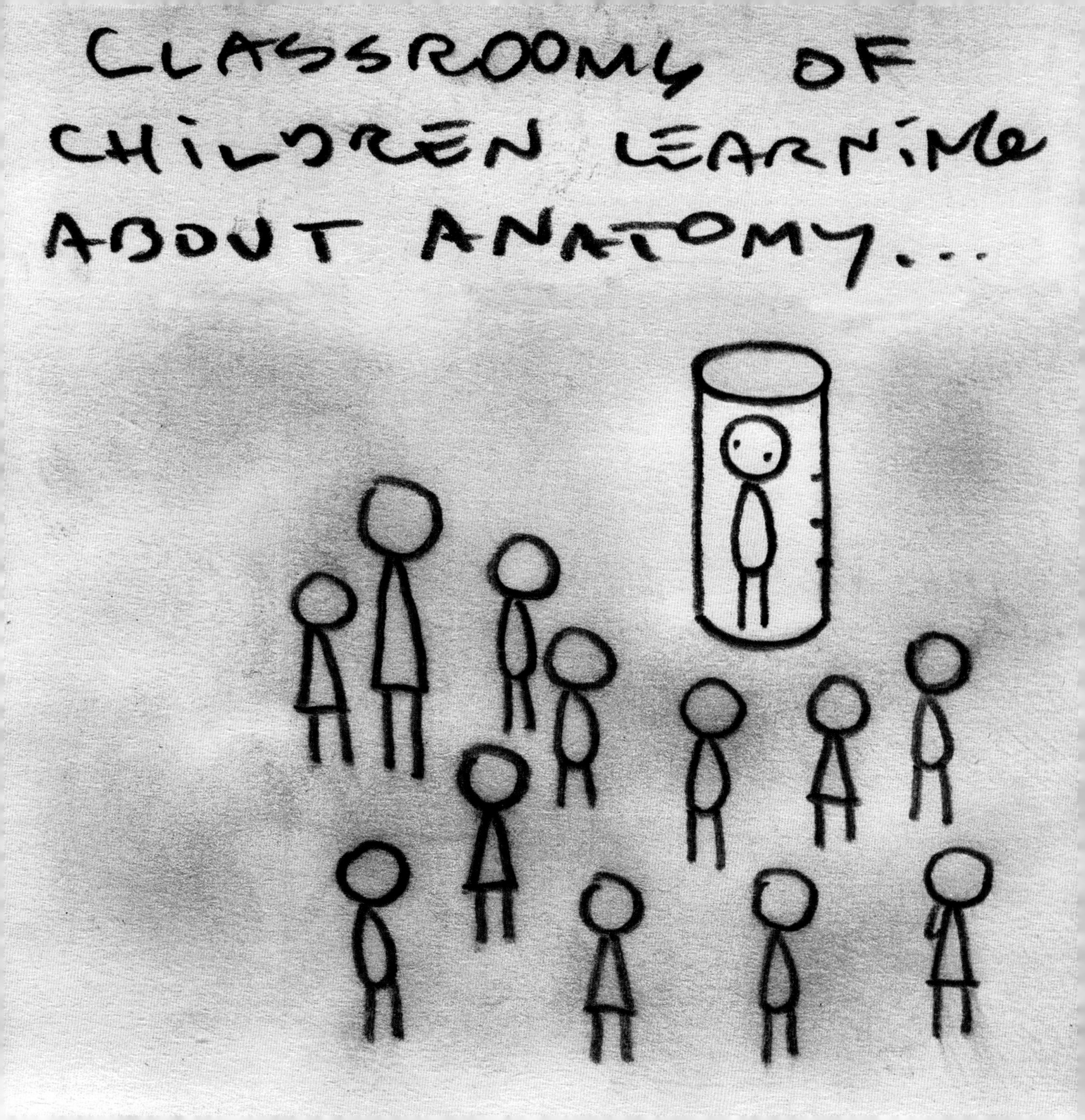
CLASSROOMS OF CHILDREN LEARNING ABOUT ANATOMY...

PEOPLE WHO SPEAK
QUIETLY TO HIM IN
the NIGHT...

PEOPLE WHO ONLY KNEW LIFE WITH HIM IN IT... PEOPLE WHO'D PAY HIM A VISIT WHENEVER THEY FOUND THEMSELVES BACK IN THE CITY AND REMEMBERED HE WAS THERE.

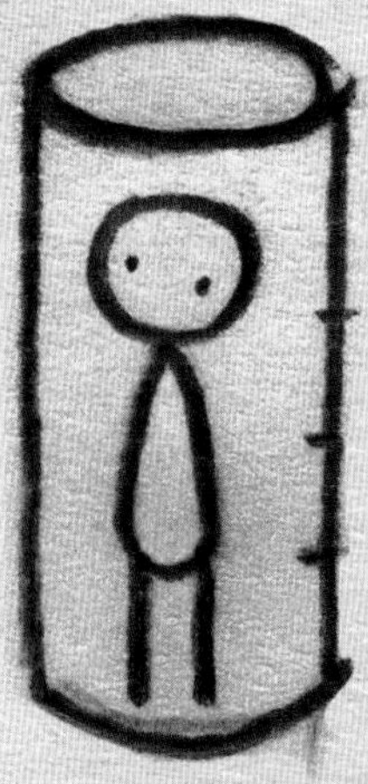

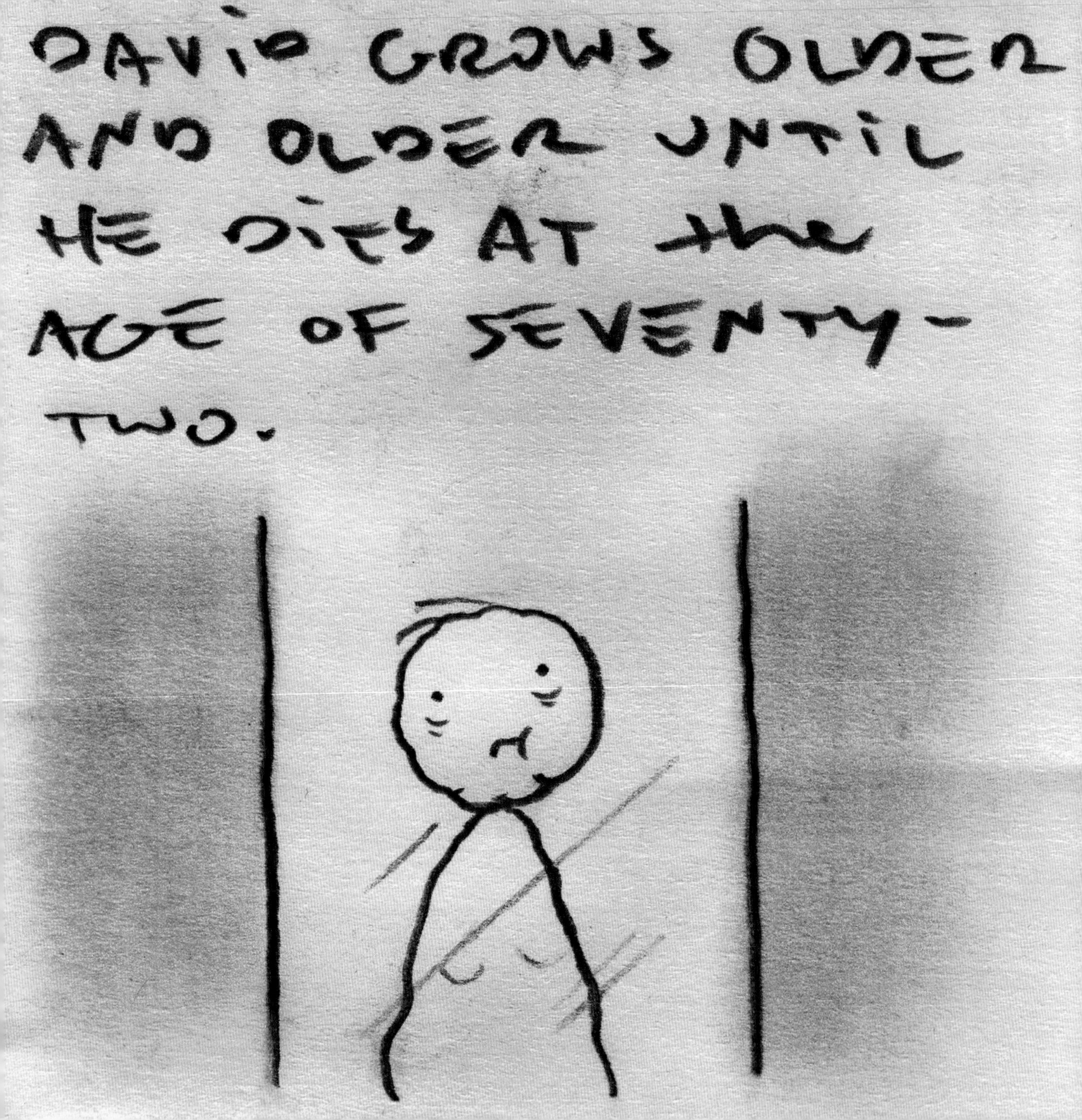
DAVID GROWS OLDER AND OLDER UNTIL HE DIES AT THE AGE OF SEVENTY-TWO.

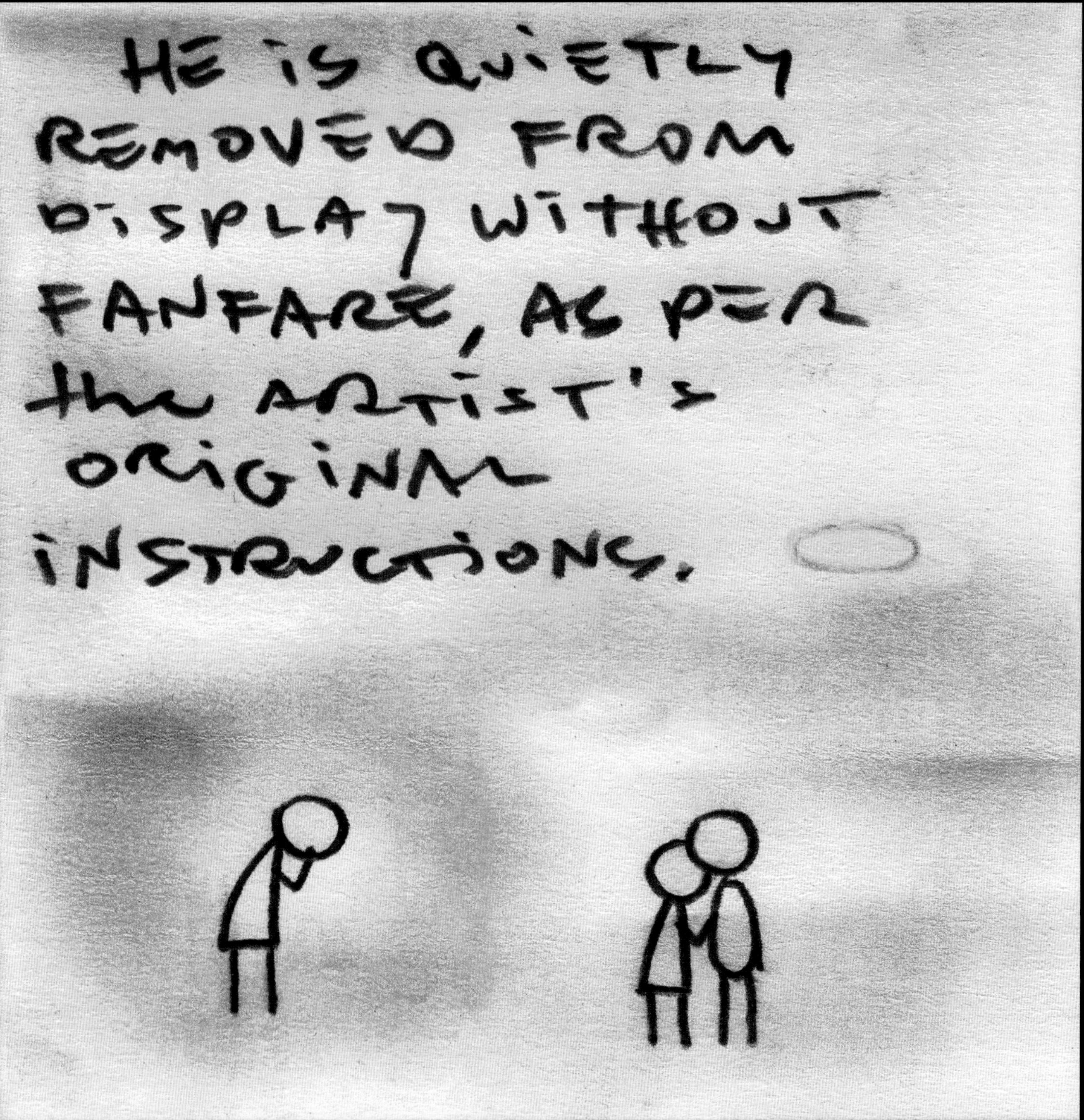
HE IS QUIETLY REMOVED FROM DISPLAY WITHOUT FANFARE, AS PER the ARTIST'S ORIGINAL INSTRUCTIONS.

HE IS MOURNED AND DEEPLY MISSED THROUGHOUT the CITY.

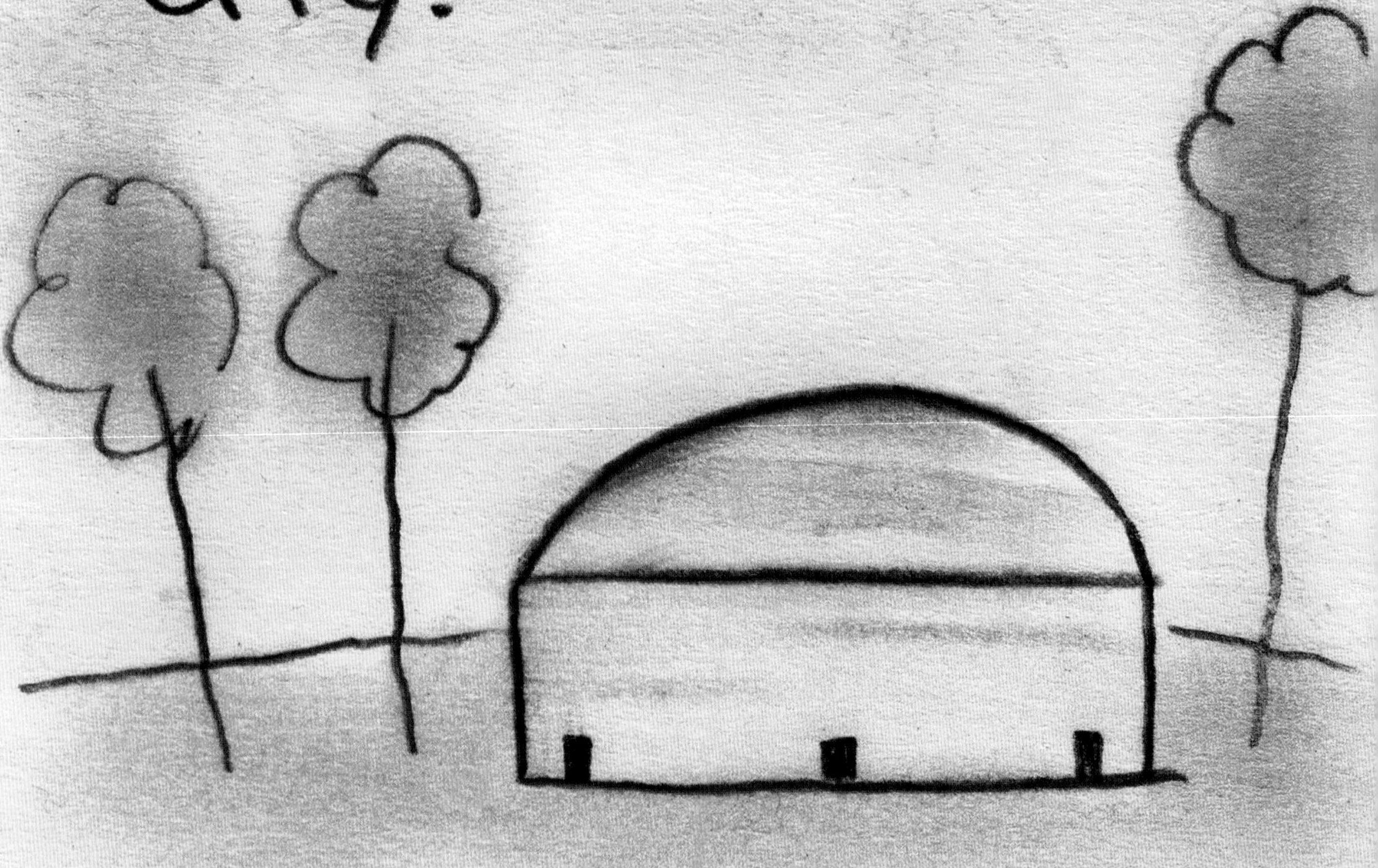

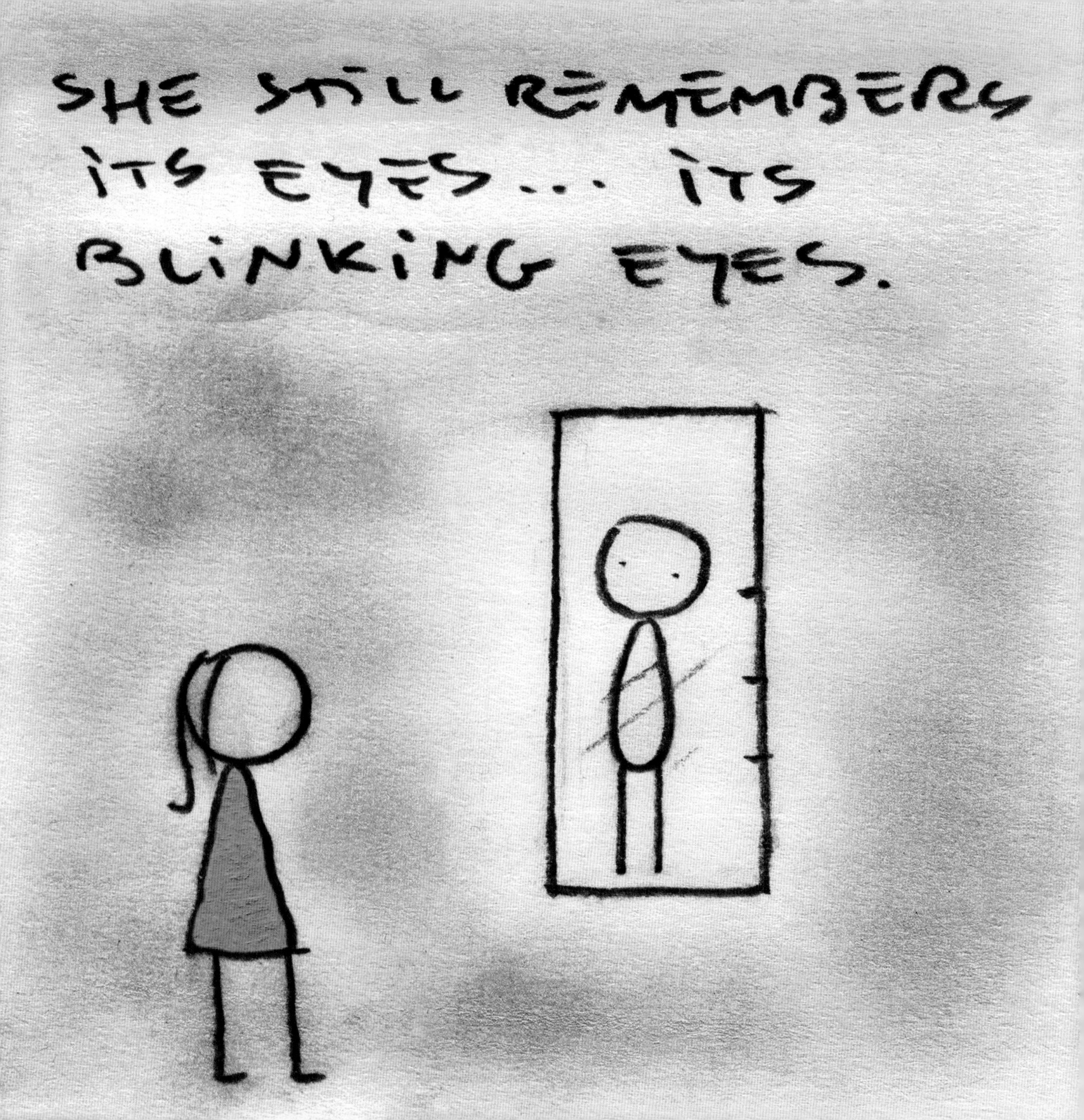
SHE STILL REMEMBERS ITS EYES... ITS BLINKING EYES.

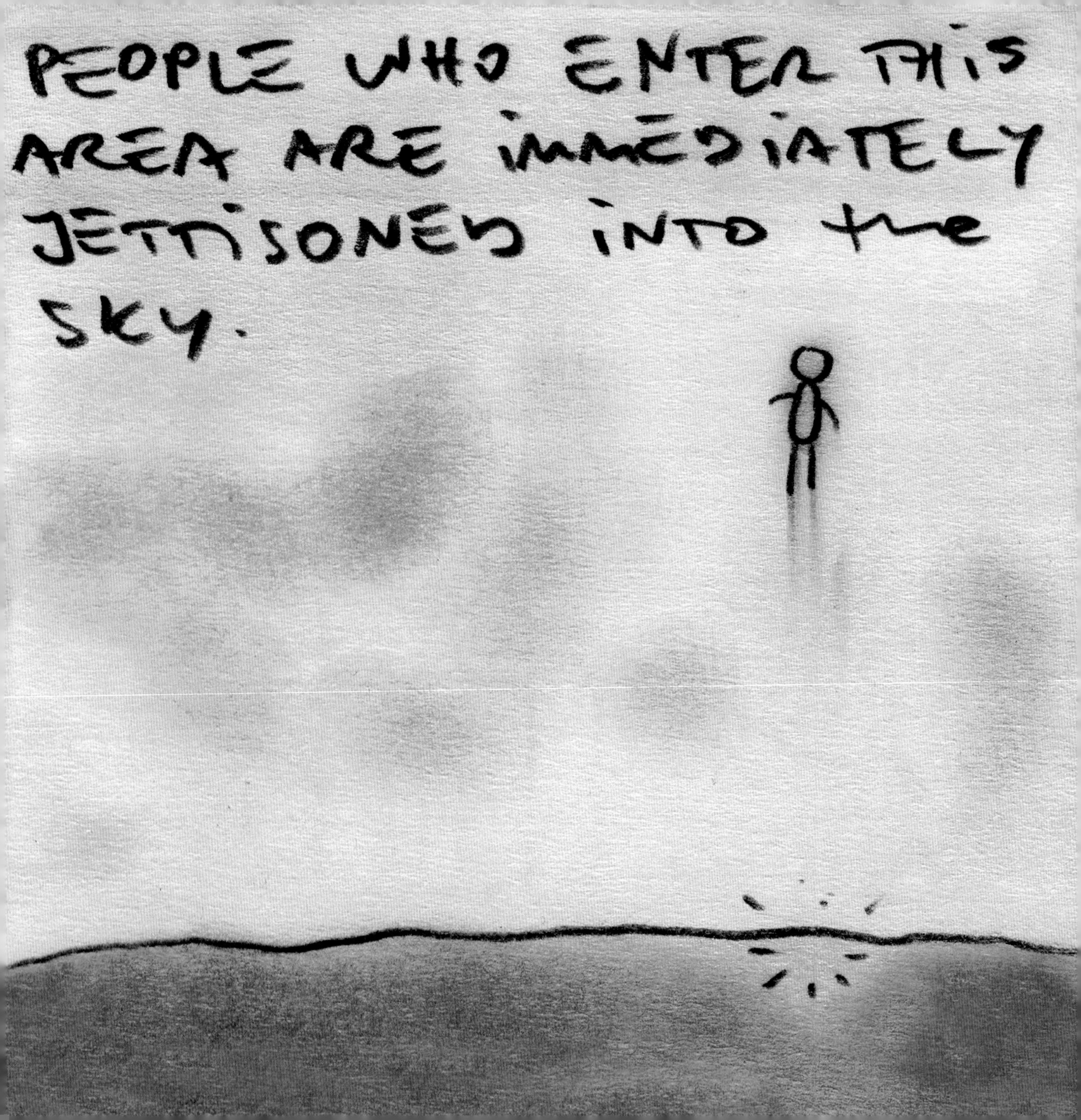
PEOPLE WHO ENTER THIS AREA ARE IMMEDIATELY JETTISONED INTO THE SKY.

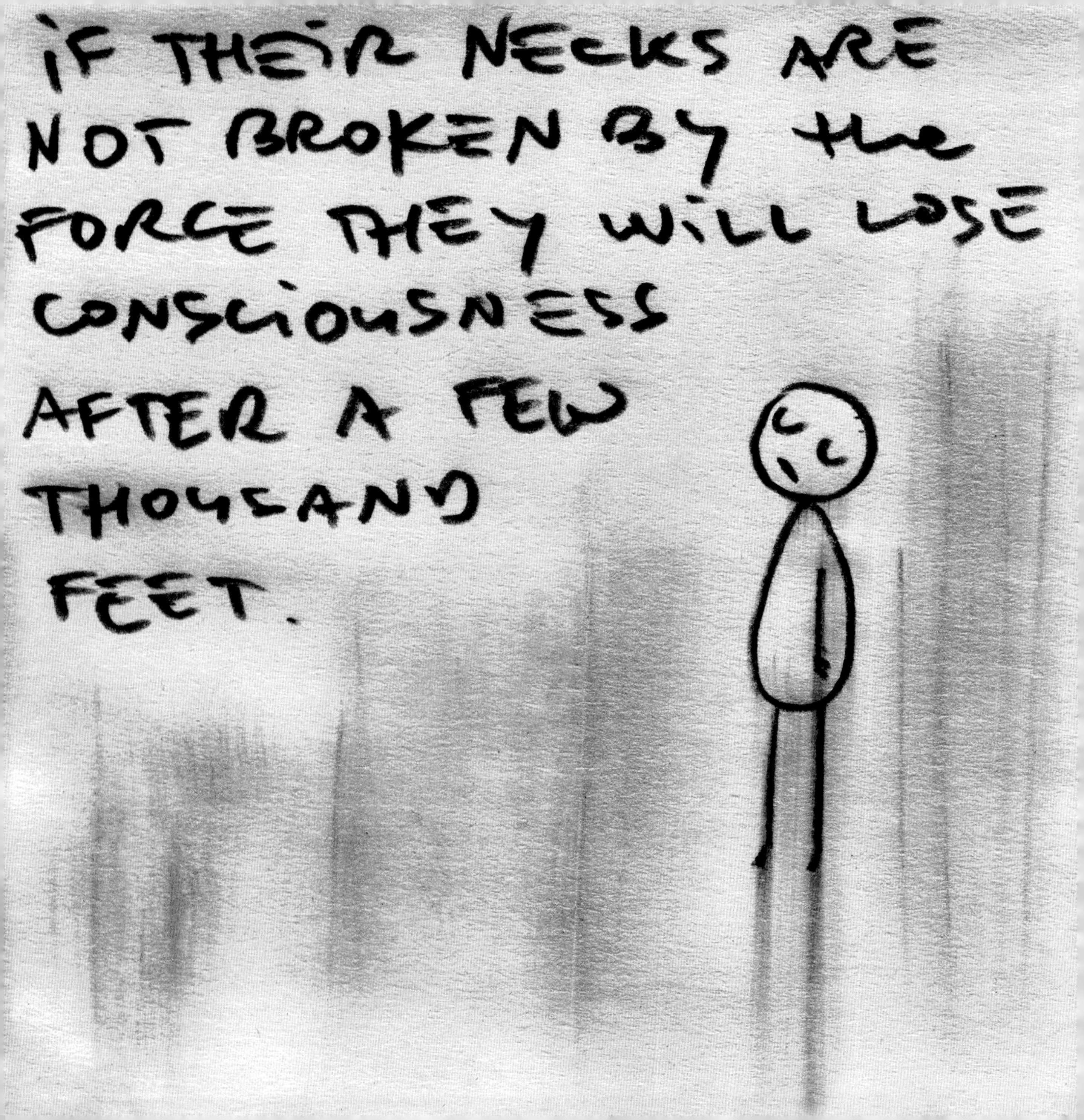
IF THEIR NECKS ARE NOT BROKEN BY the FORCE THEY WILL LOSE CONSCIOUSNESS AFTER A FEW THOUSAND FEET.

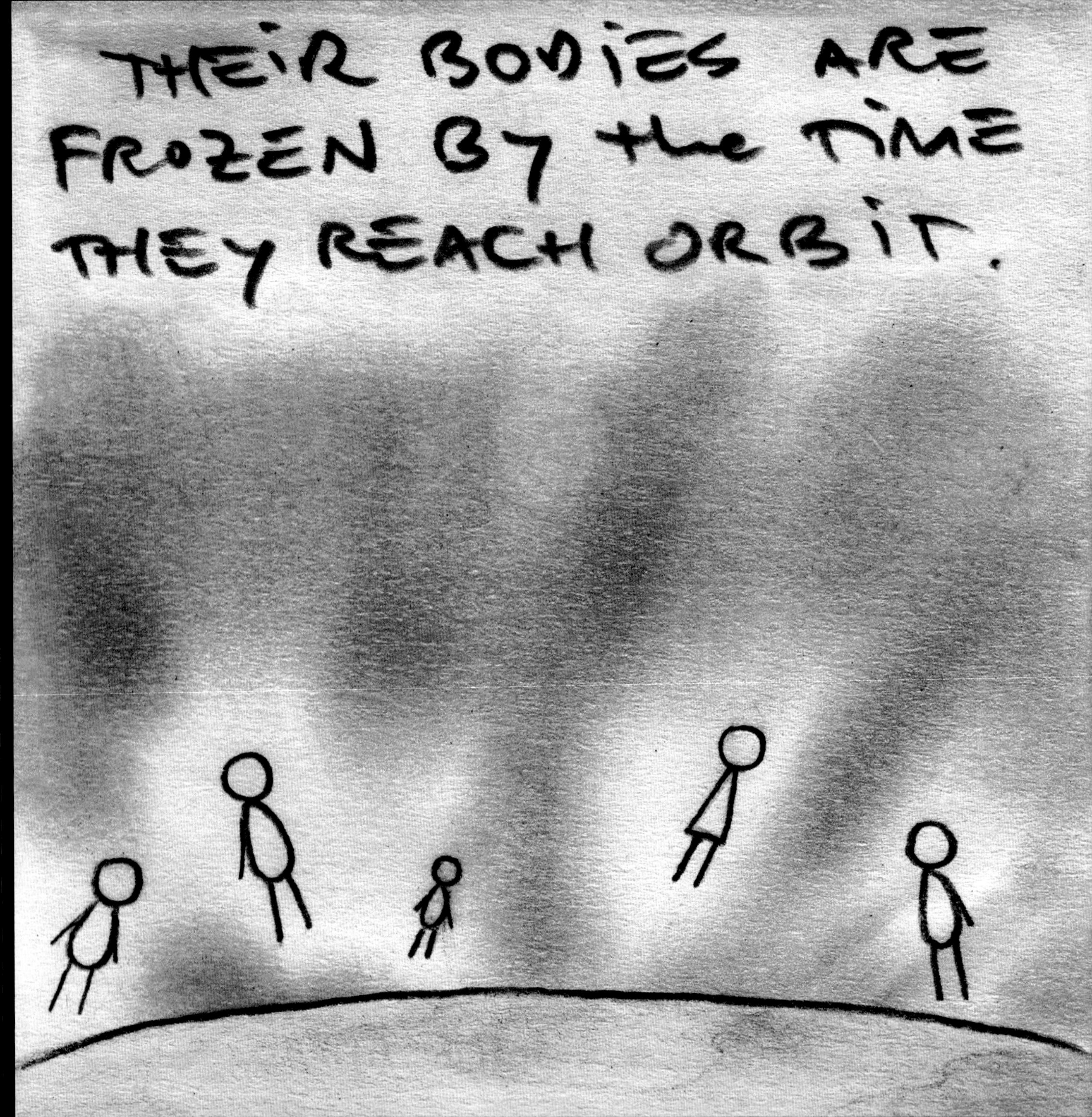
THEIR BODIES ARE FROZEN BY the TIME THEY REACH ORBIT.

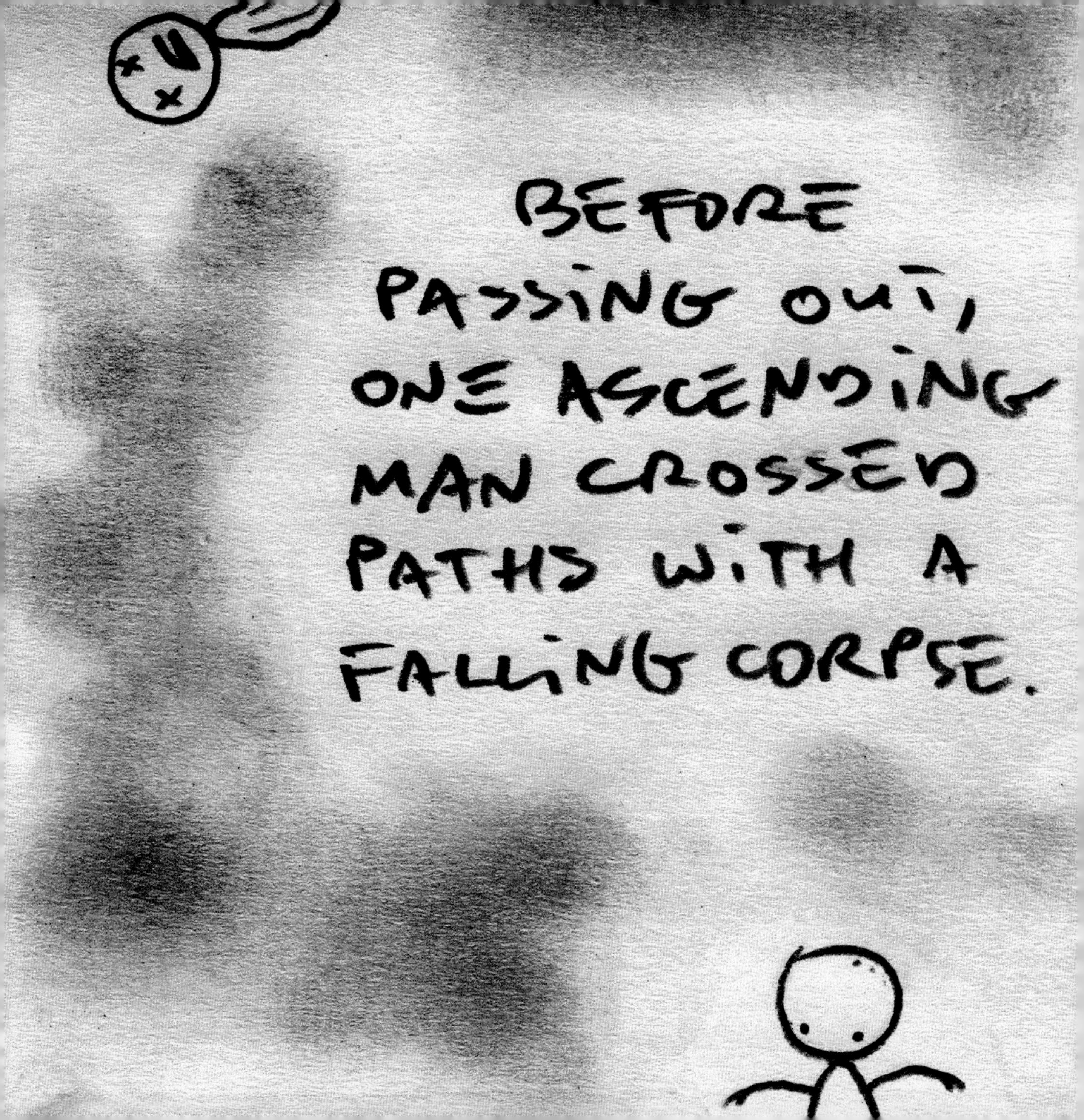
BEFORE PASSING OUT, ONE ASCENDING MAN CROSSED PATHS WITH A FALLING CORPSE.

FOR A SPLIT SECOND
AS THEY PASSED, the
ASCENDING MAN FELT
MOTIONLESS.

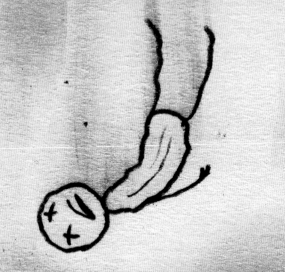
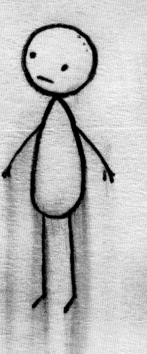

IT WAS the
STRANGEST
SENSATION.

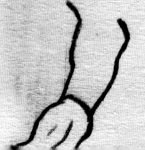

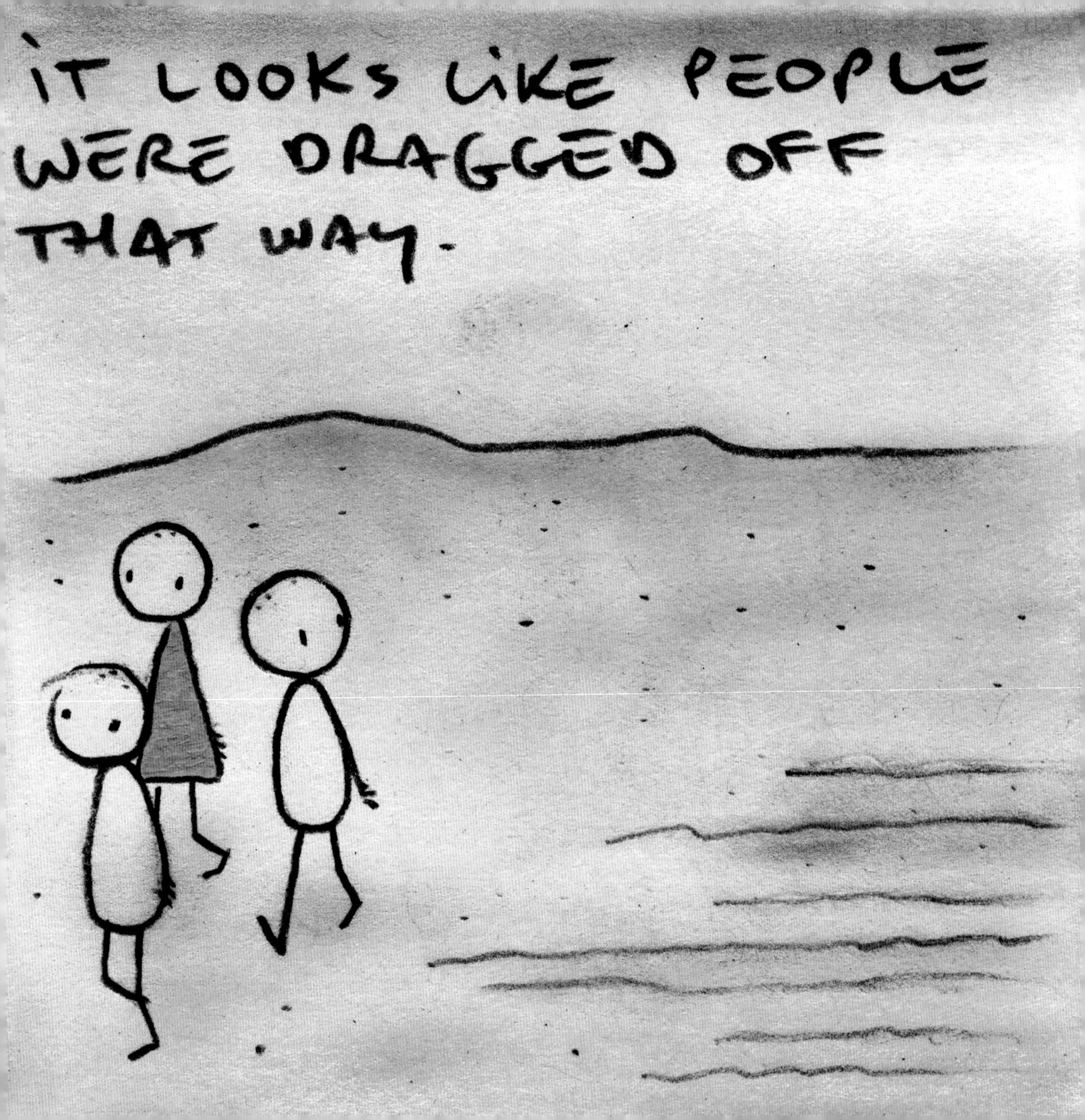
IT LOOKS LIKE PEOPLE WERE DRAGGED OFF THAT WAY.

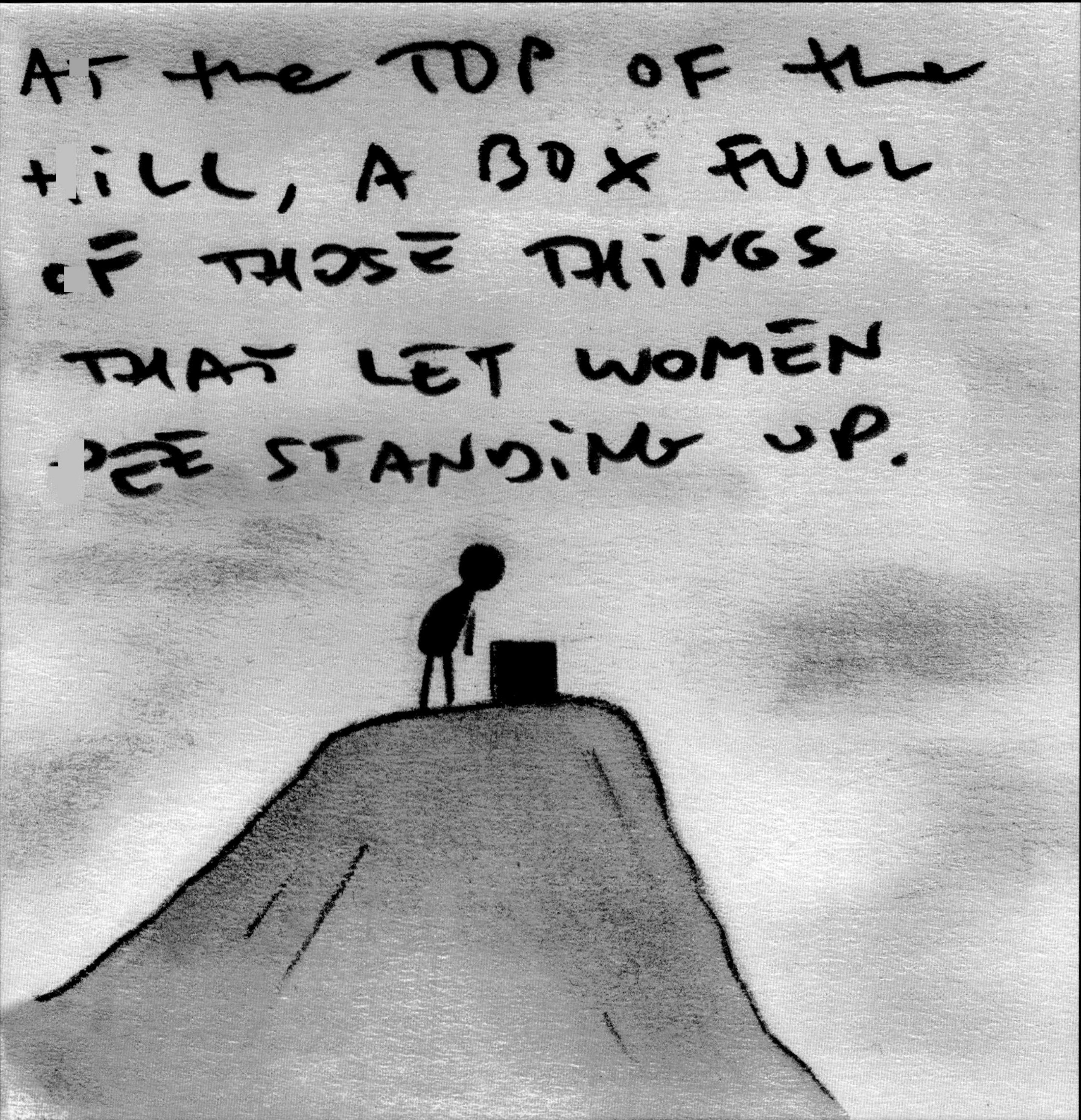
AT THE TOP OF THE HILL, A BOX FULL OF THOSE THINGS THAT LET WOMEN PEE STANDING UP.

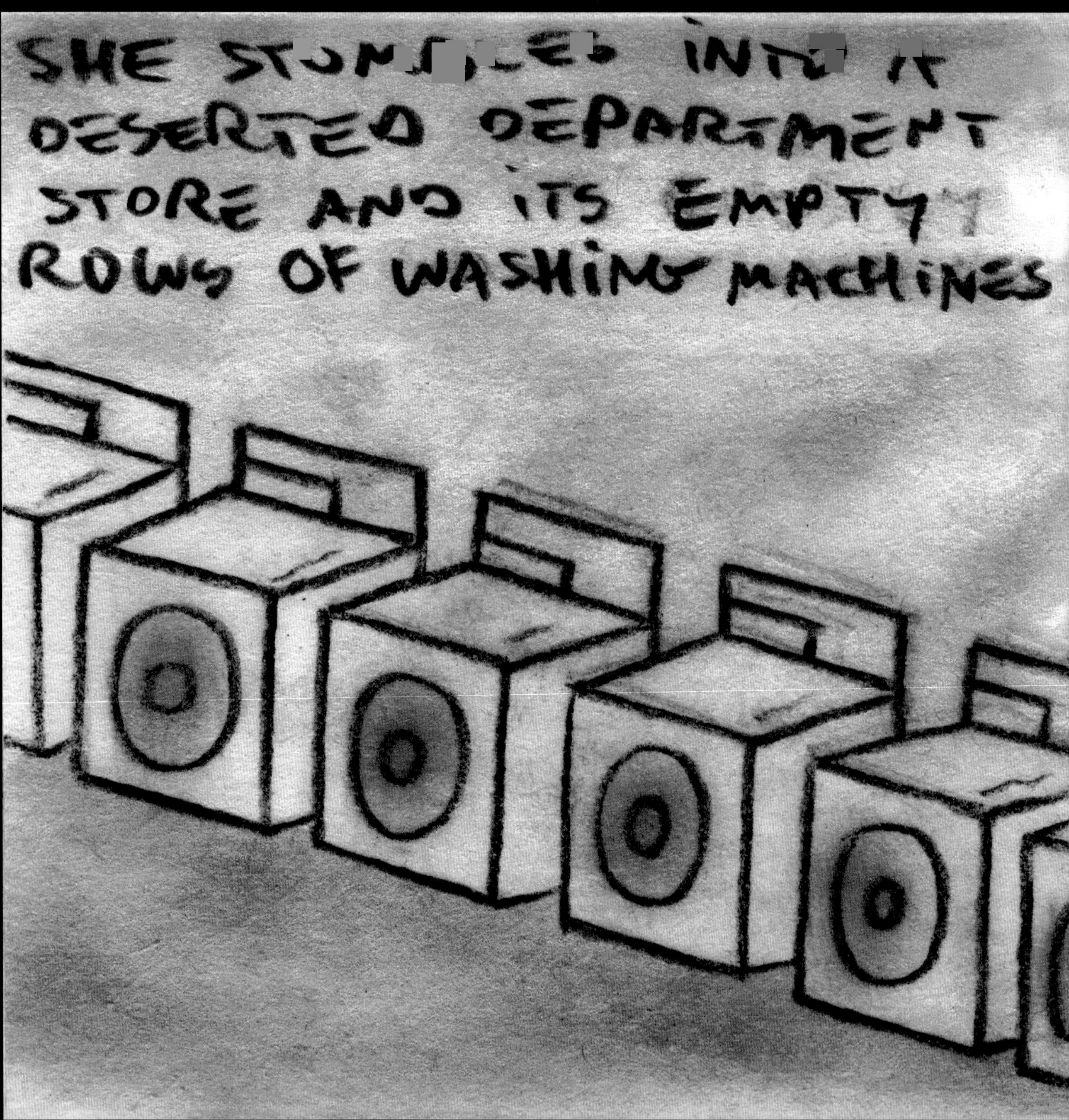
SHE STUMBLED INTO A DESERTED DEPARTMENT STORE AND ITS EMPTY ROWS OF WASHING MACHINES

BEFORE the ELECTRICITY DIED, SOMEBODY HAD REPEATEDLY FAXED the SAME COORDINATES ON A DOZEN PAGES

"TONGS! I'VE FOUND TONGS!"

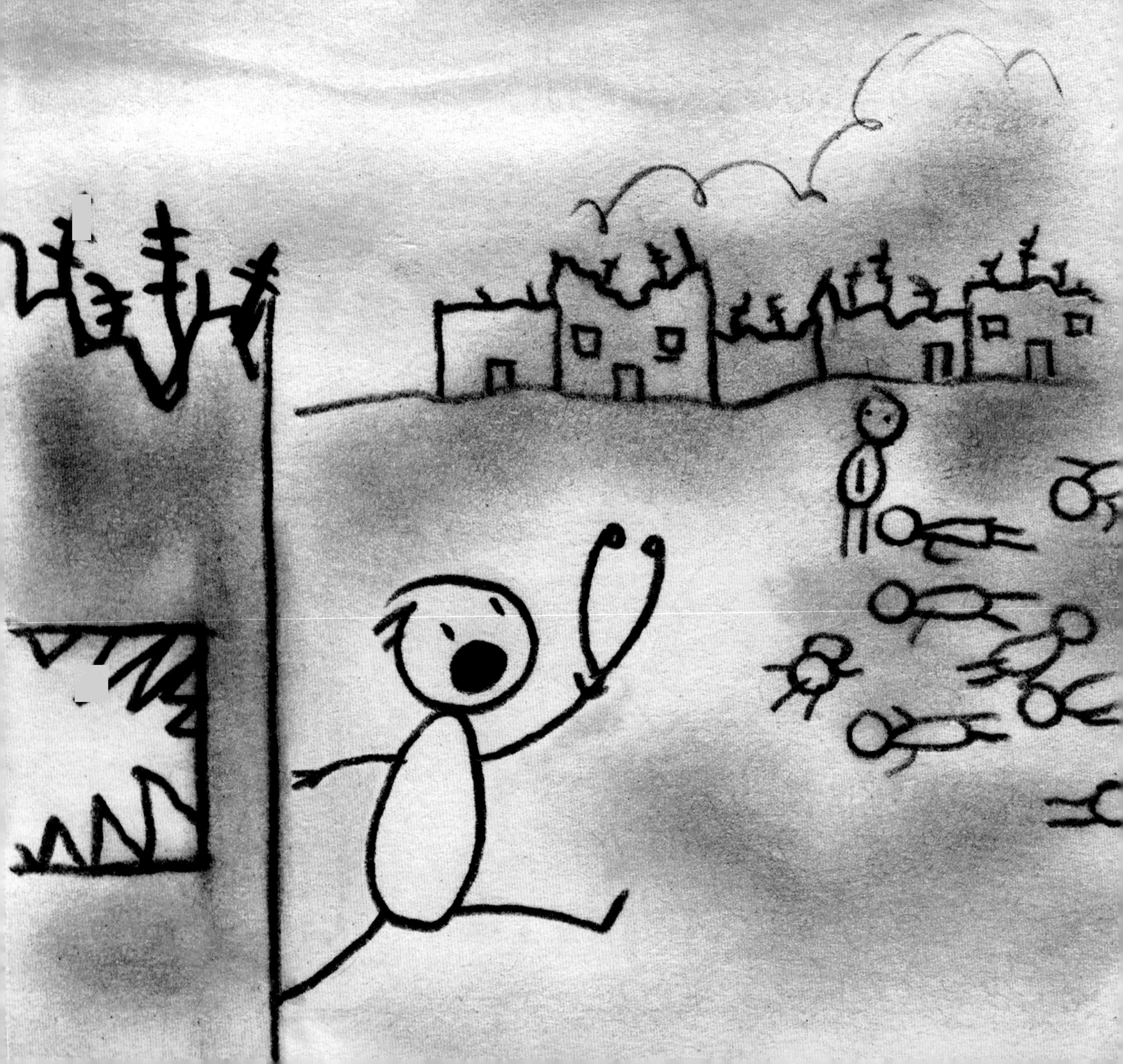

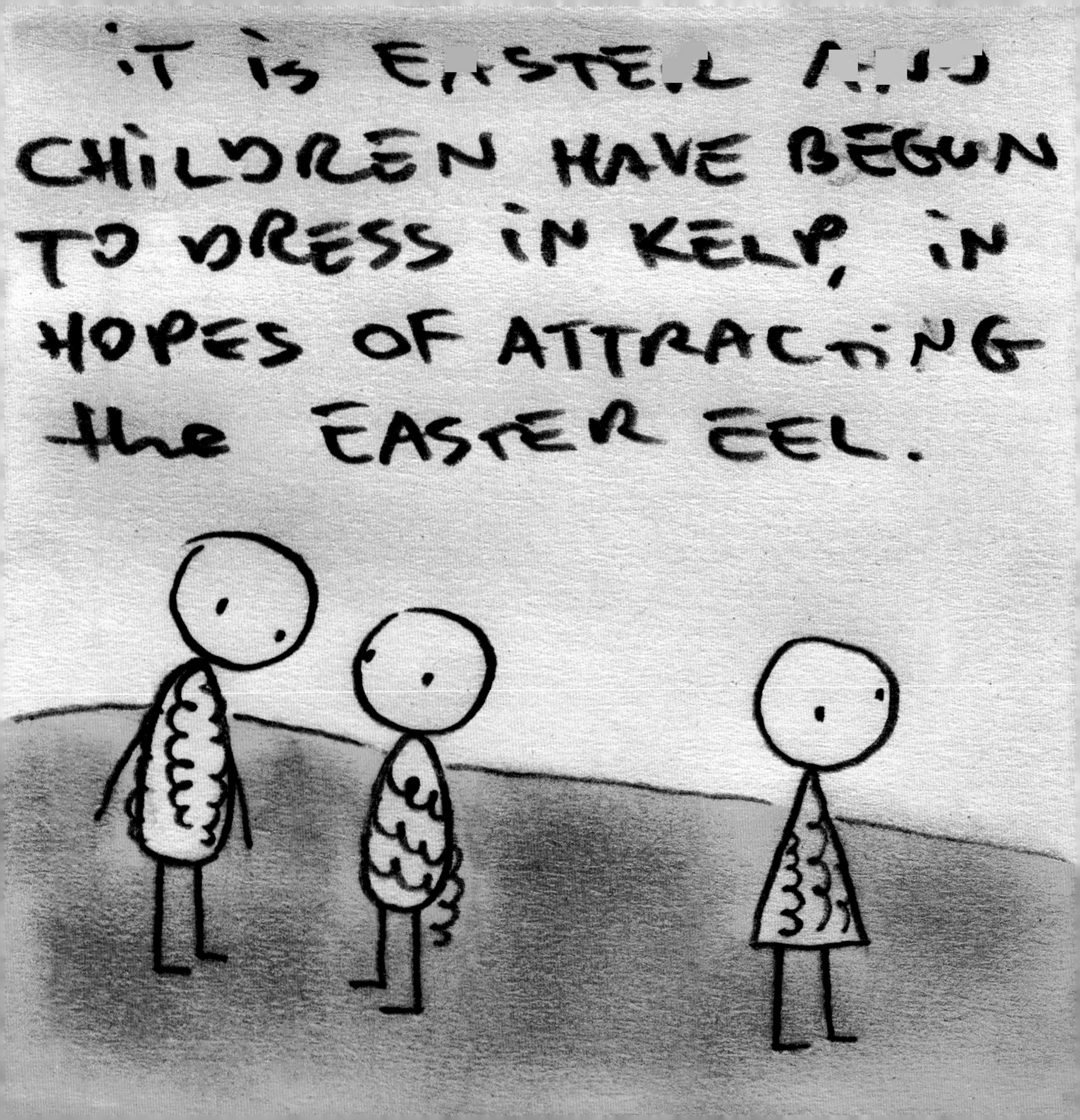
IT IS EASTER AND CHILDREN HAVE BEGUN TO DRESS IN KELP, IN HOPES OF ATTRACTING the EASTER EEL.

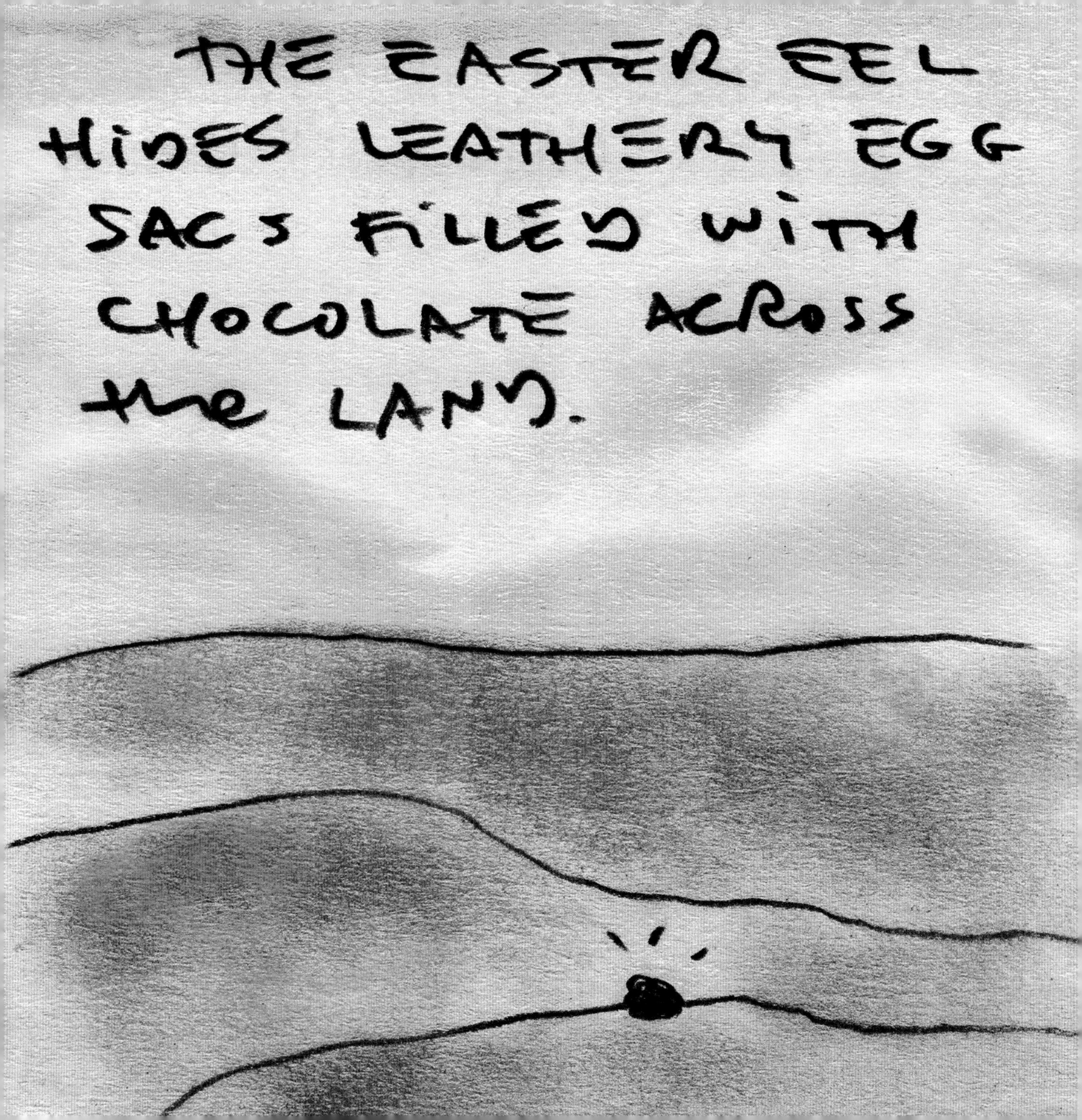
THE EASTER EEL HIDES LEATHERY EGG SACS FILLED WITH CHOCOLATE ACROSS the LAND.

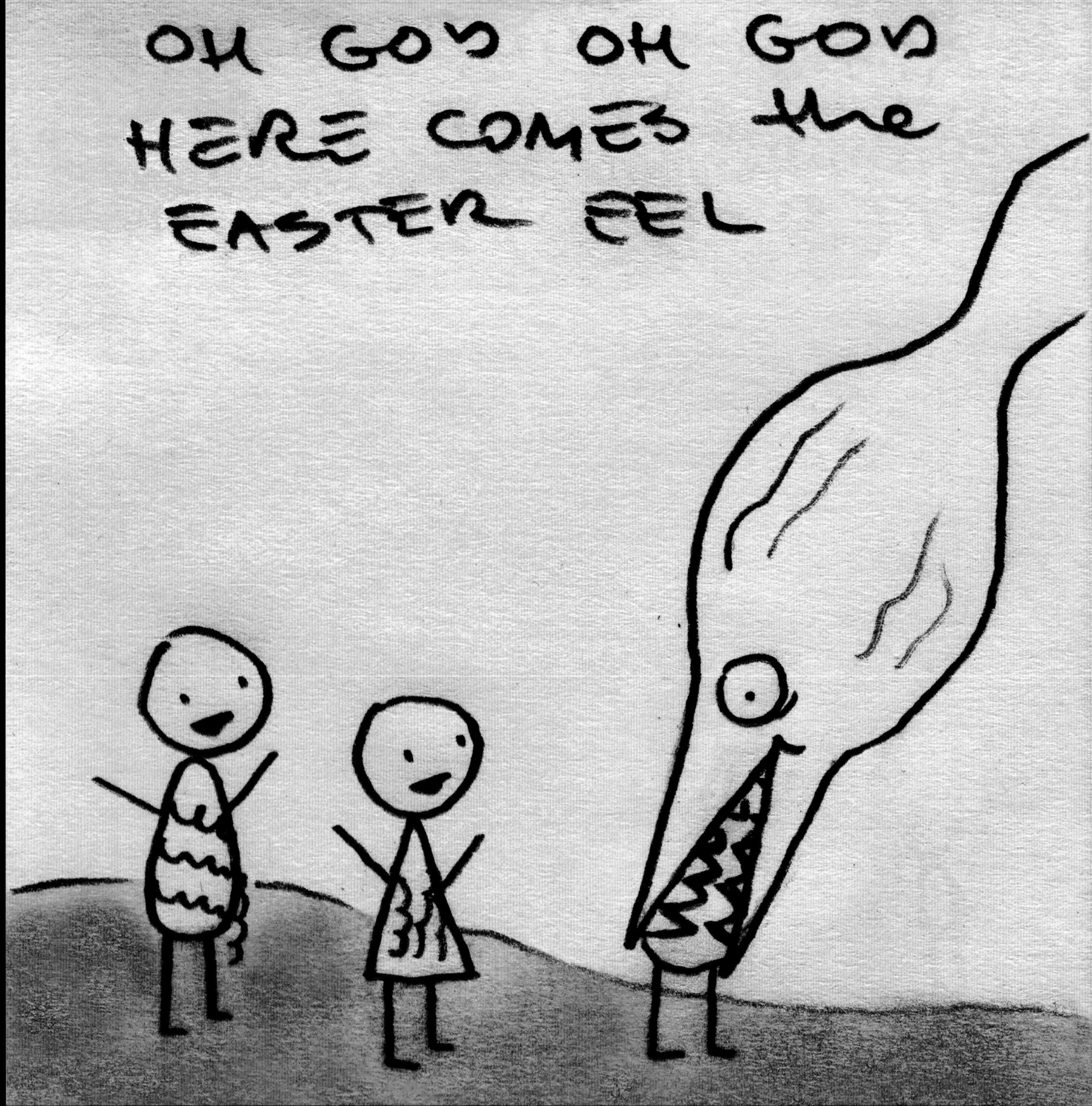
OH GOD OH GOD
HERE COMES the
EASTER EEL

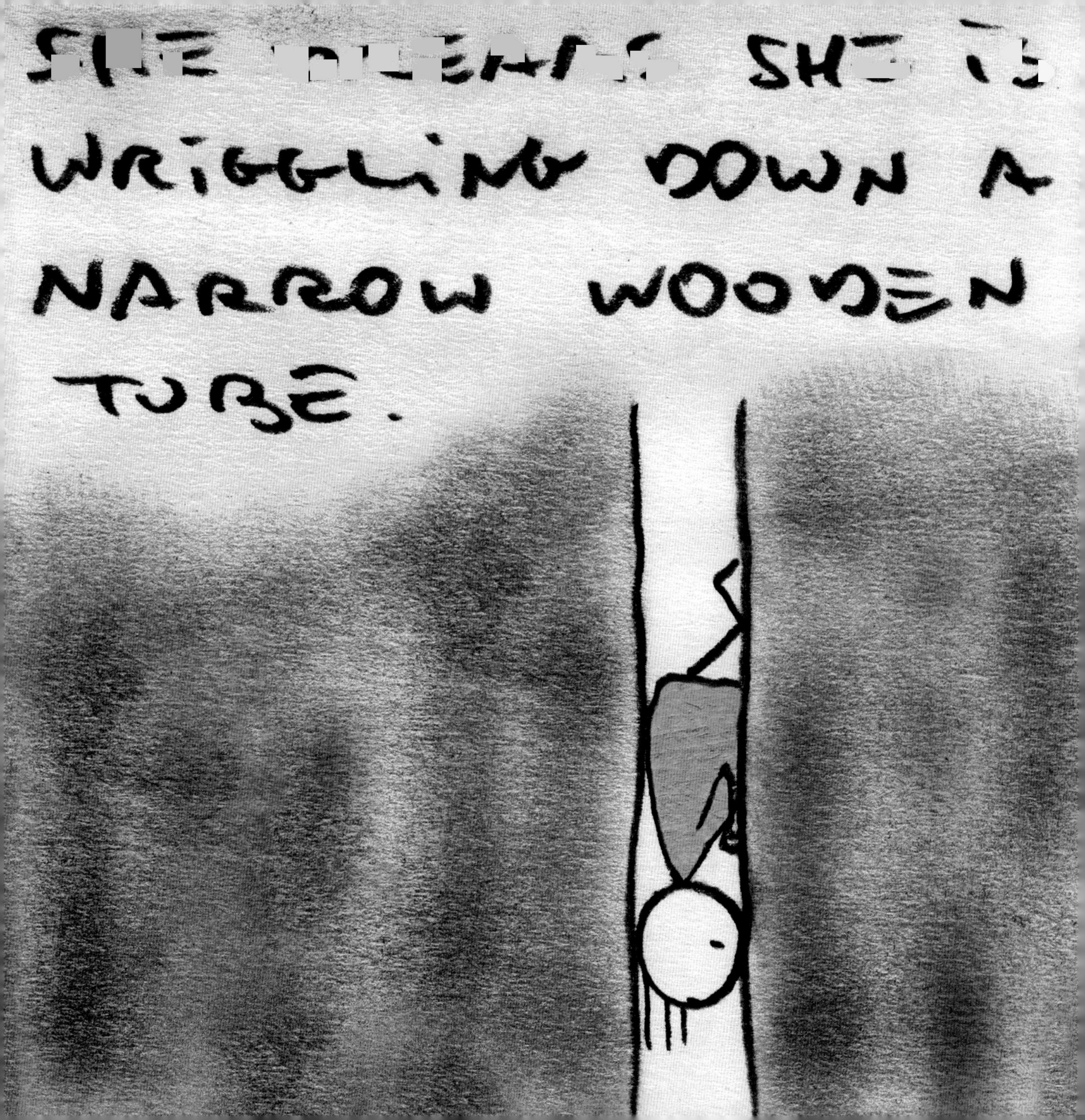
SHE DREAMS SHE IS WRIGGLING DOWN A NARROW WOODEN TUBE.

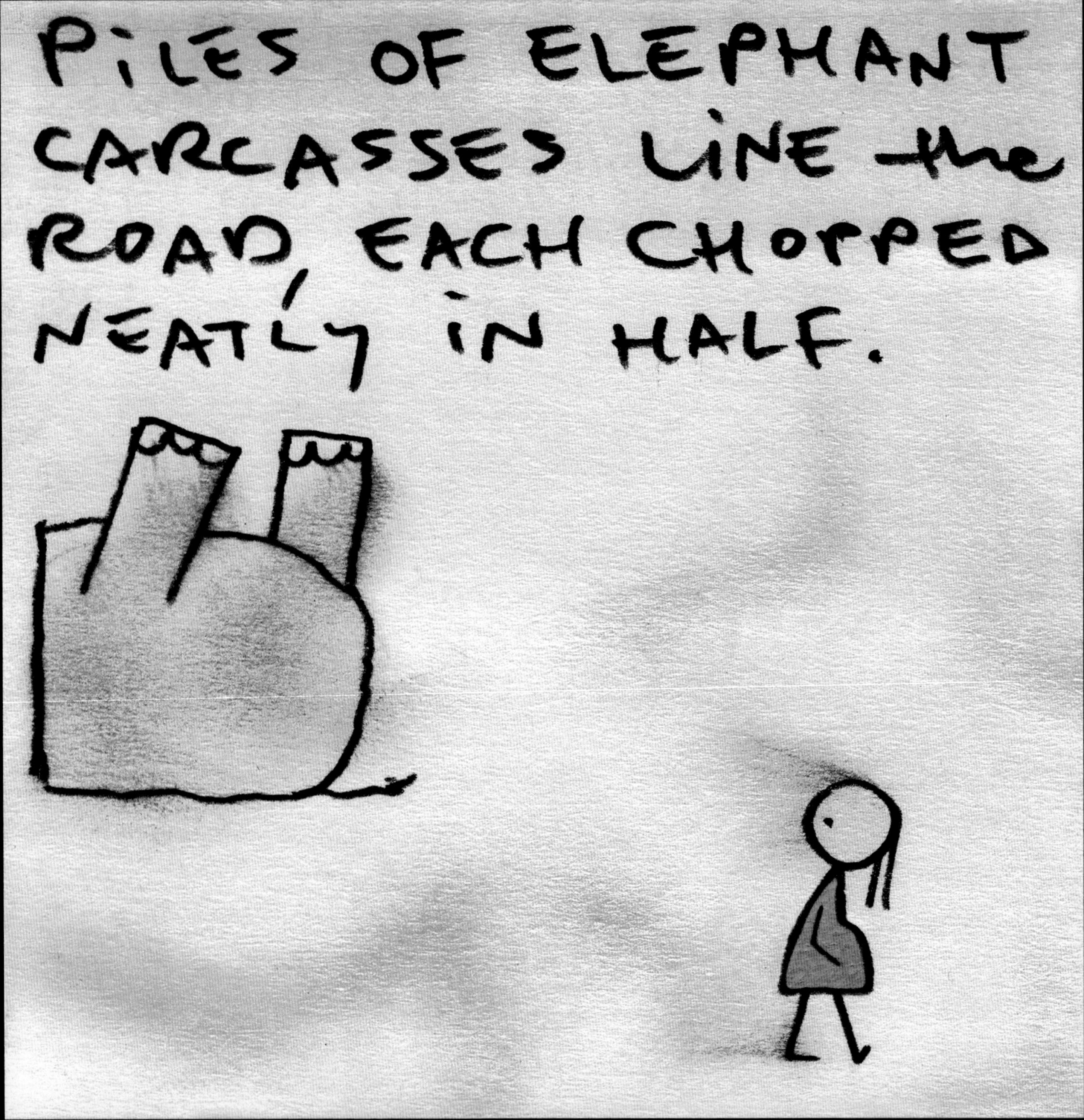
PILES OF ELEPHANT CARCASSES LINE the ROAD, EACH CHOPPED NEATLY IN HALF.

A LITTLE MAN EXPLAINS HOW THE LOCAL CORPORATION BISECTS ELEPHANTS IN THEIR MANUFACTURING OF CHEAP PEANUT BUTTER.

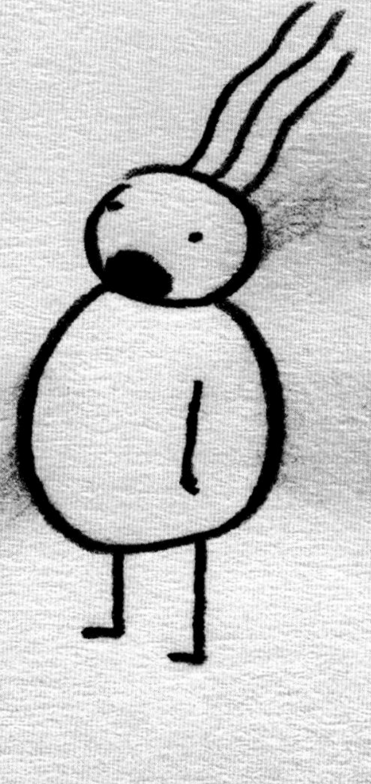

'IT SEEMS WASTEFUL,' SHE SAYS, 'WHY NOT MAKE the PEANUT BUTTER FROM the PEANUTS THEY FEED the ELEPHANTS?'

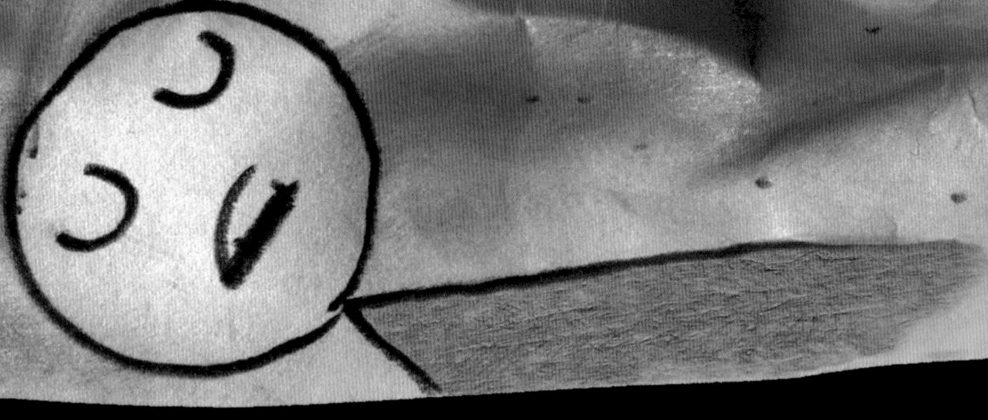

HE SAYS SOMETHING
FLIPPANT ABOUT
FEEDING GLUE TO
HORSES.

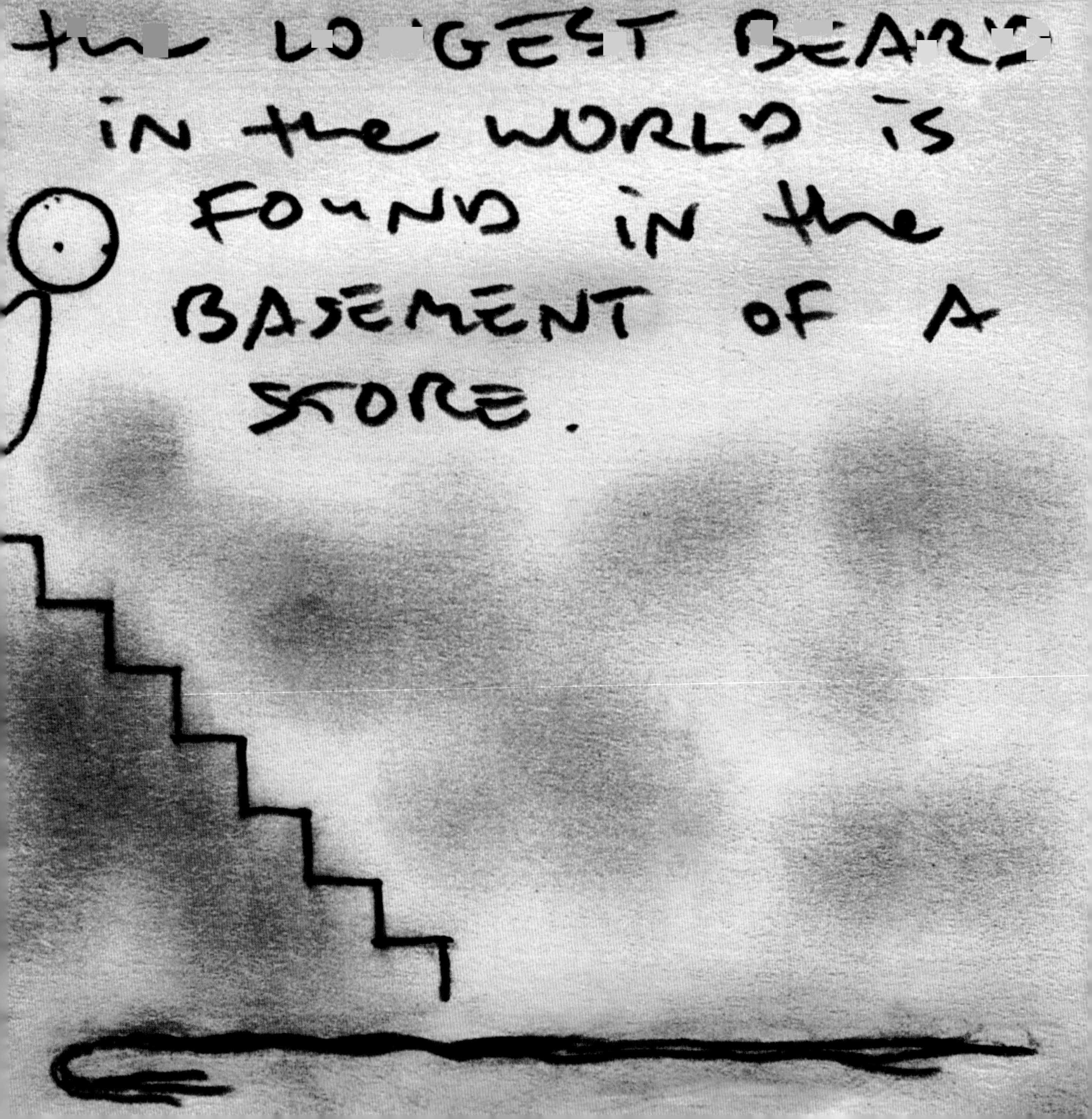
the LONGEST BEARD
in the WORLD is
FOUND in the
BASEMENT OF A
STORE.

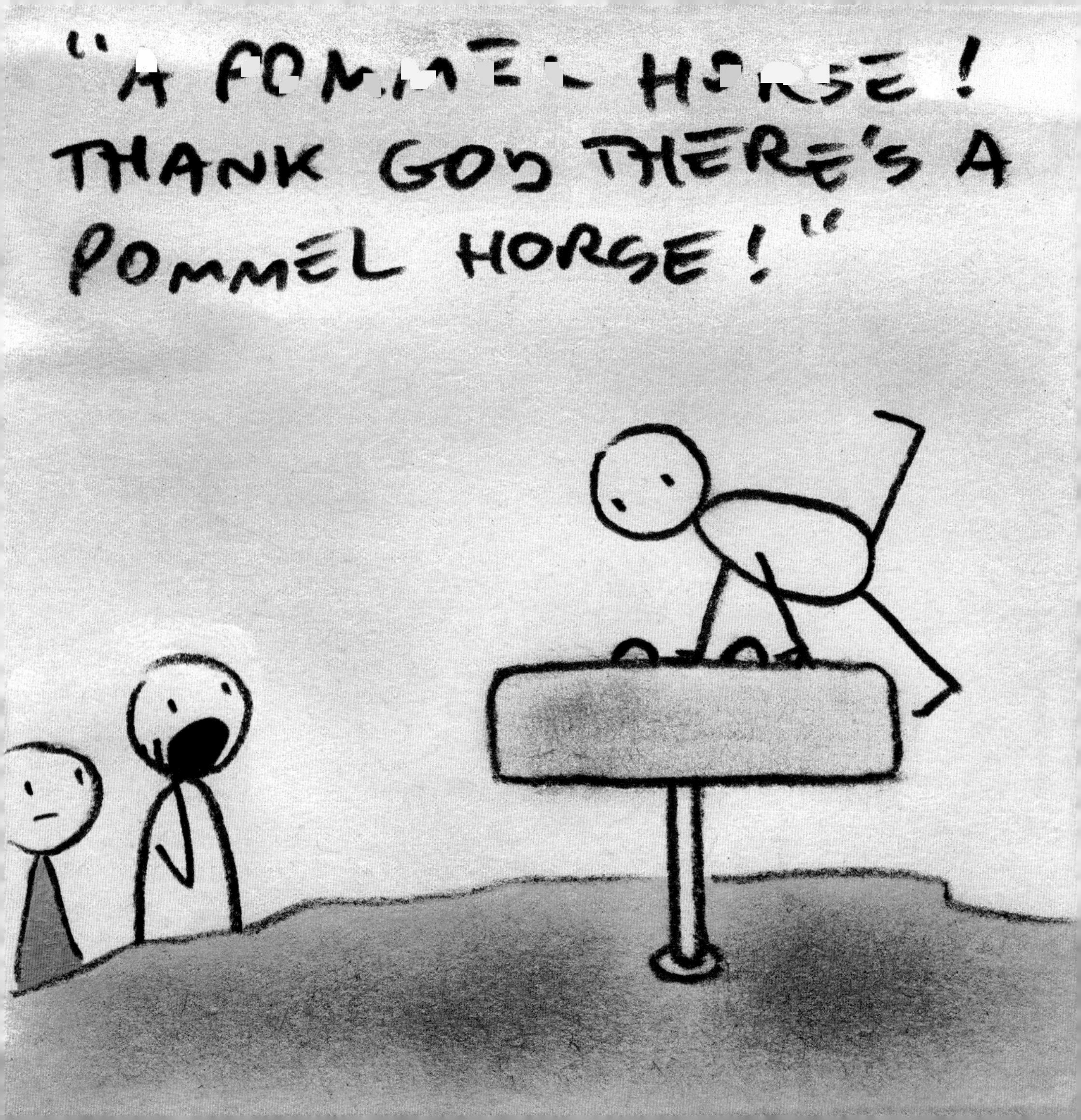
"A POMMEL HORSE! THANK GOD THERE'S A POMMEL HORSE!"

THE SAND HERE IS FLOATING IN A FINE LAYER.

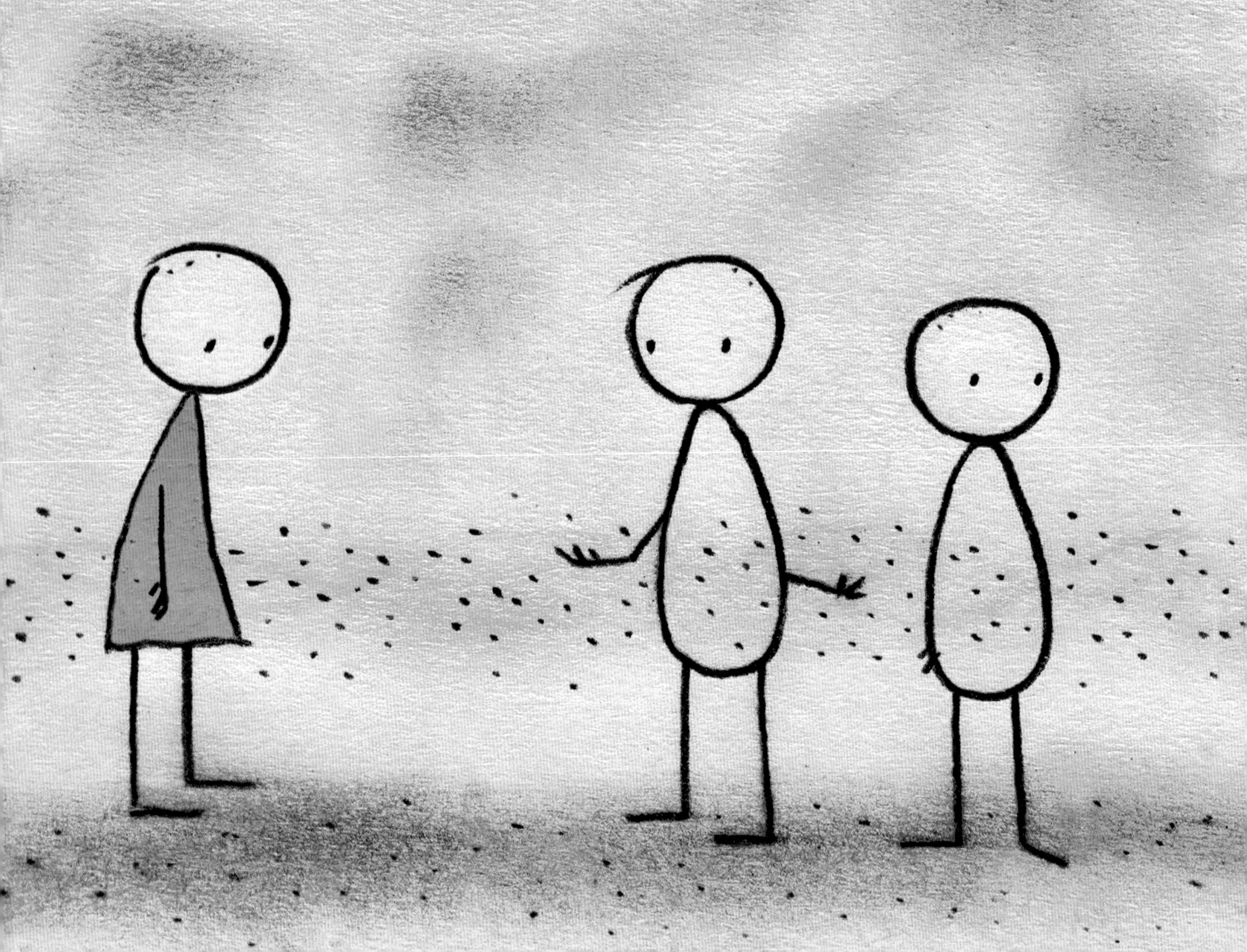

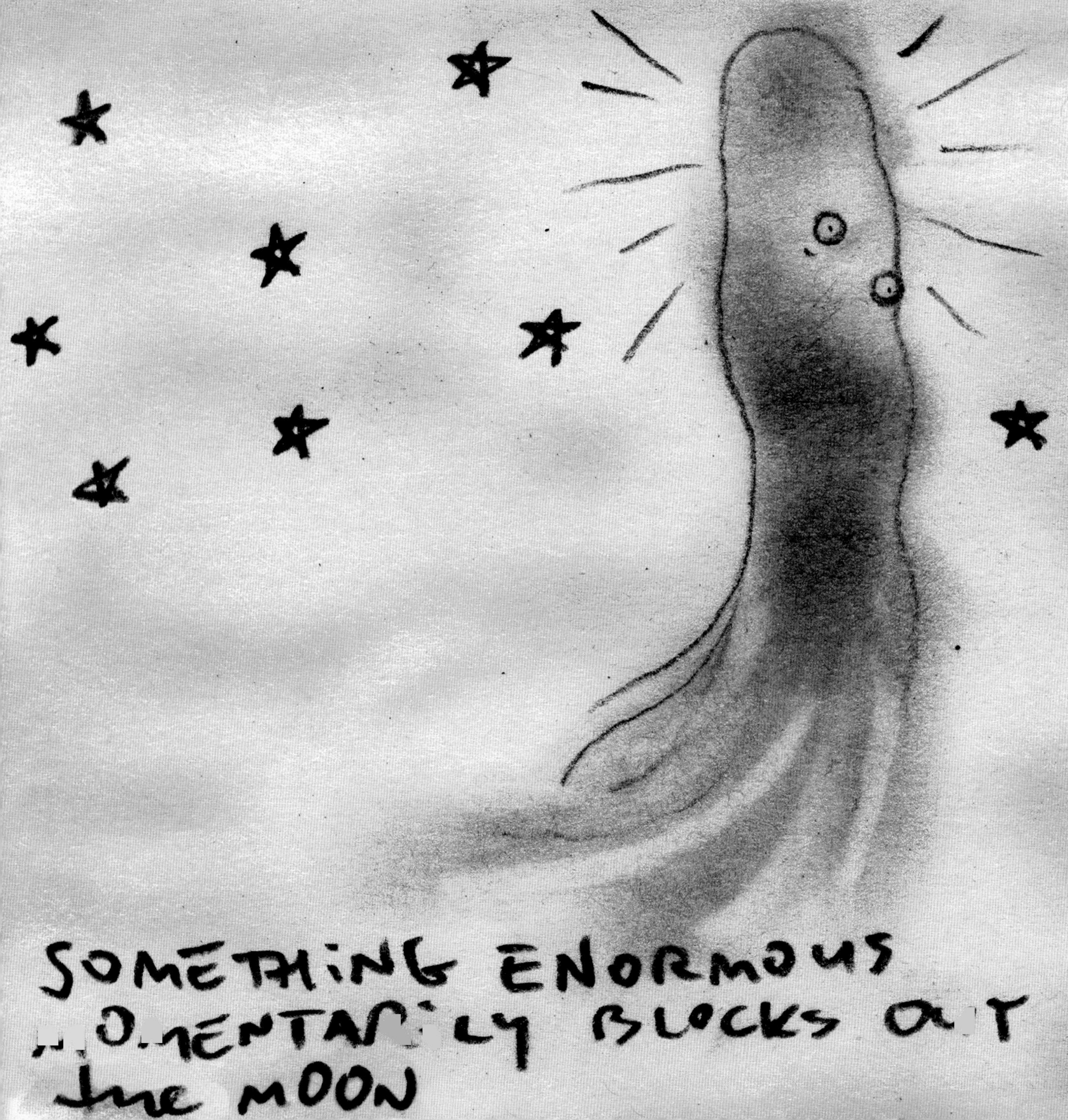
SOMETHING ENORMOUS MOMENTARILY BLOCKS OUT the MOON

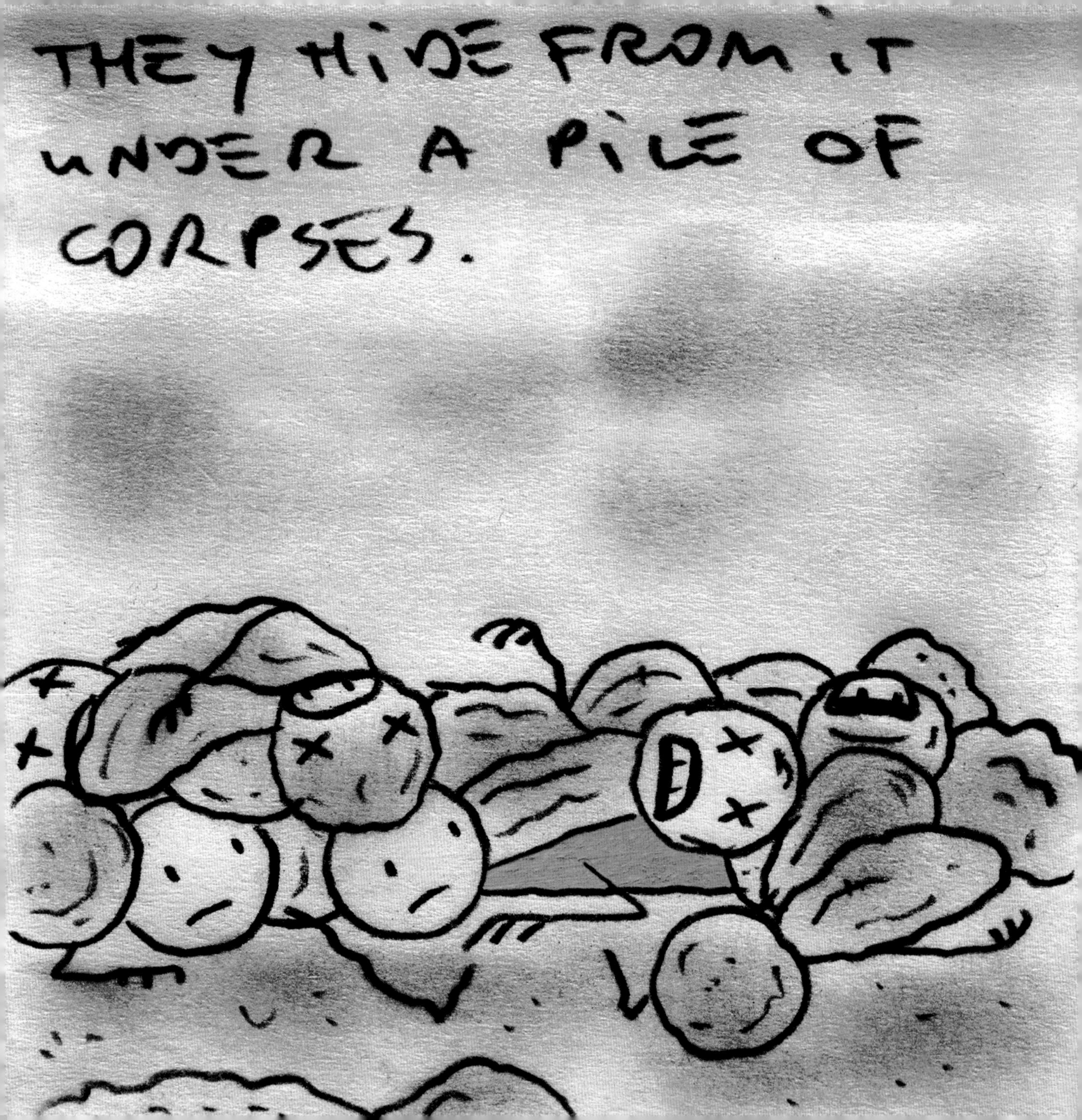
THEY HIDE FROM IT
UNDER A PILE OF
CORPSES.

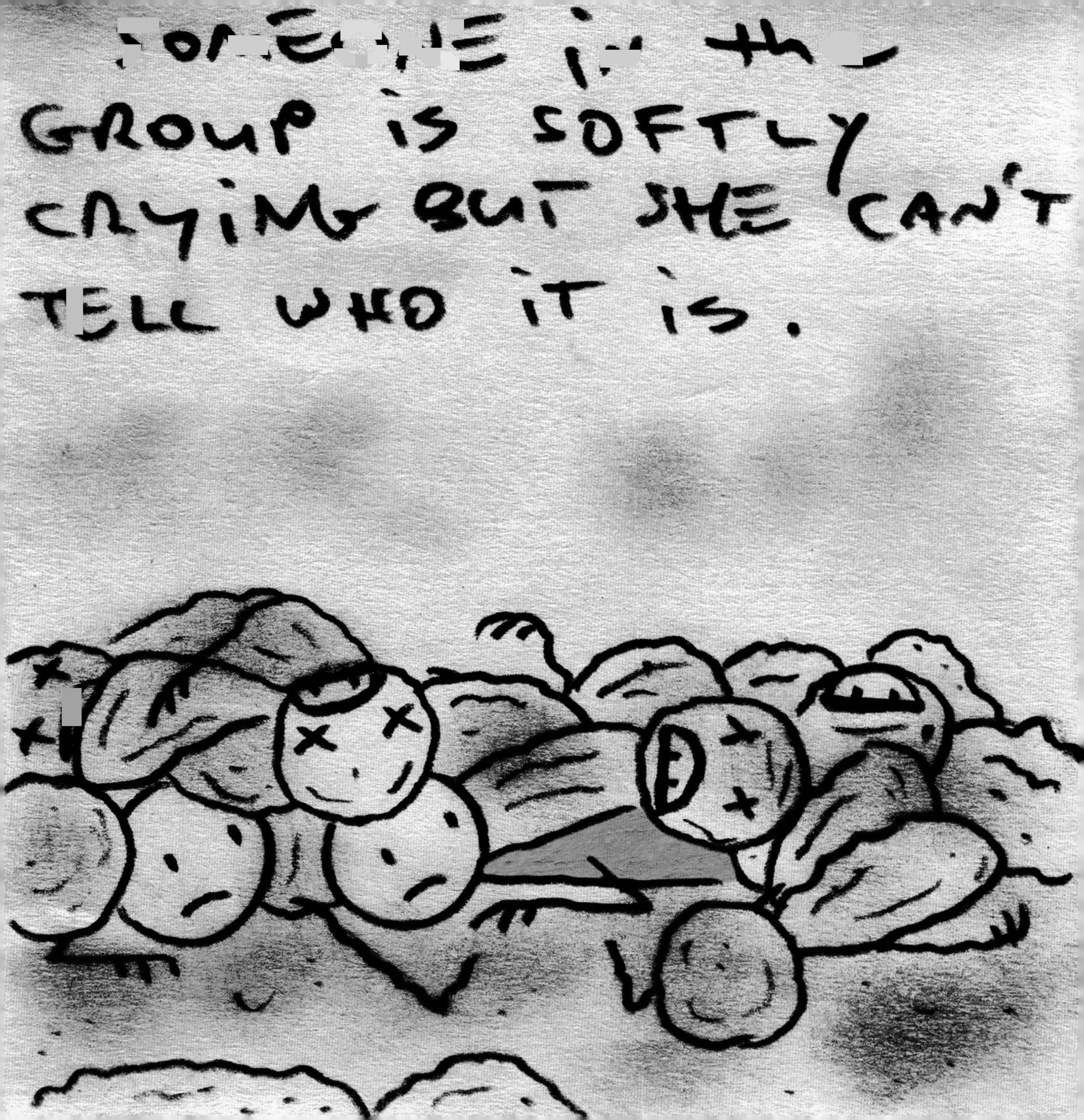
SOMEONE in the GROUP IS SOFTLY CRYING BUT SHE CAN'T TELL WHO IT IS.

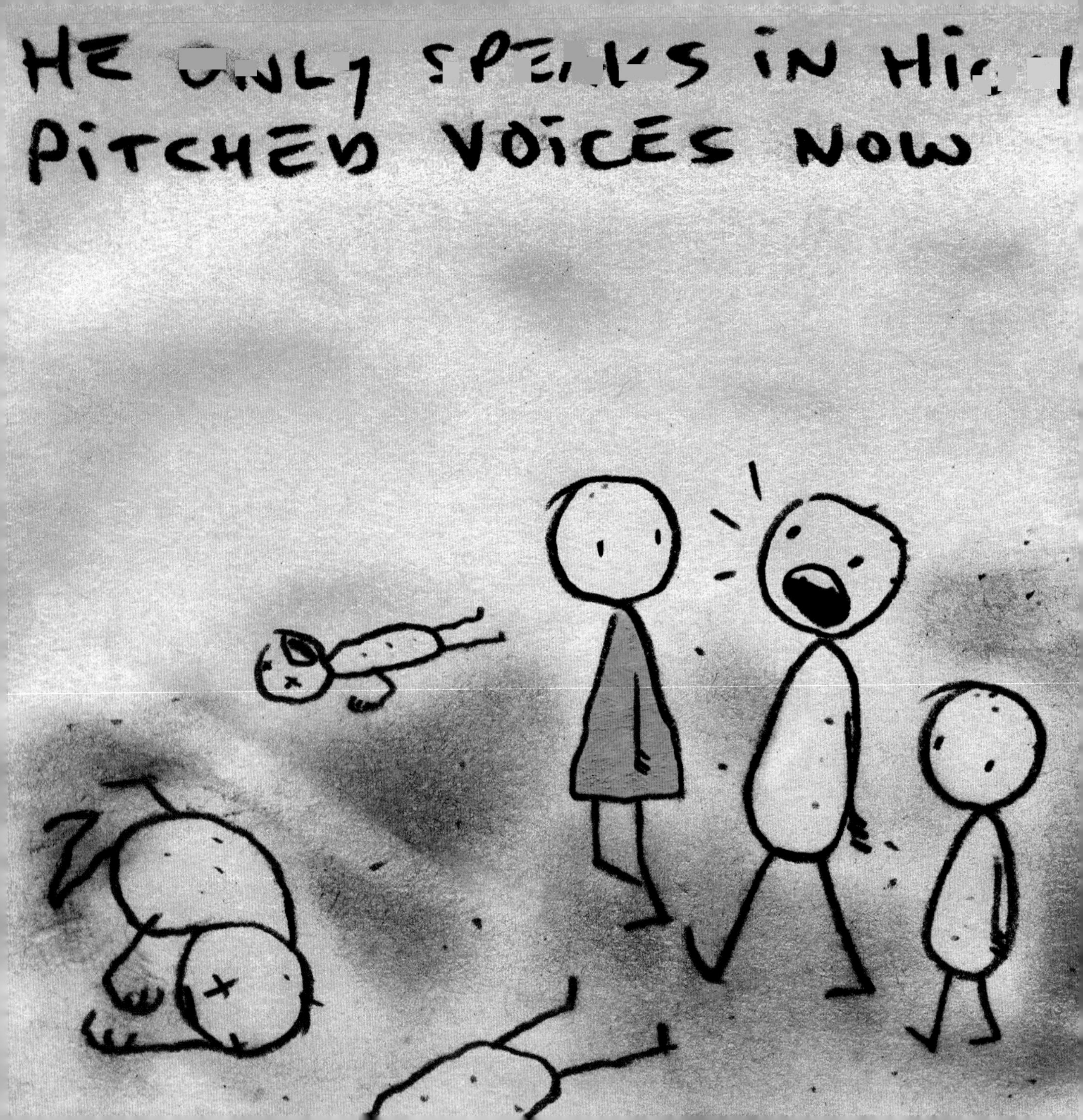
HE ONLY SPEAKS IN HIGH PITCHED VOICES NOW

THIS SQUID HAS ELBOWS

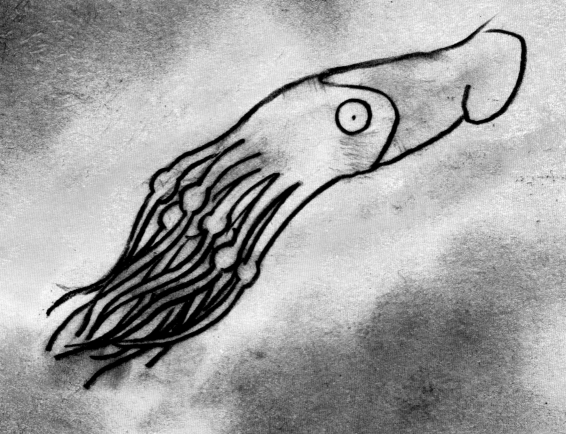

THE ONE NAMED PAUL HAS COLLAPSED FROM EXHAUSTION.

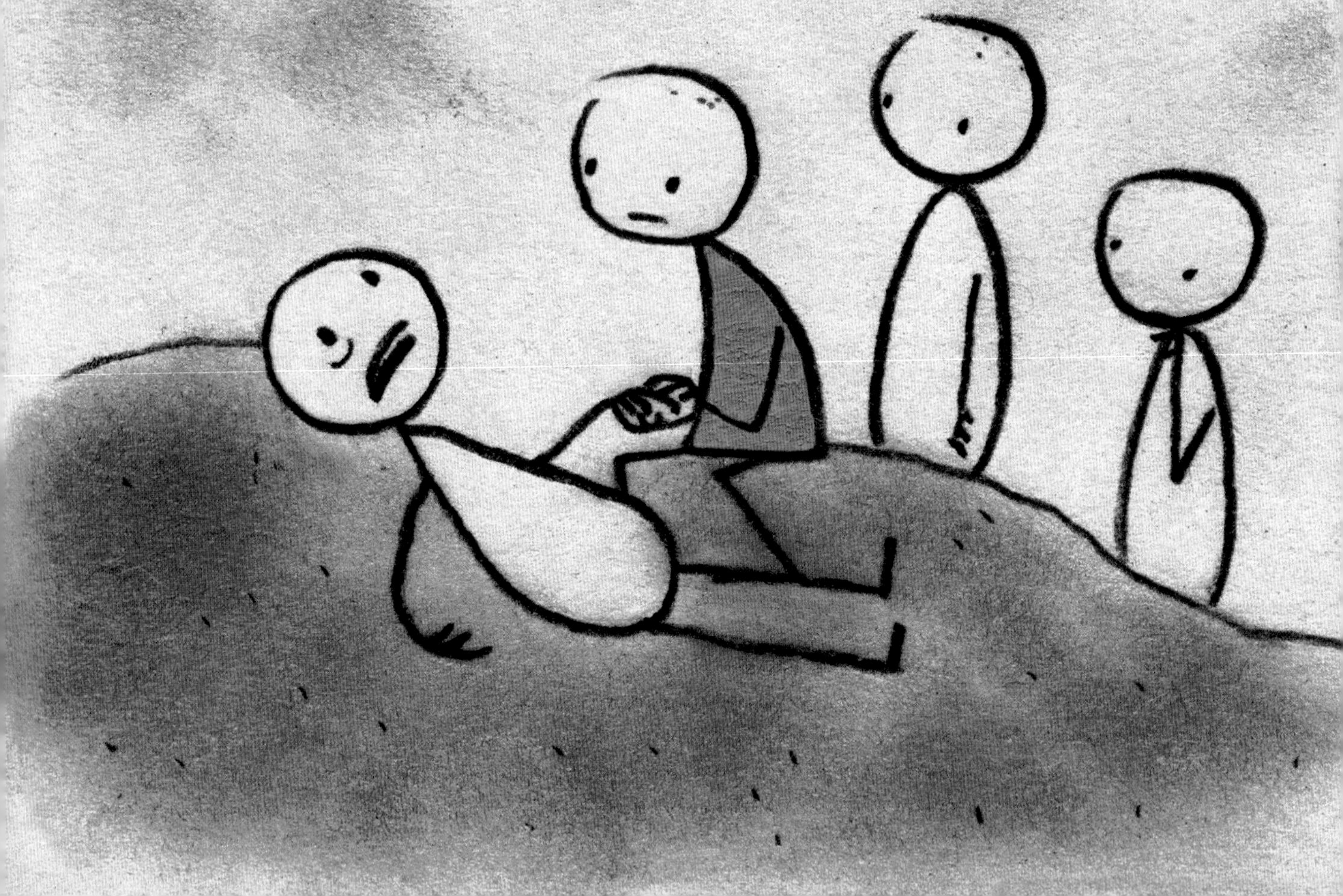

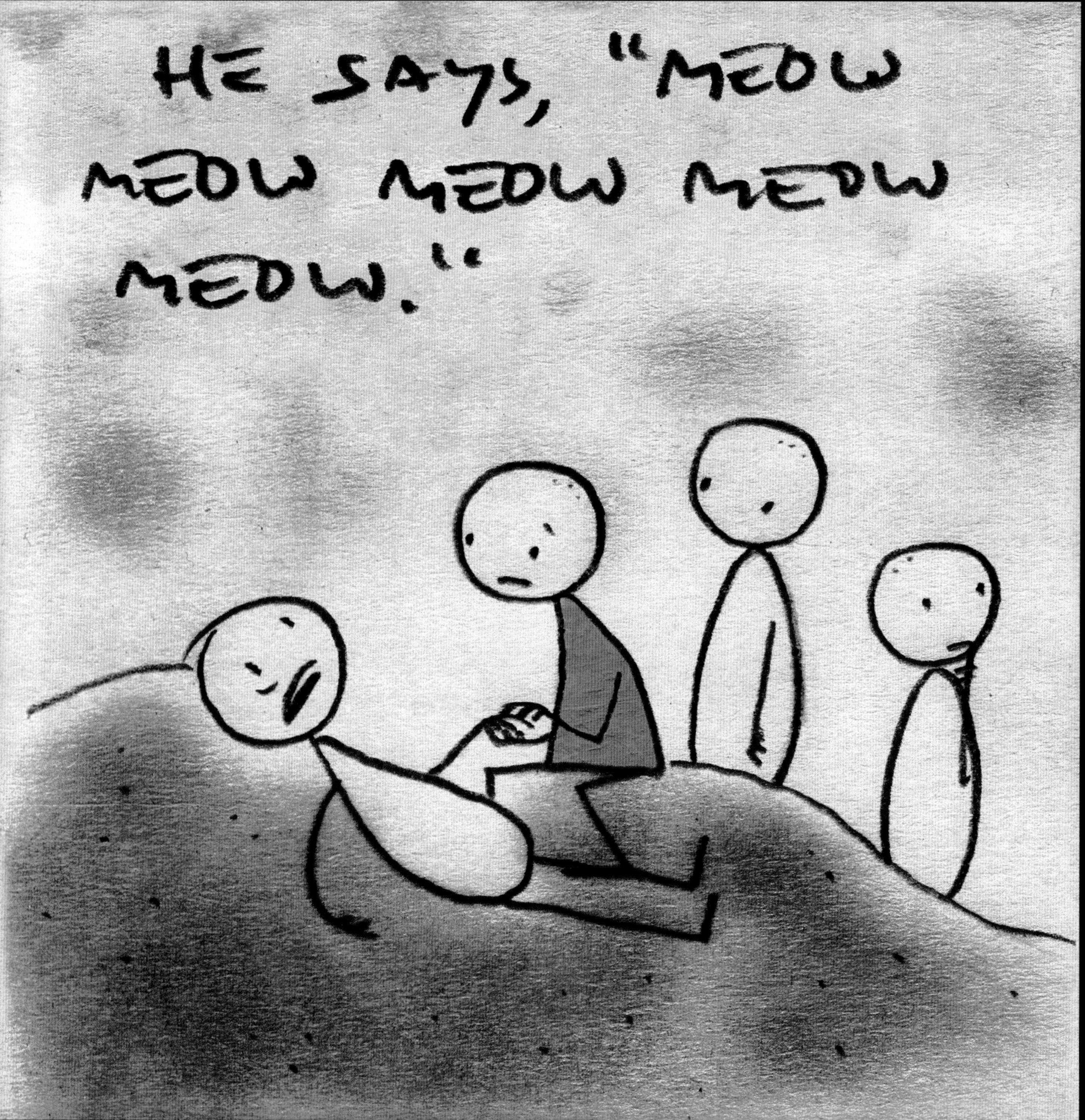
HE SAYS, "MEOW MEOW MEOW MEOW MEOW."

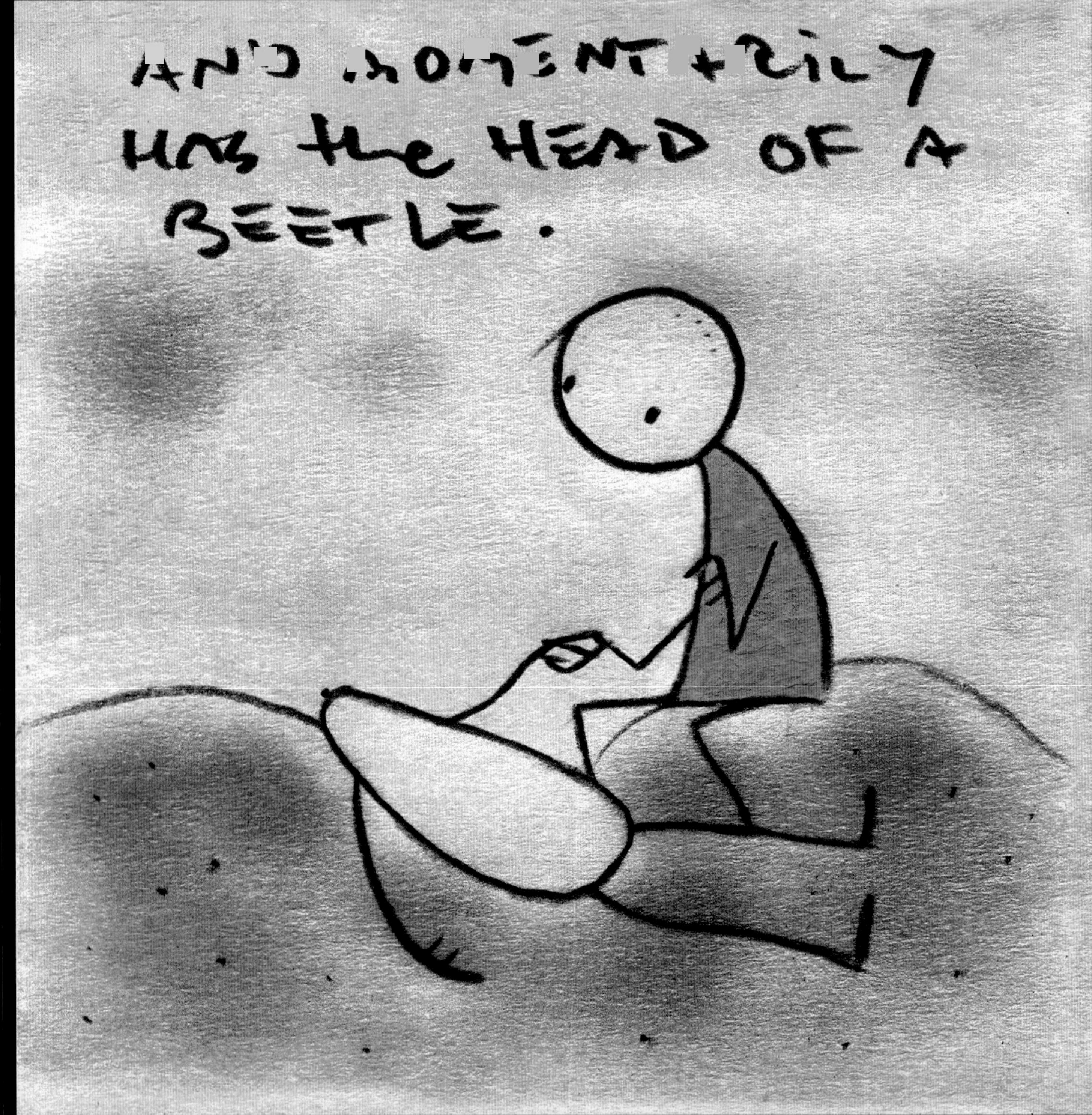
AND MOMENTARILY
HAS the HEAD OF A
BEETLE.

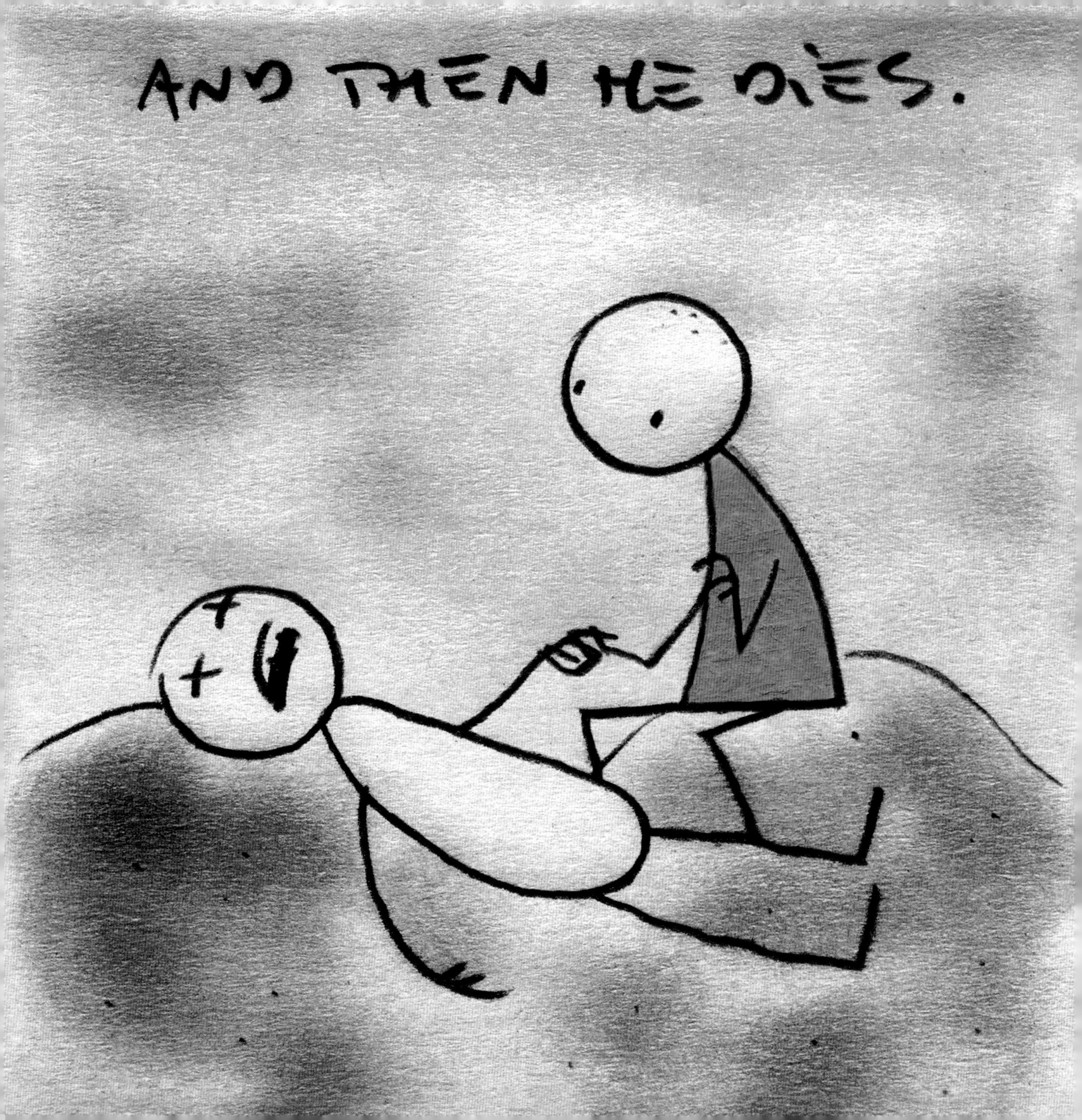
AND THEN HE DIES.

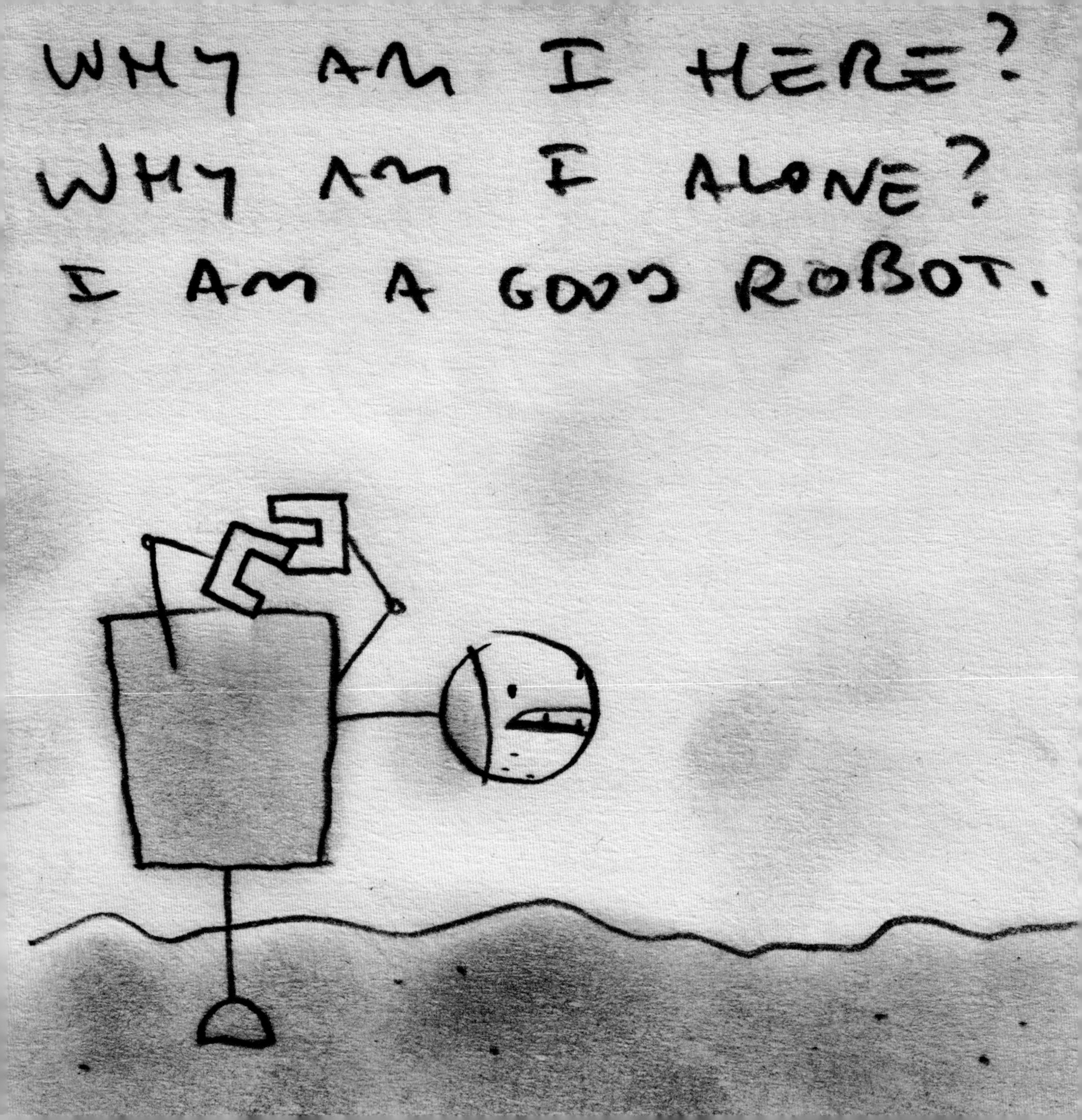
WHY AM I HERE?
WHY AM I ALONE?
I AM A GOOD ROBOT.

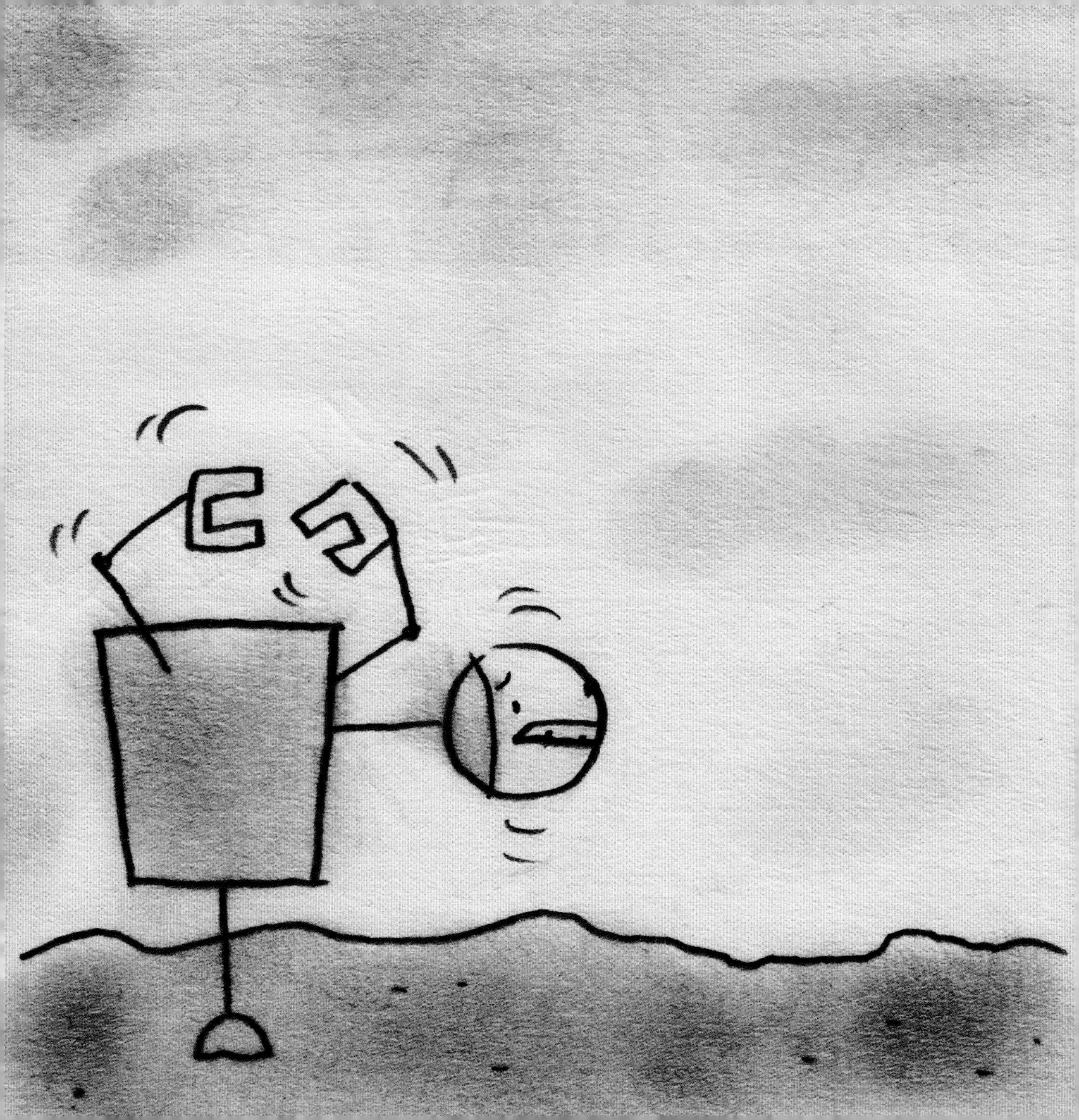

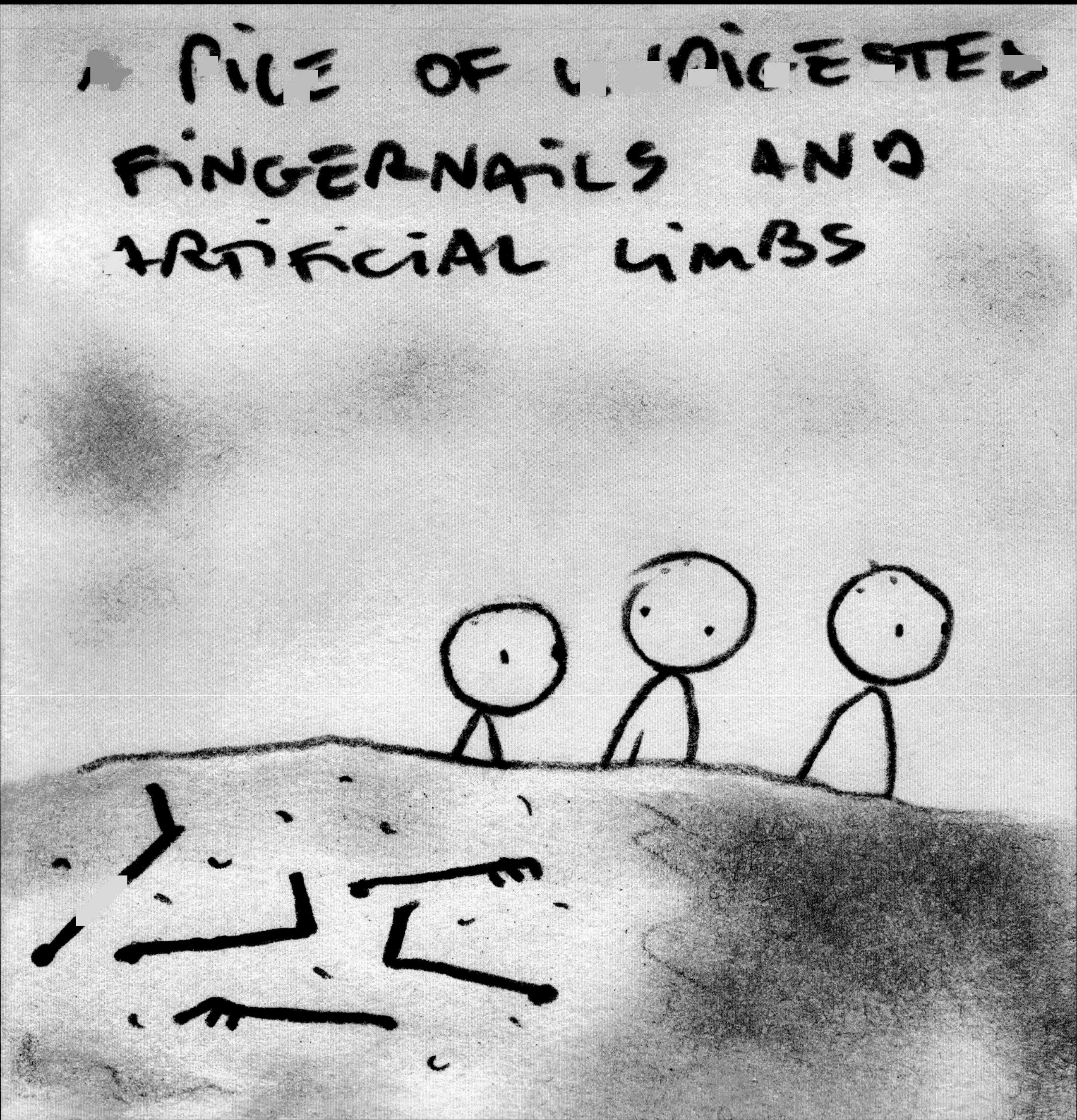
A PILE OF UNDIGESTED FINGERNAILS AND ARTIFICIAL LIMBS

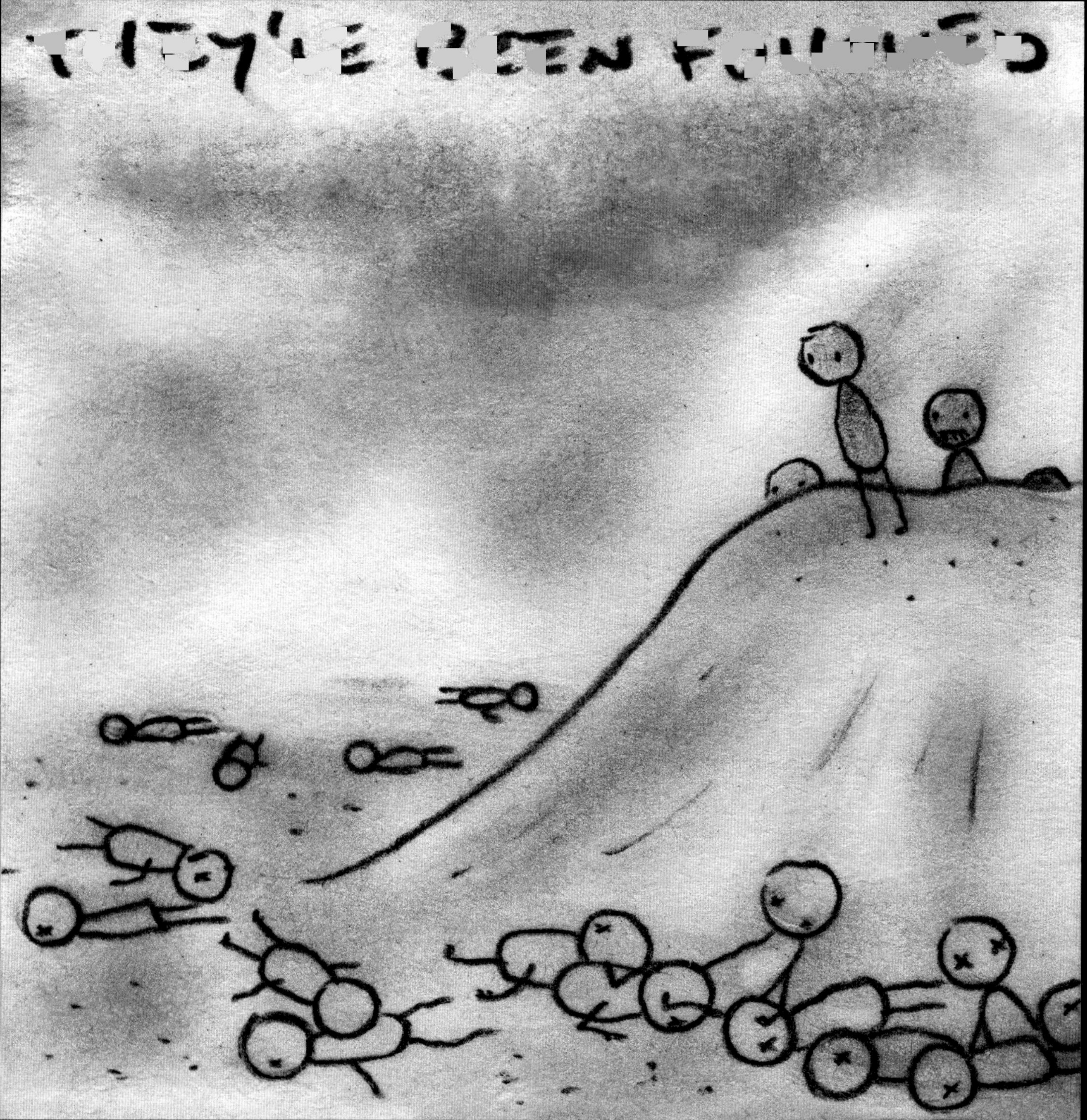

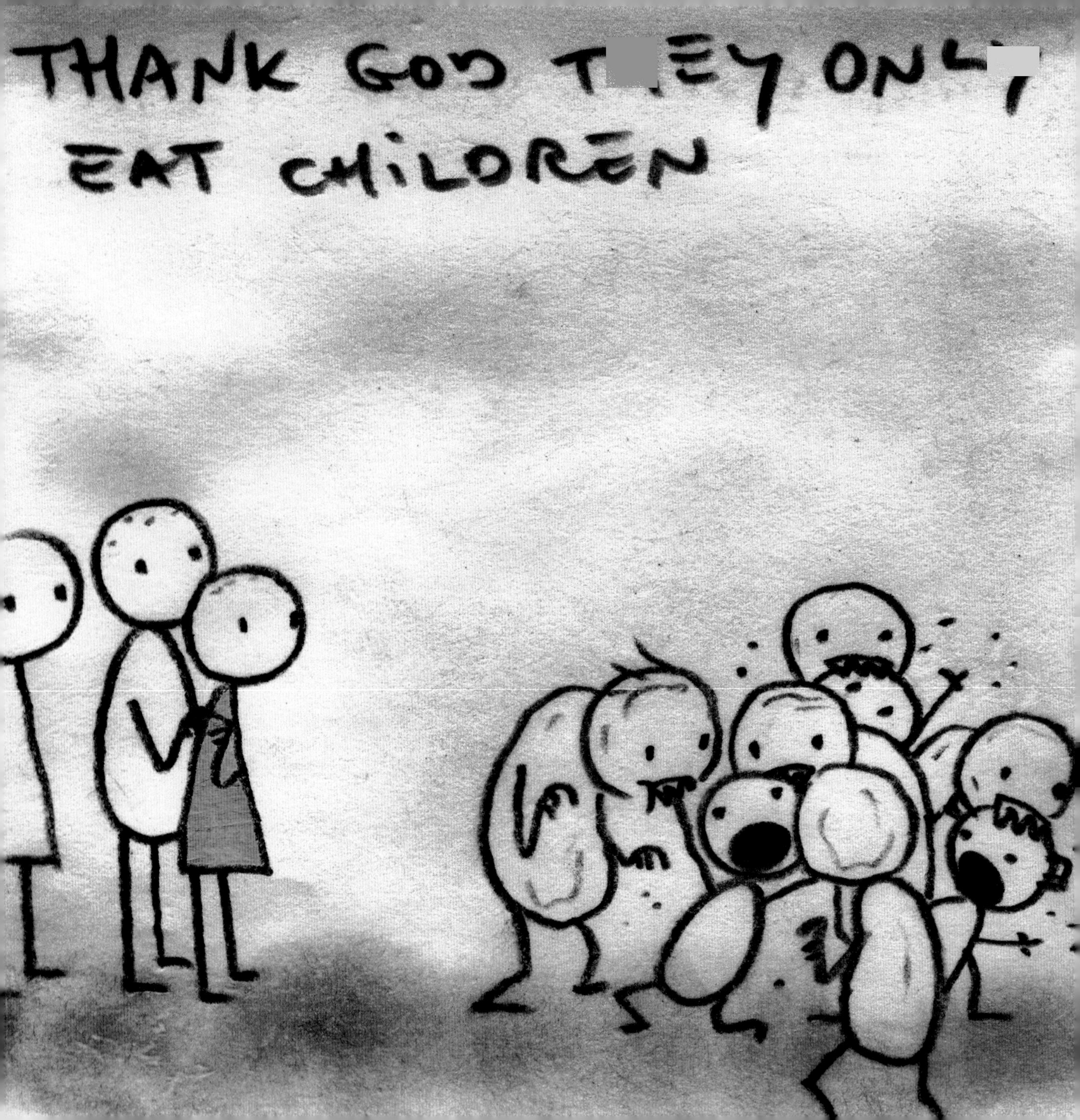
THANK GOD THEY ONLY EAT CHILDREN

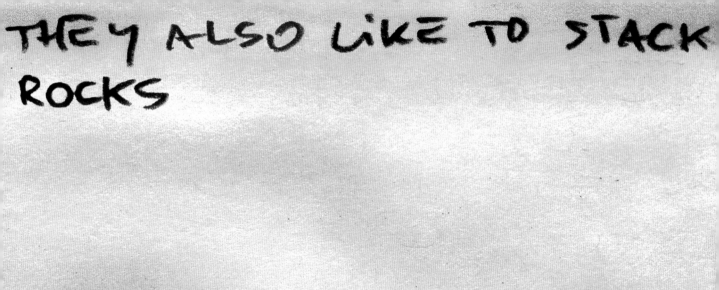

THEY ALSO LIKE TO STACK
ROCKS

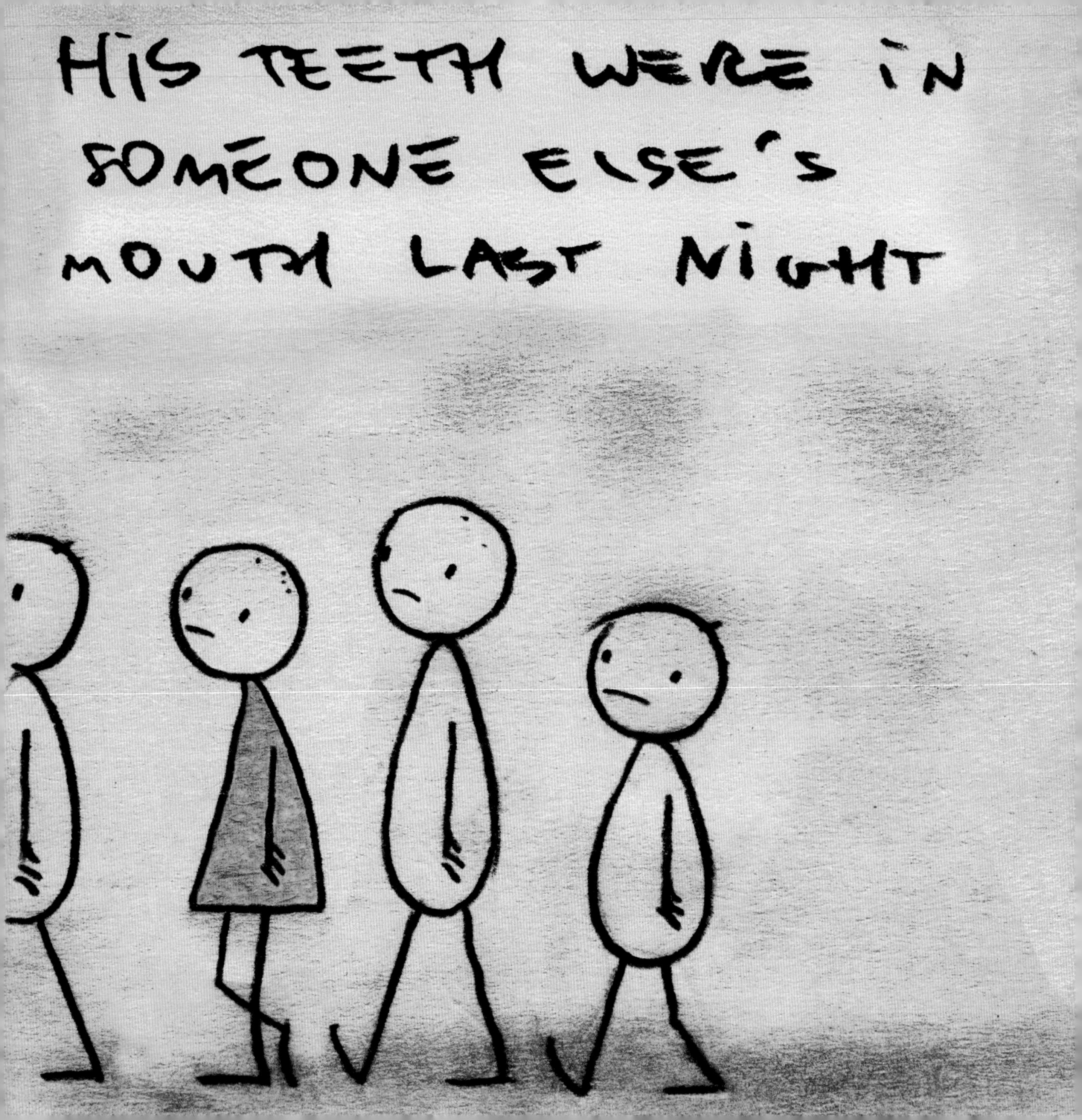
HIS TEETH WERE IN
SOMEONE ELSE'S
MOUTH LAST NIGHT

BALLOONS ARE the
OFFSPRING OF
GHOSTS AND TIRES

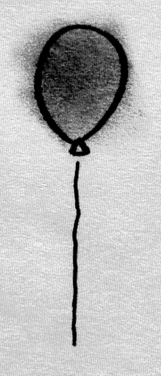

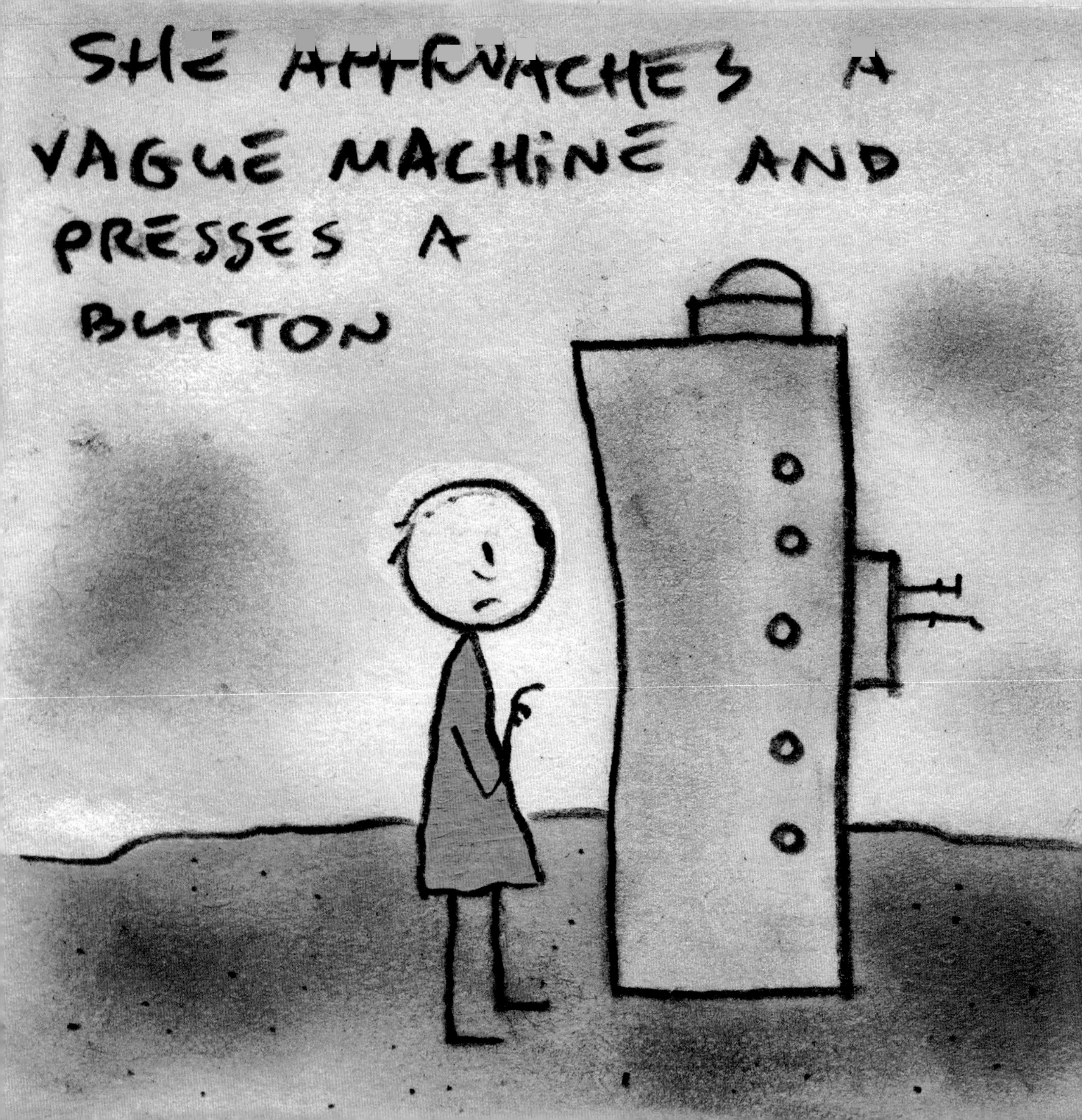
SHE APPROACHES A VAGUE MACHINE AND PRESSES A BUTTON

TONIGHT SHE DREAMT
OF A LAKE COVERED
WITH FLOWERS.

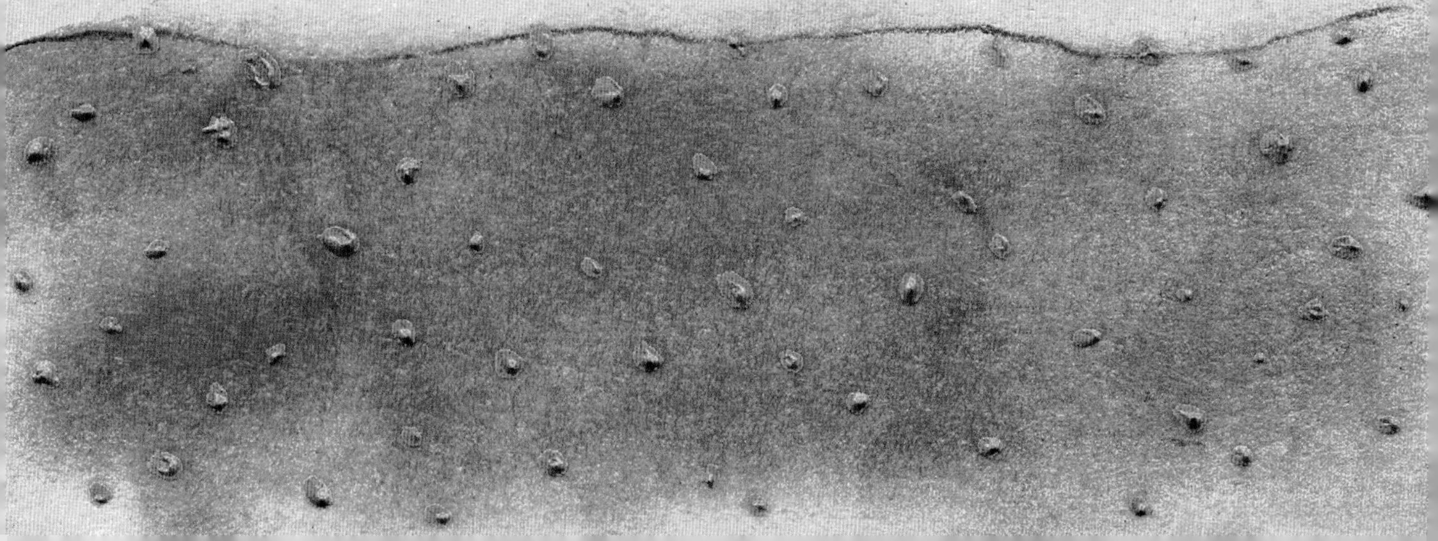

LIMBLESS BODIES FLOATED
AND SWAM UNDERNEATH,
CONTENT IN the SILENCE.

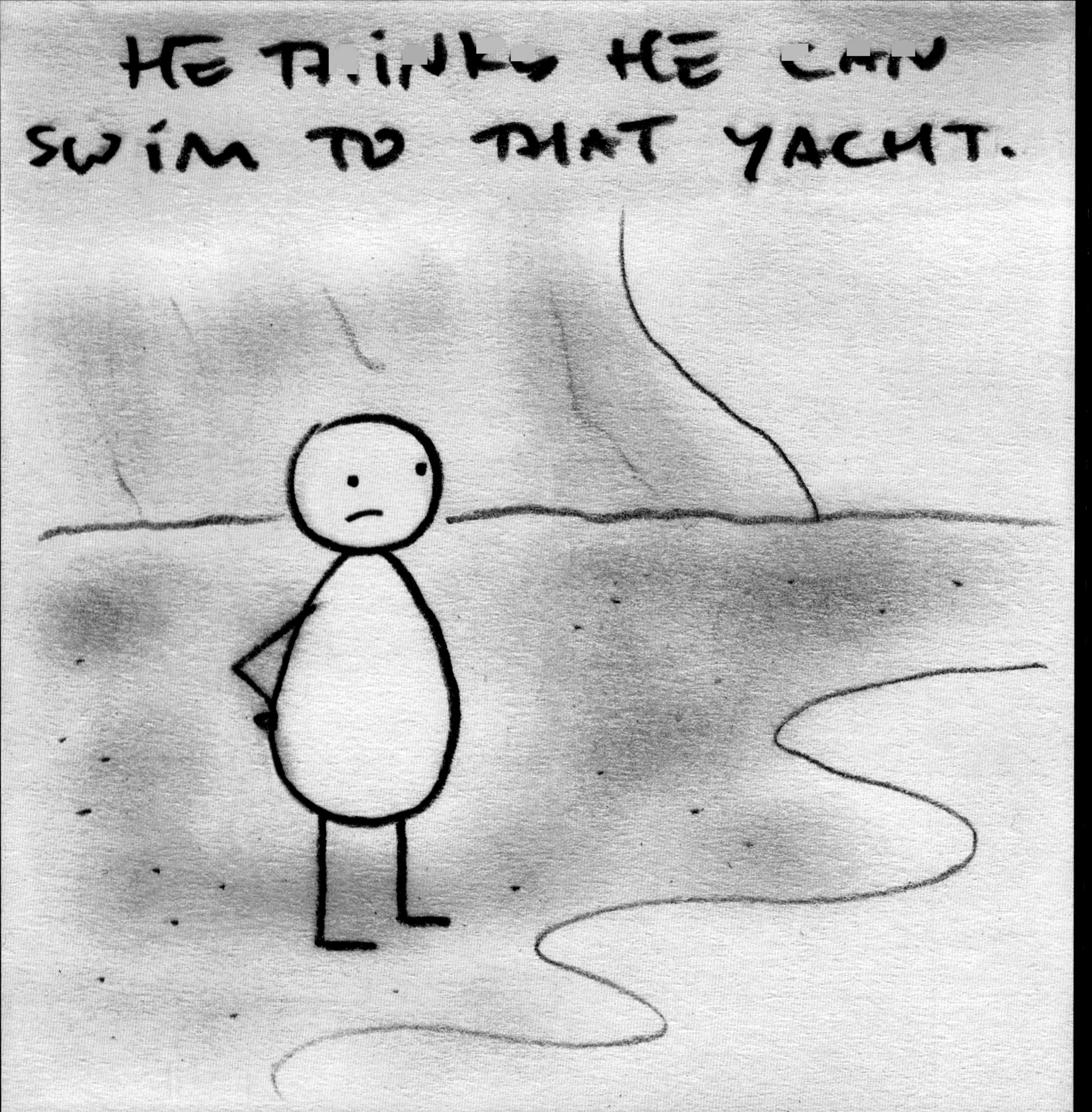
HE THINKS HE CAN SWIM TO THAT YACHT.

IT LOOKS EMPTY AND IN GOOD CONDITION.

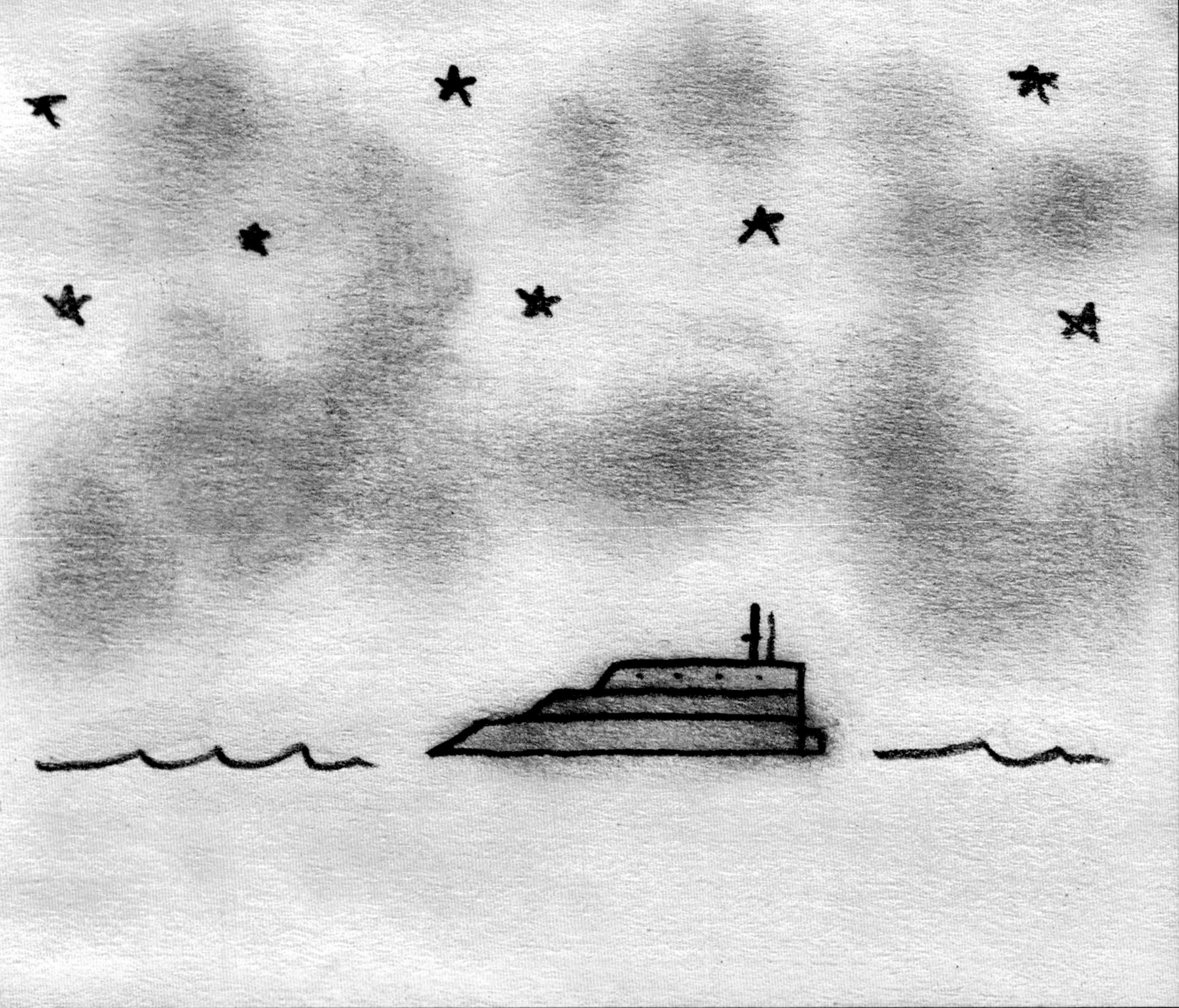

THE SWIM TEAM USED
TO CALL HIM MOBY DICK.

HIGH SCHOOL WAS A LONG TIME AGO.

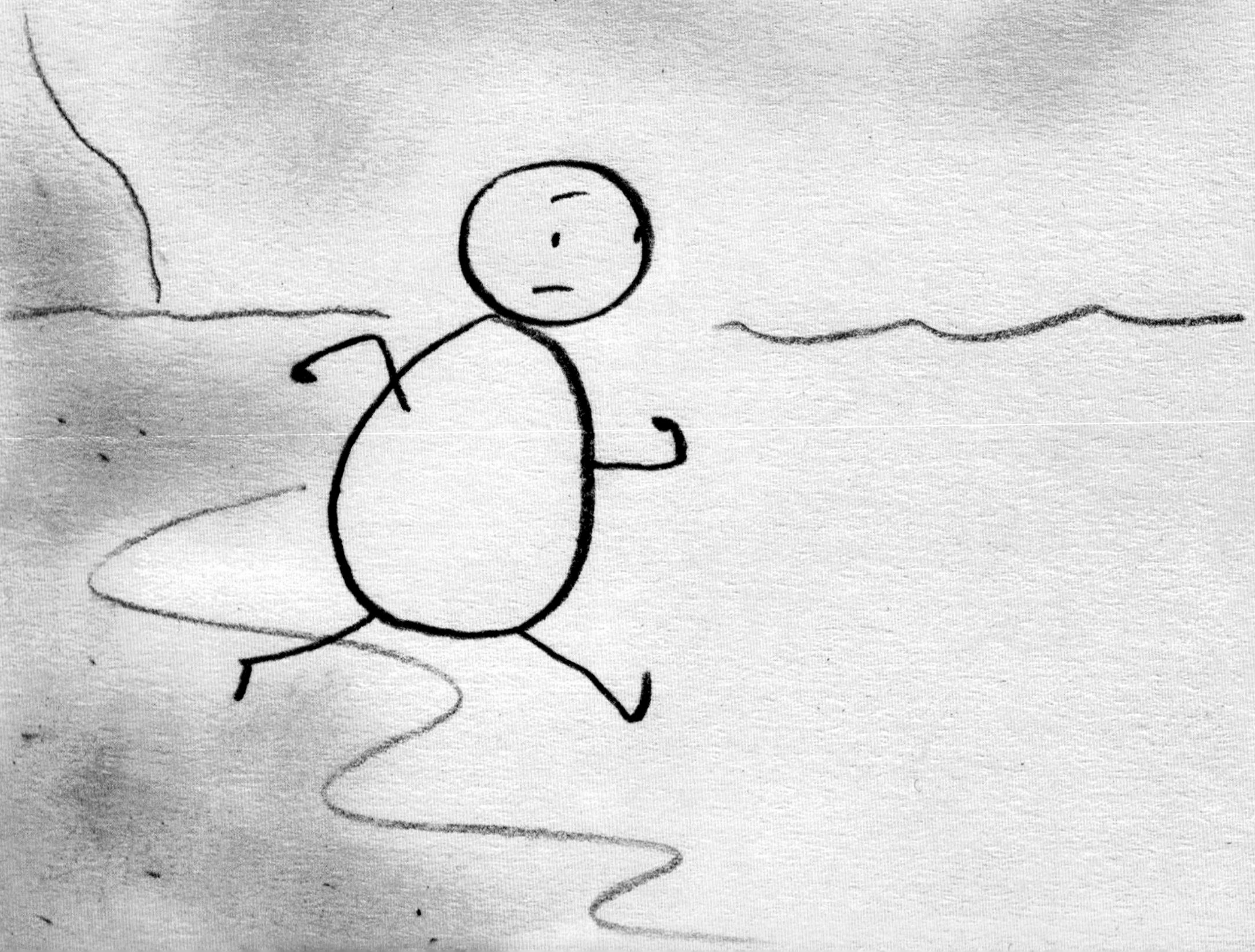

THE WATER IS UNBEARABLY COLD.

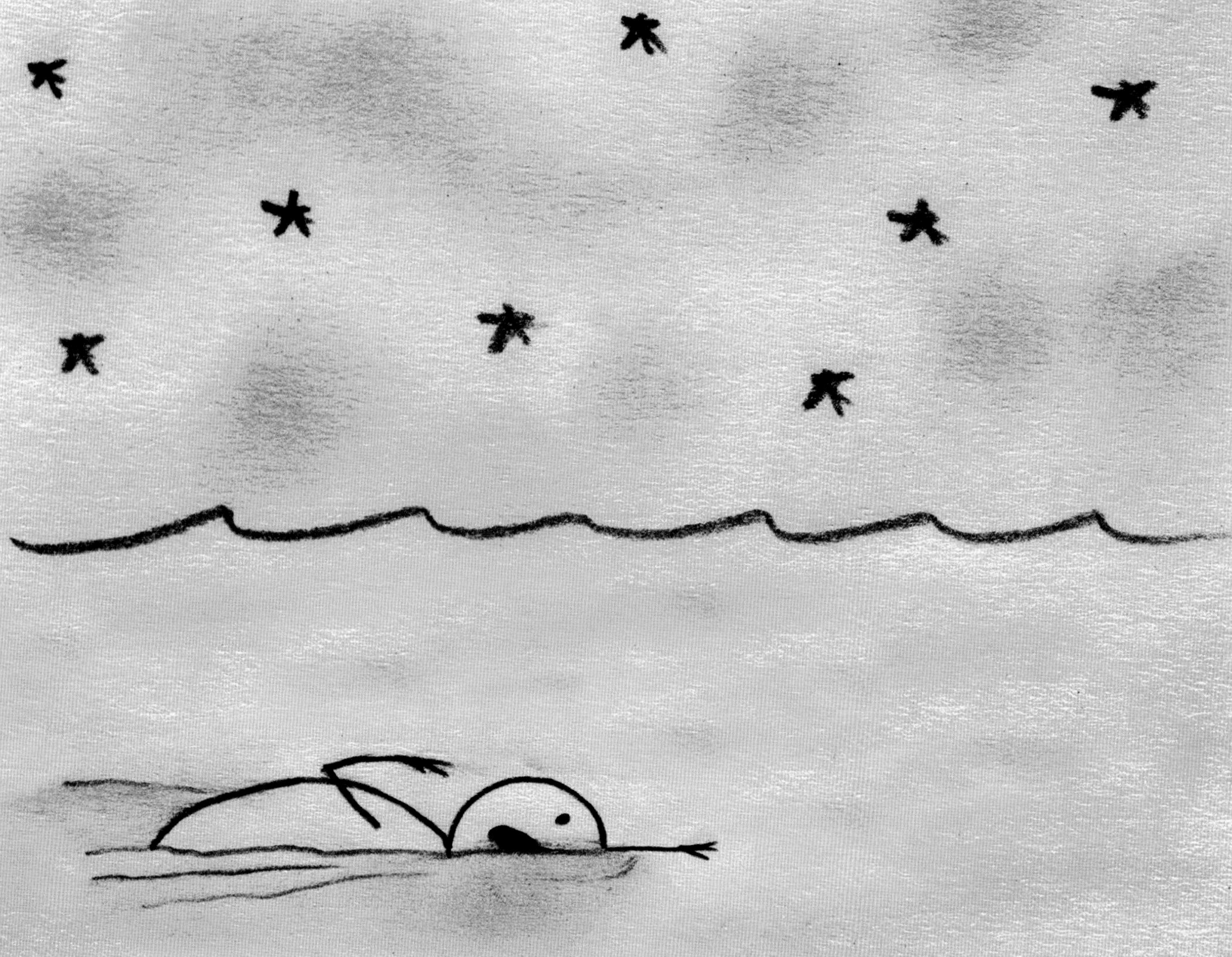

SOMETHING STICKS INTO HIS LEG AND TEARS IT FROM THE SOCKET IN TWO QUICK THRASHES.

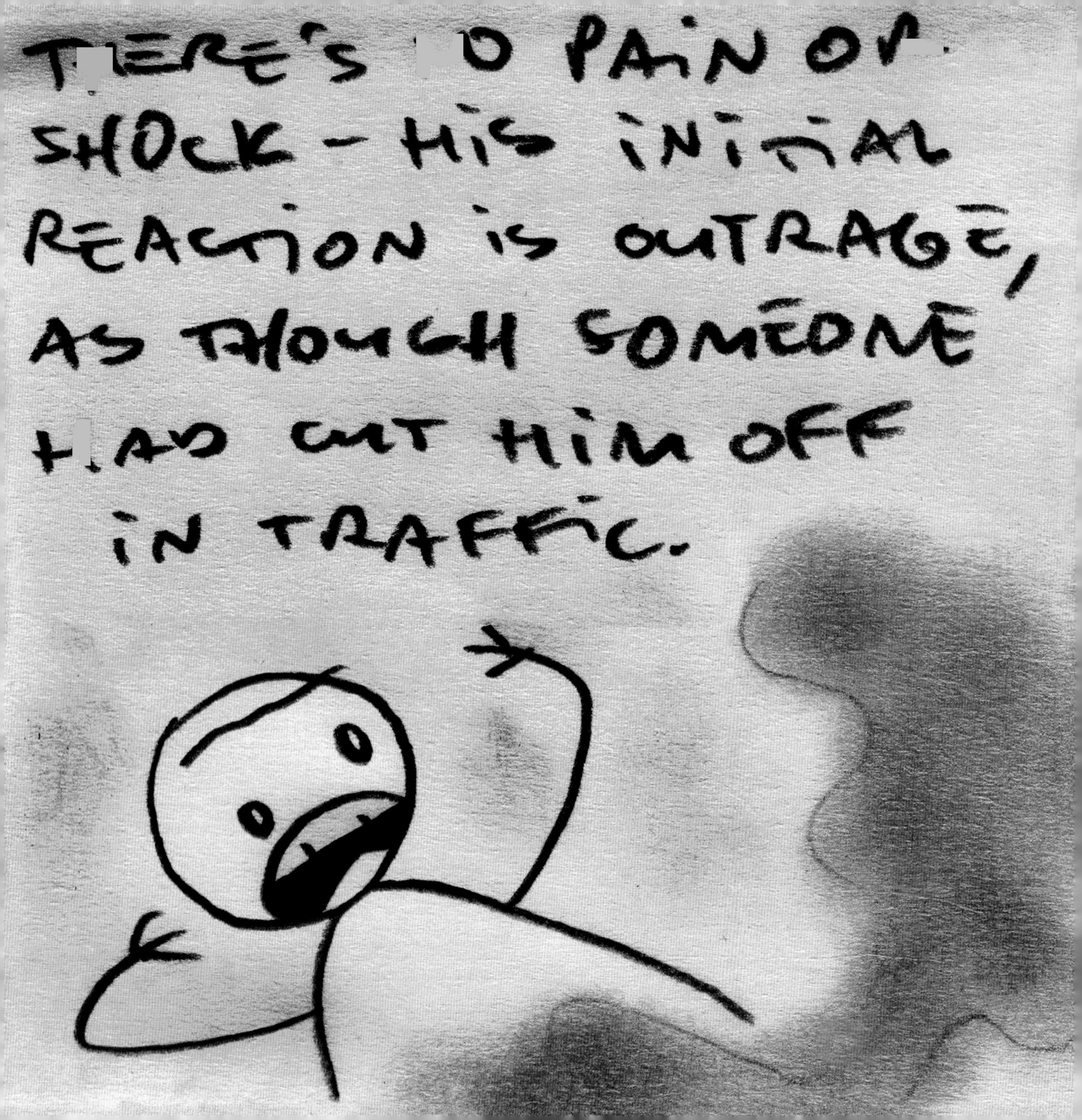
THERE'S NO PAIN OR SHOCK—HIS INITIAL REACTION IS OUTRAGE, AS THOUGH SOMEONE HAD CUT HIM OFF IN TRAFFIC.

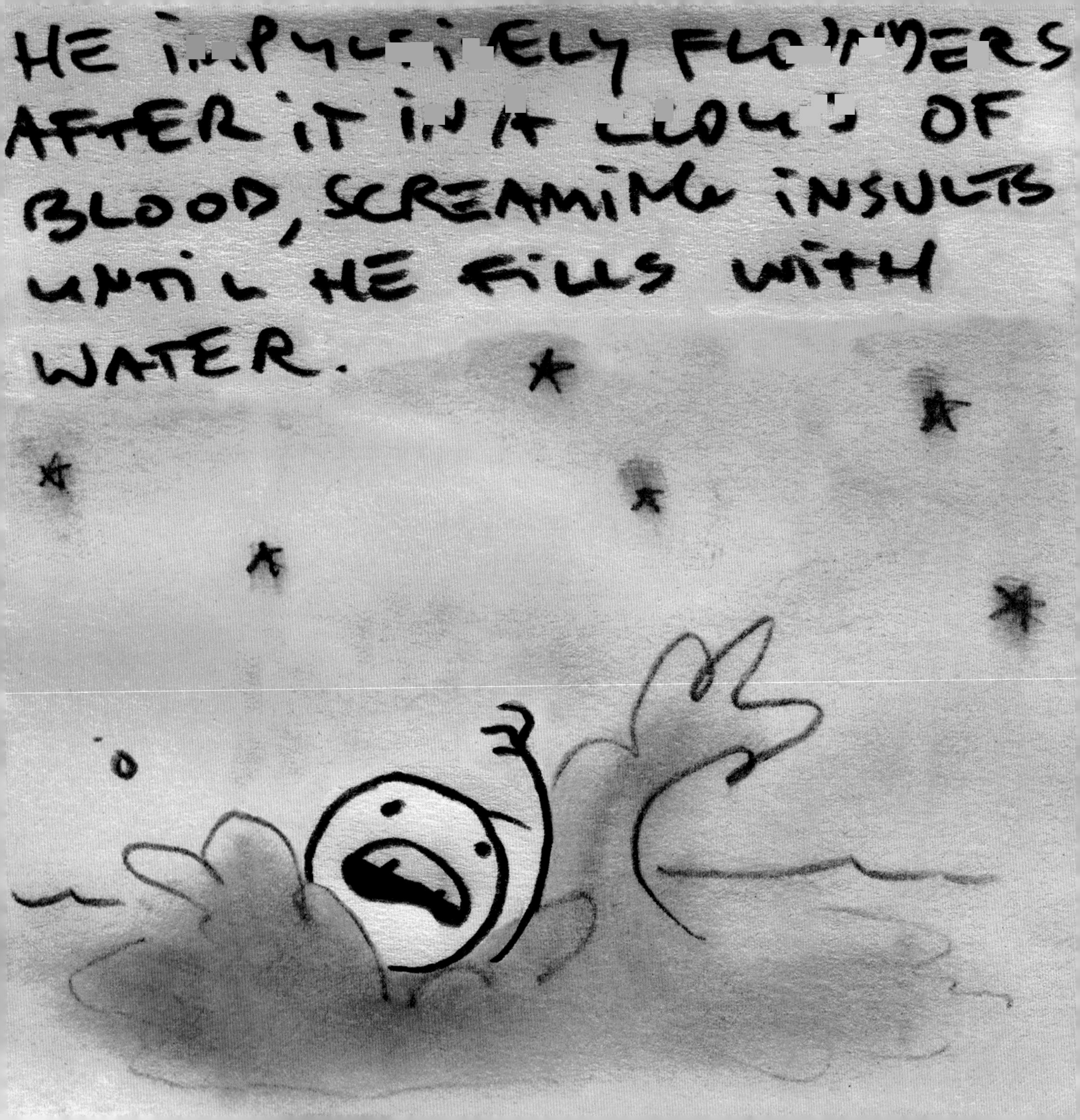
HE IMPULSIVELY FLOUNDERS AFTER IT IN A CLOUD OF BLOOD, SCREAMING INSULTS UNTIL HE FILLS WITH WATER.

HE SEES LIGHTS THAT LOOK LIKE STARS AND IS CONFUSED WHICH WAY IS UP.

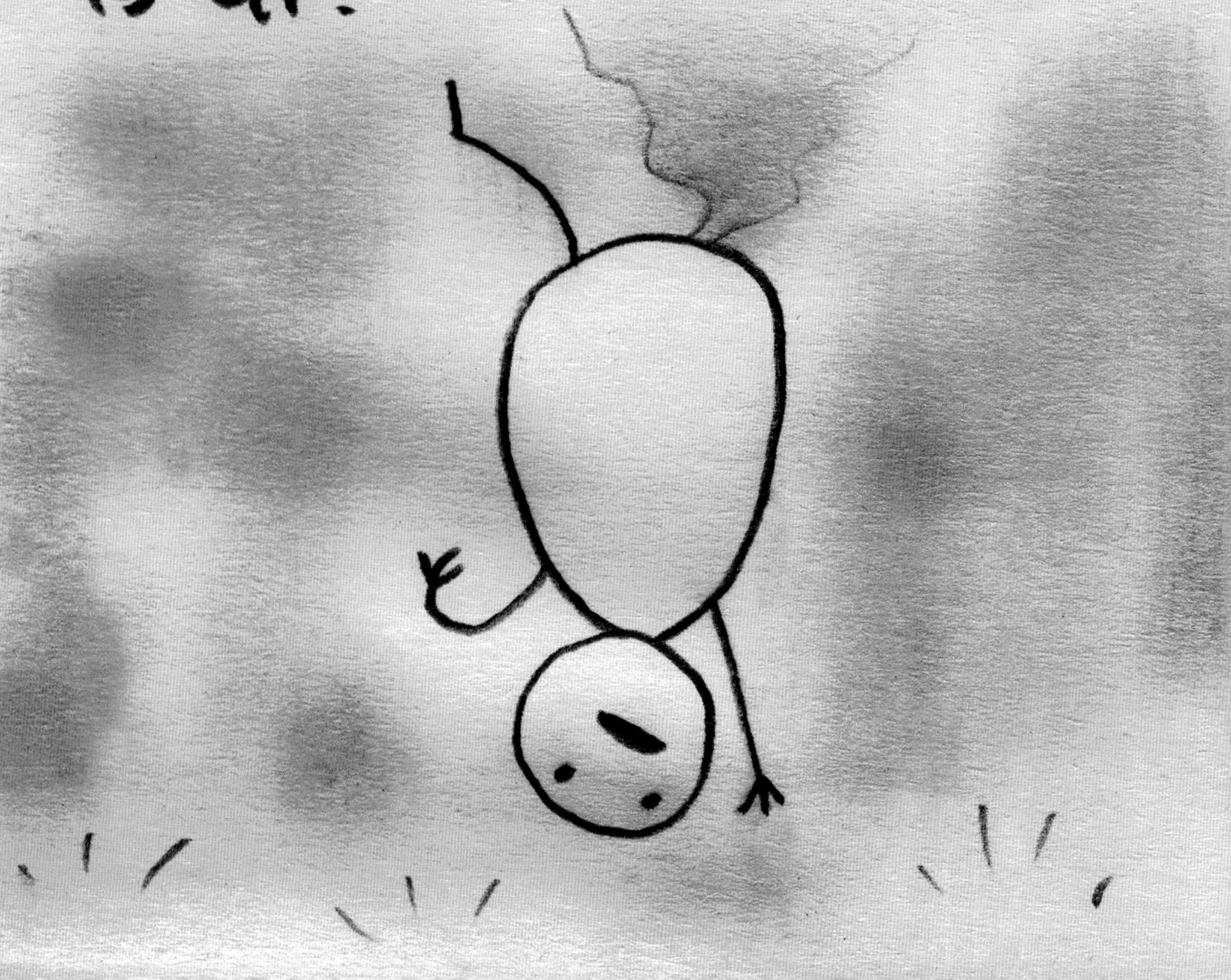

HE COMES UP FOR AIR
AND SUDDENLY HIS LEG
IS REALLY HURTING.

WAIT, DID IT REALLY TAKE HIS GODDAMN LEG?.

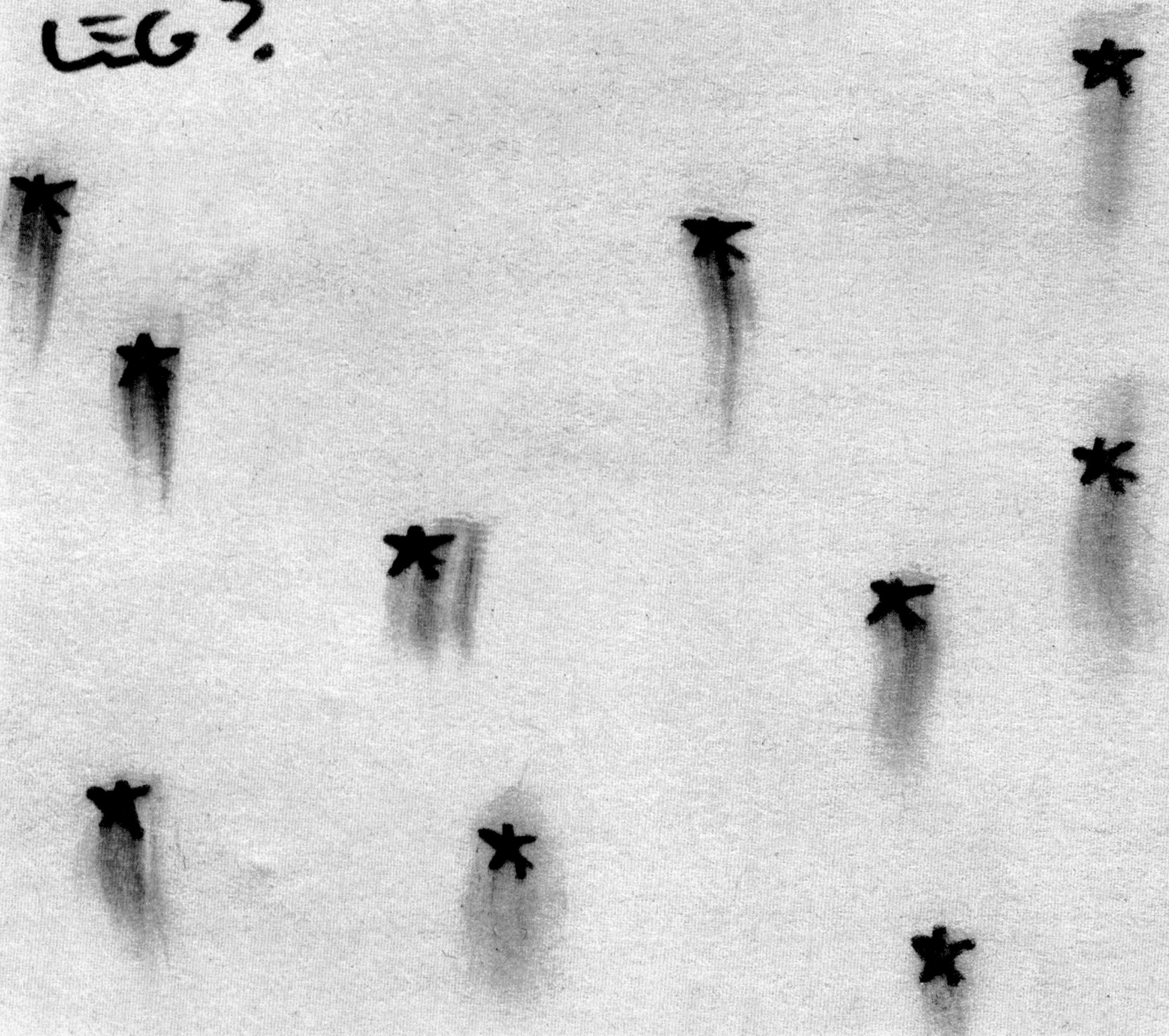

HIS ARMS STOP WORKING
AND HE SEES HIS
DAUGHTER.

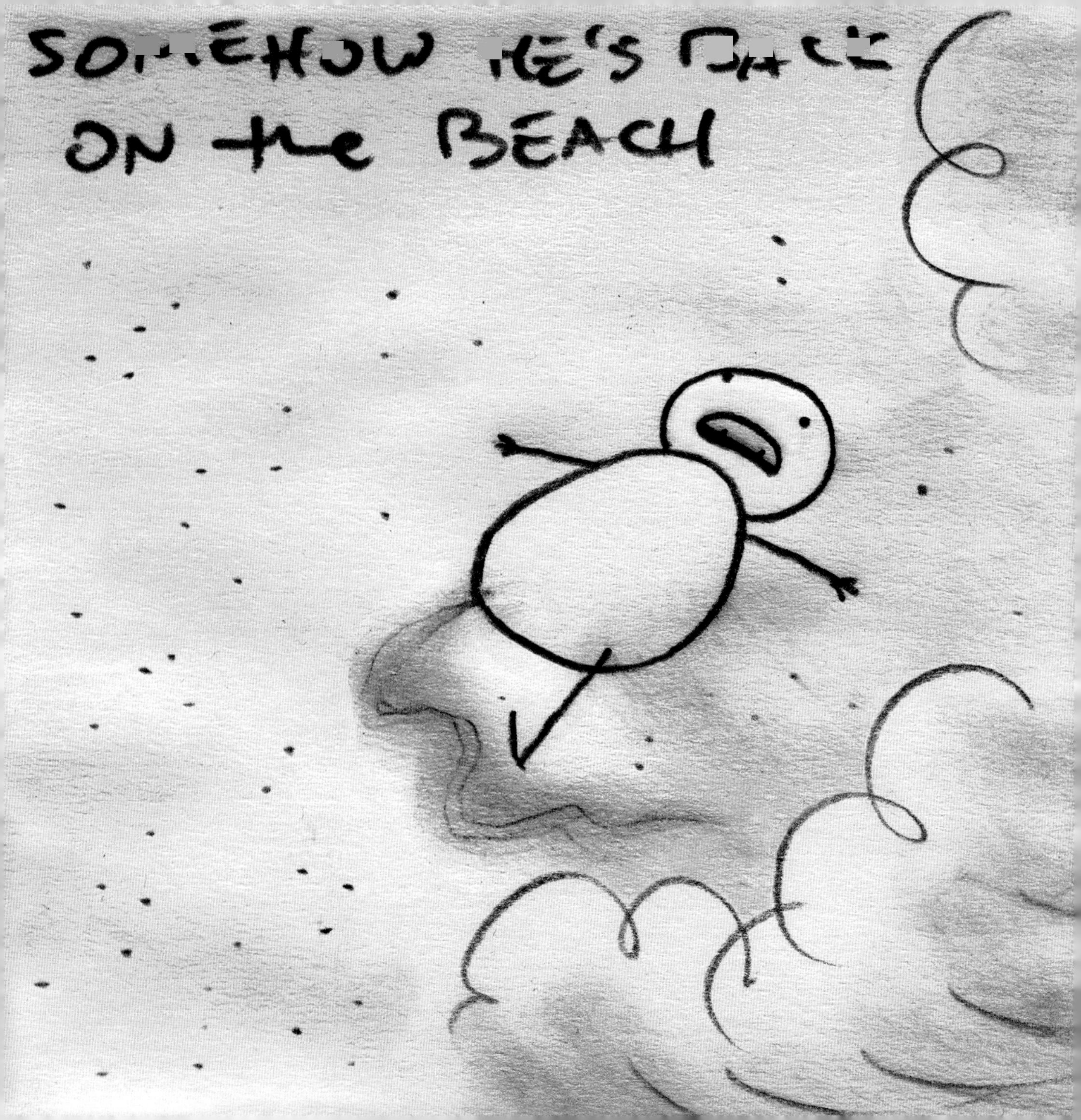
SOMEHOW HE'S BACK ON THE BEACH

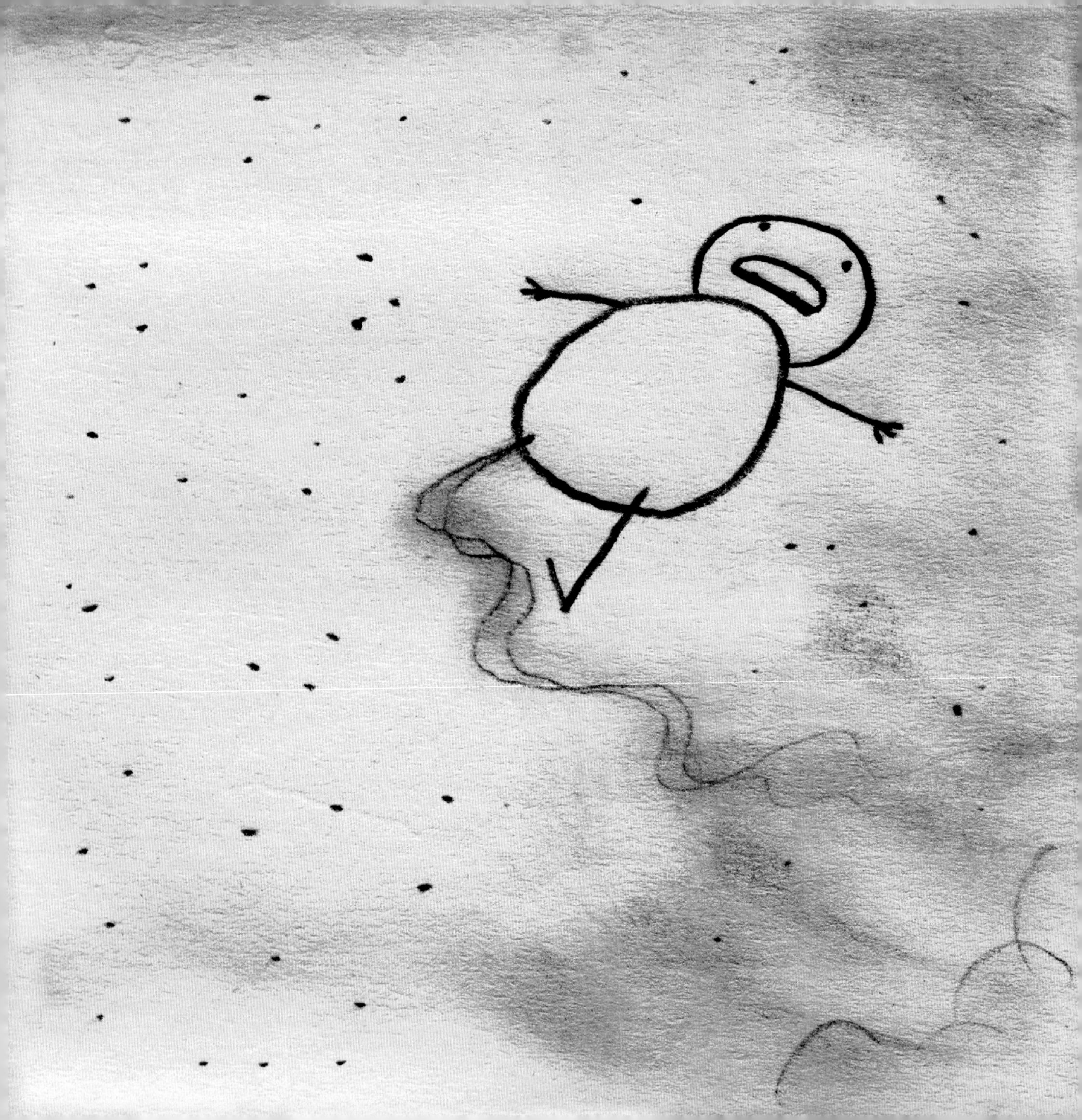

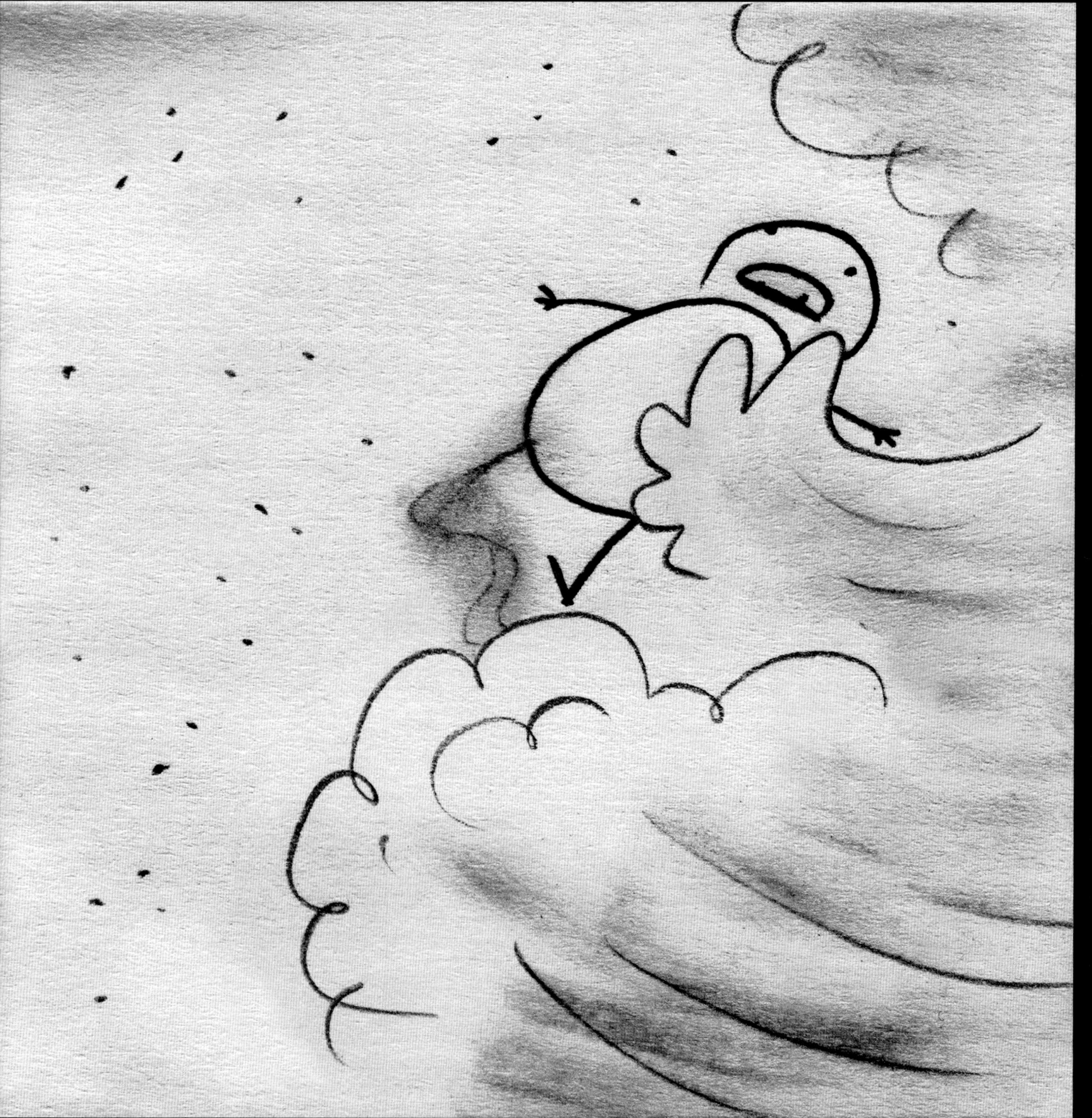

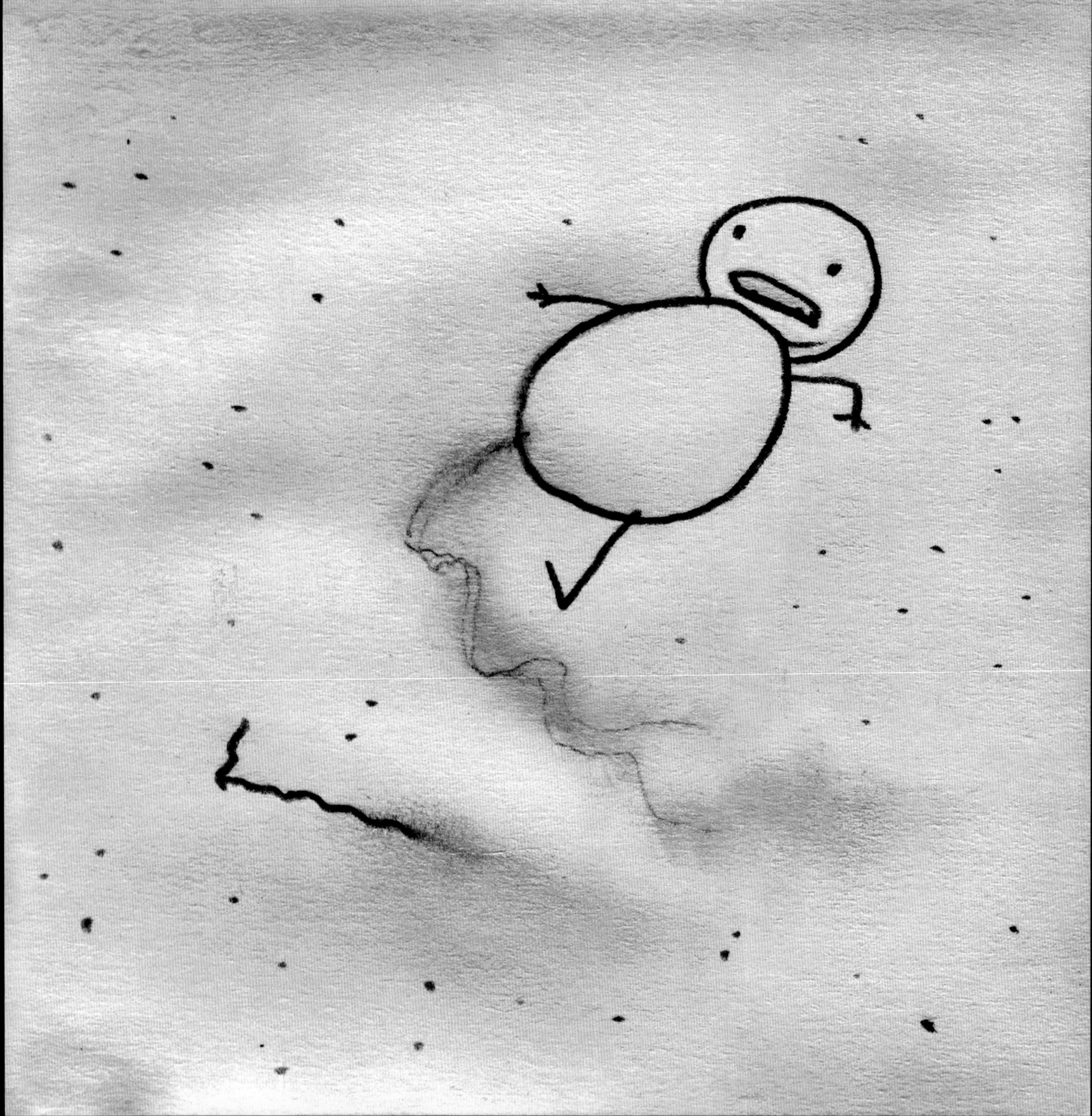

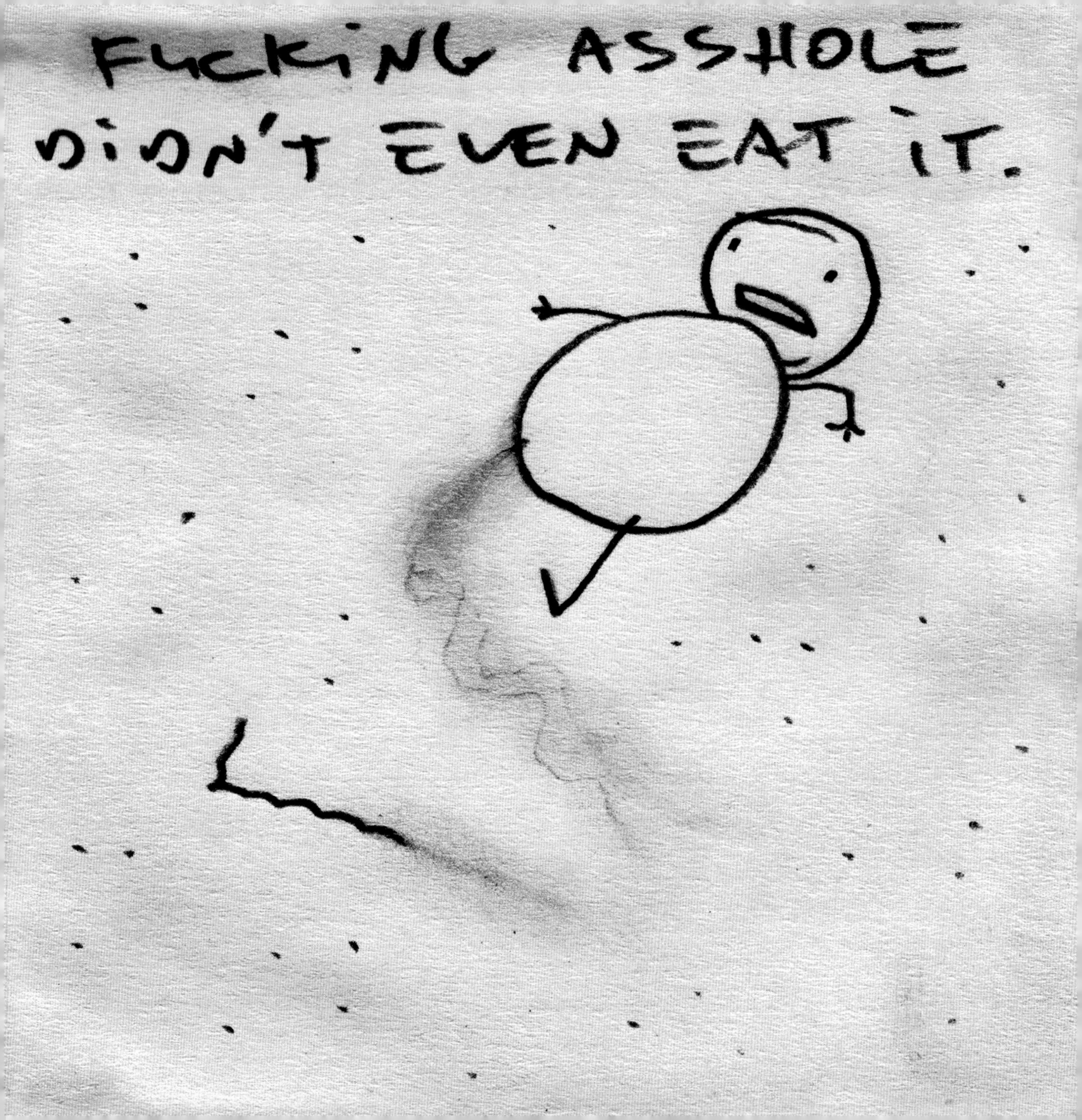
FUCKING ASSHOLE
DIDN'T EVEN EAT IT.

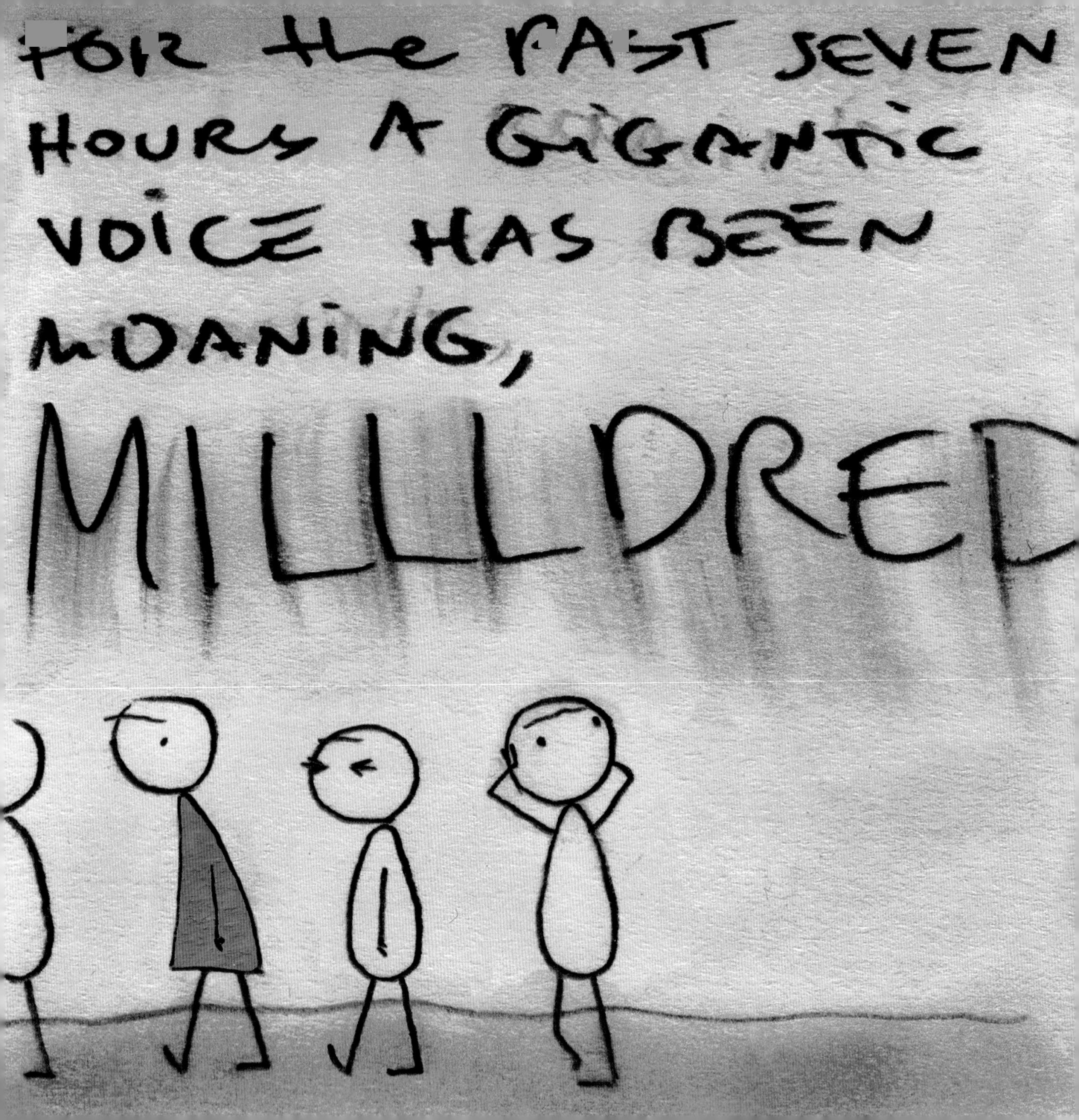
FOR THE PAST SEVEN HOURS A GIGANTIC VOICE HAS BEEN MOANING,
MILLLDRED

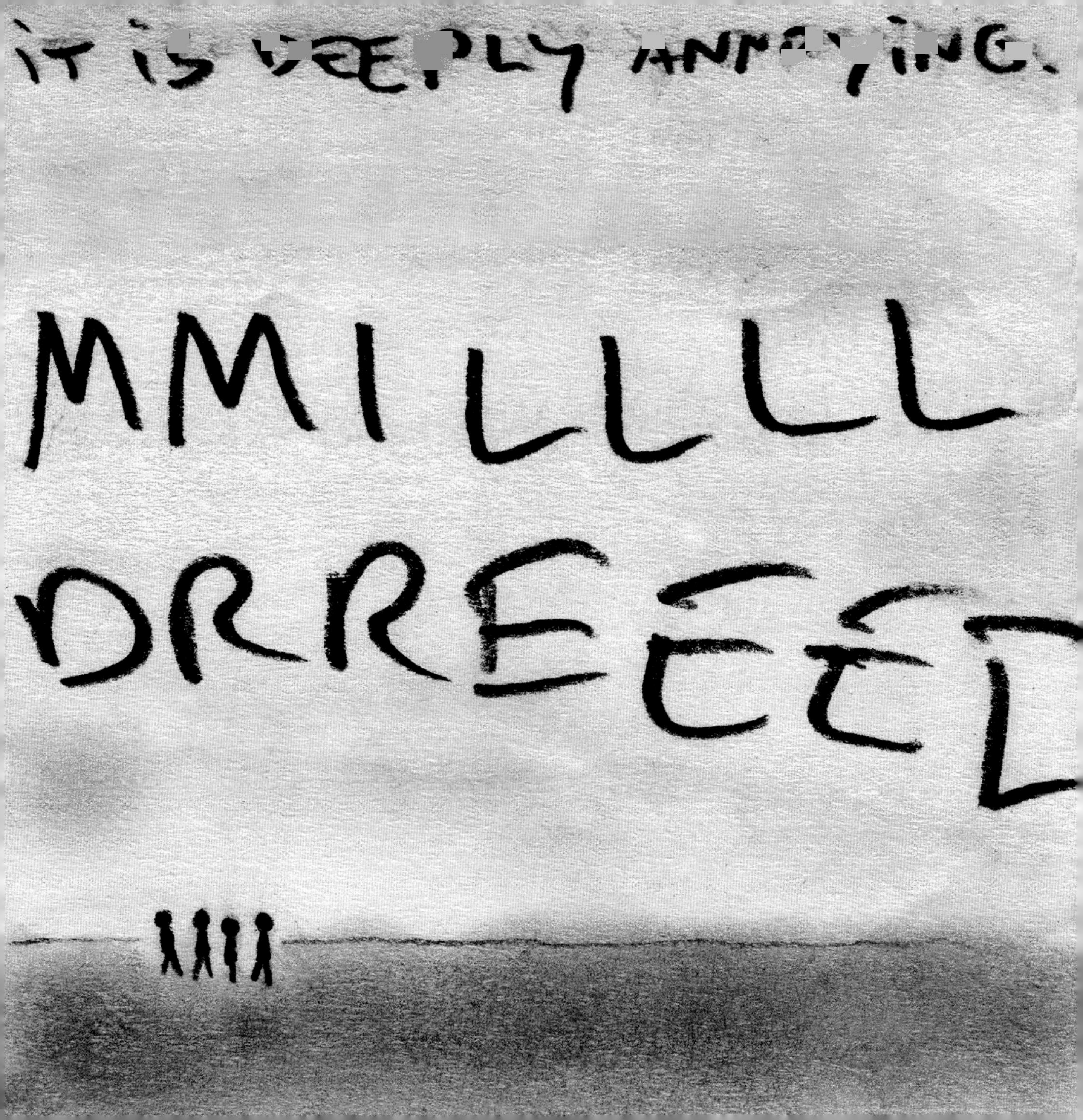
IT IS DEEPLY ANNOYING.
MMILLLL
DRREEED

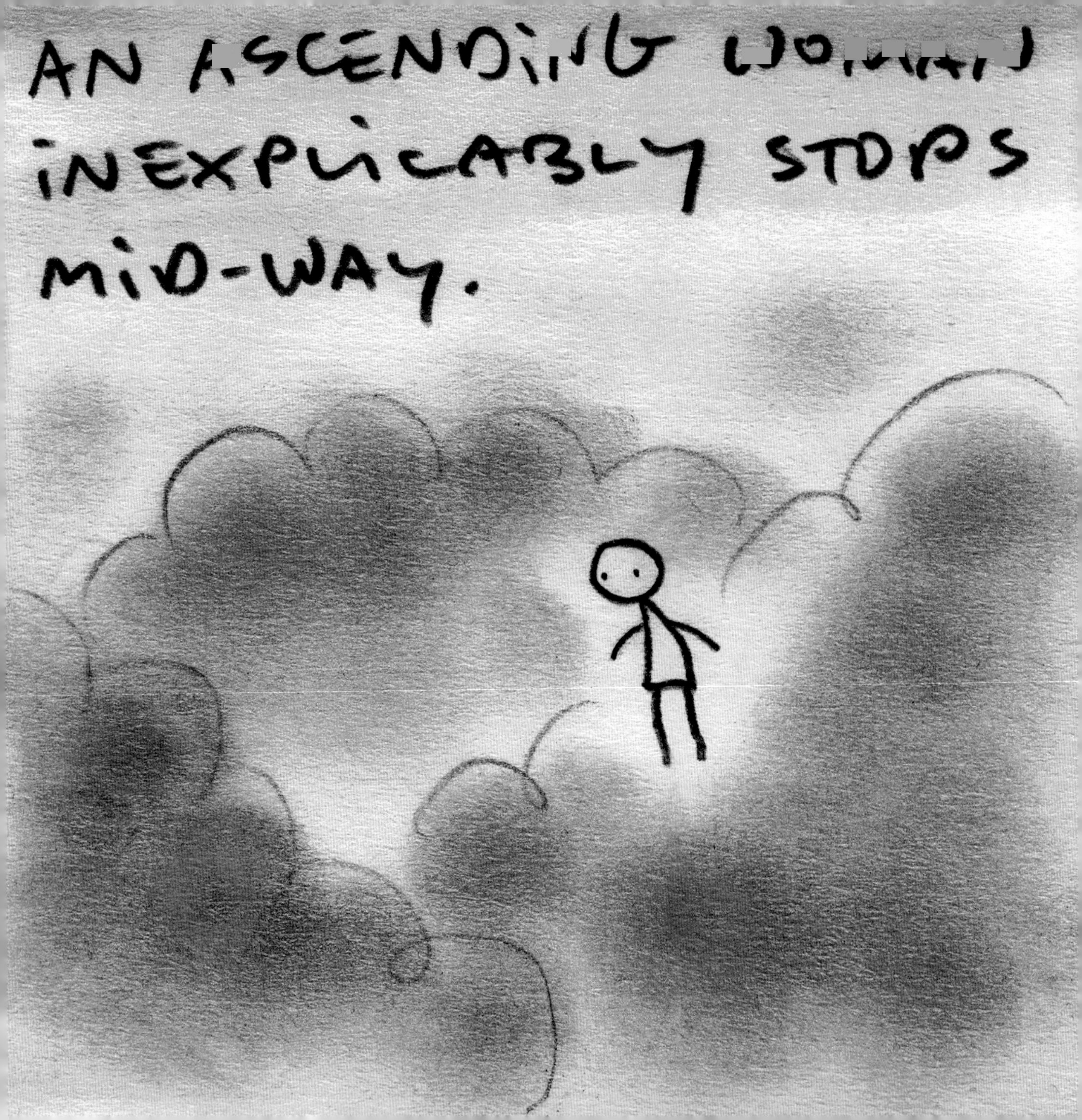
AN ASCENDING WOMAN INEXPLICABLY STOPS MID-WAY.

SHE HANGS IN THE AIR AS THE WINDS CARRY HER OVER THE MOUNTAINS.

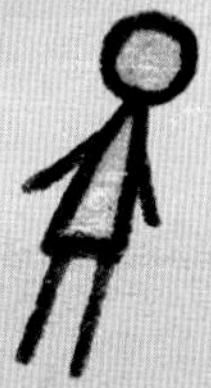

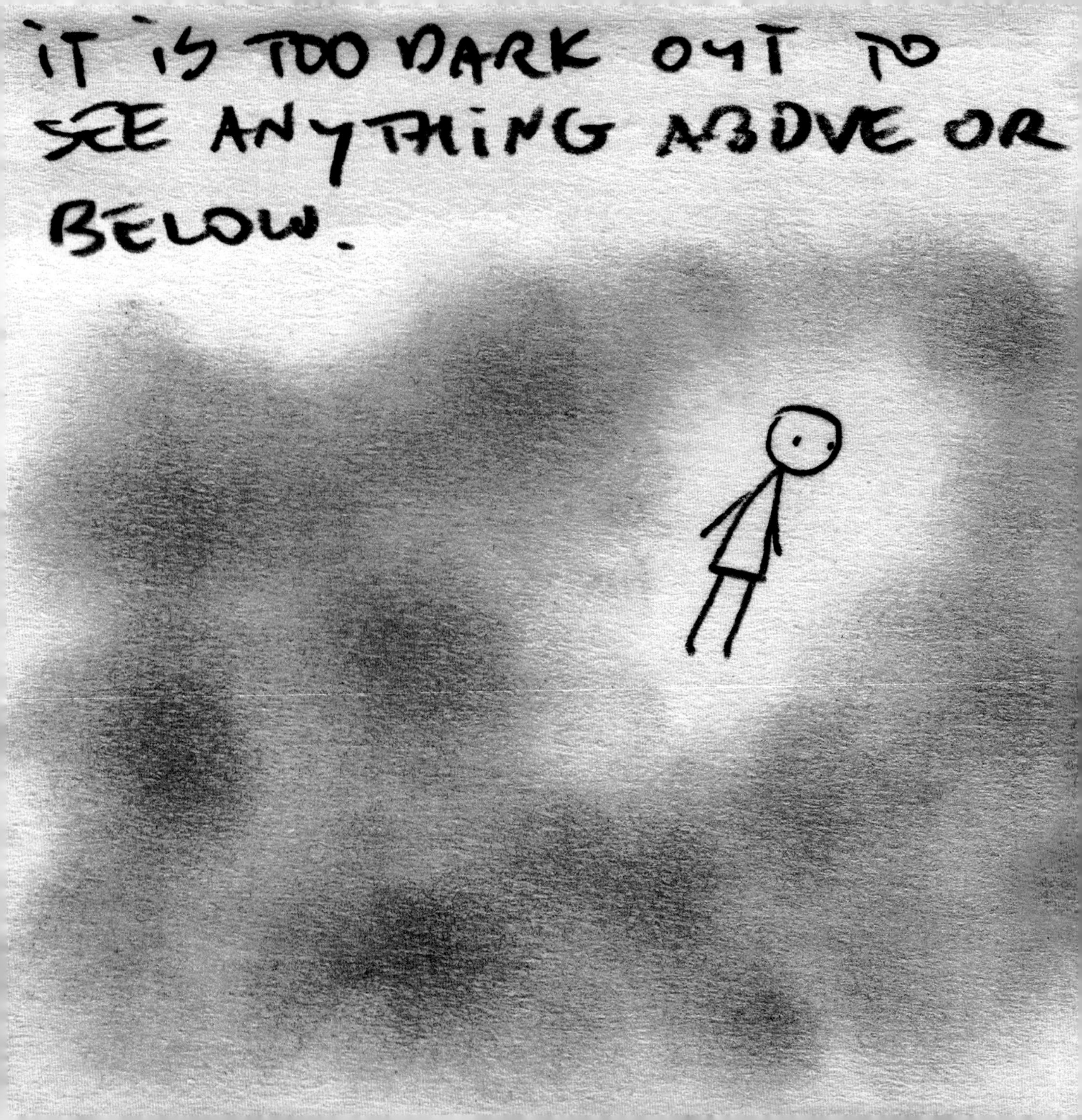
IT IS TOO DARK OUT TO SEE ANYTHING ABOVE OR BELOW.

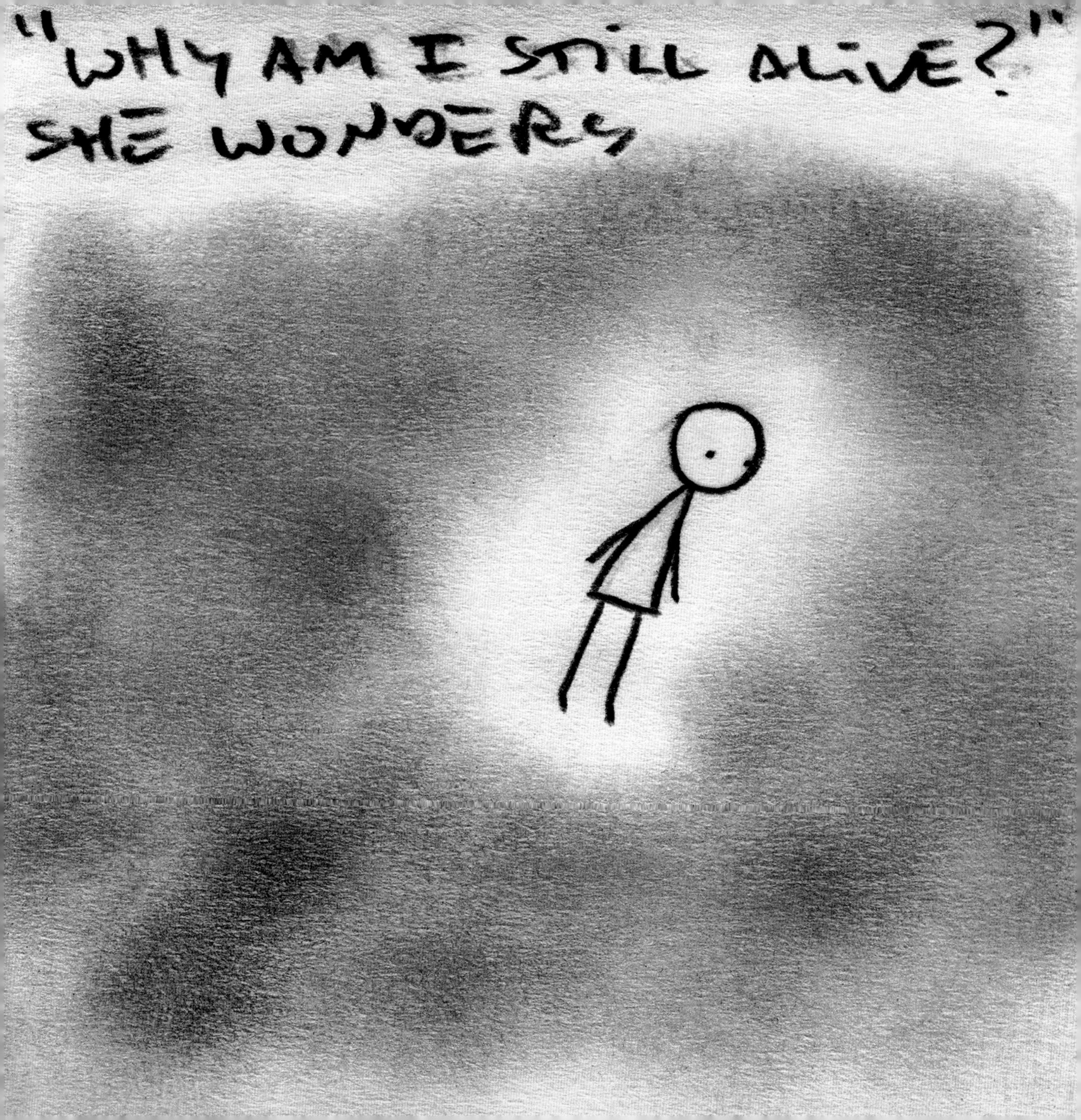
"WHY AM I STILL ALIVE?"
SHE WONDERS

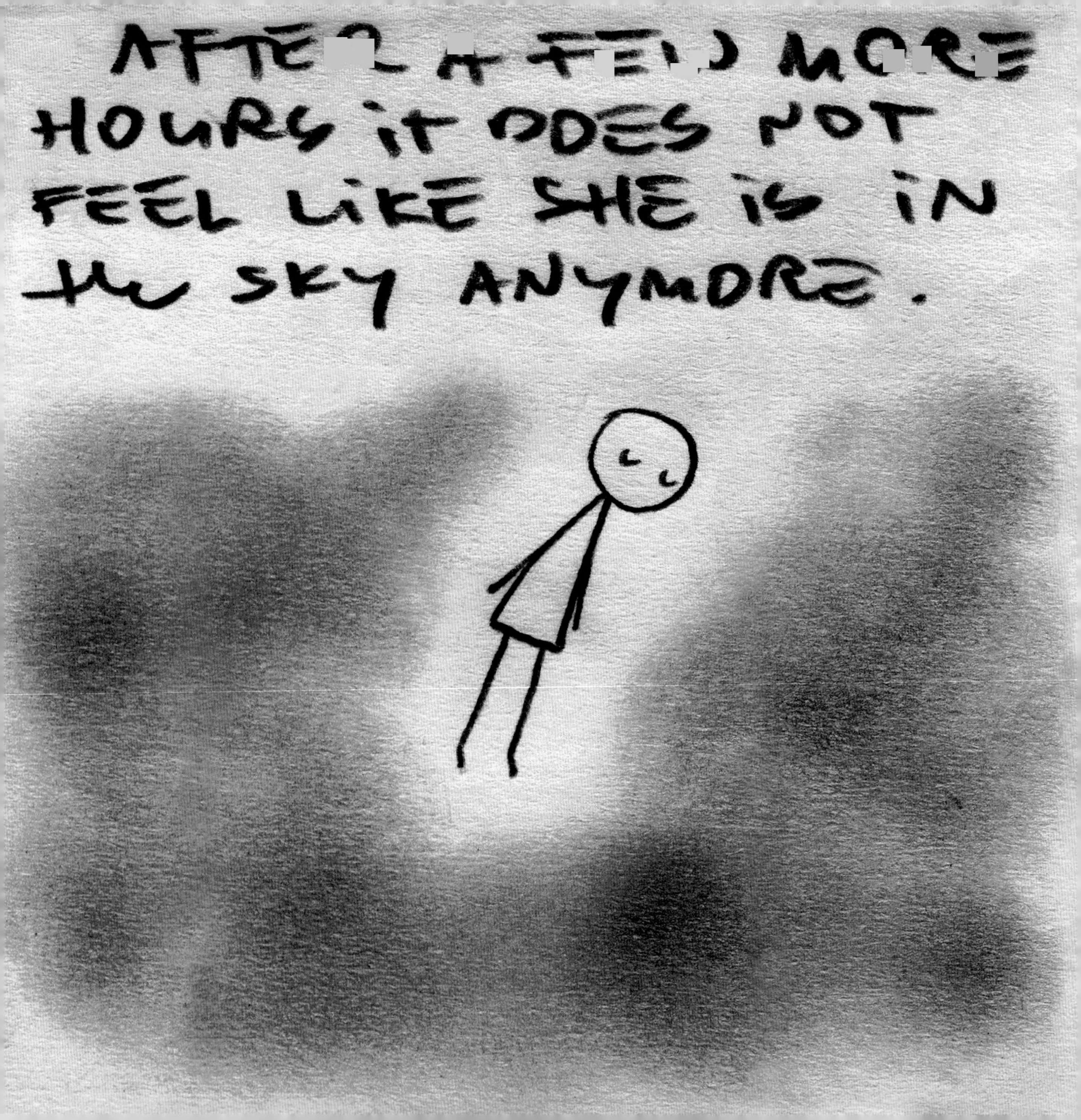
AFTER A FEW MORE HOURS IT DOES NOT FEEL LIKE SHE IS IN THE SKY ANYMORE.

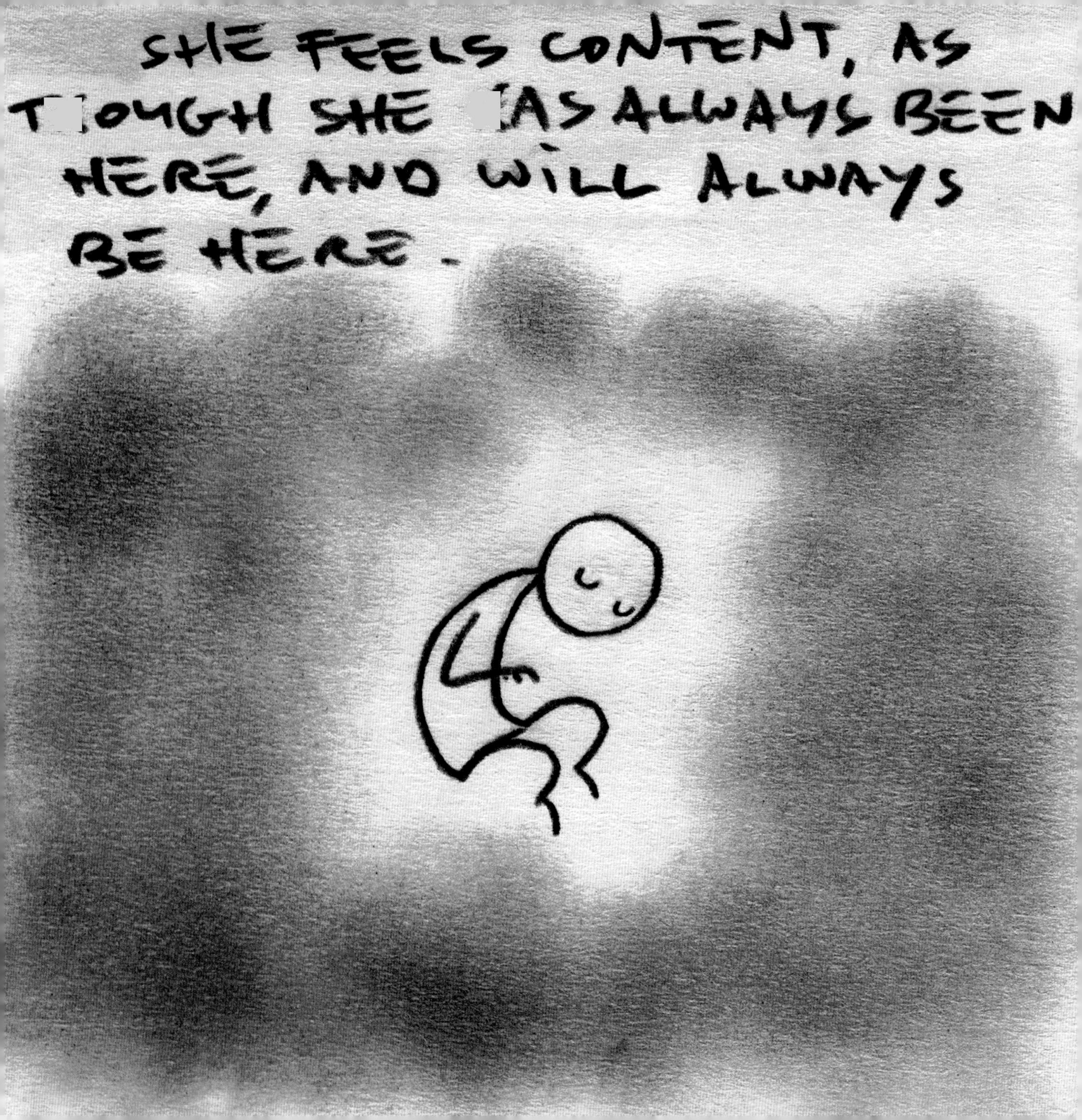
SHE FEELS CONTENT, AS THOUGH SHE HAS ALWAYS BEEN HERE, AND WILL ALWAYS BE HERE.

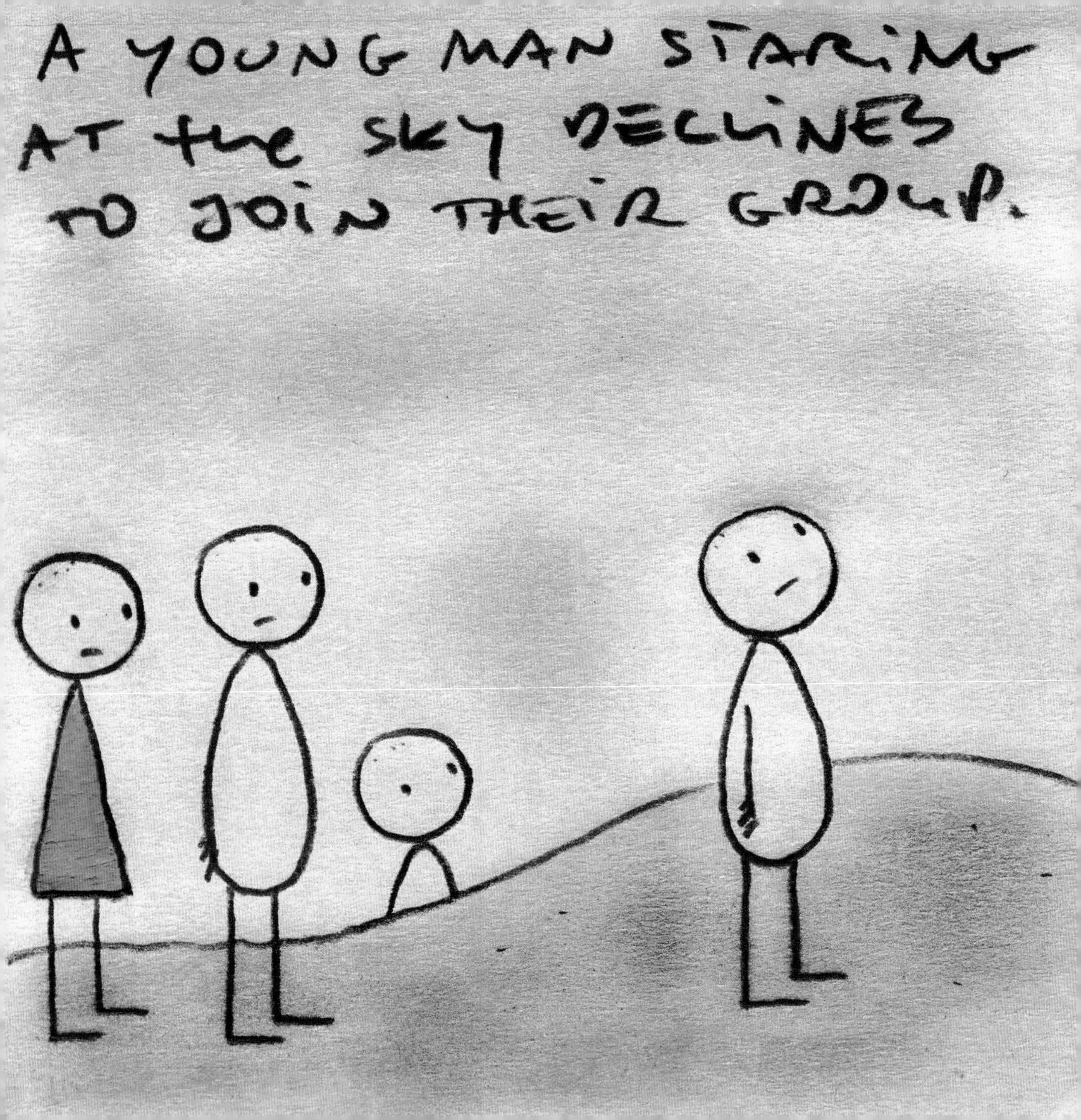
A YOUNG MAN STARING AT THE SKY DECLINES TO JOIN THEIR GROUP.

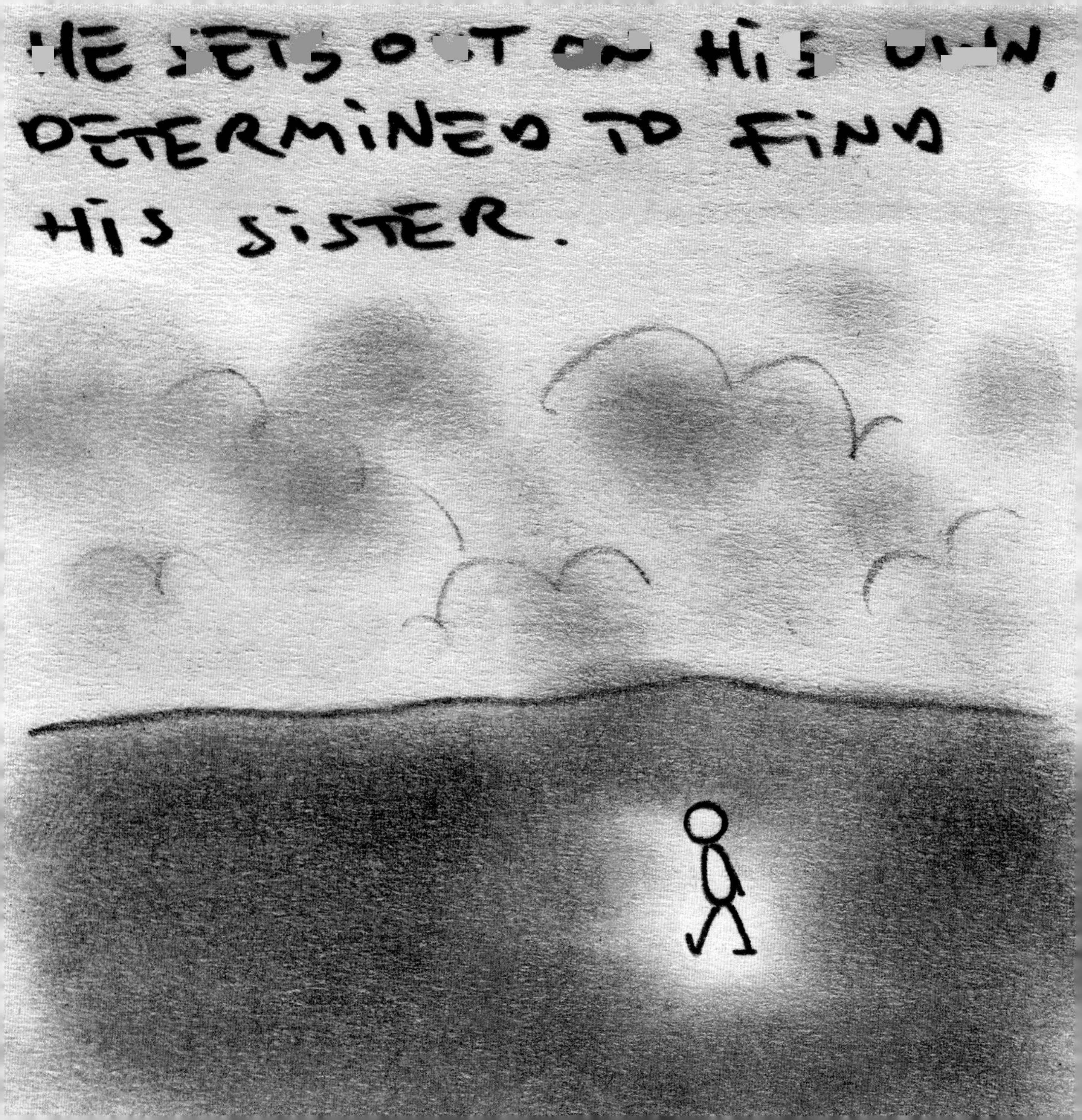
HE SETS OUT ON HIS OWN, DETERMINED TO FIND HIS SISTER.

THE LAST TIME HE SAW HER SHE WAS WEARING A RUBBER MASK OF A DOG.

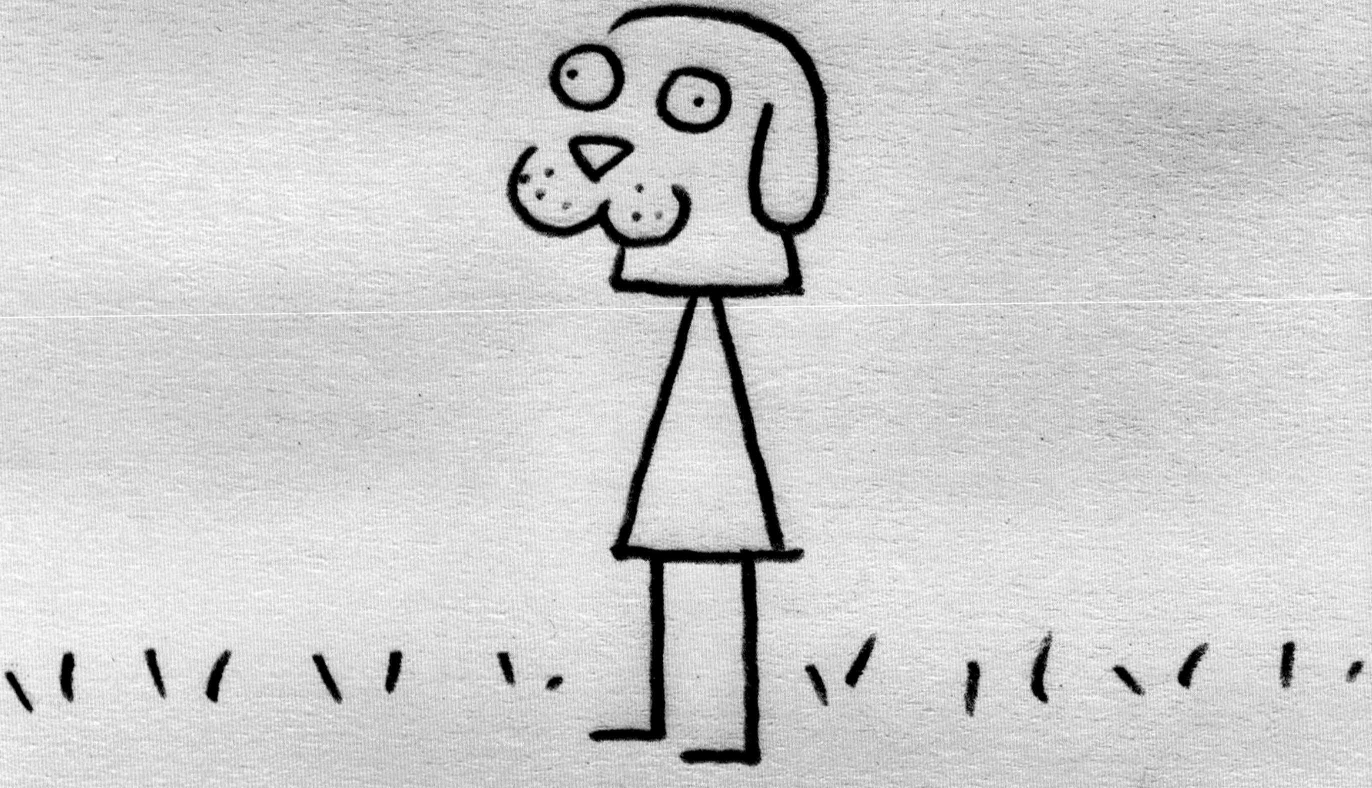

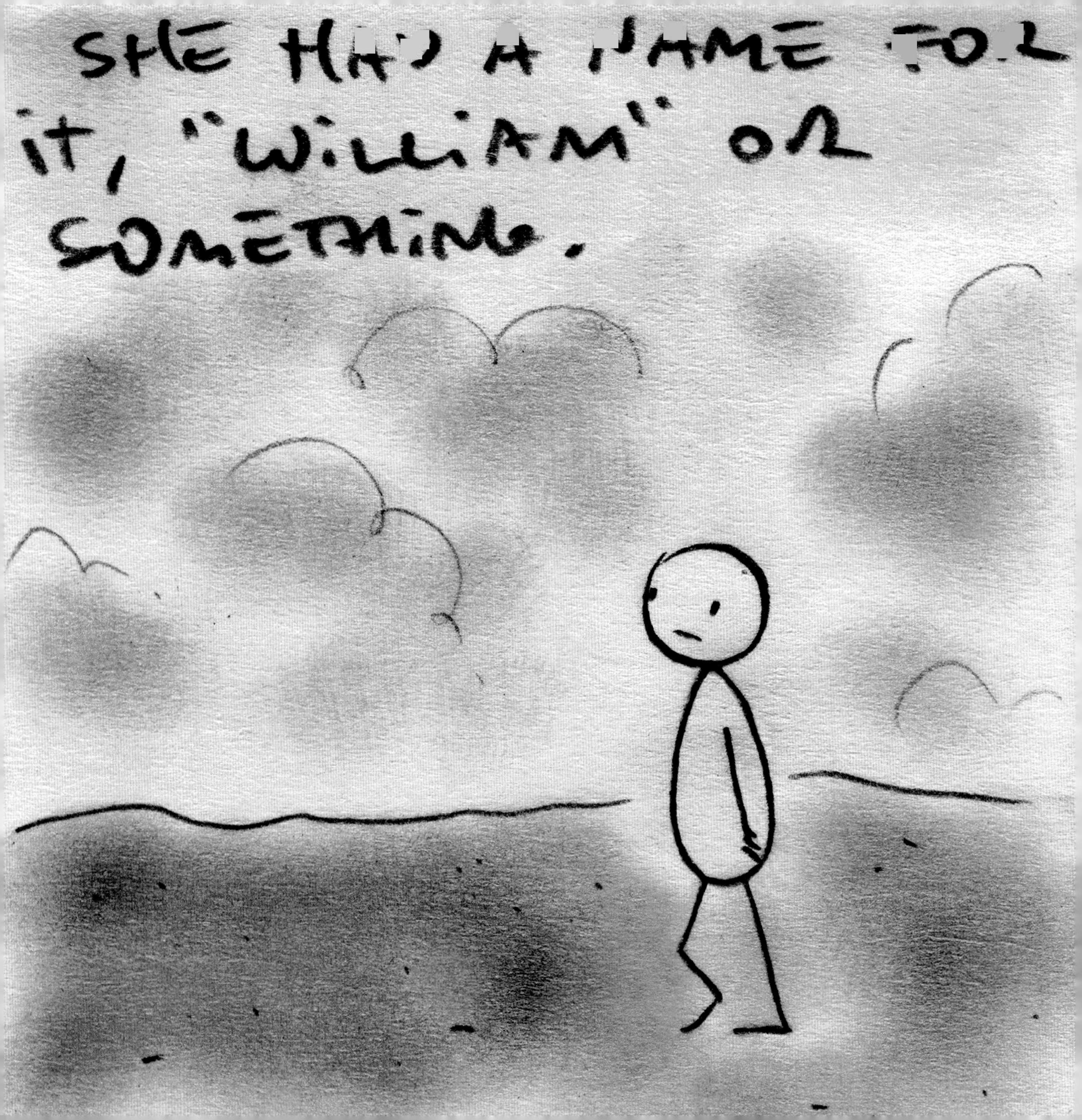
SHE HAD A NAME FOR IT, "WILLIAM" OR SOMETHING.

LORD KNOWS WHERE SHE
FOUND IT BUT SHE WORE
IT EVERYWHERE.

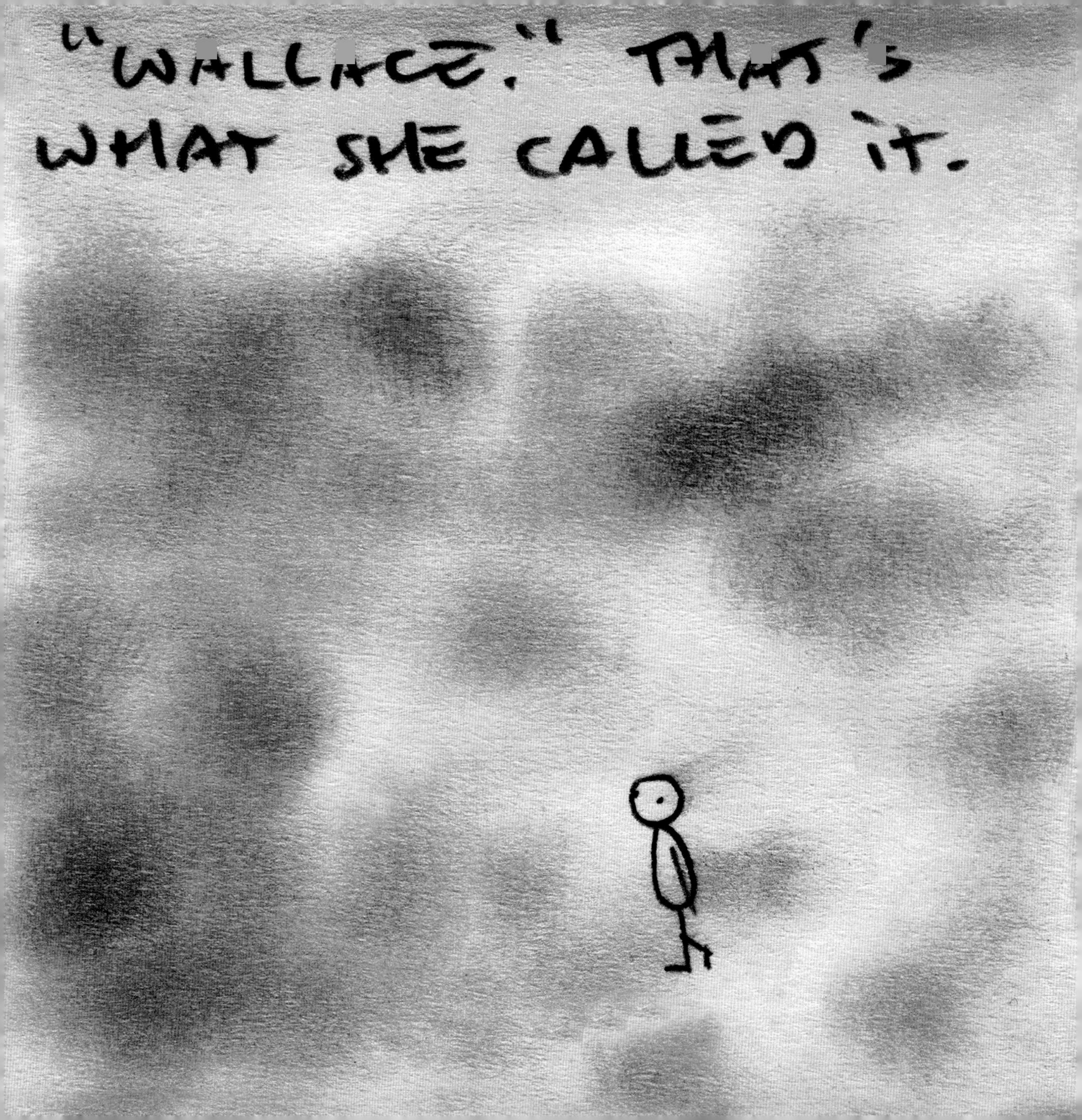
"WALLACE." THAT'S WHAT SHE CALLED IT.

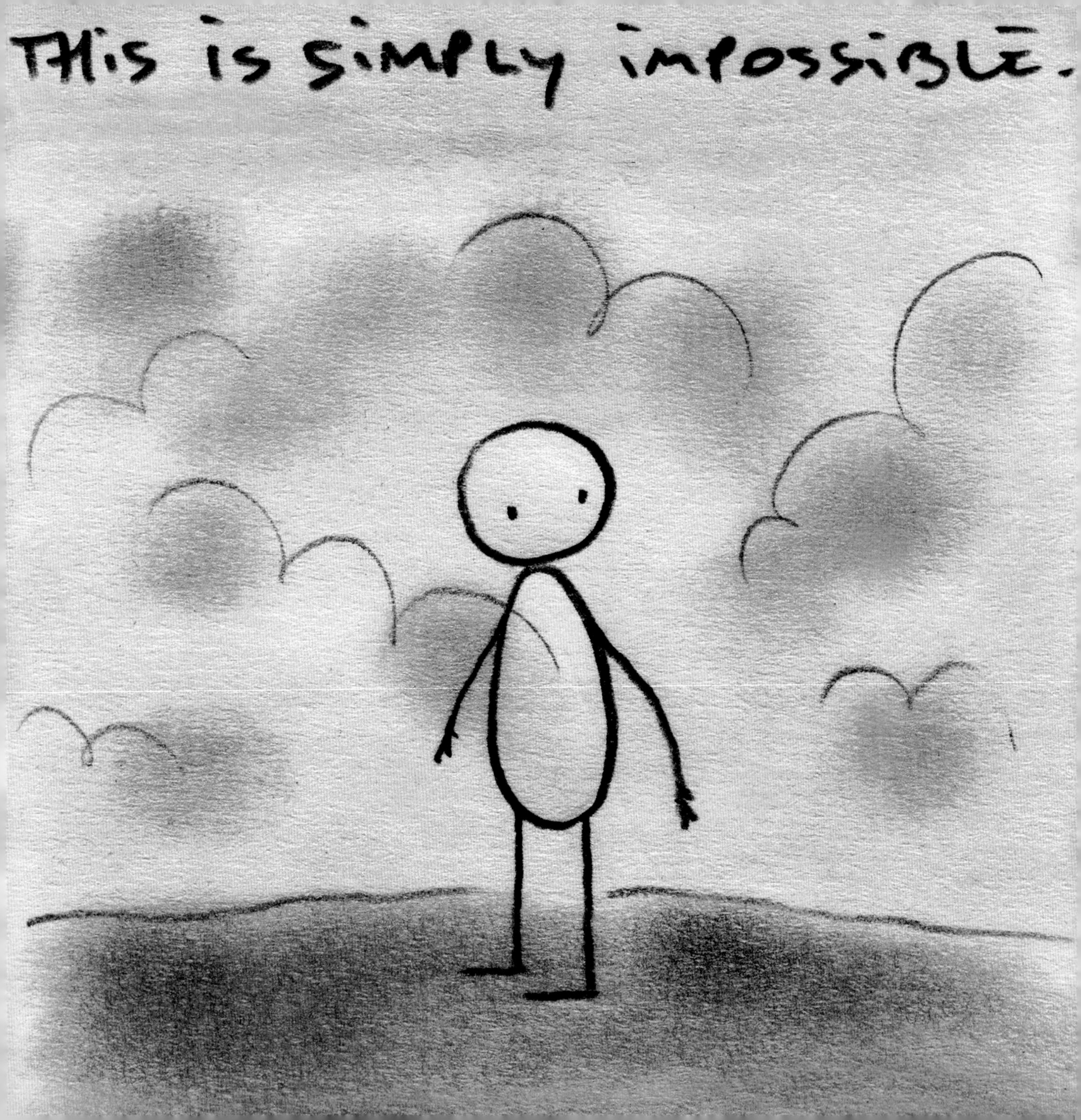
This is simply impossible.

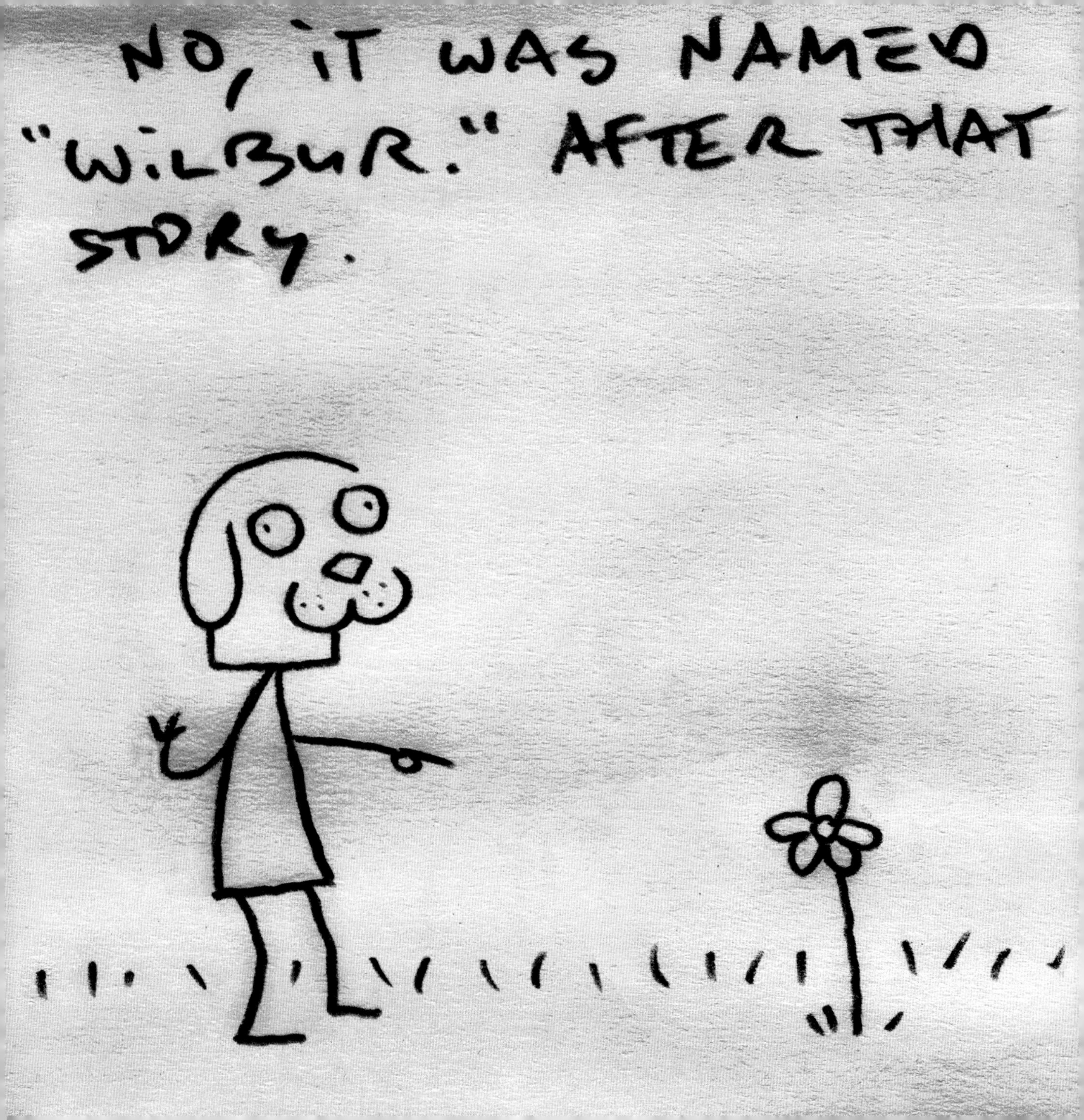
NO, IT WAS NAMED "WILBUR." AFTER THAT STORY.

SHE COLLECTS MARBLES.
HE HOPES SHE'S NOT
TOO SCARED.

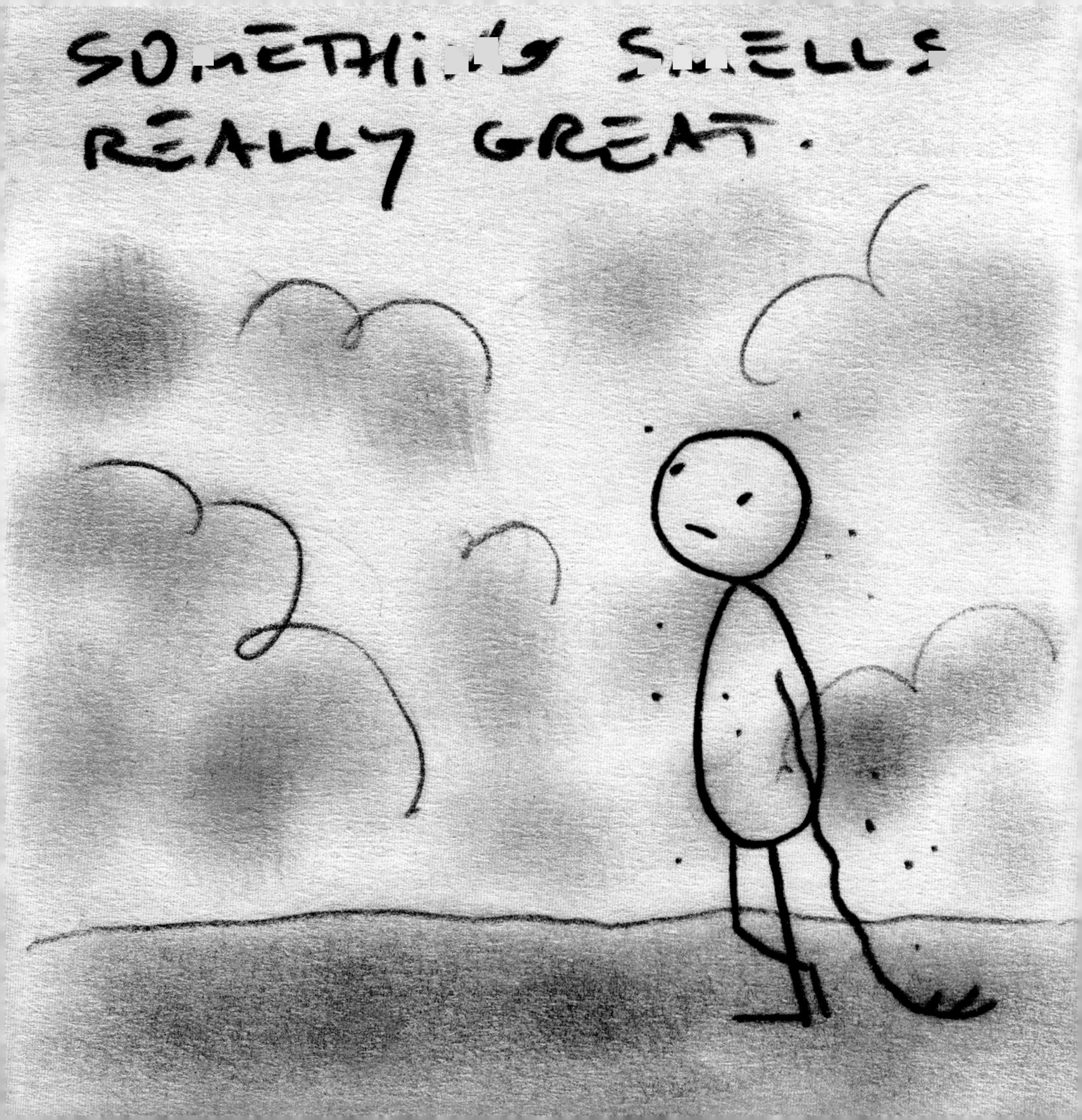
SOMETHING SMELLS
REALLY GREAT.

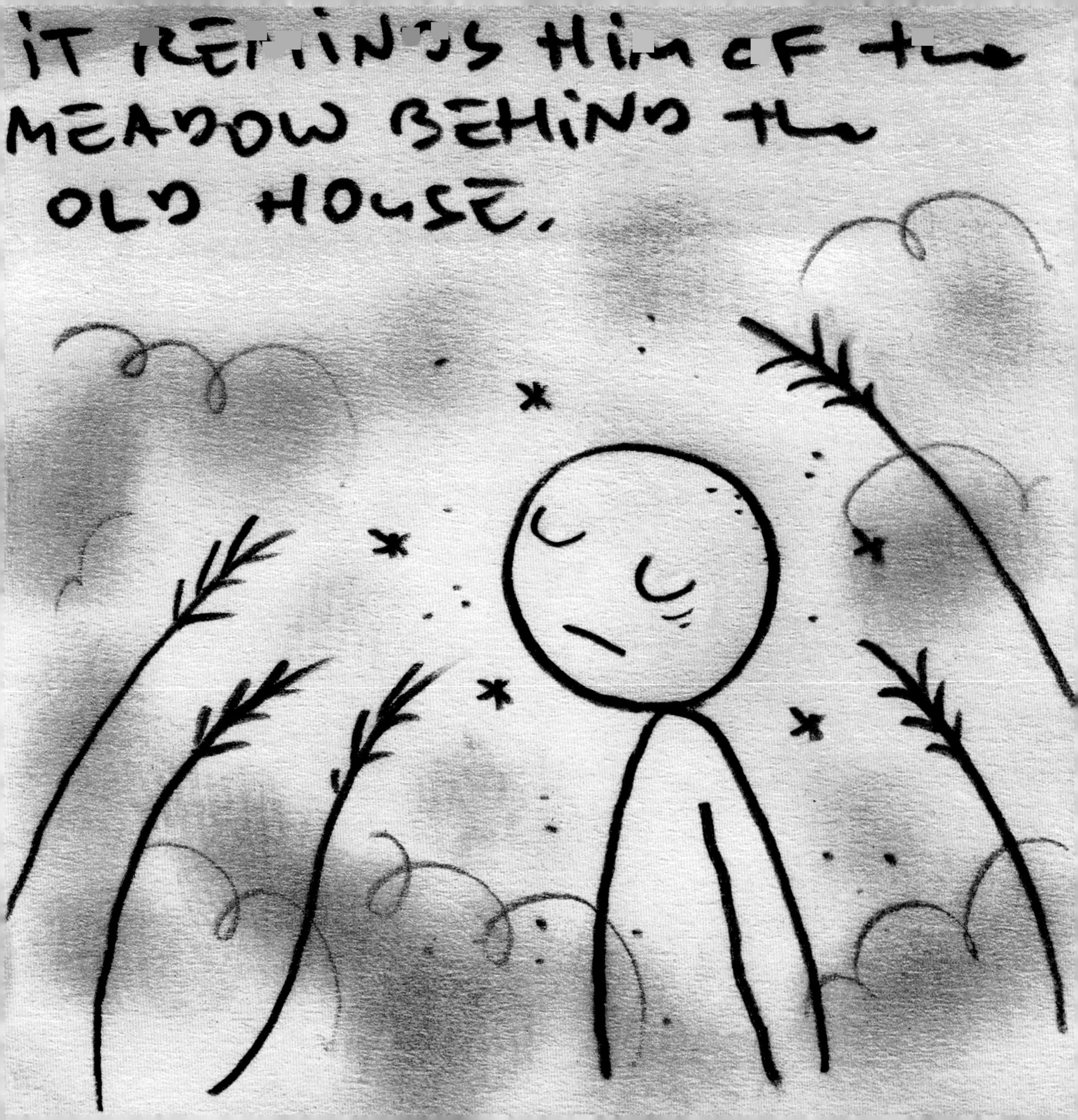
IT REMINDS HIM OF THE MEADOW BEHIND THE OLD HOUSE.

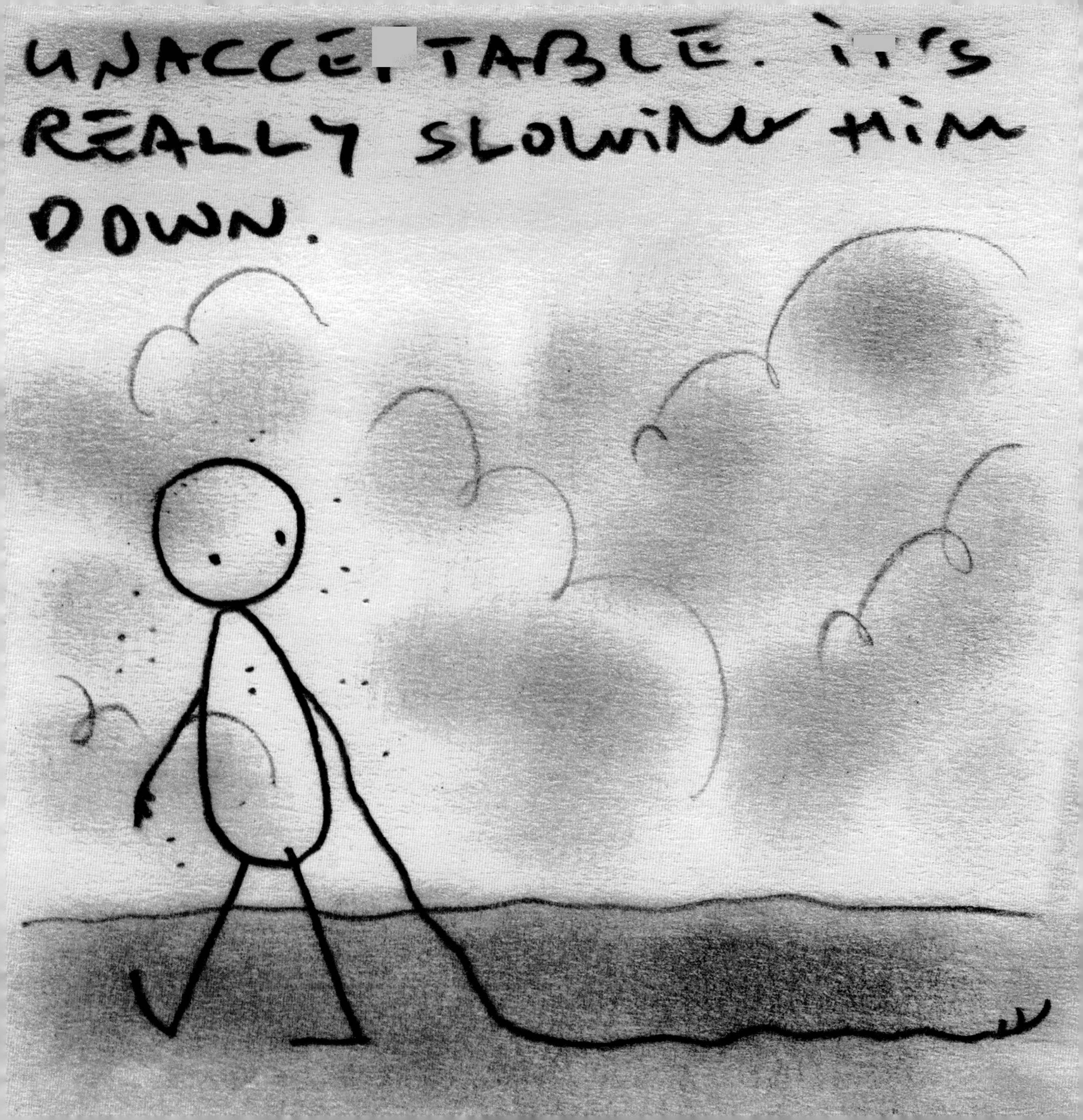
UNACCEPTABLE. IT'S REALLY SLOWING HIM DOWN.

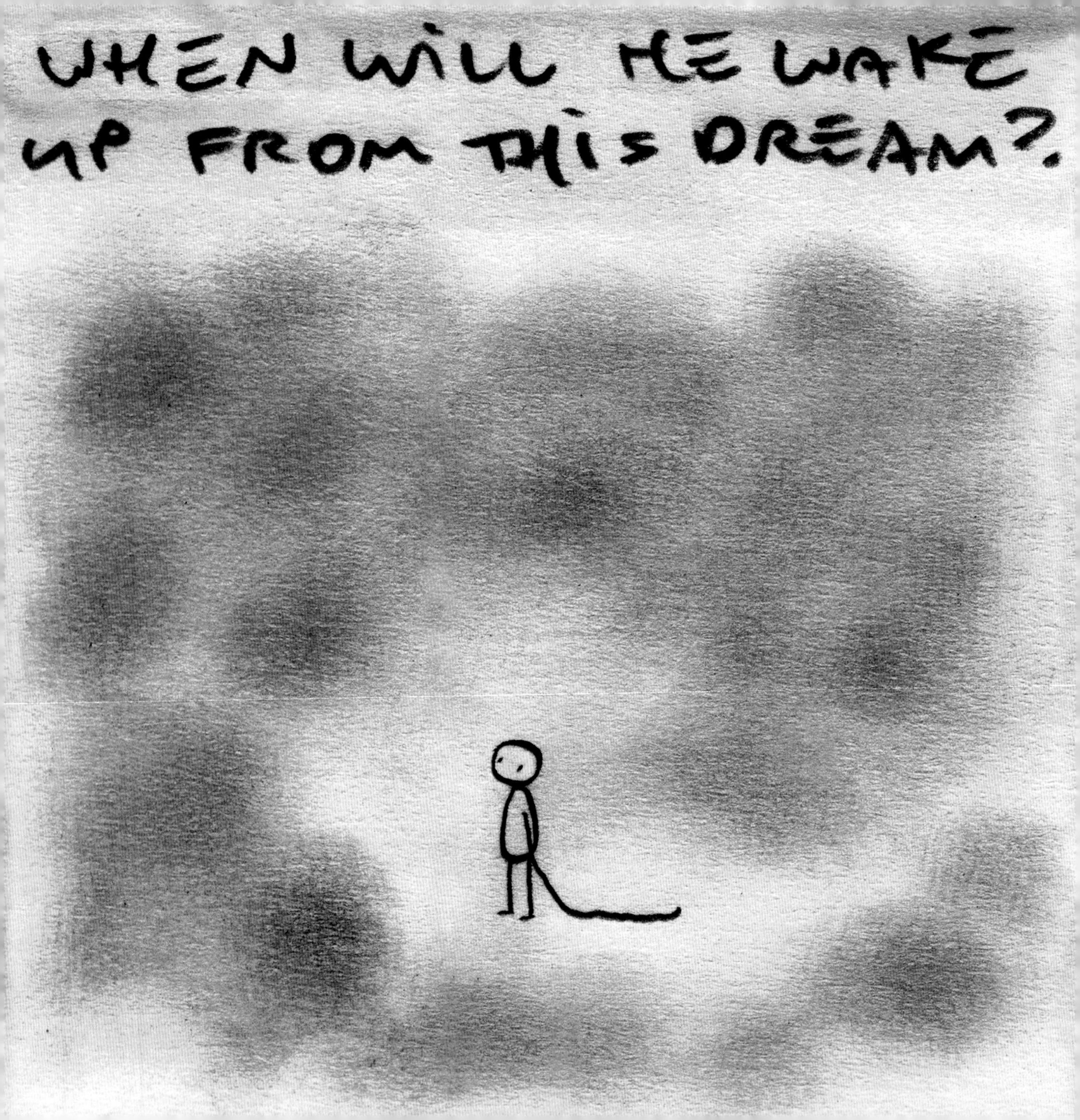
WHEN WILL HE WAKE
UP FROM THIS DREAM?.

HOW IS HE GOING TO FIND HIS LITTLE DOG NOW?

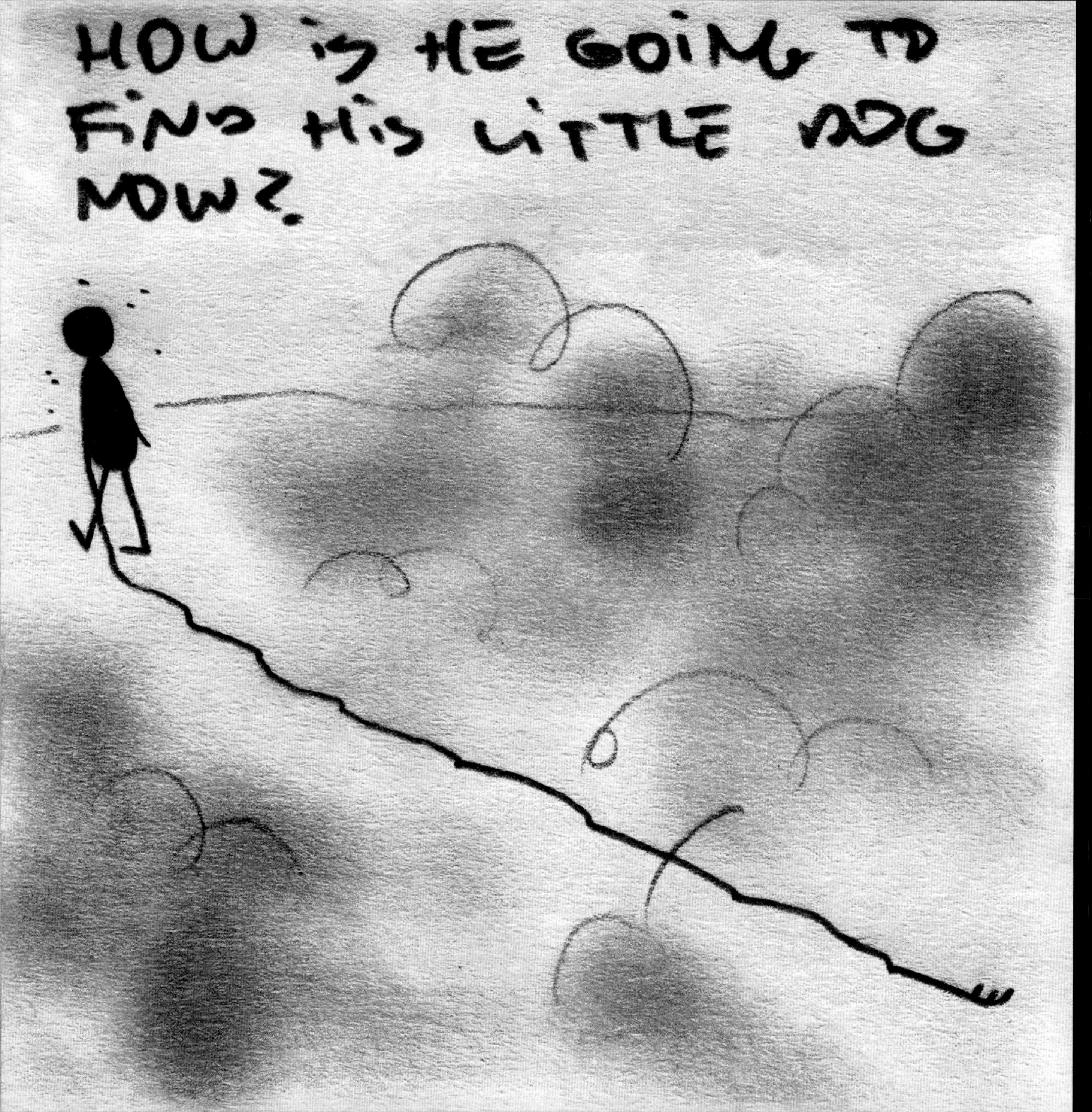

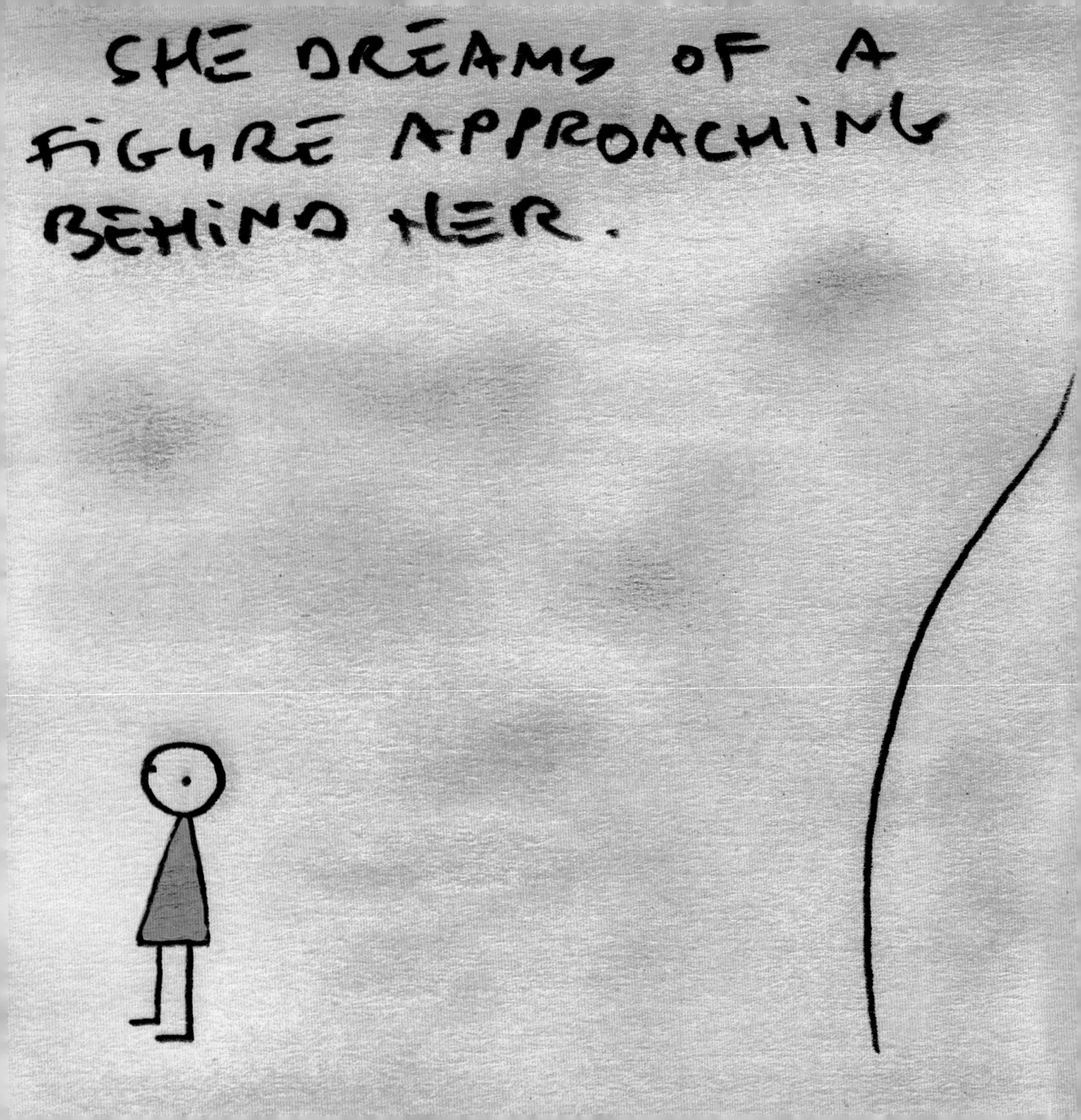
SHE DREAMS OF A FIGURE APPROACHING BEHIND HER.

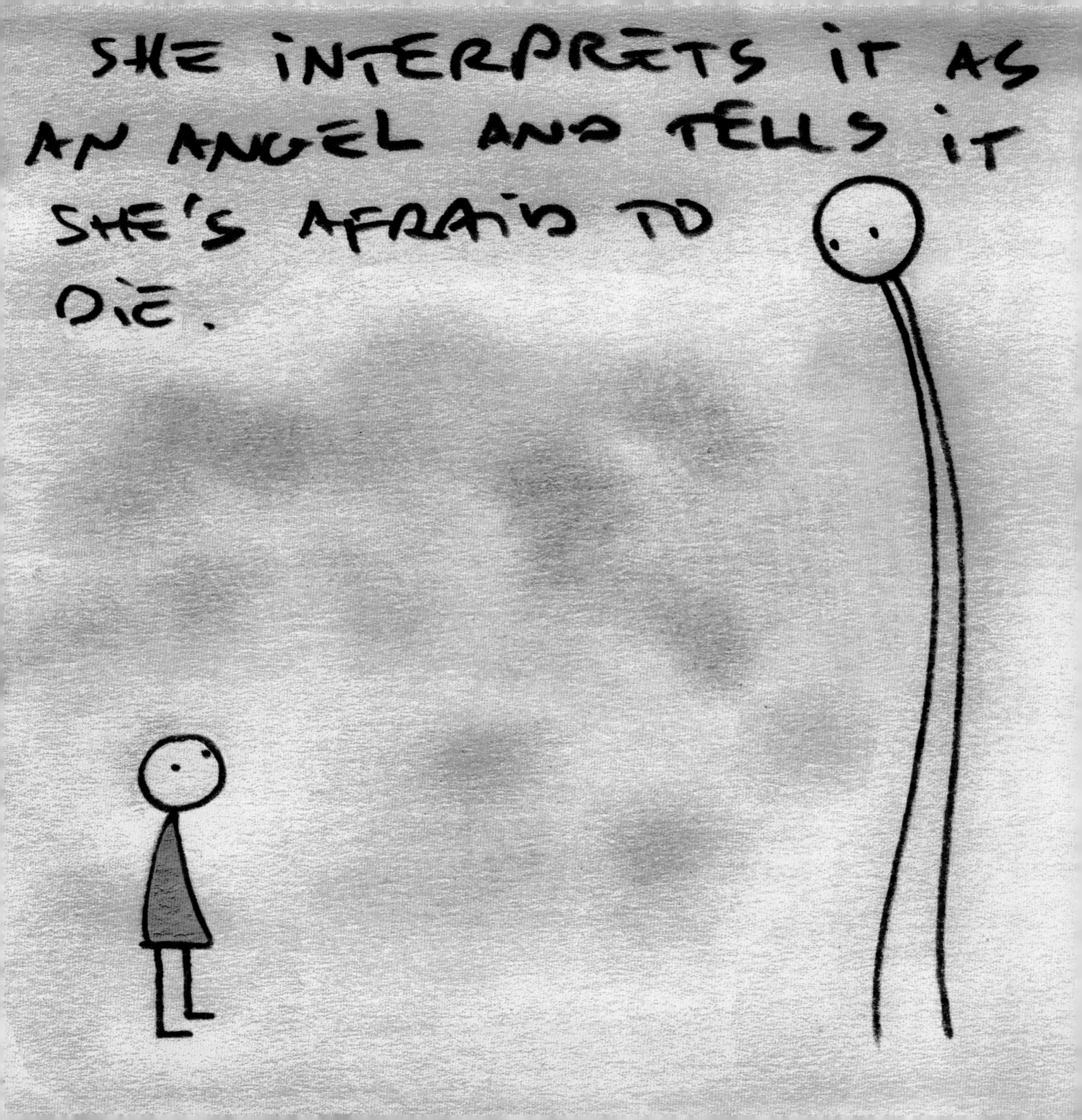
SHE INTERPRETS IT AS AN ANGEL AND TELLS IT SHE'S AFRAID TO DIE.

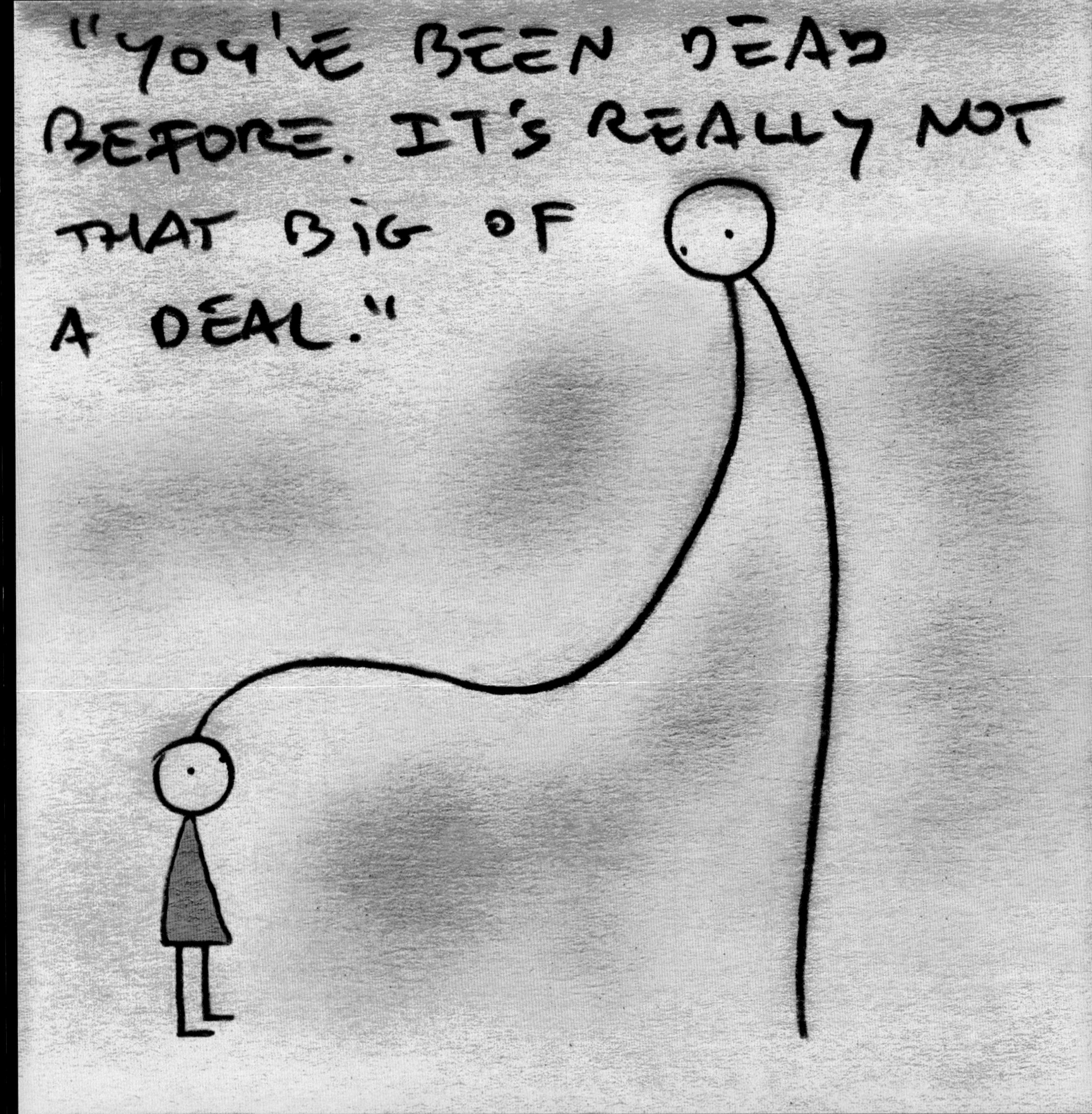
"YOU'VE BEEN DEAD BEFORE. IT'S REALLY NOT THAT BIG OF A DEAL."

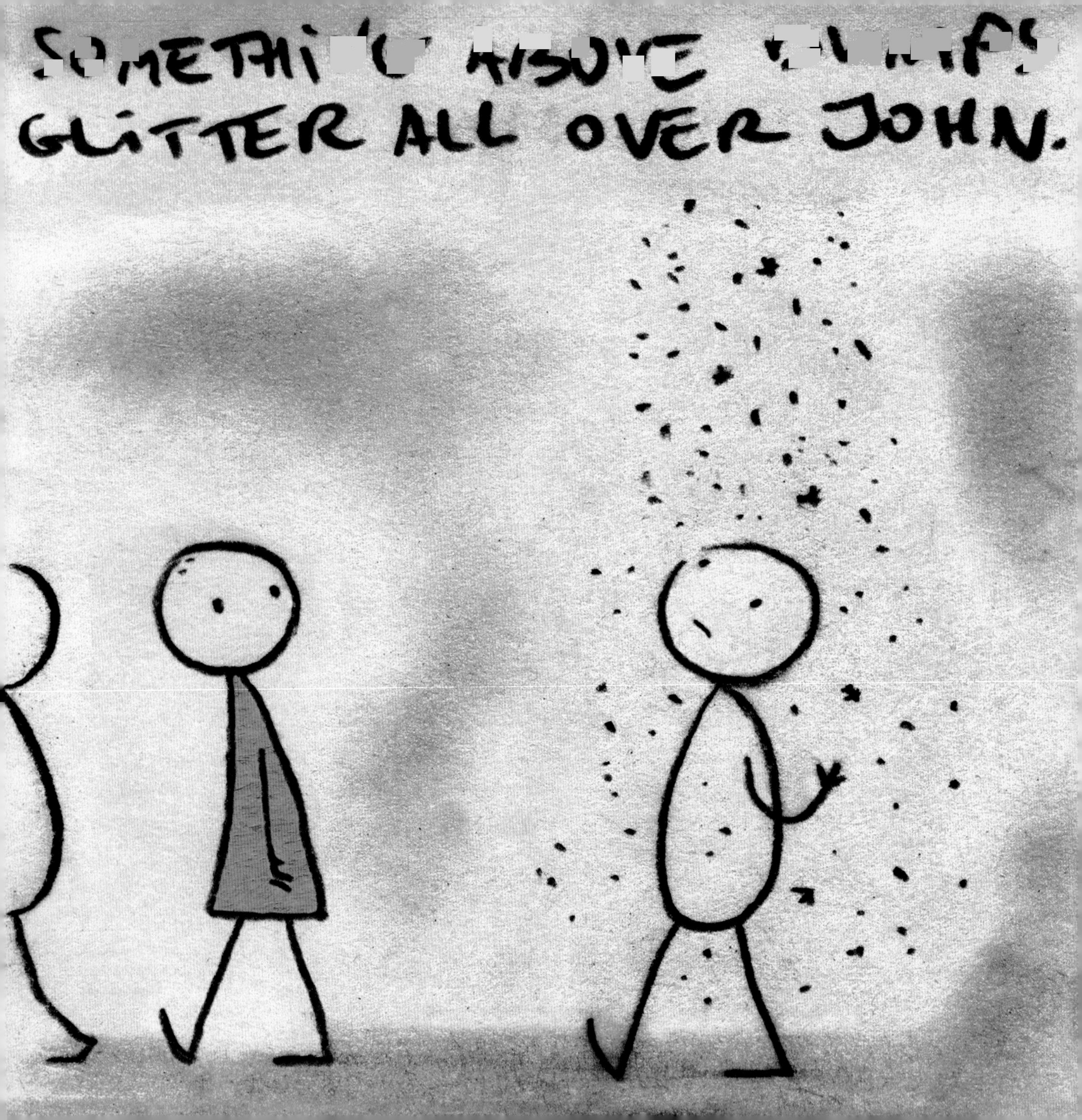
SOMETHING ABOVE DUMPS GLITTER ALL OVER JOHN.

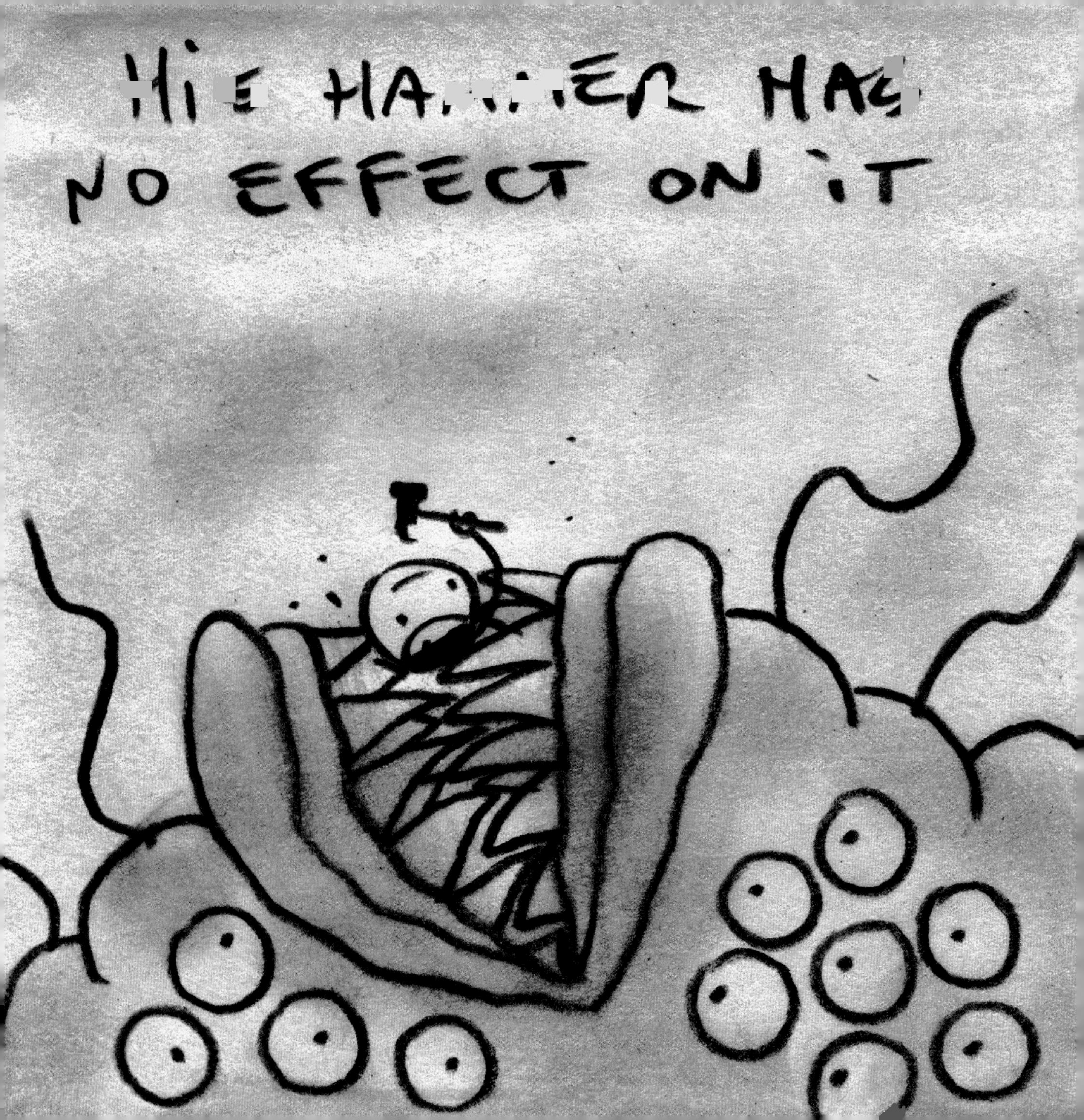
HIS HAMMER HAS NO EFFECT ON IT

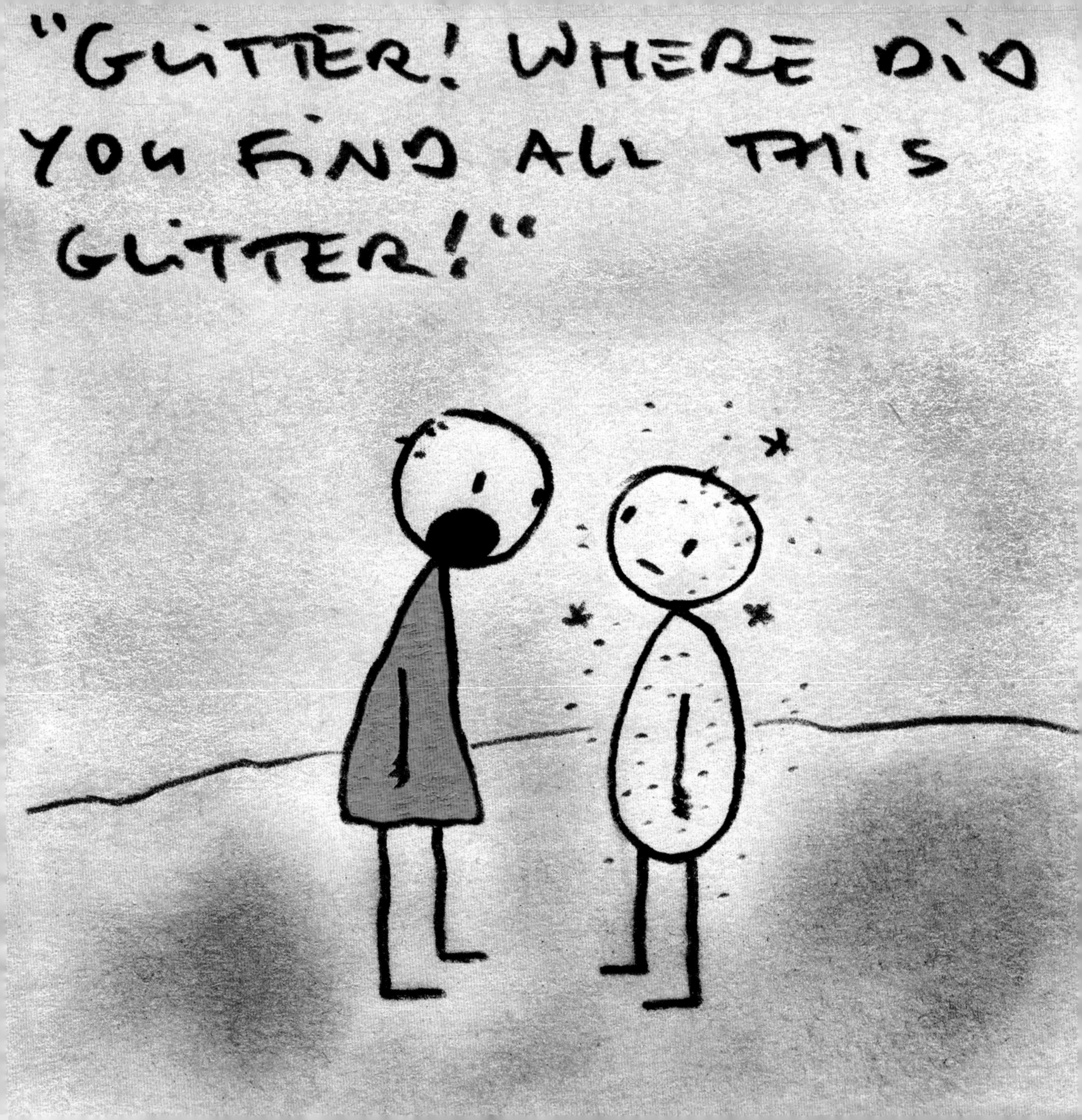
"GLITTER! WHERE DID YOU FIND ALL THIS GLITTER!"

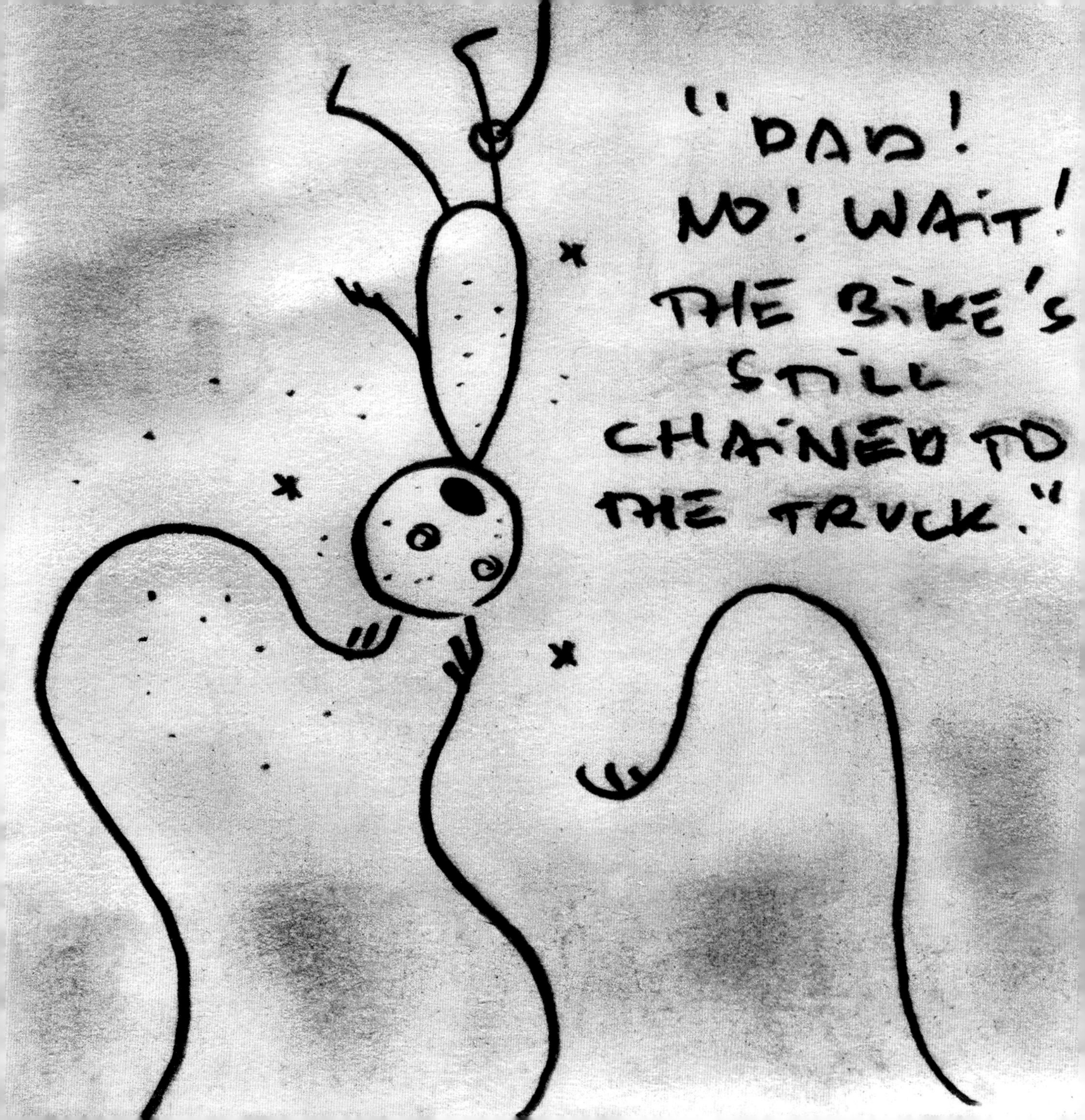
"DAD!
NO! WAIT!
THE BIKE'S
STILL
CHAINED TO
THE TRUCK."

"THOSE CLOUDS MAY HAVE SEEN US! RUN! RUN TO THE SHORE!"

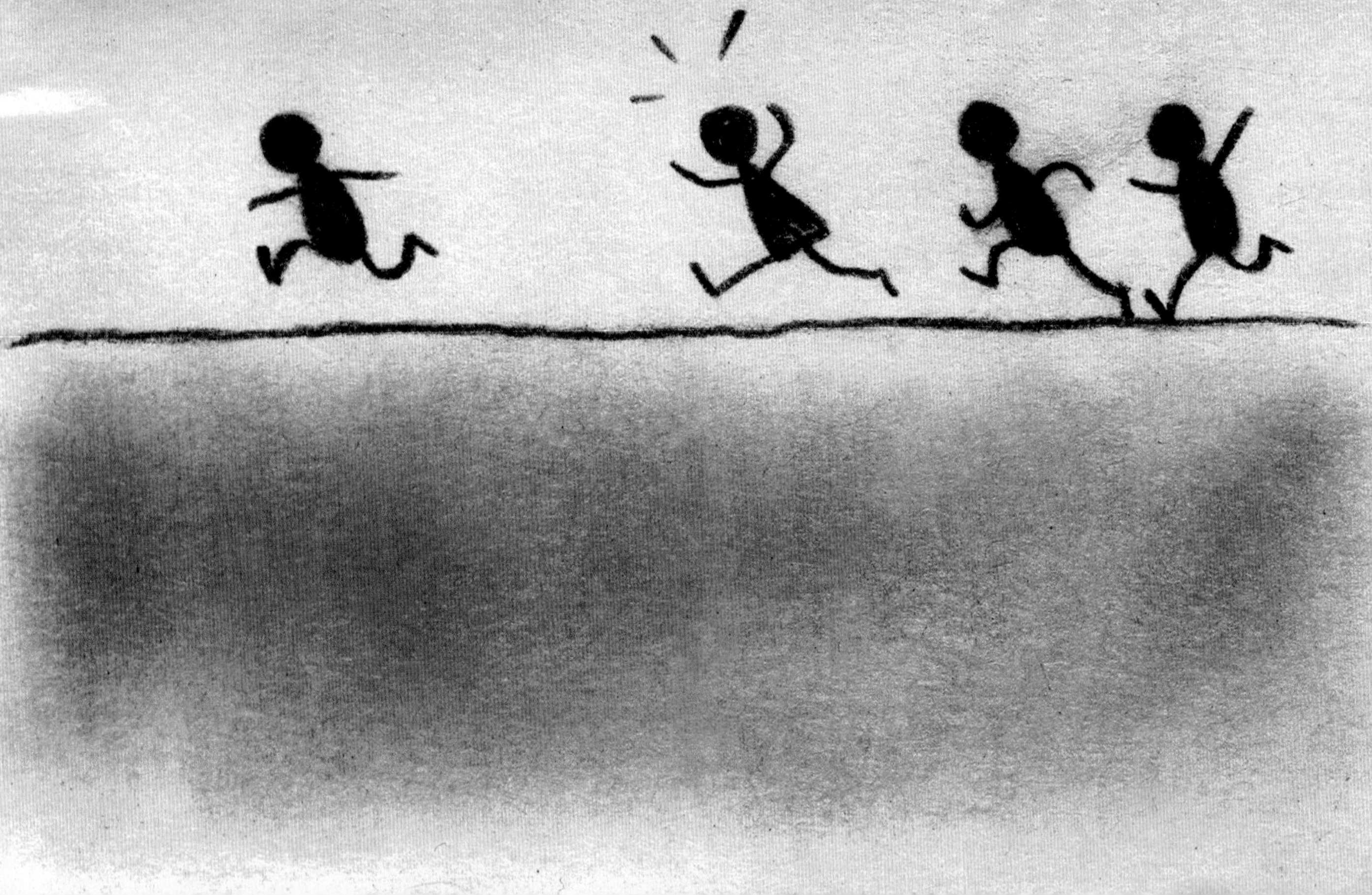

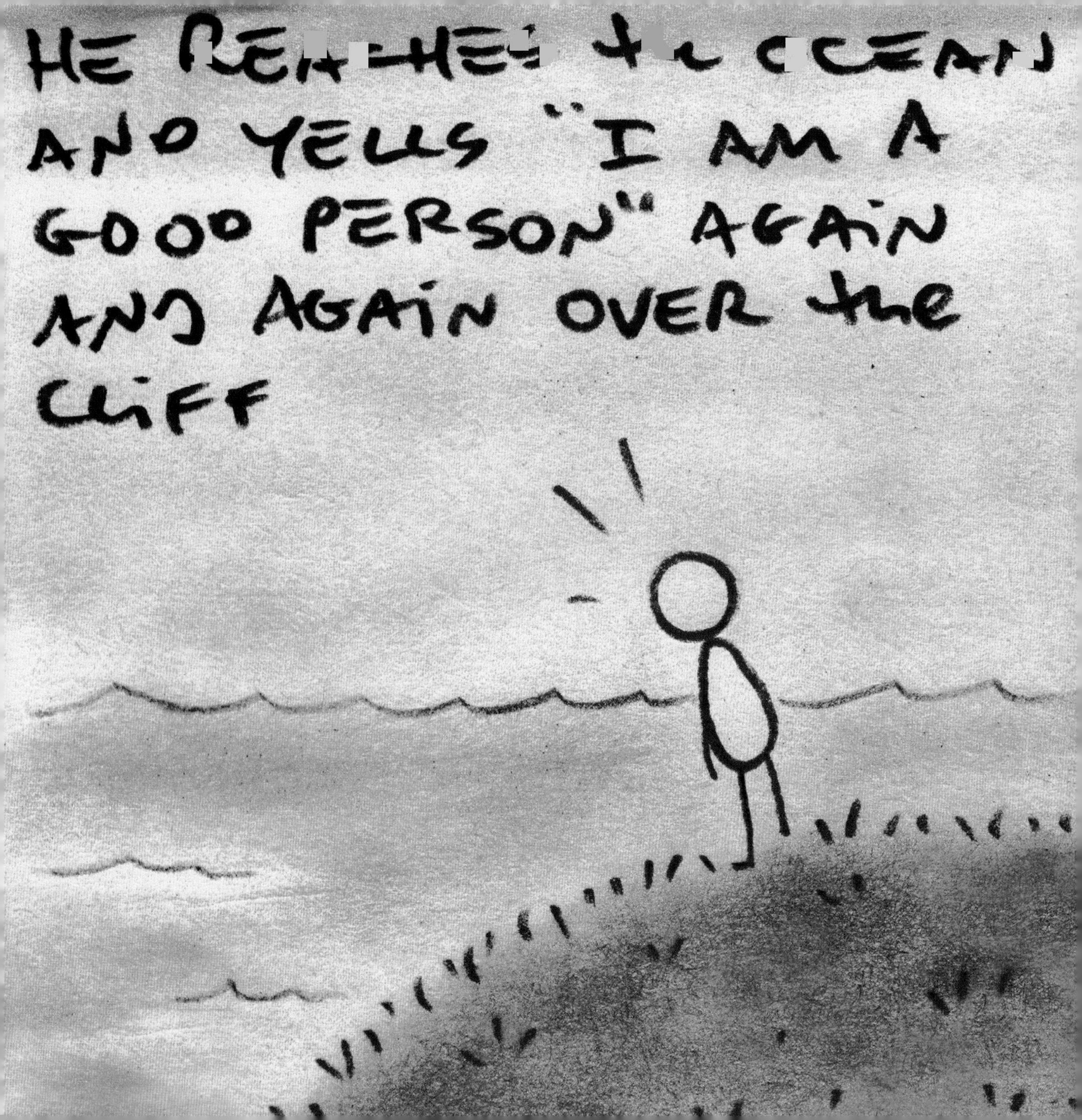
HE REACHES the OCEAN AND YELLS "I AM A GOOD PERSON" AGAIN AND AGAIN OVER the CLIFF

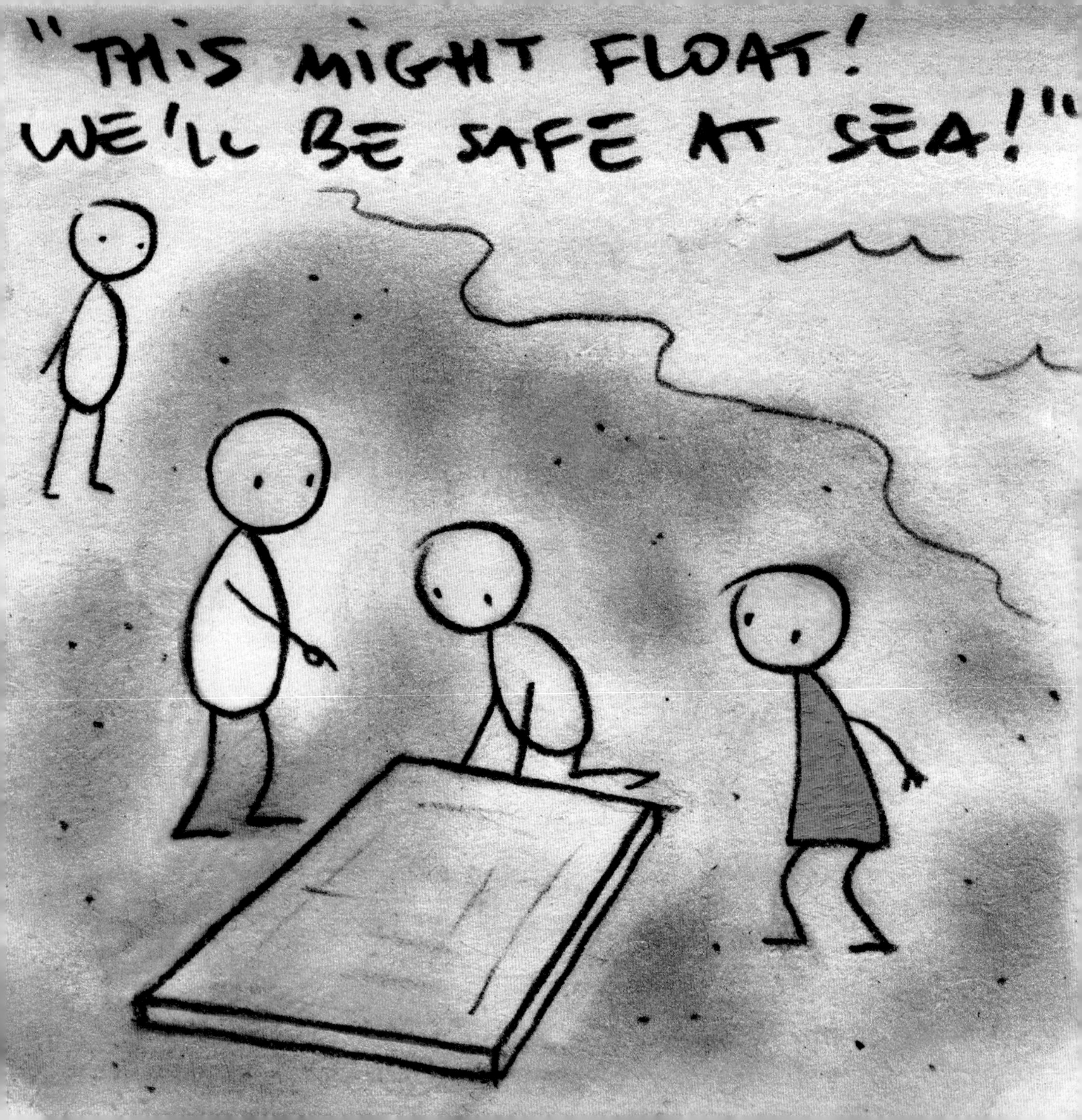
"THIS MIGHT FLOAT!
WE'LL BE SAFE AT SEA!"

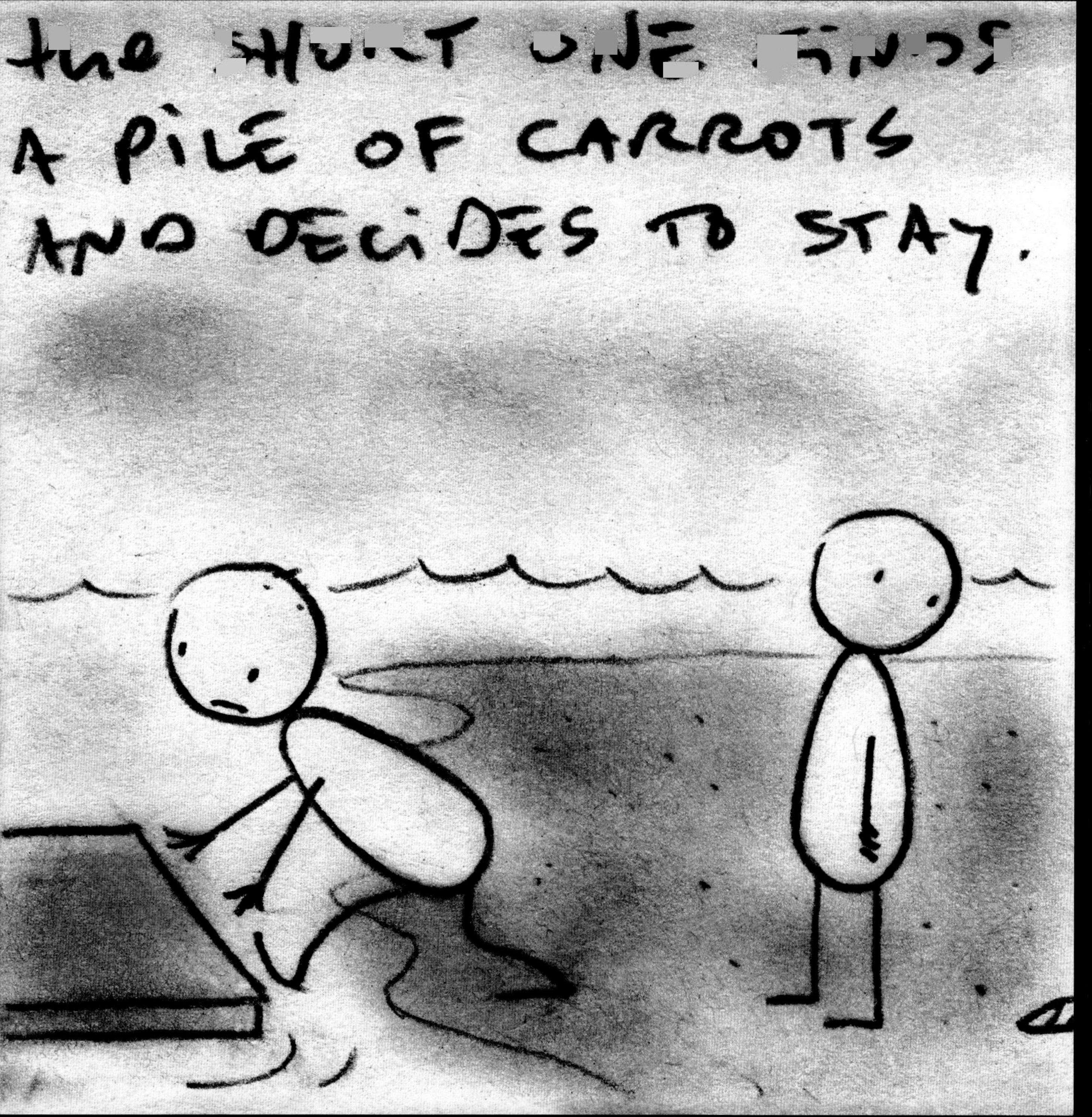
the SHORT ONE FINDS
A PILE OF CARROTS
AND DECIDES TO STAY.

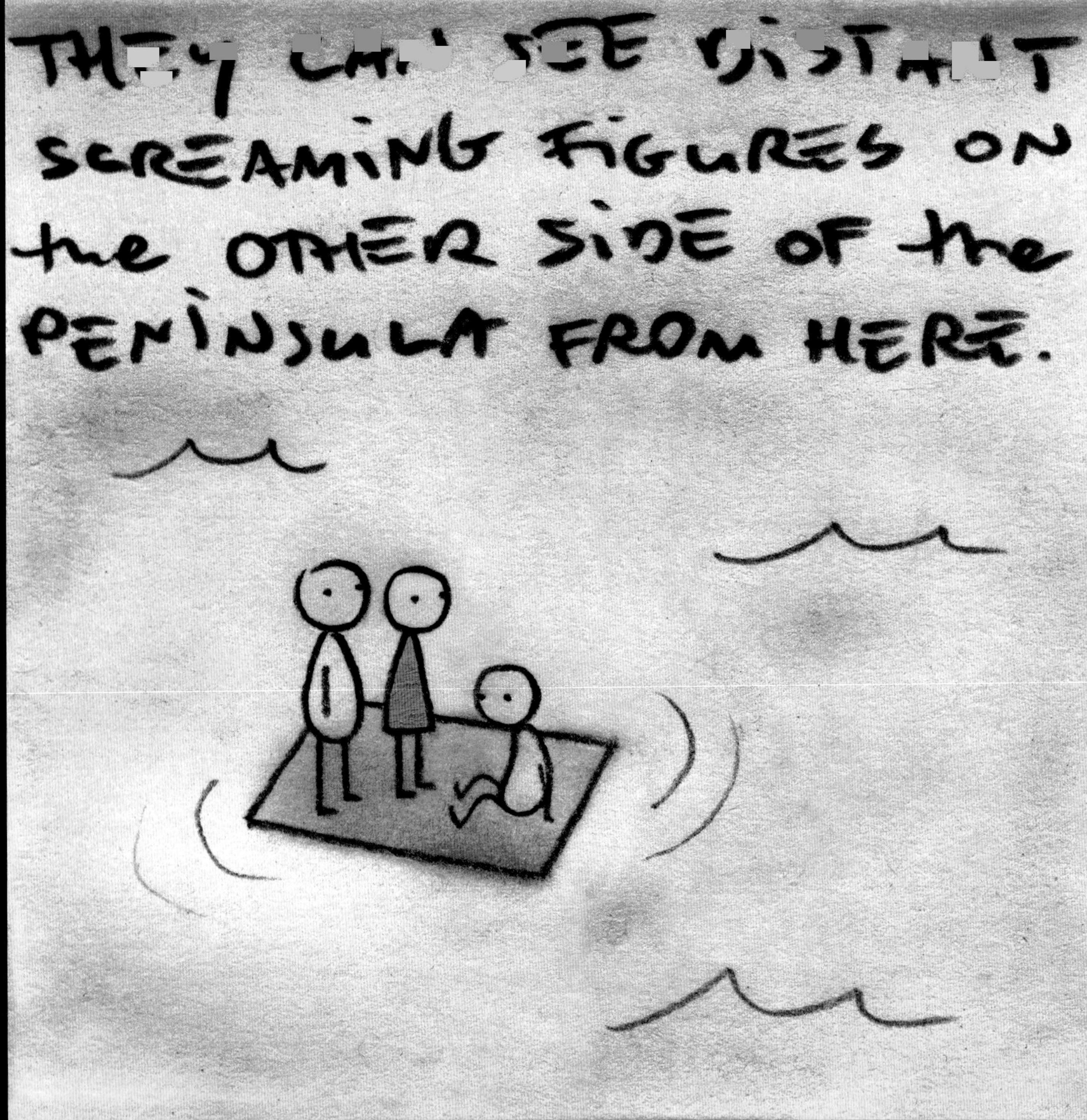
THEY CAN SEE DISTANT SCREAMING FIGURES ON THE OTHER SIDE OF THE PENINSULA FROM HERE.

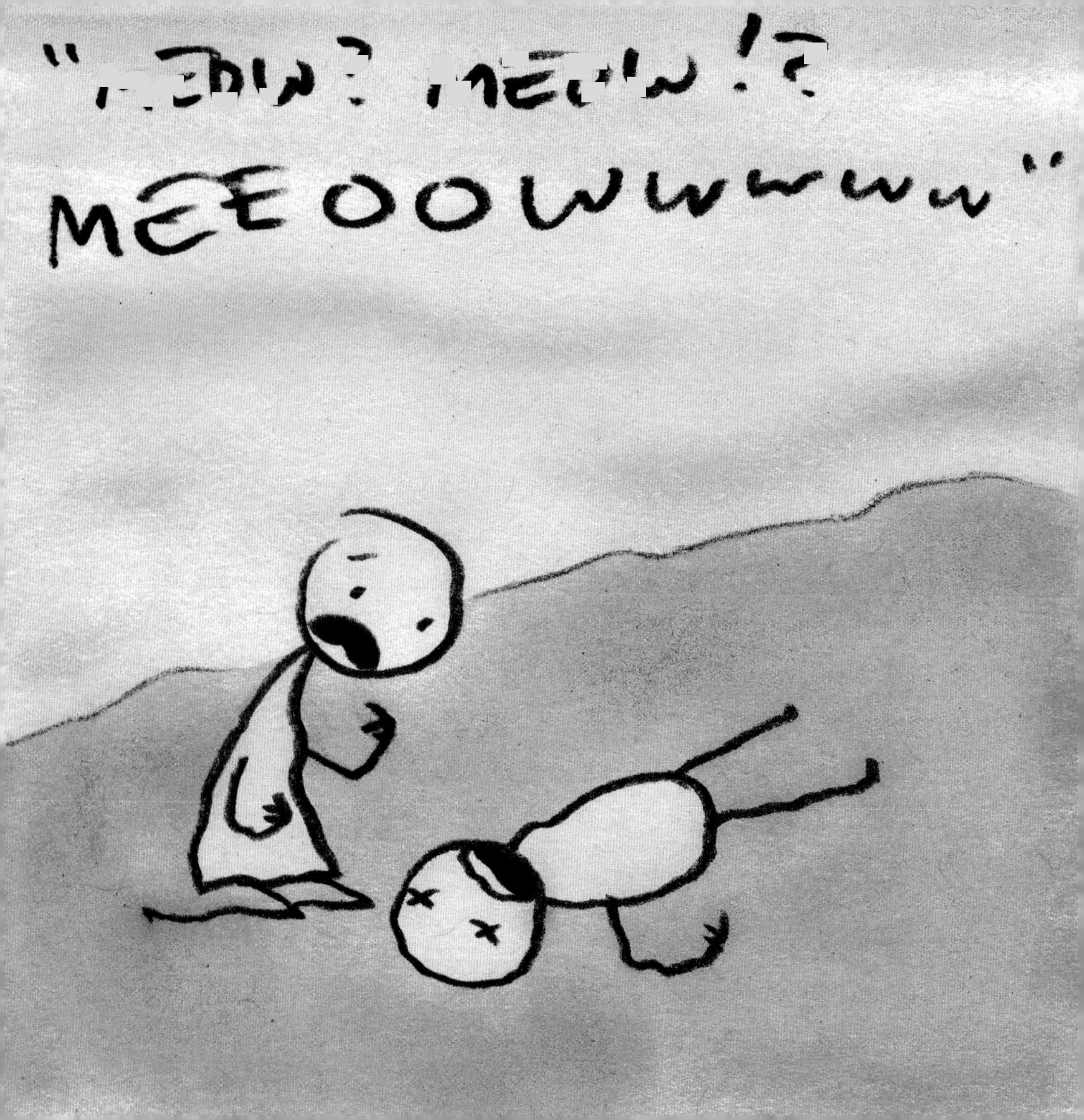
MEEOOWWWWW"

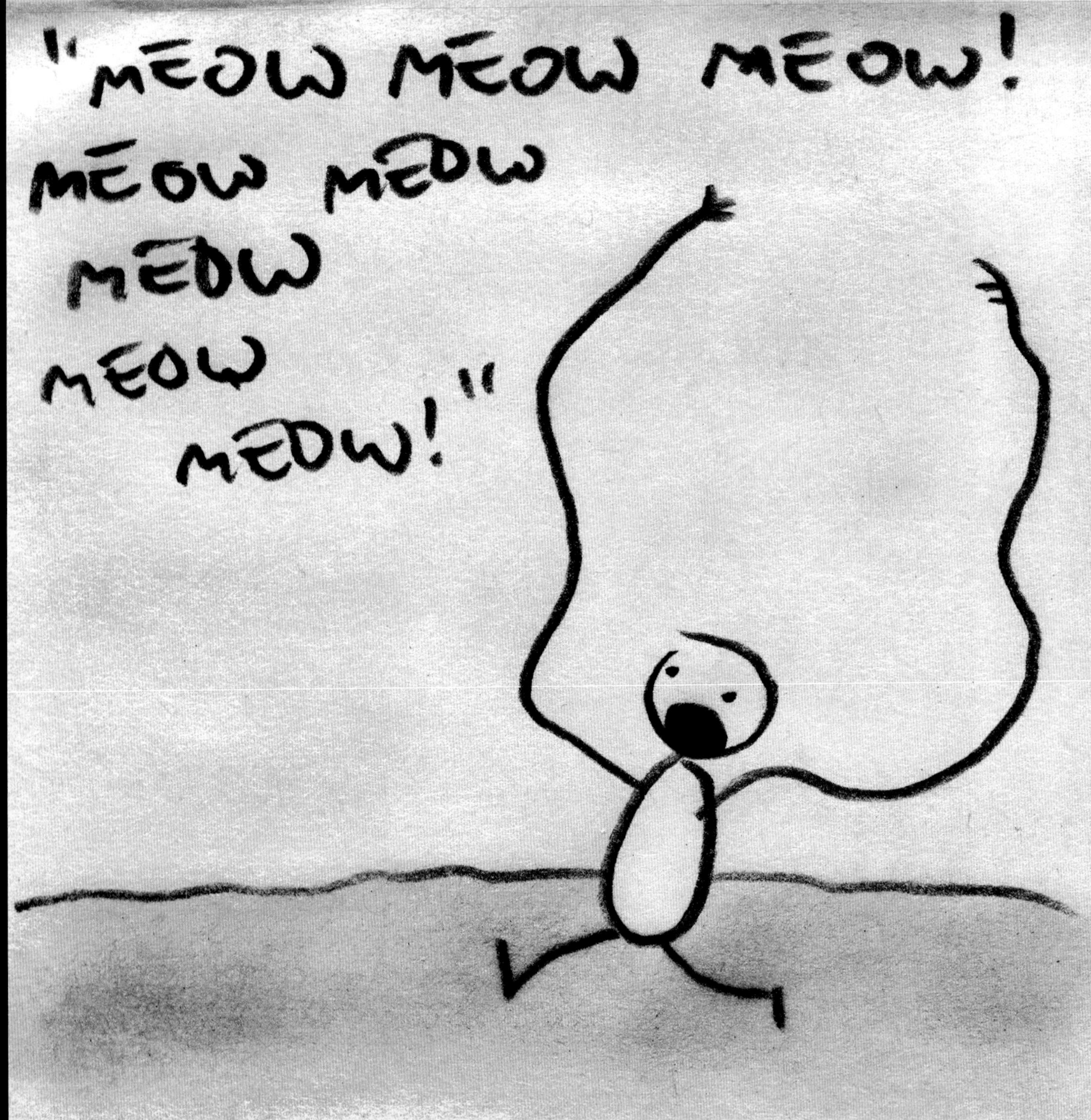
"MEOW MEOW MEOW!
MEOW MEOW
MEOW
MEOW
MEOW!"

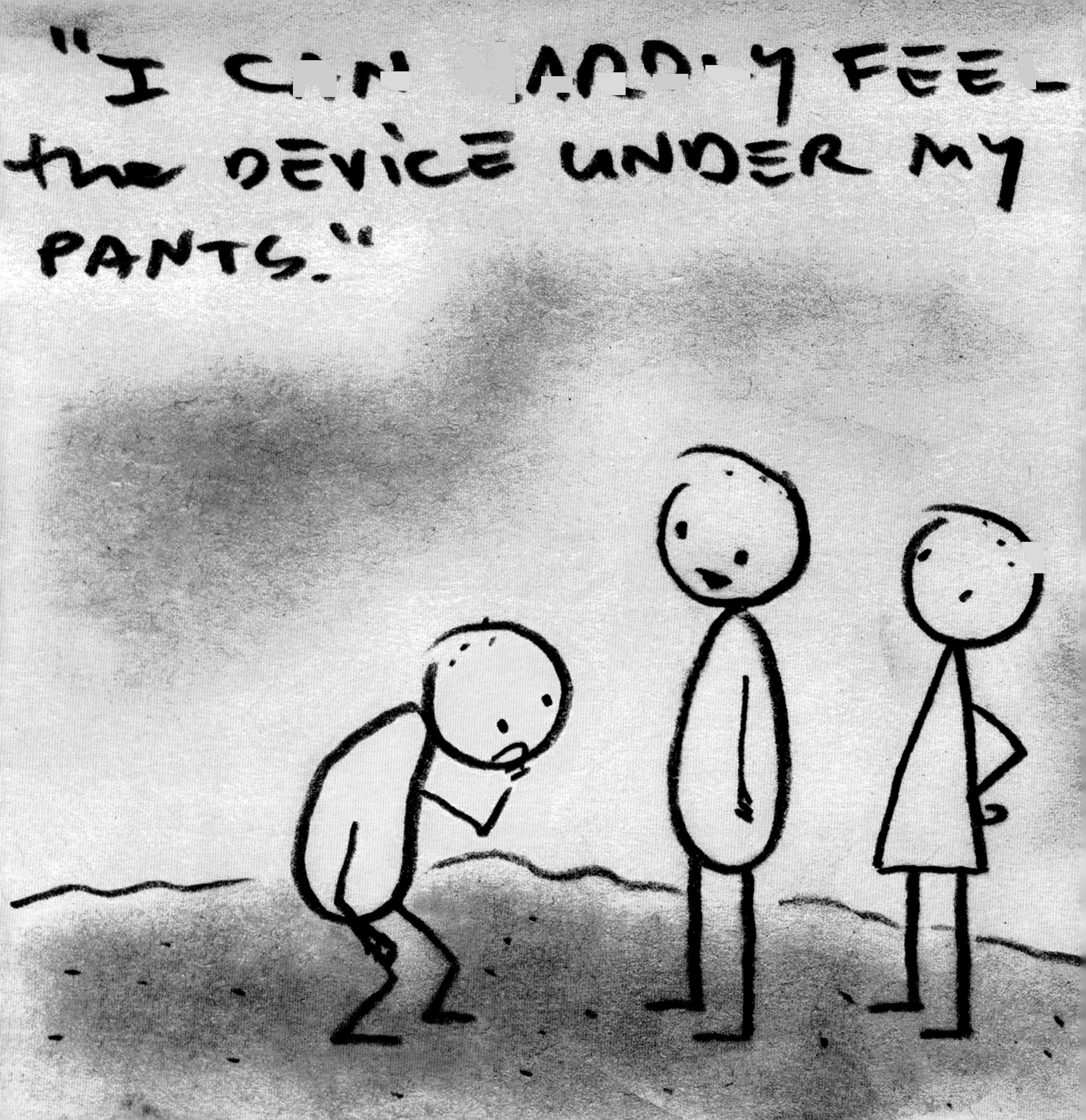
"I CAN HARDLY FEEL the DEVICE UNDER MY PANTS."

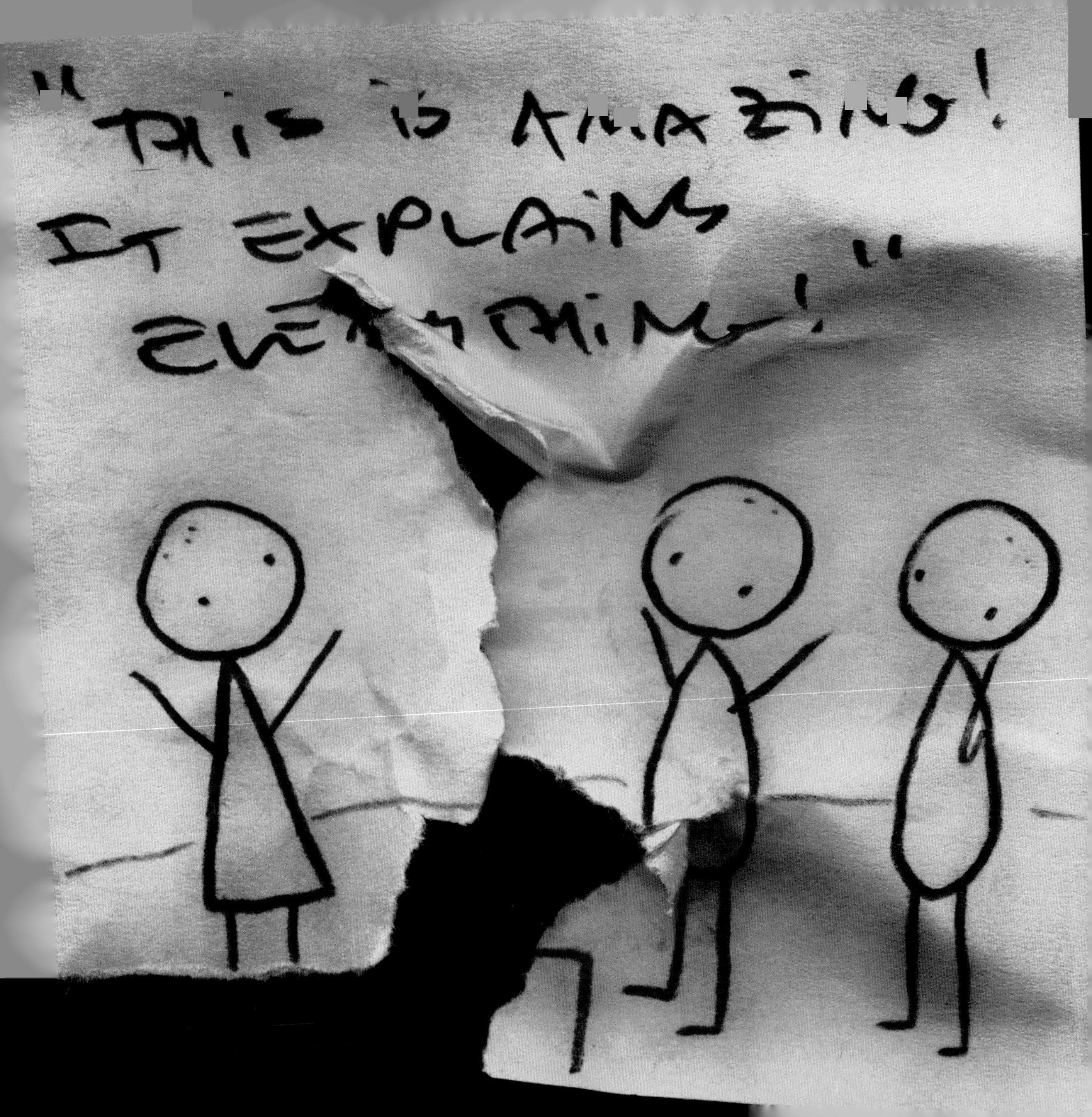
"THIS IS AMAZING!
IT EXPLAINS
EVERYTHING!"

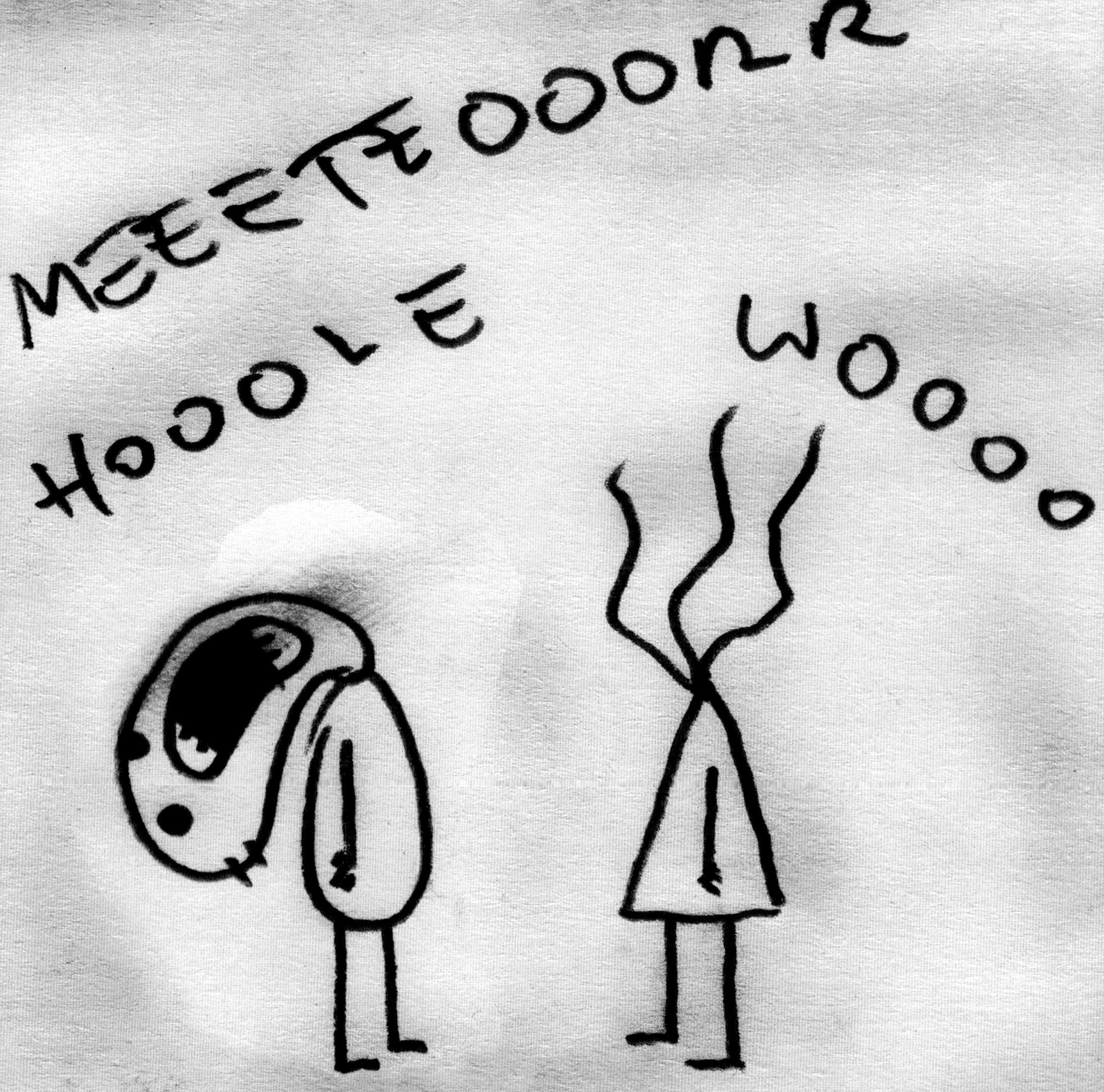
MEEETEOOORR
HOOOLE
WOOOO

HE CURLS UP HIS GIANT ARM AND OFFERS THEM A CARROT

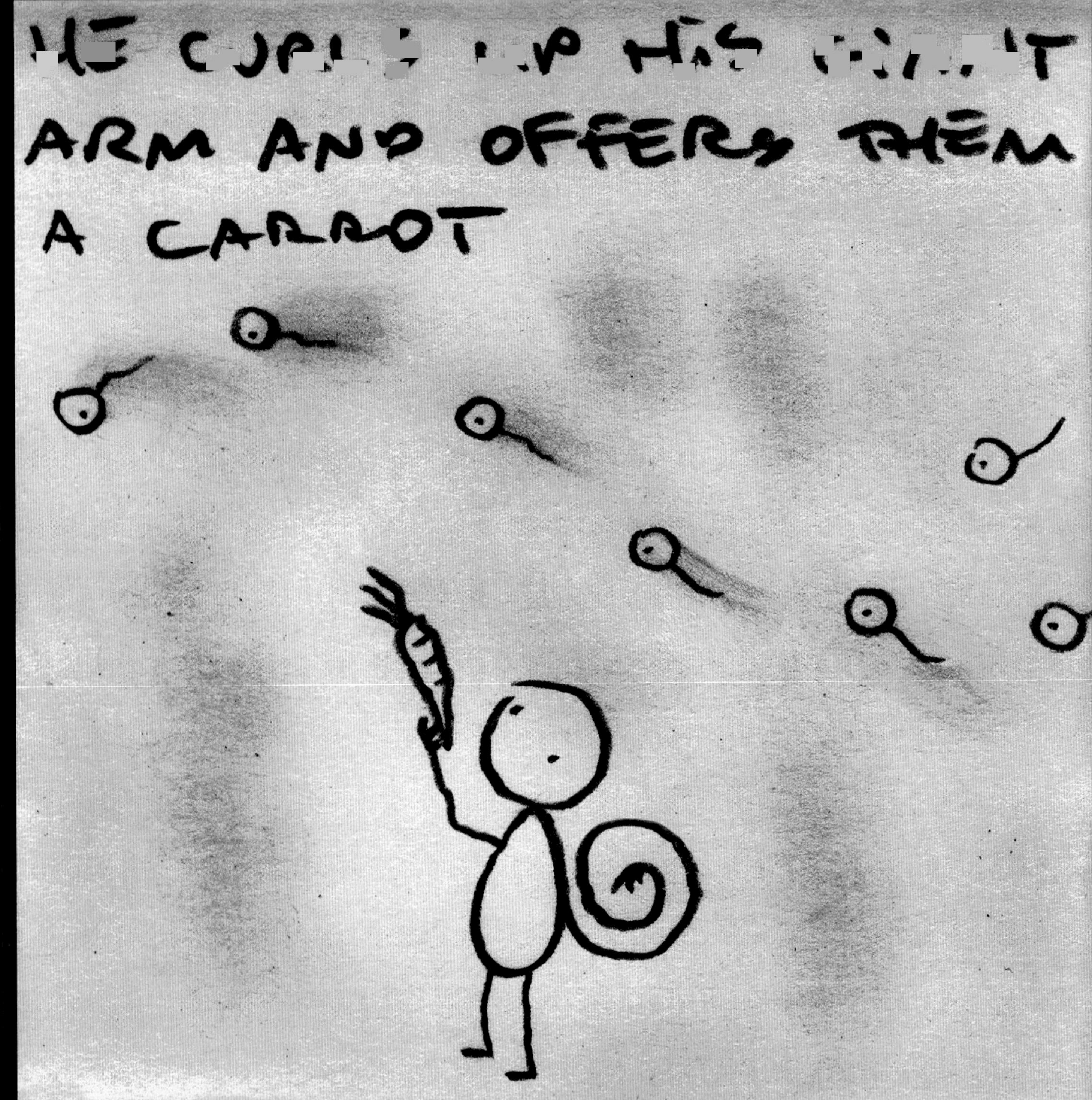

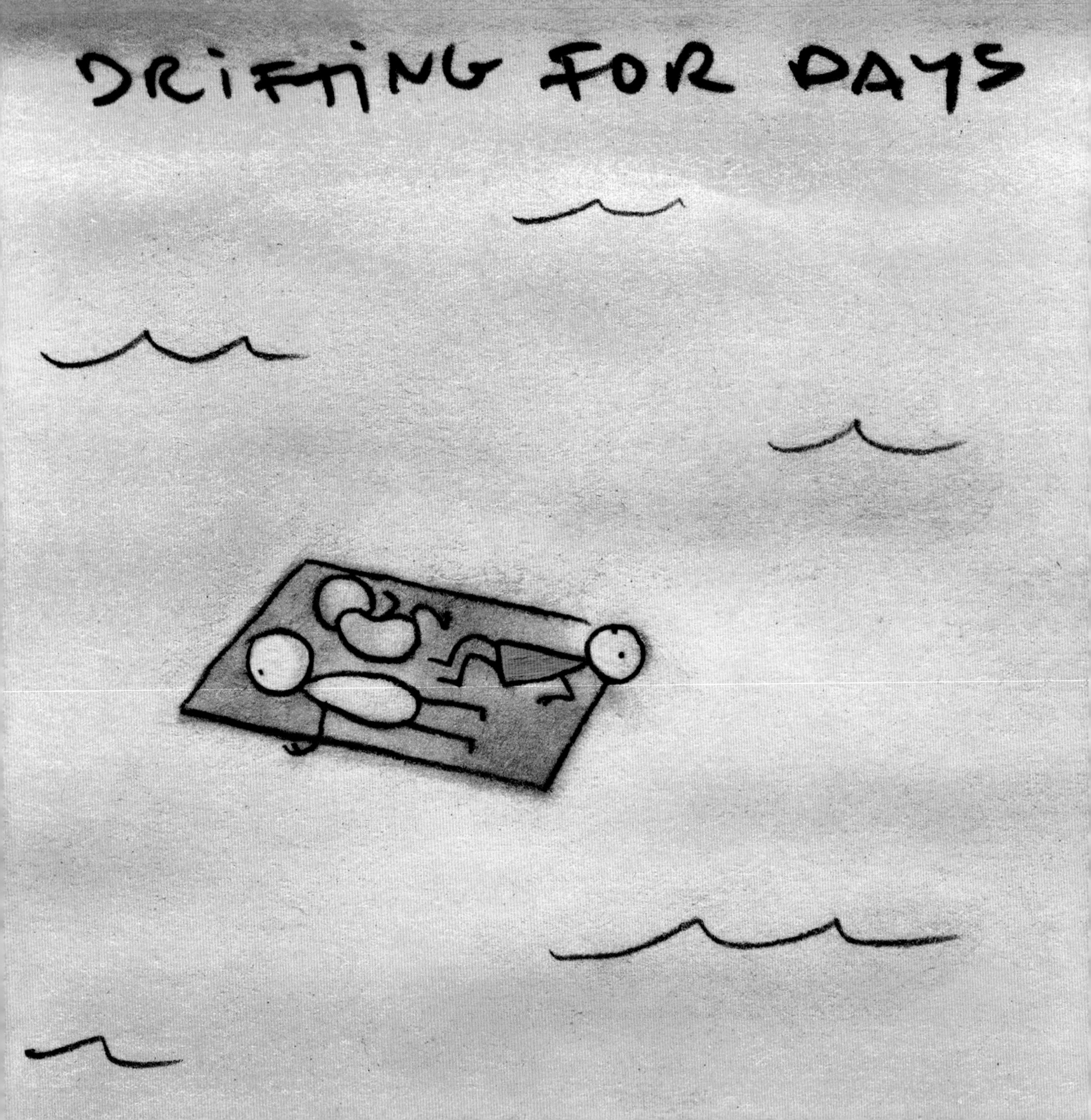
DRIFTING FOR DAYS

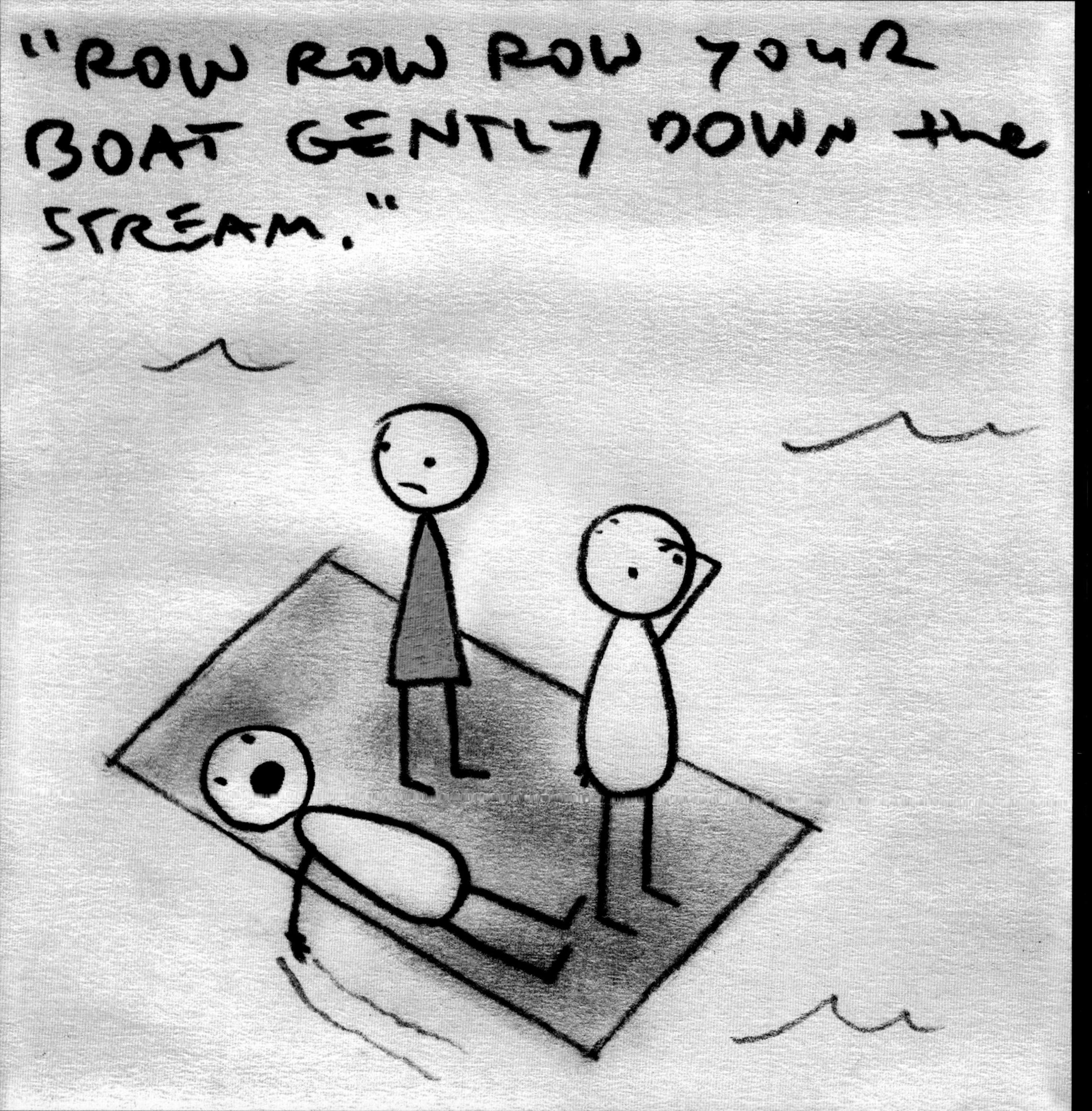
"ROW ROW ROW YOUR BOAT GENTLY DOWN the STREAM."

THERE IS NOTHING TO EAT.

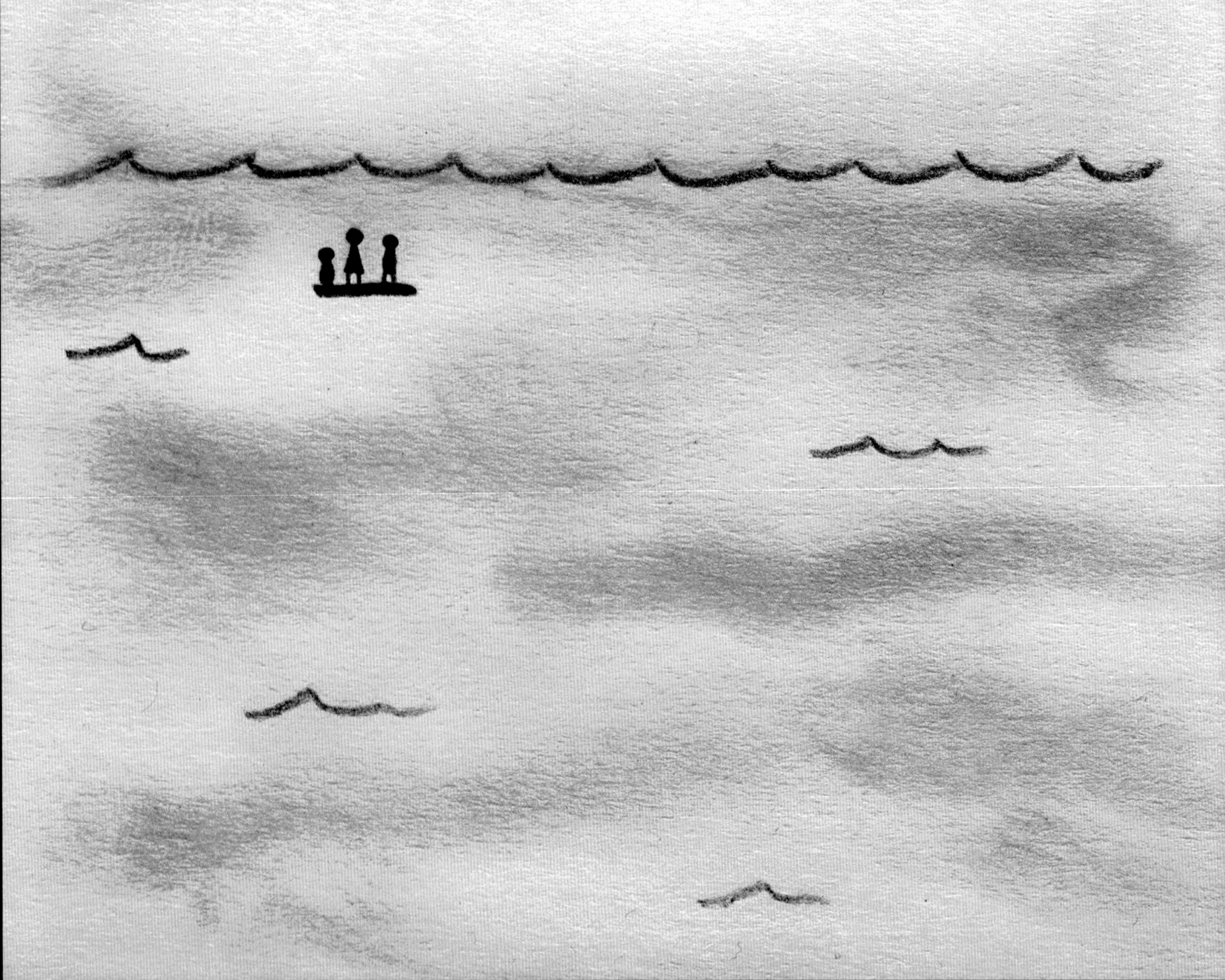

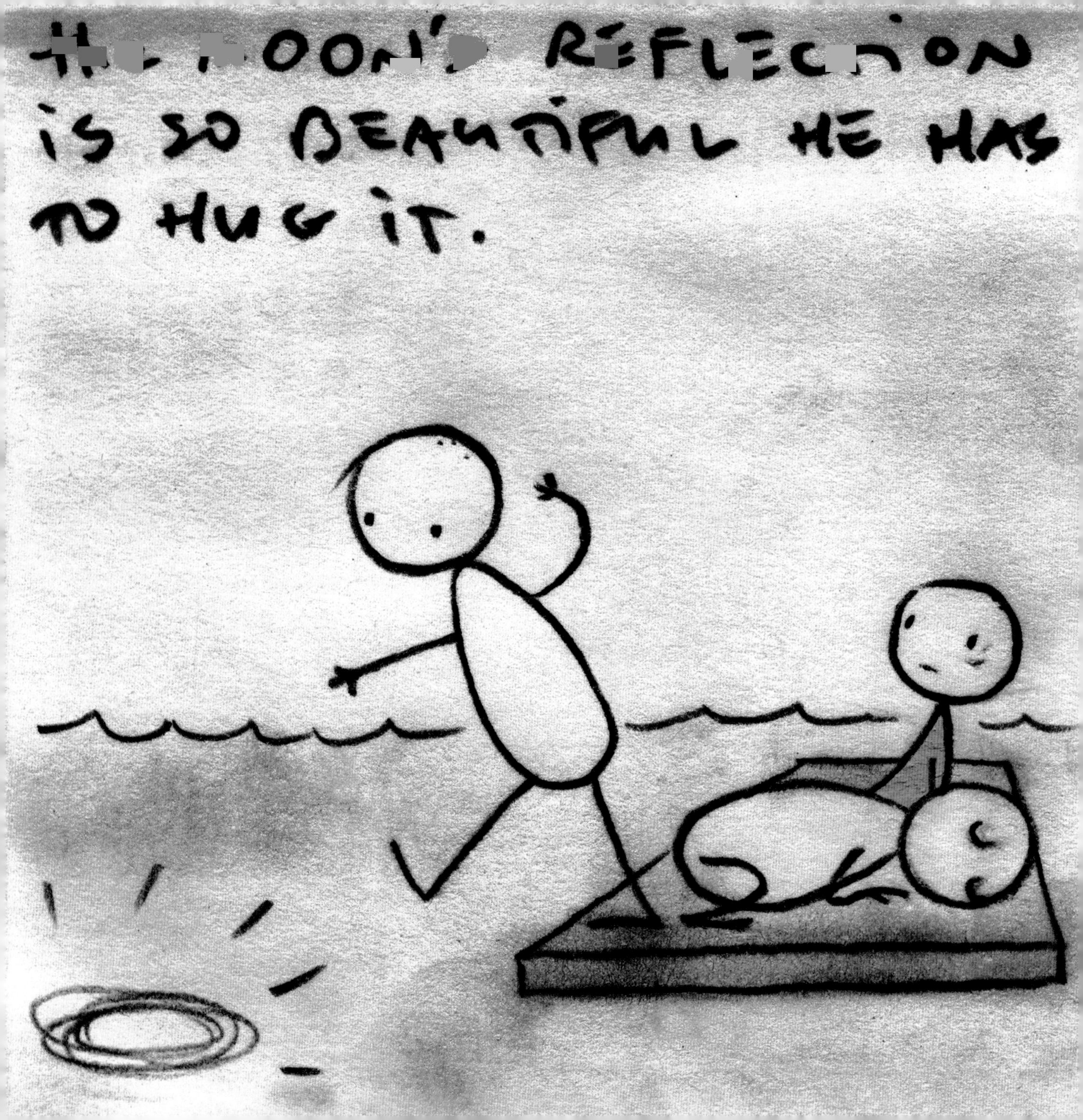
THE MOON'S REFLECTION IS SO BEAUTIFUL HE HAS TO HUG IT.

THERE IS AN ENORMOUS SWIMMING HEAD

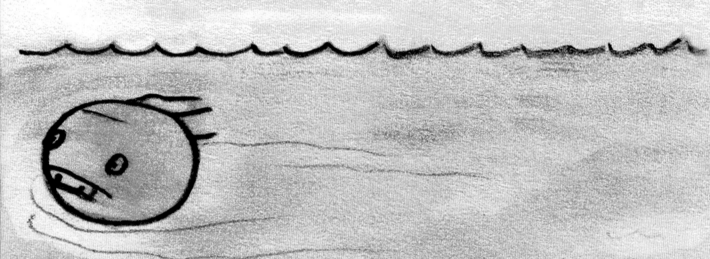

SHE DREAMS OF PURPLE DREAMING ANGRILY.

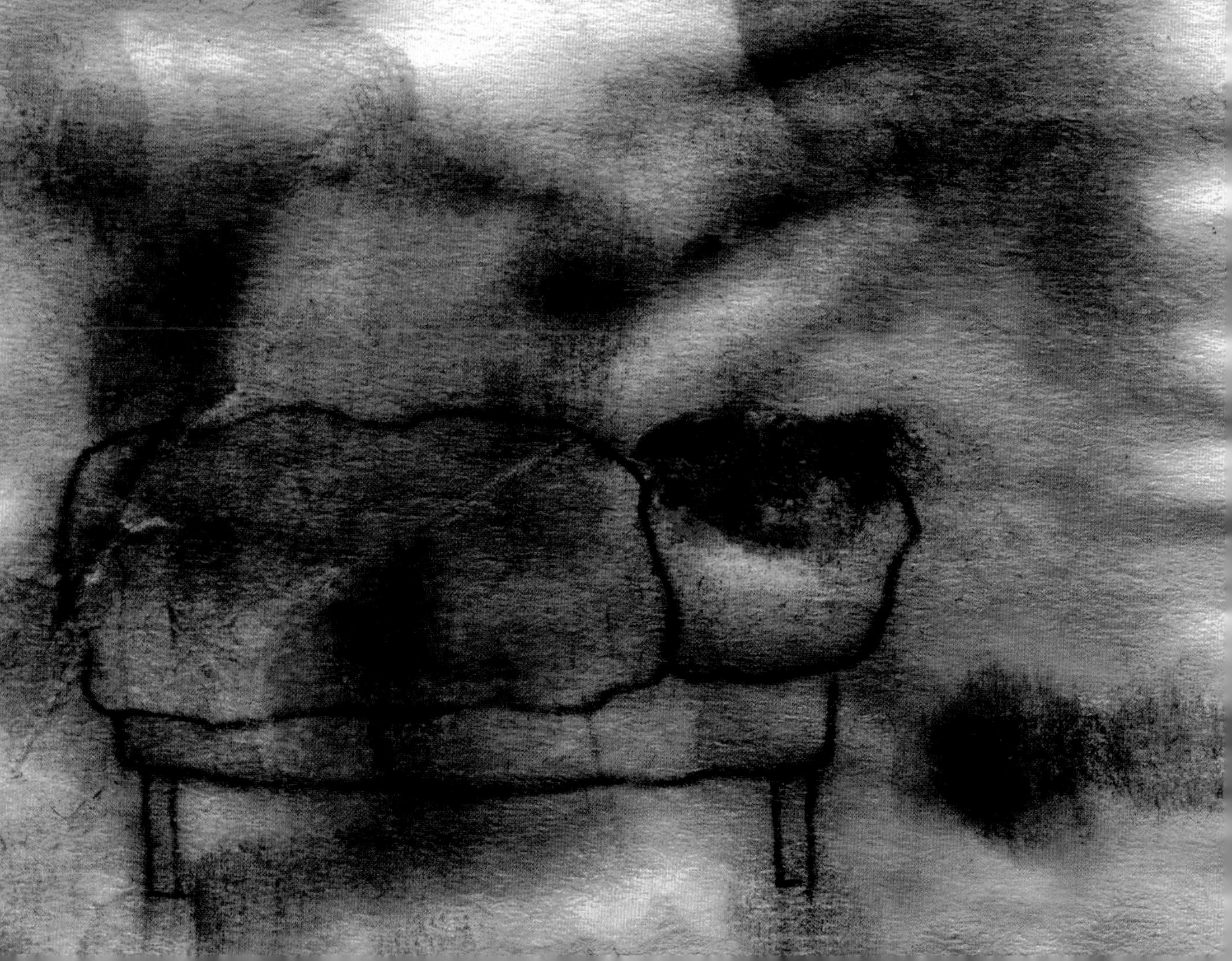

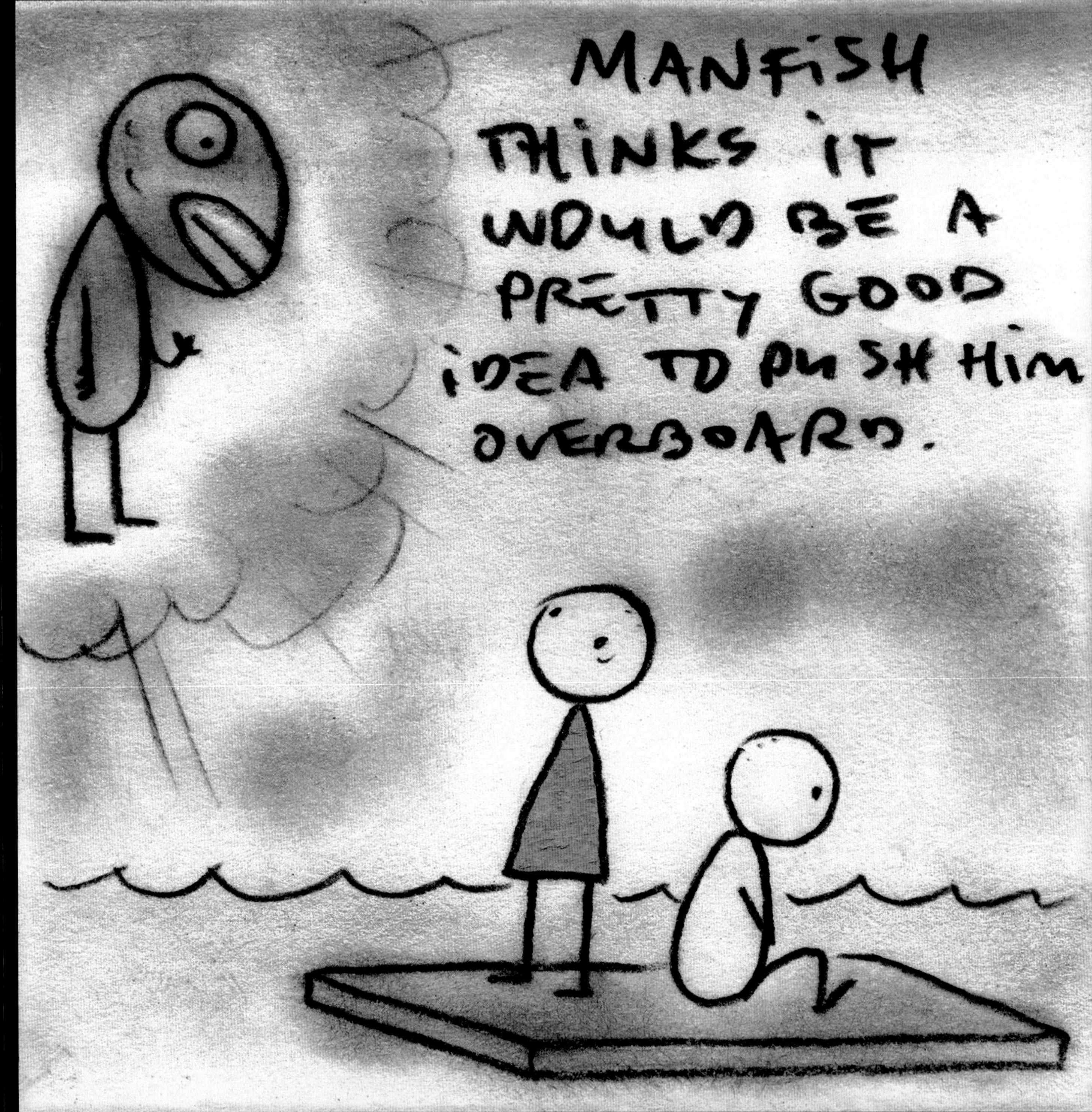
MANFISH
THINKS IT
WOULD BE A
PRETTY GOOD
IDEA TO PUSH HIM
OVERBOARD.

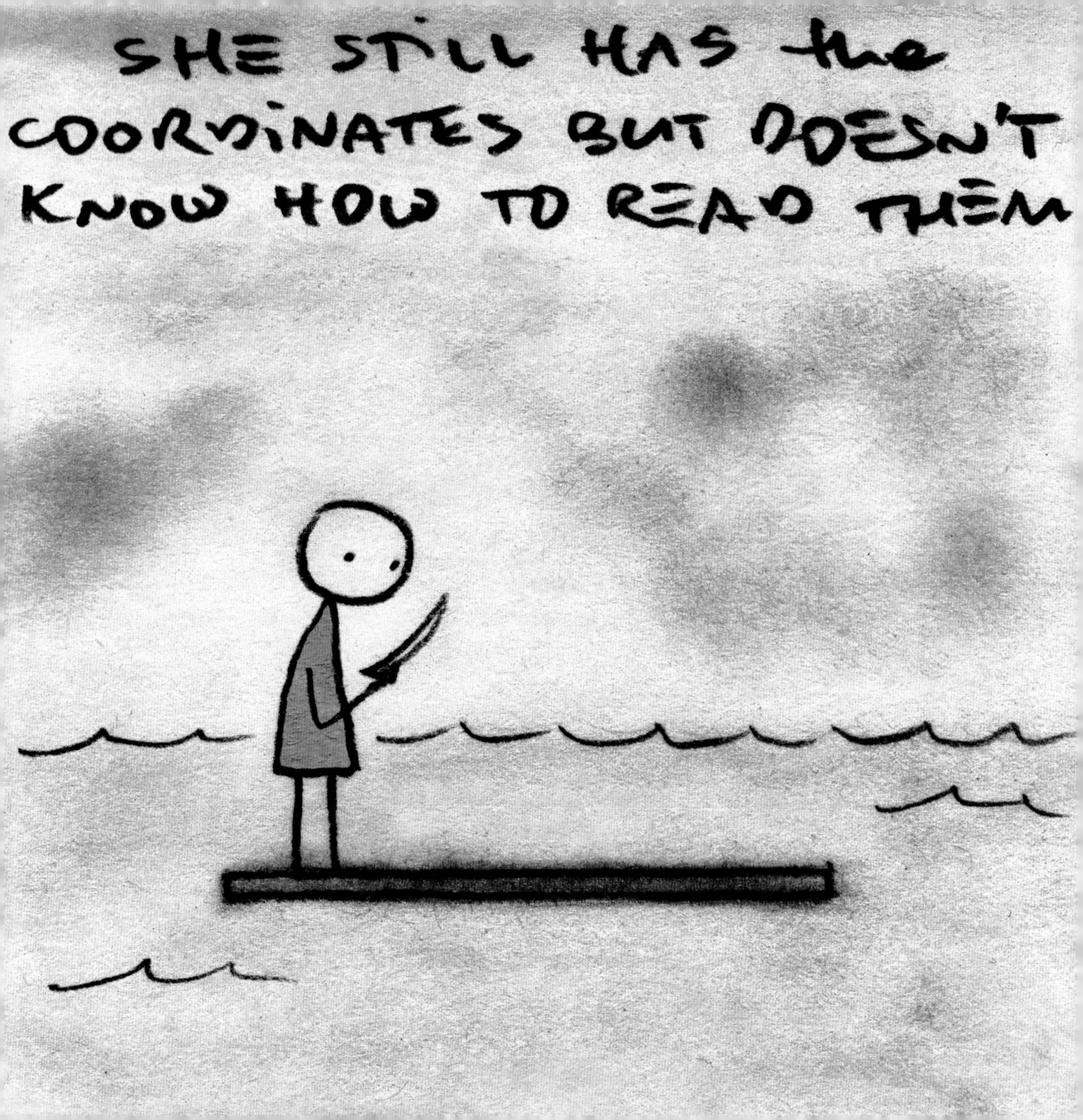
SHE STILL HAS the COORDINATES BUT DOESN'T KNOW HOW TO READ THEM

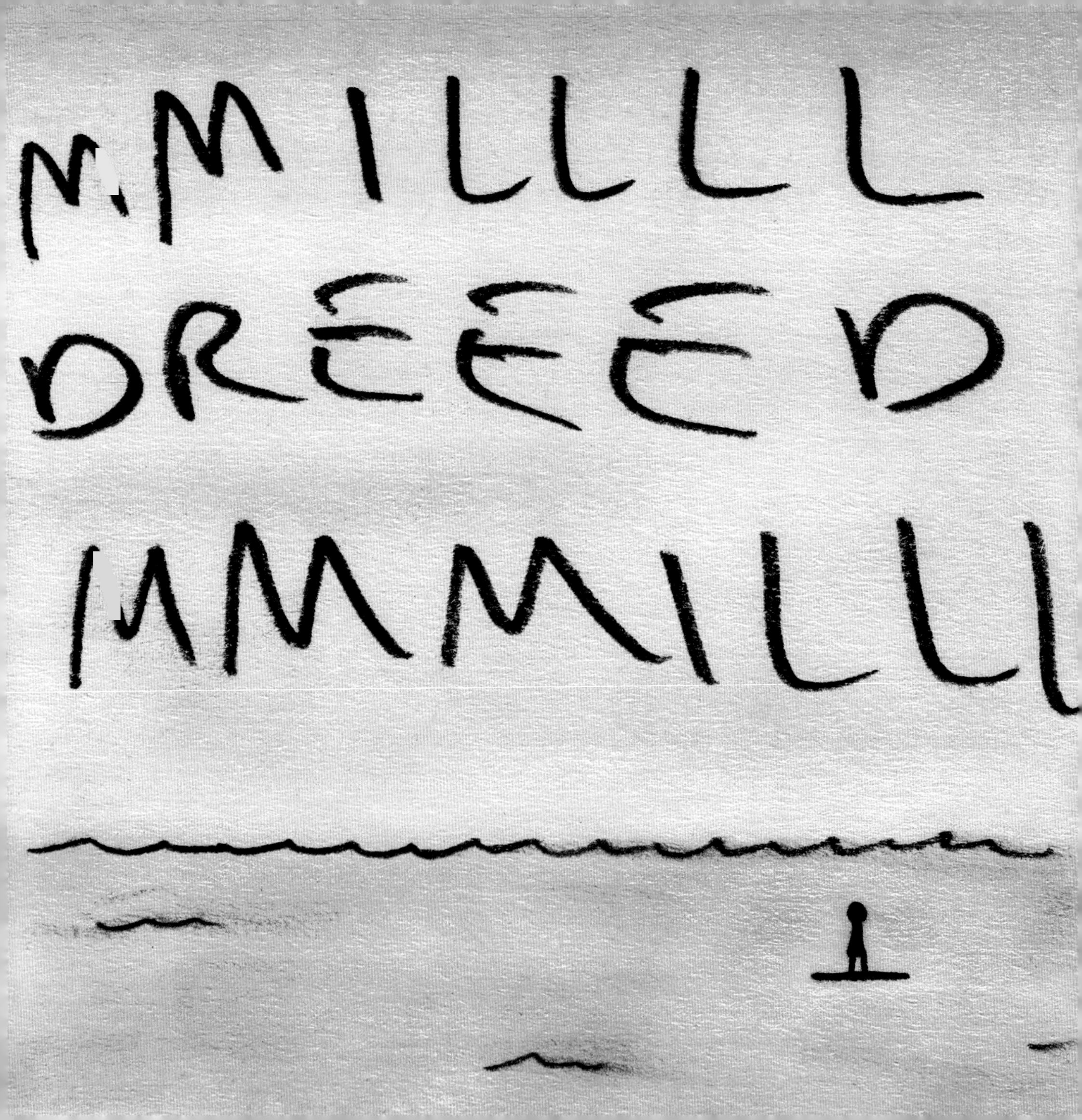
MMILLLL
DREEED
MMMILLL

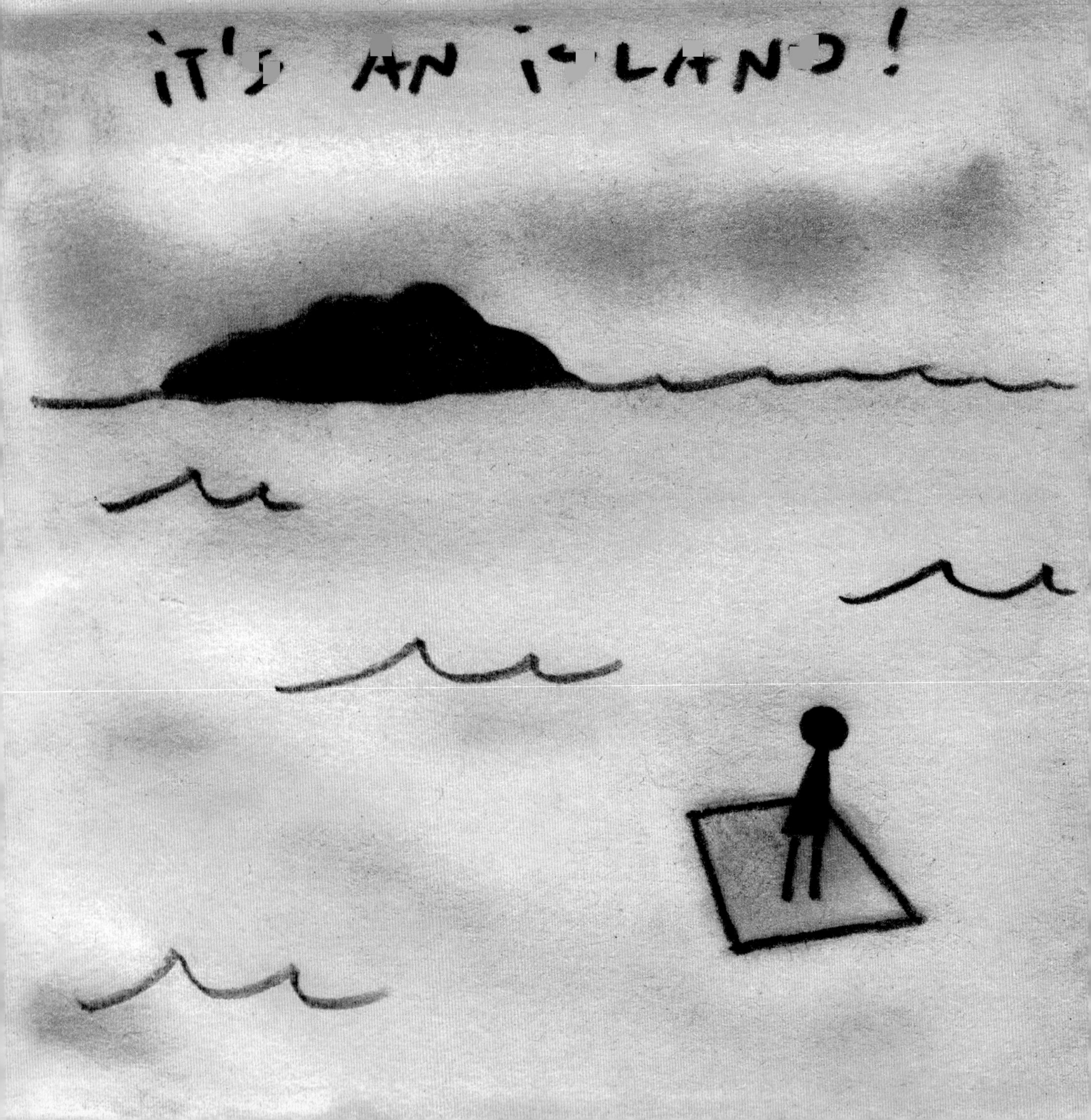
IT'S AN ISLAND!

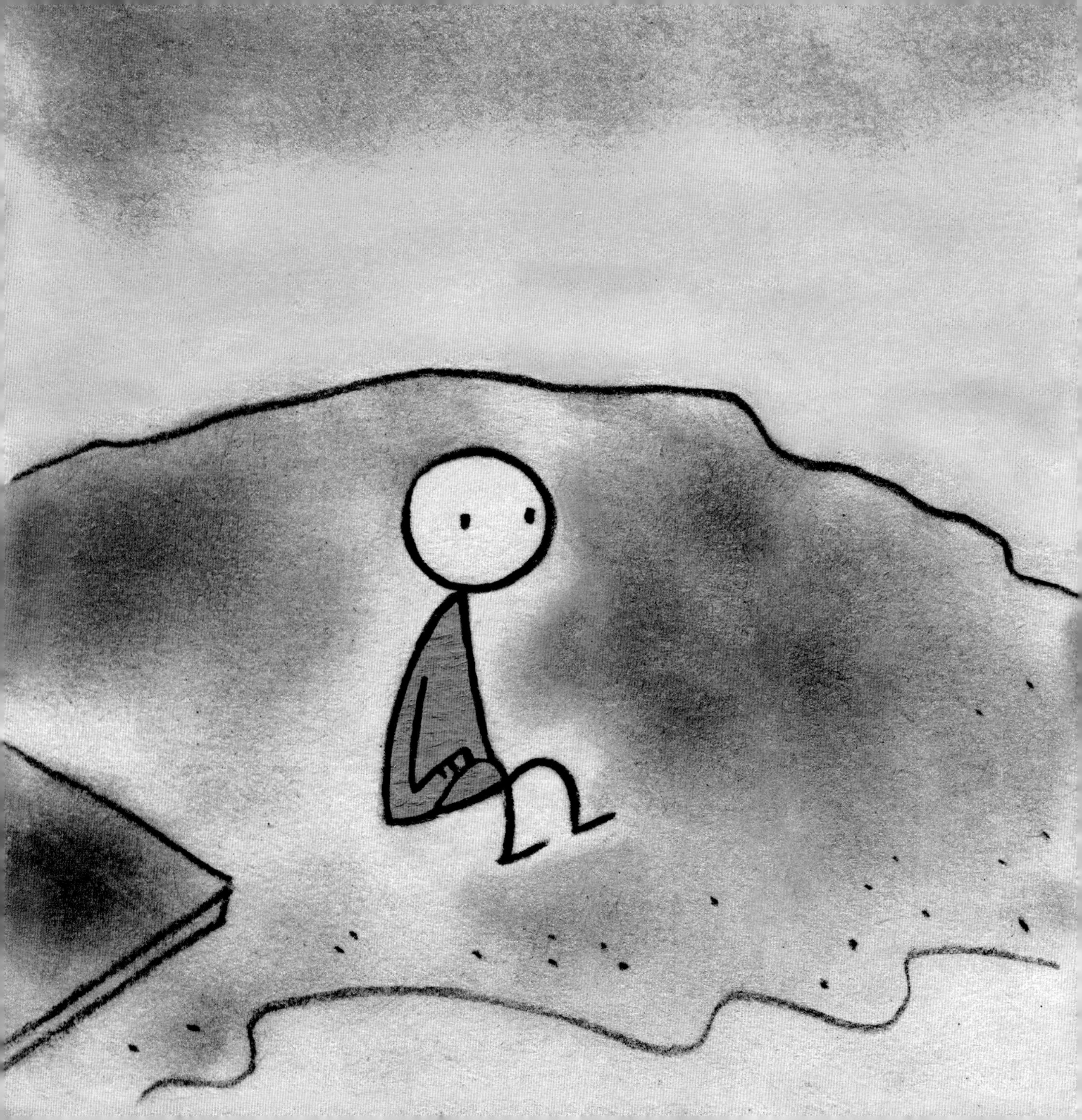

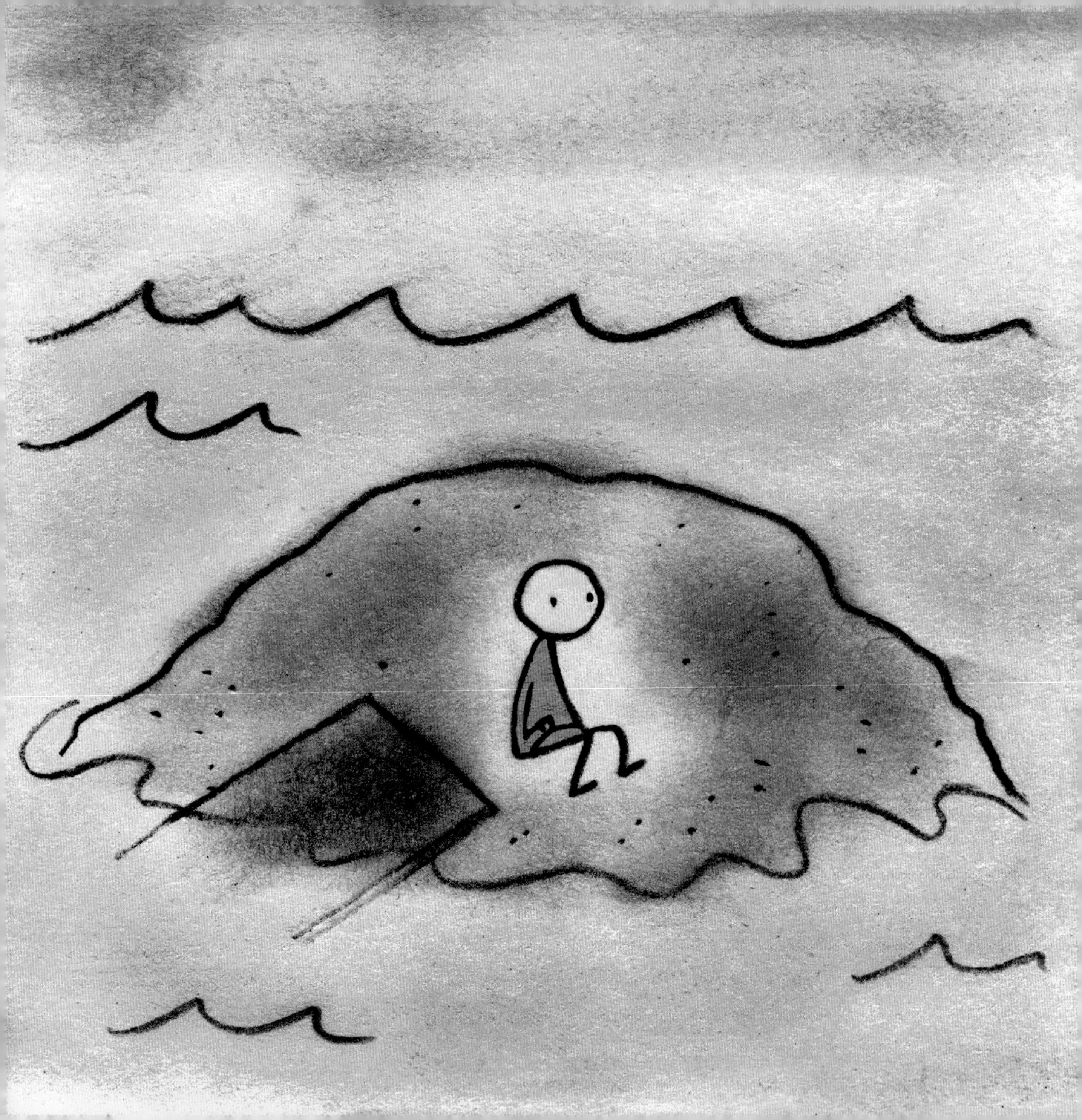

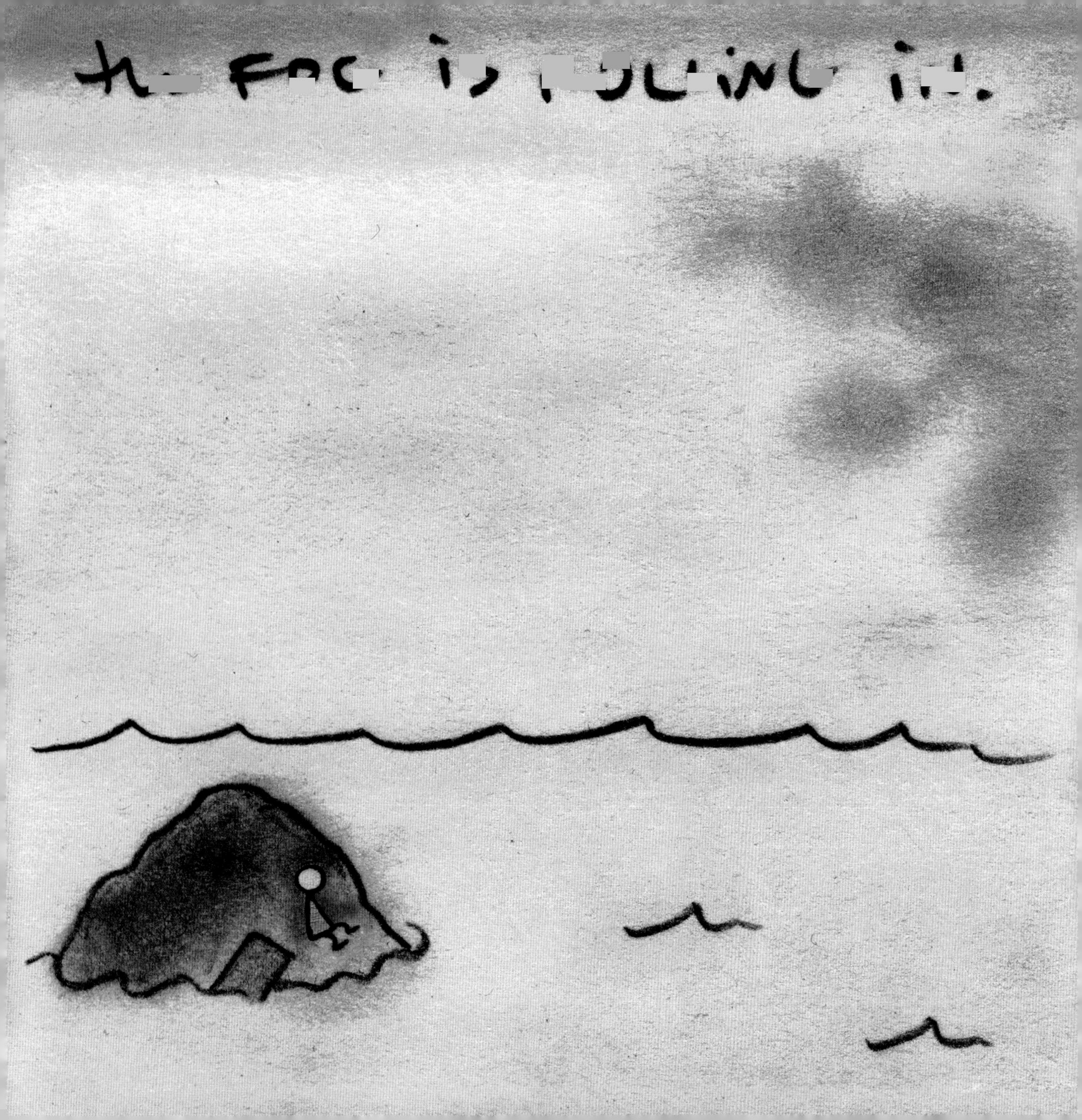
the fog is rolling in.

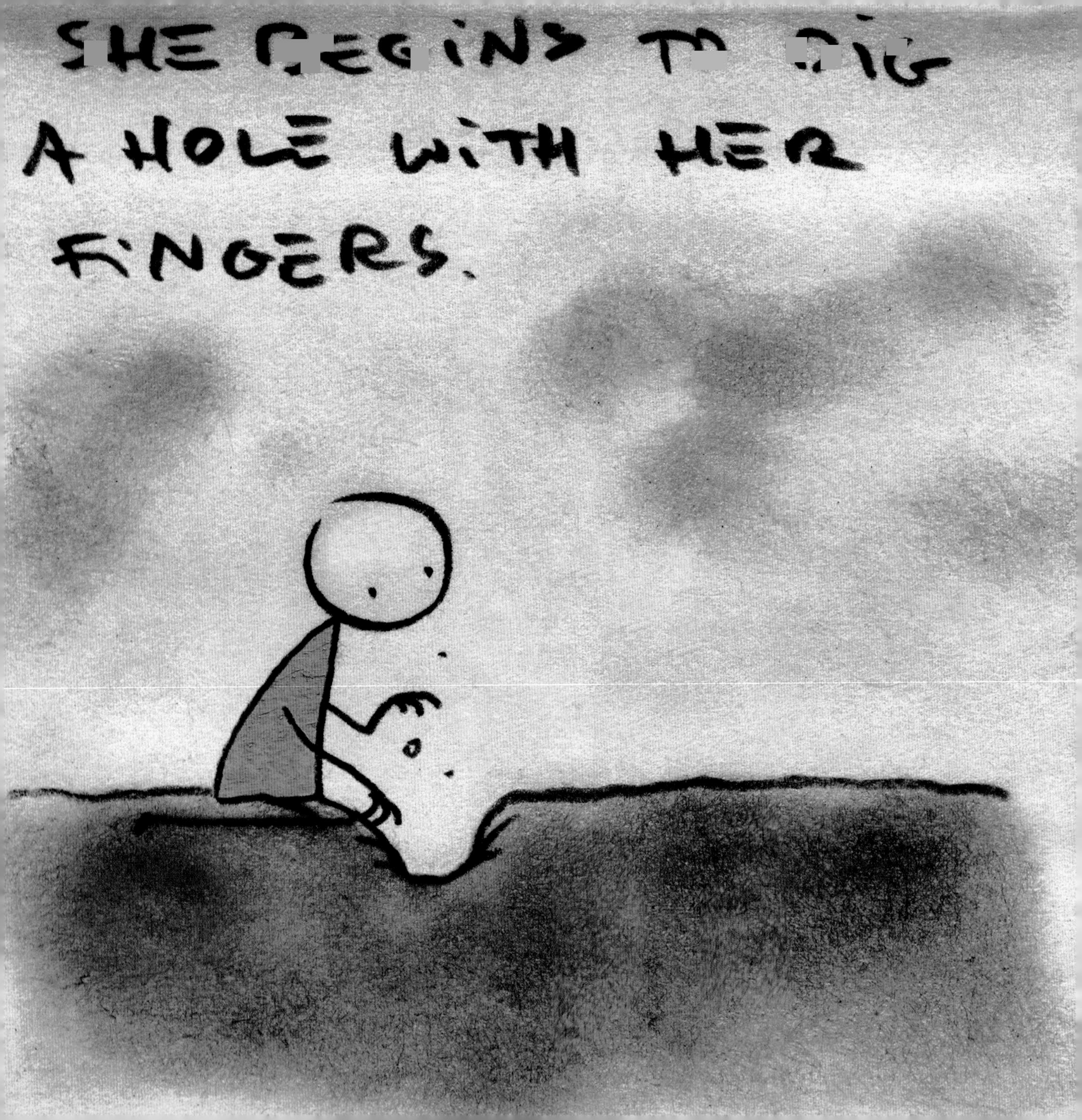
SHE BEGINS TO DIG
A HOLE WITH HER
FINGERS.

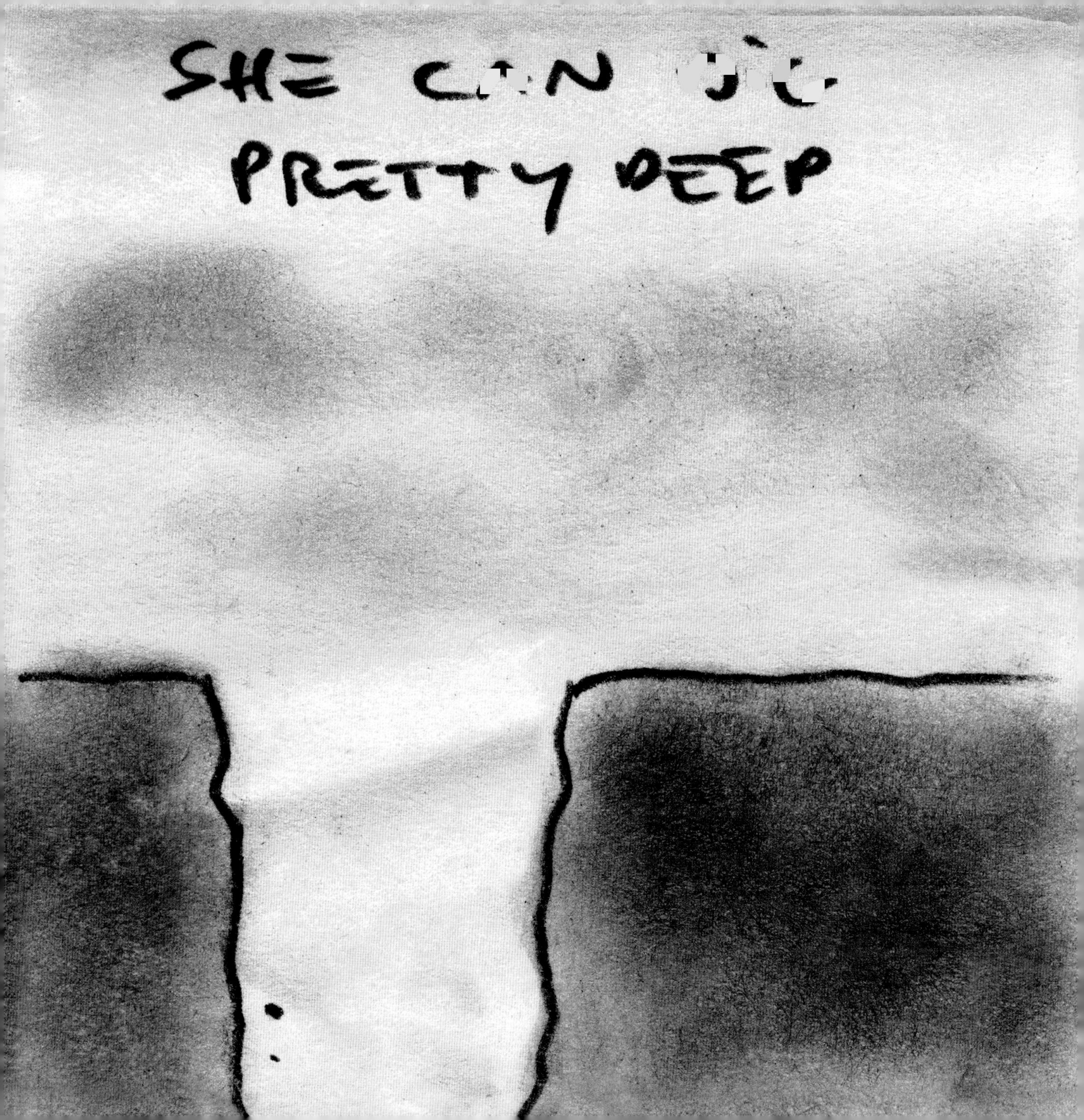
SHE CAN
PRETTY DEEP

A GHOST FACE IN the DARKEST WALL OF HER PARENT'S OLD HOUSE HAS DEPOSITED A PEAR.

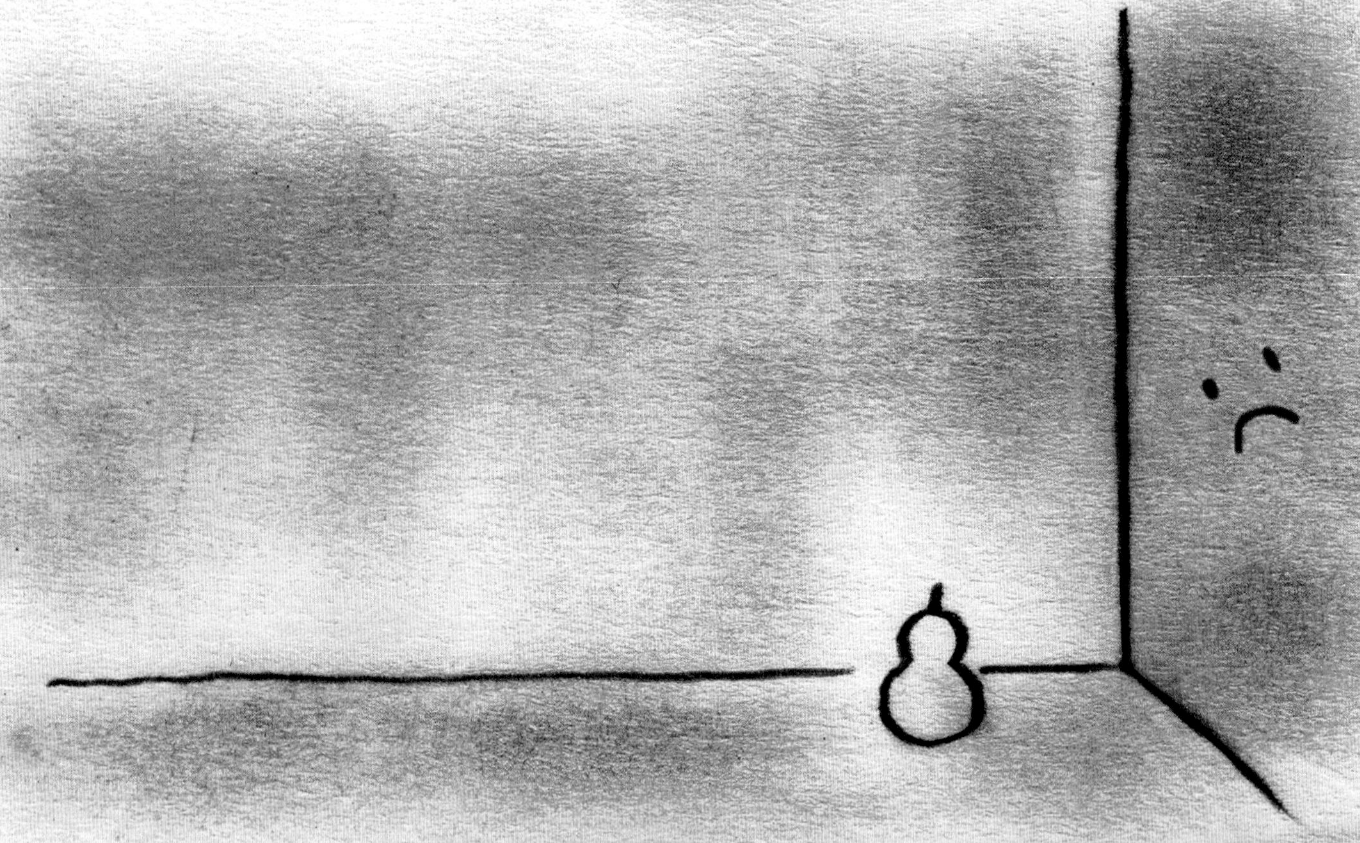

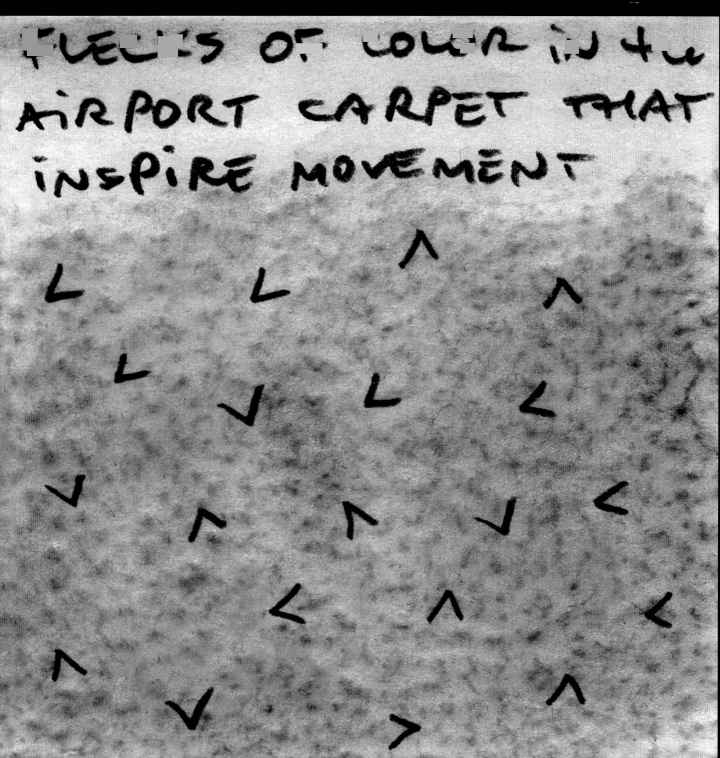

FIELDS OF COLOR IN the
AIRPORT CARPET THAT
INSPIRE MOVEMENT

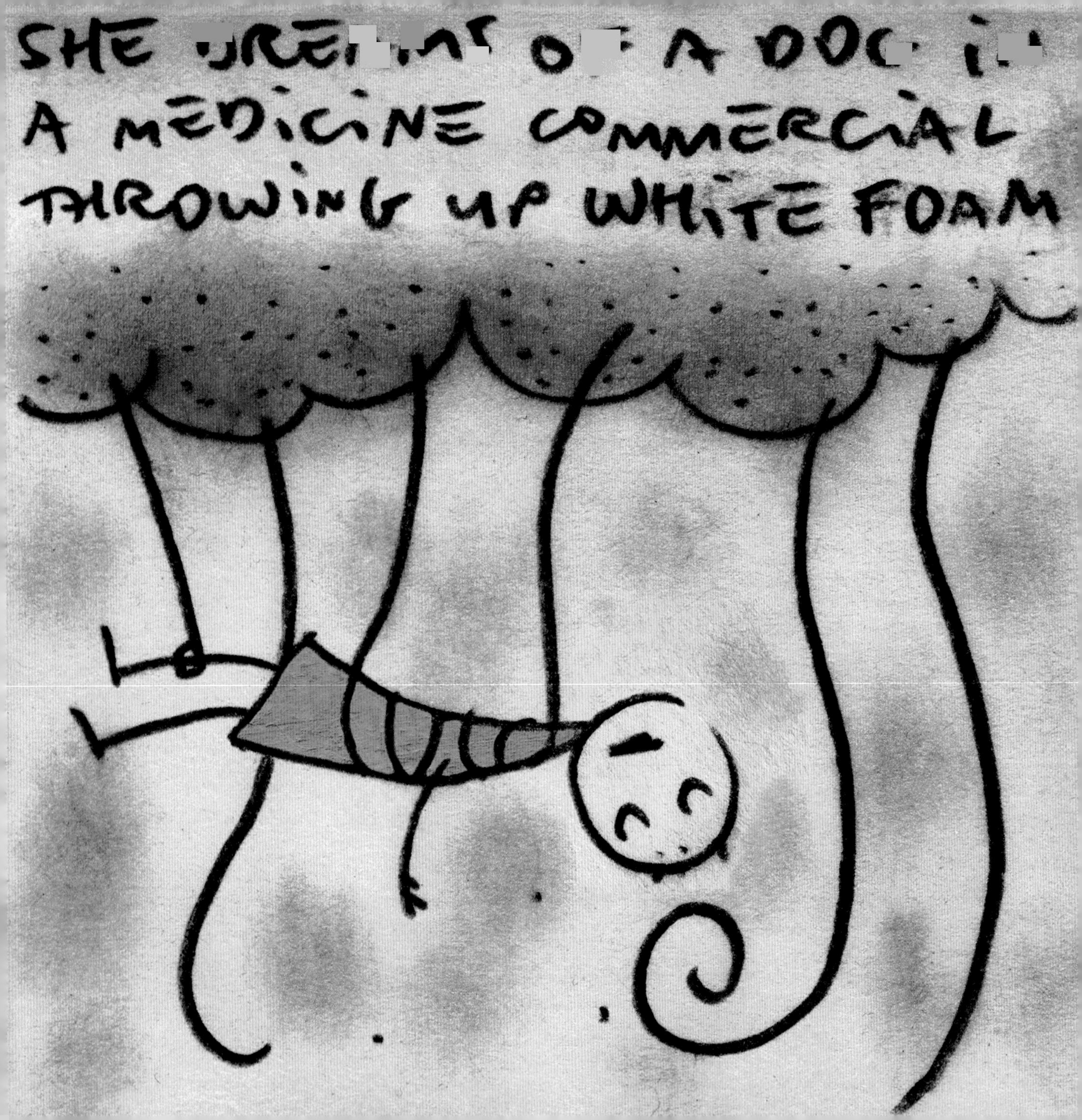
SHE DREAMS OF A DOG IN
A MEDICINE COMMERCIAL
THROWING UP WHITE FOAM

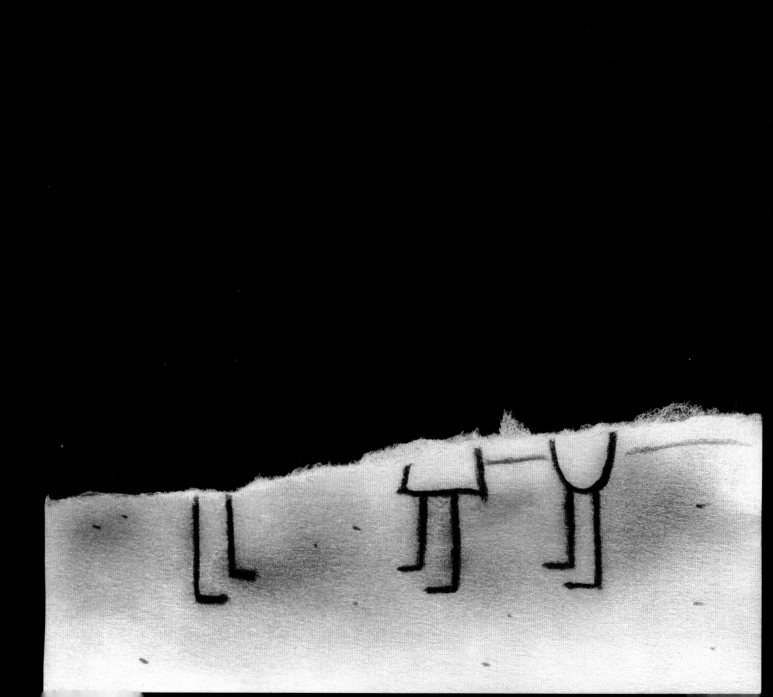

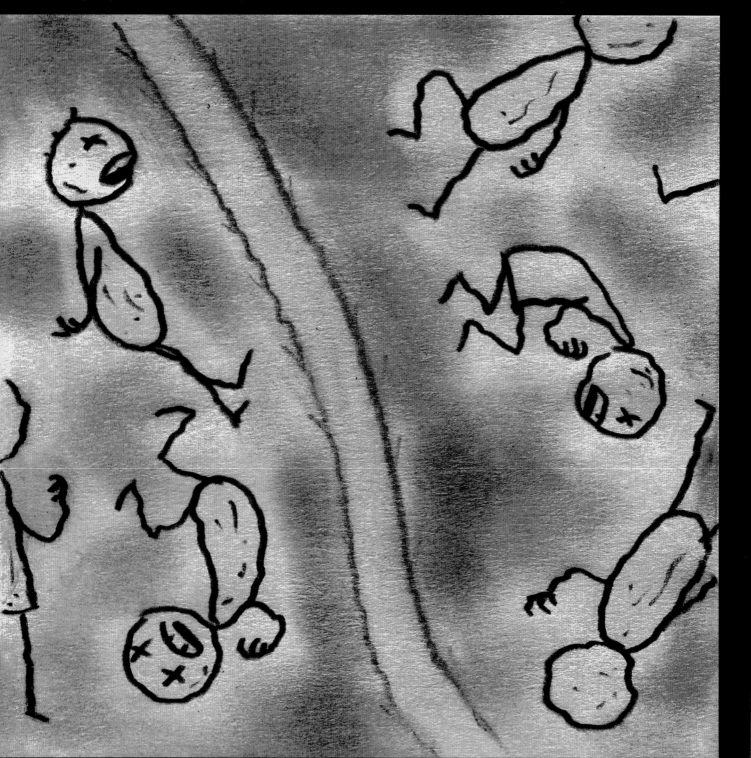

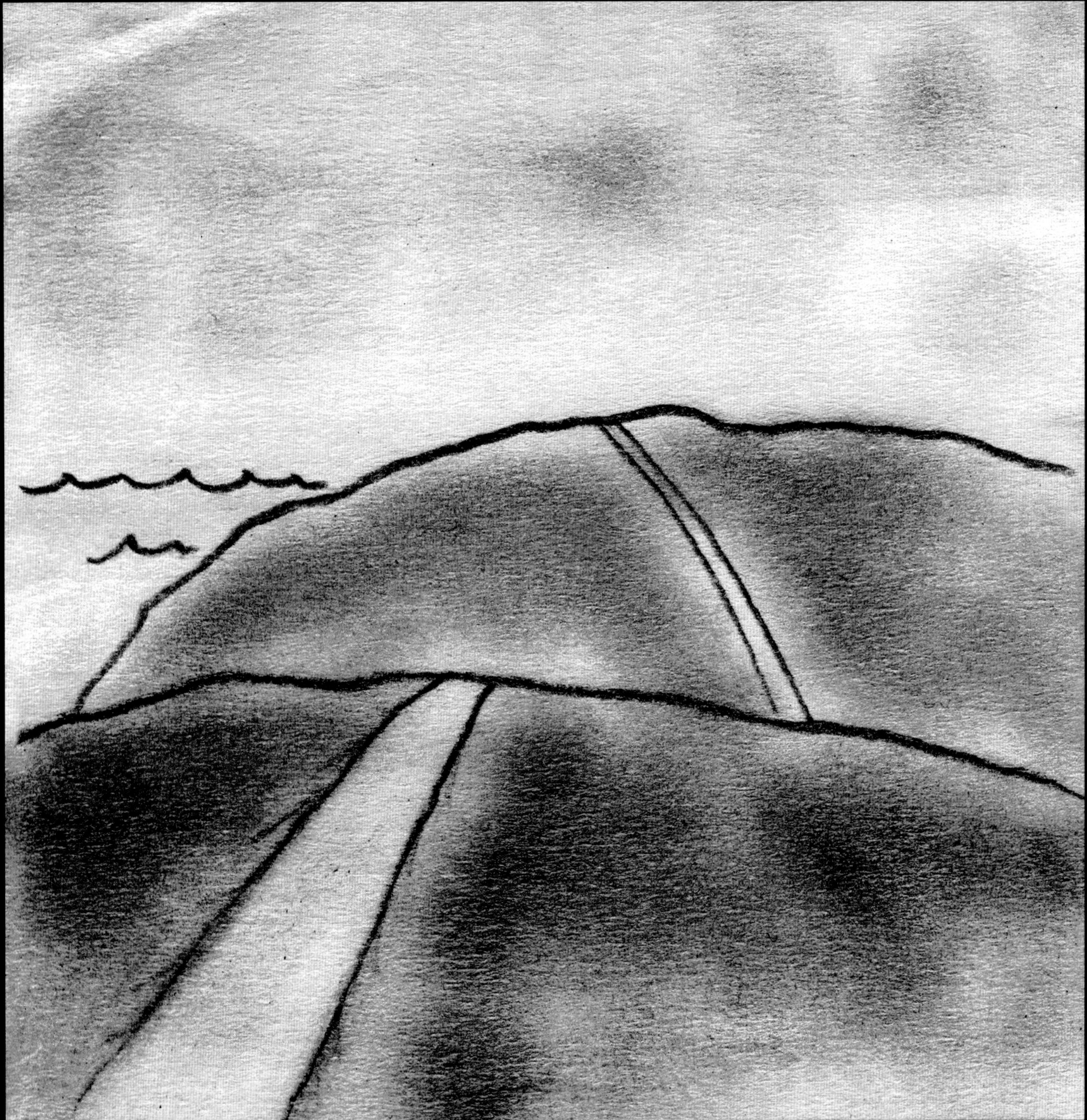

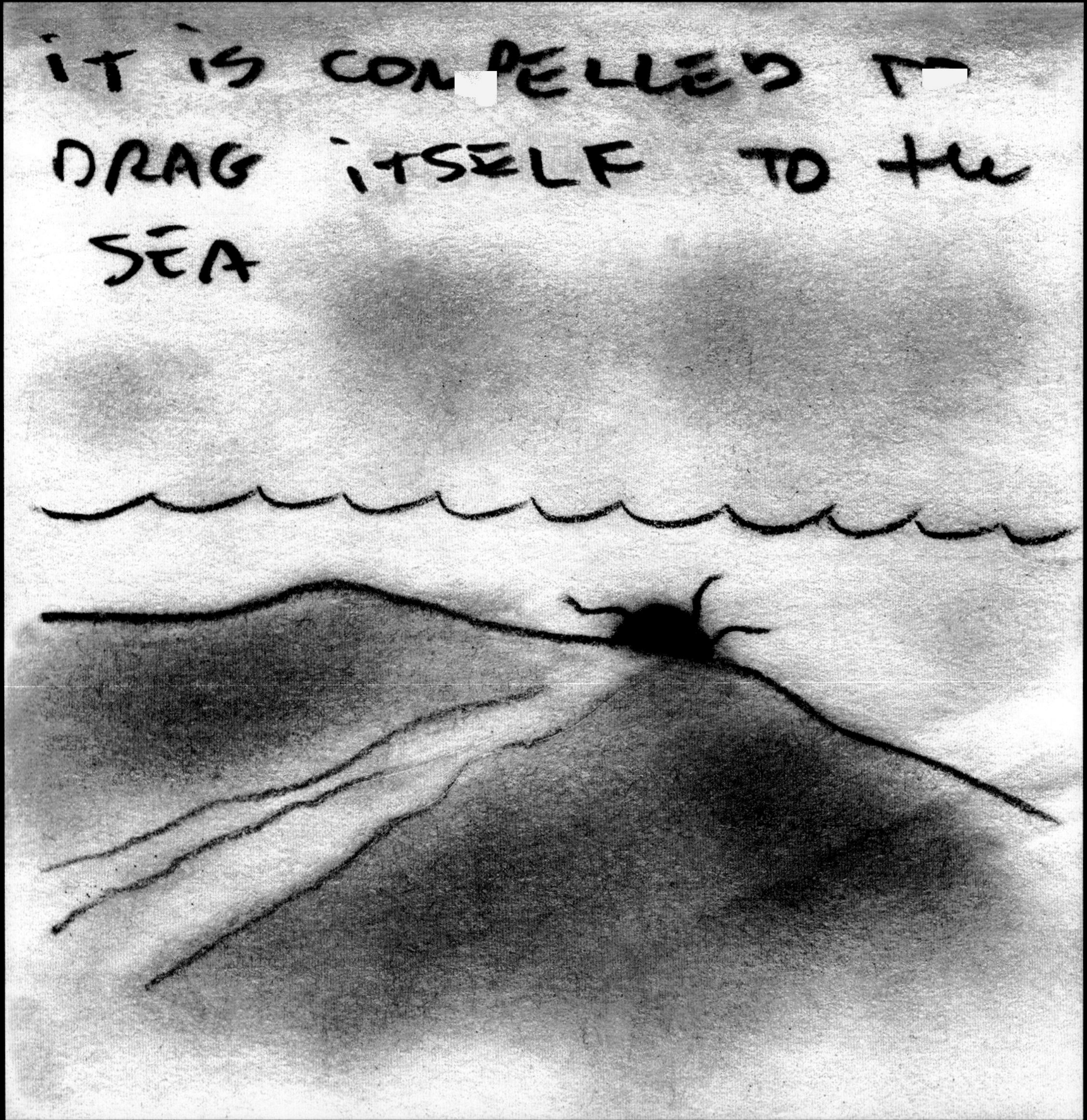
IT IS COMPELLED TO
DRAG ITSELF TO THE
SEA

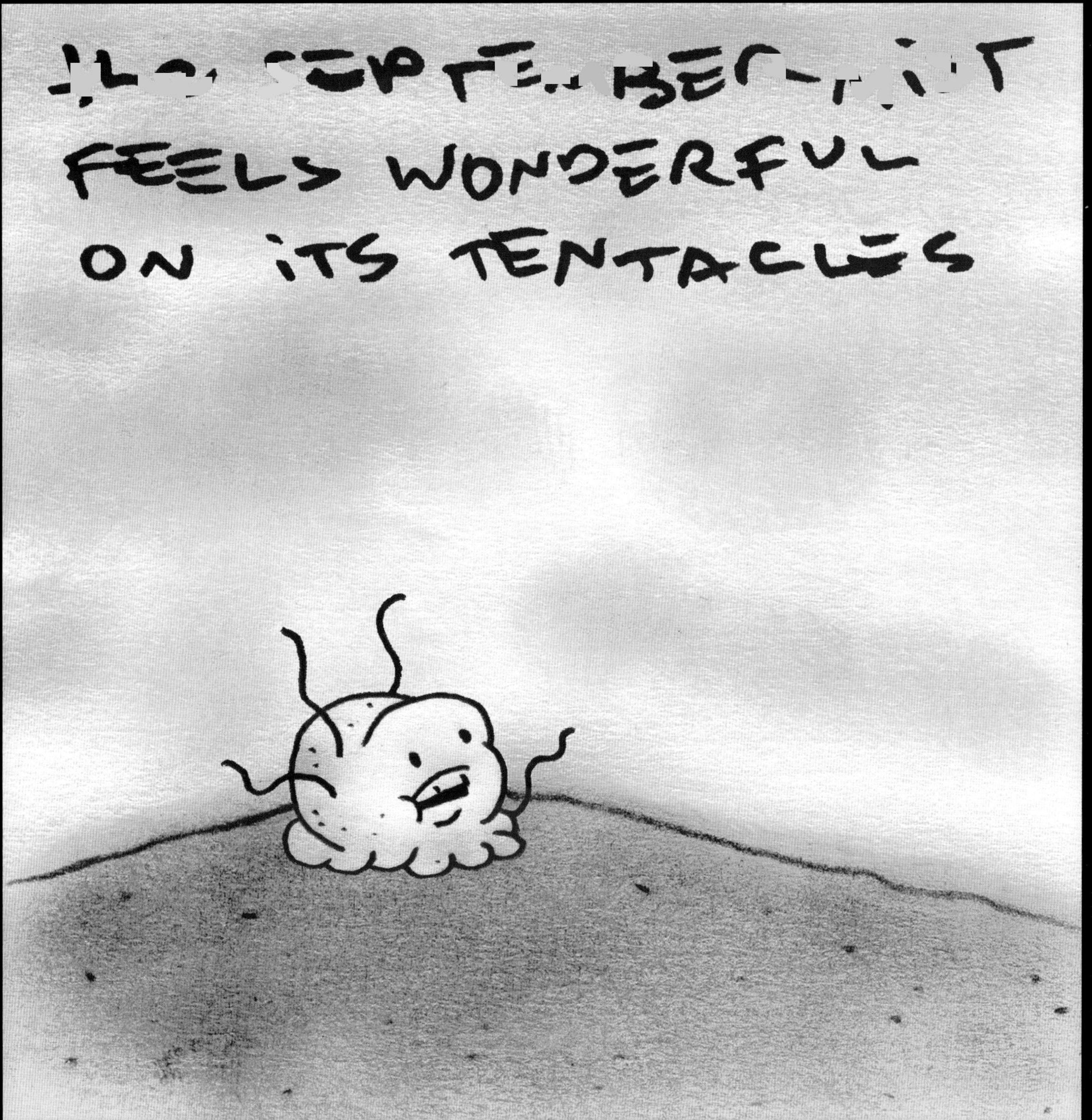
FEELS WONDERFUL
ON ITS TENTACLES